GREEN

teddekker.com

DEKKER FANTASY

BOOKS OF HISTORY CHRONICLES

THE LOST BOOKS
Chosen
Infidel
Renegade
Chaos
Lunatic
Elyon

THE CIRCLE SERIES
Green
Black
Red
White

THE PARADISE BOOKS
Showdown
Saint
Sinner

Skin
House
(WITH FRANK PERETTI)

DEKKER MYSTERY

Blink of an Eye
Kiss
(WITH ERIN HEALY)
Burn
(WITH ERIN HEALY—JANUARY 2010)

MARTYR'S SONG SERIES
Heaven's Wager
When Heaven Weeps
Thunder of Heaven
The Martyr's Song

THE CALEB BOOKS
Blessed Child
A Man Called Blessed

DEKKER THRILLER

THR3E
Obsessed
Adam

THE CIRCLE SERIES

GREEN

THE BEGINNING AND THE END

TED DEKkER

THOMAS NELSON
Since 1798

NASHVILLE DALLAS MEXICO CITY RIO DE JANEIRO BEIJING

Published in Nashville, Tennessee, by Thomas Nelson. Thomas Nelson is a registered trademark of Thomas Nelson, Inc.

Published in association with Thomas Nelson and Creative Trust, Inc., 5141 Virginia Way, Suite 320, Brentwood, TN 37027.

Thomas Nelson, Inc., titles may be purchased in bulk for educational, business, fund-raising, or sales promotional use. For information, please e-mail SpecialMarkets@ThomasNelson.com.

Publisher's Note: This novel is a work of fiction. Names, characters, places, and incidents are either products of the author's imagination or used fictitiously. All characters are fictional, and any similarity to people living or dead is purely coincidental.

ISBN 978-1-59554-739-2 (IE)

Library of Congress Cataloging-in-Publication Data

Dekker, Ted, 1962–
    Green : the beginning and the end / Ted Dekker.
      p. cm. — (The circle ; bk. zero)
    ISBN 978-1-59554-288-5
    I. Title.
PS3554.E43G74 2009
813'.54—dc22   2009024590

Printed in the United States of America

09 10 11 12 13 RRD 6 5 4 3 2

The Beginning and the End

In times past, our history has been retold using simple metaphors. Light coming into the darkness. A land called Narnia set free by a lion. A Ring that would enslave the hearts of all.

But our generation looks to a new mythology to peel back the layers of truth. Dive deep into a world of colors. Of *Green*, of *Black*, of *Red*, and of *White*.

According to the Books of History, everything that happened following the year 2010 actually began in the year 4036 AD. It began in the future, not the past. Earth had been destroyed once during the twenty-first century, an apocalypse foretold by the ancient prophets. But the time for history was not yet finished, and Elyon, in his great wisdom, set upon the Earth a new firstborn named Tanis. This time Elyon gave humans an advantage. This time what was once spiritual and unseen became physical and seen. All that was good and evil could be watched and touched. The Roush and the great lions roamed the forests. Humans knew no pain, no fear, no sadness. And everywhere was the color of intoxicating pleasure, of Elyon Himself.

Yet evil also remained. Teeleh and his minions bided their time in a Black Forest.

And that time came. When least expected, through a bridging of space and time, a twenty-four-year-old man named Thomas Hunter fell asleep in Denver, Colorado, and woke up in the Black Forest, two thousand years in the future. A gateway was opened for the dark powers to ravage the land.

Now wars, betrayal, disease, and death threaten to once again destroy every living soul. Only a small band of rebels called The Circle, led by Thomas Hunter, stand in the way. But The Circle is fracturing. Betrayal is in the air as the forces of evil gather to crush all that remains of good

Welcome, lovers and fighters, to The Circle.

Welcome to Book Zero.

Welcome to *Green*.

WHERE DOES THE CIRCLE START?

Unlike most series, the Circle Series is truly circular, meaning *Green*, Book Zero, both begins the series for those who have not yet read *Black*, *Red*, or *White*, and it ends the series for those who have read *Black*, *Red*, and *White*. Have no fear, the story works seamlessly either way, like a circle or a zero. The choice is yours. Start with *Black*, then read *Red*, *White* and end with *Green*. Or start with *Green* and move on to *Black*, *Red* and *White*.

Dive Deep.

Prologue

ACCORDING TO the Books of History, everything that happened after the year 2010 actually began in the year 4036 AD. It began in the future, not the past. Confusing perhaps, but perfectly understandable once you realize that some things are as dependent on the future as on the past.

The world's history was written in the Books of History, those magnificent volumes that recorded only the truth of all that happened. Earth was destroyed once during the twenty-first century, in an apocalypse foretold in the books of the ancient prophets Daniel and John, and then recorded as history in the Books of History. But the time for history was not yet finished, and Elyon in his great wisdom set upon the earth a new firstborn named Tanis.

This time, Elyon gave humans an advantage: What had been spiritual and unseen became physical and seen. All good and evil could be watched and felt and touched and tasted. As time passed, however, mankind closed its eyes to what was real and became blind to the forces that surrounded it.

But there remained a small band of rebels who longed to see Elyon as they once had. They were led by one man who claimed to have visited the twenty-first century in his dreams.

His name was Thomas Hunter.

This is his story.

0

The Future

CHELISE HUNTER, wife of Thomas Hunter, stood beside her son, Samuel, and gazed over the canyon now flooded with those who'd crossed the desert for the annual Gathering. The sound of pounding drums echoed from the cliff walls; thousands milled in groups or danced in small circles as they awaited the final ceremonies, which would commence when the sun settled beyond the horizon. The night would fill with cries of loyalty and all would feast on fatted cows and hopes for deliverance from their great enemy, the Horde.

But Samuel, a warrior with a heavy sword and angry glare, had evidently put his hope in something entirely different. He stood still, but she knew that under the leather chest-and-shoulder armor his muscles were tense and, in his mind's eye, moving already. Racing off to make war.

Chelise let the breeze blow her hair about her face and tried to calm herself with steady breathing. "This is impossible, Samuel. Complete foolishness."

"Is it? Say that to Sacura."

"She would agree with me."

Sacura, mother of three just a few days earlier, was now mother of two. Her fifteen-year-old son, Richard, had been caught and hung by a Horde scouting party when he'd straggled behind his tribe as it made its way to the Gathering.

"Then she's the fool, not me."

"You think our nonviolent ways are just a haphazard strategy to gain us the upper hand?" Chelise demanded. "You think returning death with more death will bring us peace? Nearly everyone in the valley was once Horde, including me, in case I need to remind you—now you want to hunt their families because they haven't converted to our ways?"

"And you would let them slaughter us instead? How many of us do they need to kill before you shed this absurd love you have for our enemy?"

Chelise could take his backtalk no longer. It took all of her strength to resist the temptation to slap his face, here and now. But it occurred to her that using violence at precisely this moment would strengthen his point.

And knowing Samuel, he would only grin. She knew how to fight, they all did as a matter of tradition, but next to Samuel she was the butterfly and he the eagle.

Chelise settled. For the sake of Jake, her youngest, they must follow the ways of Elyon. For the sake of her father, Qurong, commander of the Horde, and her mother. For the sake of the *world*, they had to cling to what they knew, not what their emotions demanded from them. To take up arms now would make an unforgivable mockery of all the Circle stood for.

She faced Samuel and saw that his sleeve was hitched up under his left arm guard. She pulled it down and brushed it flat. "It's hard, I know," she said, casting a glance back at the three mounted guards who waited behind them. Samuel's band numbered a couple dozen, all sharing his hatred. Honorable men who were tired of seeing loved ones die at the hands of the Horde.

"He's larger-than-life, we all know that. Just because you're his son doesn't mean you have to blaze his trail."

She'd meant to console him, but he stiffened and she knew her words had done the opposite. "Not that you feel like you have to measure up to Thomas, but—"

"This has nothing to do with Thomas!" he snapped, pulling away. "Nobody could possibly measure up to a man with his past. My concern is the future, not some crazy history bounding between the worlds through those dreams of his."

Odd that he would refer to the time when Thomas claimed to have traveled back in time through dreams. Thomas so rarely referred to it himself those days.

"Forget his dreams. My husband is the leader of the Circle. He carries the burden of keeping twelve thousand hearts in line with the truth, and you, his son, would undermine that?"

Samuel's jaw knotted. "The truth, Mother?" he bit off. He shoved a hand south, in the direction of Qurongi Forest, once controlled by Thomas and the Forest Guard, now inhabited by her father, leader of the Horde, Qurong. "The truth is, your precious Horde hates us and butchers us wherever they find us."

"What do you suggest?" she cried. "Run off now, on the eve of our greatest celebration, in search of a few Scabs who are likely back in the city by now?"

Samuel lowered his hand and looked back at his men. Then to the south again. "We have him now."

"You have who now?"

"The Scab who killed Sacura's son. We have him captive in a canyon."

Chelise didn't know what to say to this. They had taken a Scab captive? Who'd ever heard of such a thing?

"We're going to give him a trial in the desert," Samuel said.

"For what purpose?"

"For justice!"

"You cannot kill him, Samuel! The Gathering would come undone! I don't have to tell you what that would do to your father."

"To my father?" He looked at her. "Or to you, Mother, the daughter of Qurong, supreme commander of all that is wicked and vile?"

Chelise slapped him. Nothing more than a flat palm to his cheek, but the crack of the blow sounded like a whip.

Samuel grinned. She immediately wished to take her anger back.

"Sorry. Sorry, I didn't mean that. But you're speaking of my father!"

"Yes, you did mean that, Mother." He turned and strode toward his horse.

"Where are you going?"

"To conduct a trial," he said.

"Then at least bring him in, Samuel." She started after him, but he was already swinging into the saddle. "Think!"

"I'm done thinking." He pulled his horse around and brushed past his men, who turned with him. "It's time to act."

"Samuel . . ."

"Keep this between us, will you?" he said, looking over his shoulder. "I'd hate to put a damper on such a wonderful night of celebration."

"Samuel. Stop this!"

He kicked his horse and left her with the sound of pounding hooves.

Dear Elyon . . . the boy would be the ruin of them all.

1

THOMAS HUNTER stood next to his wife, Chelise, facing the shallow canyon lined by three thousand of Elyon's lovers, who'd drowned in the red lakes to rid their bodies of the scabbing disease that covered the skin of all Horde.

The reenactment of the Great Wedding had taken an hour, and the final salute, which would usher the Gathering into a wild night of celebration, was upon them.

As was customary, both he and Chelise were dressed in white, because Elyon would come in white. She with lilies in her hair and a long, flowing gown spun from silk; he in a bleached tunic, dyed red around the collar to remind them of the blood that had paid for this wedding.

This was their great romance, and there could not possibly be a dry eye in the valley.

Six maidens also in white faced Chelise and Thomas on their knees and sang the Great Wedding's song. Their sweet, yearning voices filled the valley as they cried the refrain in melodic unison, faces bright with an eager desperation.

You are Beautiful . . . so Beautiful . . . Beautiful . . . Beautiful . . .

The drums lifted the cry to a crescendo. Milus, one of the older children, had recounted their history earlier in the night to thundering applause. Now Thomas retraced from his own vantage all that had brought them here.

Ten years ago, most of these people had been Horde, enslaved by Teeleh's disease. The rest were Forest Dwellers who had kept the disease at bay by washing in Elyon's lakes once every day as he'd directed.

Then the Horde, led by Qurong, had invaded the forests and defiled the lakes. All had succumbed to the scabbing disease, which deceived the mind and cracked the skin.

But Elyon made a new way to defeat the evil disease: Any Horde simply had to drown in one of the red pools, and the disease would be washed away, never to return. Those who chose to drown and find new life were called albinos by the Horde, because their skin, whether dark or light, was smooth.

The albinos formed a Circle of trust and followed their leader, Thomas of Hunter.

The Horde, however, divided into two races: Purebred Horde, who'd always had the scabbing disease, and half-breeds, who'd been Forest Dwellers but turned Horde after Qurong's invasion of the forests. The full-breed Horde despised and persecuted the half-breeds because they'd once been Forest Dwellers.

Eram, a half-breed, had fled Qurong's persecution and welcomed all half-breeds to join him in the deep northern desert, where they thrived as Horde and enemies of Qurong. Nearly half a million, rumor had it.

They called the faction who followed Eram *Eramites*, remnants of the faithful who were as diseased as any other Scab. All suffered from the sickly, smelly disease that covered the skin and clouded the mind.

Thomas glanced at his bride. To look at Chelise's smooth, bronzed jaw now . . . her bright emerald eyes had once been gray. Her long blonde hair had once been tangled dreadlocks smothered in morst paste to fight the stench of the scabbing disease.

Chelise, who'd given birth to one of his three children, was a vision of perfect beauty. And in so many ways they were all perfectly beautiful, as Elyon was beautiful. *Beautiful, Beautiful, Beautiful.*

They had all once denied Elyon, their maker, their lover, the author of the Great Romance. Now they were the Circle, roughly twelve thousand who lived in nomadic tribes, fugitives from the Horde hunters who sought their deaths.

Three thousand had come together northwest of Qurongi City in a remote, shallow canyon called Paradose. They did this every year to express their solidarity and celebrate their passion for Elyon.

The Gathering, they called it. This year four Gatherings would take place near four forests, one north, one south, one east, one west. The danger of all twelve thousand crossing the desert from where they had scattered and coming to one location was simply too great.

Thomas scanned the three thousand strewn along the rocks and on the earth in a huge semicircle before him. After three days of late nights and long days filled with laughter and dancing and innumerable embraces of affection, they now stared at him in wide-eyed silence.

A large bonfire raged to his left, casting shifting shadows over their intent gazes. To his right, the red pool glistened, black in the night, one of seventy-seven they'd found throughout the land. Cliffs surrounded the hidden canyon, broken only by two gaps wide enough for four horses abreast. Guards lined the tops of the cliffs, keeping a keen eye on the desert beyond for any sign of Horde.

How many times over the past ten years had members of the Circle been found and slaughtered wholesale? Too many to count. But they had learned well, gone deep, tracked the Horde's movements, become invisible in the desert canyons. So invisible that the Scabs now often referred to the Circle as ghosts.

But Thomas now knew that the greatest danger no longer came from the Horde.

Treachery was brewing inside the Circle.

A horse snorted from the corrals around the bend behind Thomas. The fire popped and crackled as hungry flames lapped at the shimmering waves of heat they chased into the cool night air. The breathing of several thousand bodies steadied in the magic of the maiden's song.

Still no sign of his elder son, Samuel.

An echo followed the last note, and silence fell upon the Gathering as the maidens backed slowly into the crowd. Thomas lifted his gray chalice, filled to the brim with Elyon's red healing waters from the pool.

As one, the followers of Elyon lifted their chalices out to him, level with their steady gazes. The Salute. Their eyes held his, some defiant in their determination to stay true, many wet with tears of gratitude for the great sacrifice that had first turned the pools red.

The leaders stood to his left. Mikil and Jamous, her husband, side by side, goblets raised, staring forward, waiting for Thomas. Susan, one of the many colored albinos, and her lover, Johan, who had been a mighty warrior—was a mighty warrior—gripped each other's hands and watched Thomas.

Marie, his daughter from his first wife, who was now with Elyon, stood next to his youngest child, Jake, who was five years old one month ago. Where had all the years gone? The last time he'd taken a breath, Marie had been sixteen; now she was twenty-five. A hundred boys would have wed her years ago if Thomas hadn't been so stuffy, as she put it. At eighteen Marie had lost interest in boys and taken up scouting with Samuel. Her betrothal to Vadal, the dark-skinned man next to her, had occurred only after she abandoned her old passions.

Samuel, on the other hand, still pursued his, with enough eagerness to keep Thomas pacing late into the night on occasion.

And still, no sign of the boy. He'd been gone for a day.

The Circle waited, and he let the moment stretch to the snapping point. A presence here warmed the back of his neck with anticipation. They couldn't see him, hadn't seen him for many years, but Elyon was near.

Elyon—as the boy, as the warrior, as the lion, the lamb, the giver of life and the lover of all. Their Great Romance was for him. He'd given his life for them, and they for him.

They all wore the symbol that represented their own history, a medallion or a tattoo shaped like a circle, with an outer ring in green to signify the beginning, the life of Elyon. Then a black circle to remember evil's crushing blow. Two straps of red crossed the black circle, the death that brought life in the red waters.

And at the center, a white circle, for it was prophesied that Elyon would come again on a white horse and rescue his bride from the dragon Teeleh, who pursued her day and night.

Soon, Thomas thought. Elyon had to come soon. If he did not, they would fall apart. They'd been wandering in the desert for ten years, like lost Israelites without a home. At celebrations like this, surrounded by song and dance, they all knew the truth. But when the singing was over . . . how quickly they could forget.

Still he held them, three minutes now, and not a man, woman, or child over the age of two spoke. Even the infants seemed to understand that they had reached the climax of the three-day celebration. Later they would feast on the fifty boar they'd slaughtered and set over fires at the back of the canyon. They would dance and sing and boast of all things worthy and some not.

But they all knew that every pleasure they tasted, every hope that filled their chests, every moment of peace and love rested firmly on the meaning behind the words that Thomas would now speak.

His low voice flooded the canyon with an assurance that brought a tremble to their limbs.

"Lovers of Elyon who have drowned in the lakes and been given life, this is our hope, our passion, our only true reason to live."

"It is as he says," Chelise said in a light voice choked with emotion.

Together the three thousand responded, "He speaks the truth." Their soft voices rumbled through the valley.

They knew Elyon by many names: the Creator, who'd fashioned them; the Warrior, who'd once rescued them; the Giver of gifts, who gave them the fruit that healed and sustained them. But they'd agreed to simply call him Elyon several years earlier, when a heretic from a southern tribe began to teach that Thomas himself was their savior.

Thomas spoke with more intensity. "He has rescued us. He has wooed us. He has lavished us with more pleasures than we can contain in this life."

"It is as he says," Chelise said.

The people's reply washed over Thomas like a wave, gaining volume. "He speaks the truth."

"Now we wait for the return of our king, the prince warrior who loved us while we were yet Horde."

"It is as he says!"

"He speaks the truth!"

"Our lives are his, born in his waters, made pure by the very blood we now raise to the sky!" Thomas thundered each word.

And Chelise cried her agreement. "It is as he says!"

"He speaks the truth." Their voices spilled over the canyon walls for any within a mile on this still night to hear.

"Remember Elyon, brothers and sisters of the Circle! Live for him! Ready the bride, make a celebration ready, for he is among us!"

"It is as he says!"

The volume rose to a crushing roar. "He speaks the truth."

"I speak the truth."

"He speaks the truth!"

"I speak the truth!"

"He speaks the truth!"

Silence.

"Drink to remember. To the Great Romance. To Elyon!"

This time their response was whispered in utmost reverence, as if each syllable was something as precious as the red water in their hands.

"To Elyon."

Thomas closed his eyes, brought the chalice to his lips, tilted it back, and let the cool water flow into his mouth. The red liquid swirled around his tongue then seeped down his throat, leaving a lingering copper taste. He let the gentle effects of the first few drops warm his belly for a second, then swallowed deep, flooding his mouth and throat with the healing waters.

They weren't nearly as strong as the green lake waters that had once flowed with Elyon's presence. And they didn't contain the same medicinal qualities of the fruit that hung from the trees around the pools, but they lifted spirits and brought simple pleasure.

He took three full gulps of the precious water, allowing some to spill down his chin, then pulled the chalice away, cleared his throat with one final swallow, and gasped at the night sky.

"To Elyon!"

As one, the Circle pulled their goblets from their mouths like parched warriors satisfied by sweet ale, and roared at the night sky.

"To Elyon!"

And with that cry, the spirit of celebration was released. Thomas turned to Chelise, drew her to him with his free arm, and kissed her wet lips. A thousand voices cried their approval, chased by undulating calls from the unwed maidens and their hopeful suitors. Chelise's laughter filled his mouth as he spun back to the crowd, goblet still raised.

He pulled her forward, so all could see his bride. "Is there anyone here who would dare not love as Elyon has loved us all? Can anyone not remember the disease that covered their flesh?" Thomas looked at Chelise and spoke his poetic offering around a subtle grin that undoubtedly failed to properly express his love for this woman.

"What beauty, what pleasure, what intoxicating love he has given me for my own ashes. In place of the stench that once filled my very own nostrils he has given me this fragrance. A princess whom I can serve. She numbs my mind with dizzying pictures of exquisite beauty."

They all knew he was speaking of Chelise, who had been the princess of the Horde, Qurong's very own daughter. Now she was the bride of Elyon, Thomas's lover, the bearer of his youngest son, who stared up at them with wonder next to Marie.

"He speaks the truth," Johan said, grinning. He took a pull from his goblet and dipped his head.

"He speaks the truth," they returned, followed by more calls and rounds of drinks.

Johan, too, had been Horde not so long ago, charged with killing hundreds—thousands by the time it was all over—of Elyon's followers.

Thomas thrust his goblet toward the Gathering, unmindful of the liquid that splashed out; there were seventy-seven pools filled with the red waters, and not one had ever showed any sign of going dry.

"To the Horde."

"To the Horde!"

And they drank again, flooding themselves with the intoxicating waters in a start to what promised to be a night of serious, unrestricted celebration.

"Aye, Father." The male voice came from behind and to his right. The husky, unmistakable sound of Samuel. "To the Horde."

Thomas lowered his chalice and turned to see his son perched atop his horse, drilling him with his bright green eyes. He rode low in the pale stallion's saddle and moved with the horse as if he'd been bred and born on the beast. His dark hair fell to his shoulders, blown by a hard ride. Sweat had mixed with the red mud that he and those of his band applied to their cheekbones; streaks etched his darkened face and neck. His leather chest guard was open, allowing the night air to cool his bared chest, still glistening in the moonlight.

He had his mother's nose and eyes.

A stab of pride sliced through Thomas's heart. Samuel might have gone astray, but this image of his boy could have been *him* fifteen years ago.

The stallion's *clip-clopping* hooves echoed as it stepped into the firelight, followed by three, then five, then nine warriors who'd taken up arms with Samuel. All were dressed in the same battle dress of the Forest Guard, largely abandoned since the Circle had laid down arms eleven years ago. Only the guards and scouts wore the protective leathers to ward off arrows and blades.

But Samuel . . . no amount of reason seemed to jar good sense into his thick skull.

His son stilled his horse with a gentle tug on its reins. His followers stopped behind him in a loose formation that left them with no weak flank, standard Guard protocol by his own orders. Samuel and his band moved with the ease of seasoned warriors.

A few catcalls from different points in the crowd raised praise for the man who scanned them without a hint of acknowledgment.

"Hear, Samuel! Elyon's strength, boy!" A pause. "Keep the boogers in their stink hole, Samuel!"

This remark was a departure from general sentiment, though not as distant from the heart of the Circle as it once had been. Thomas was all too aware of the rumblings among many clans.

"Nice of you to join us, Samuel," Thomas said, tipping his chalice in the boy's direction.

His son looked directly at Chelise, dipped his head, then looked back at the three thousand gathered in the natural amphitheater. "To the Horde," he called.

"To the Horde." But only half took up the cry. The rest, like Thomas, heard the bite in Samuel's voice.

"To the stinking, bloody Horde who butcher our children and spread their filthy disease through our forests!" Samuel cried, voice now bitter with mockery.

Only a few took him up. "Stinking, bloody Horde."

"Our friends, the Horde, have sent their apologies for taking the life of our own three days ago. They have sent us all a gift to express their remorse, and I have brought it to our Gathering."

Samuel stuck his hand out, palm up. A dark object sailed forward, lobbed by Petrus, son of Jeremiah, and Samuel snatched it out of the air as if it were a water bag needing to be refilled. He tossed it onto the ground. The object bounced once and rolled to stop where firelight illuminated the fine details of their prize.

It was a head. A human head. A Horde head with a mane of long dreadlocks, covered in disease.

A chill snaked down Thomas's spine. This, he thought, was the beginning of the end.

2

THERE WAS no gasp, no outcry, only a heavy silence. None of them was a stranger to violence. But among the Circle, taking the life of another, Scab or albino, was strictly forbidden.

This . . . this looked to be the result of an execution. Carried out by his own son. For a moment, all Thomas could hear was the pounding of his own heart.

Vadal, son of Ronin, one of the very first to drown, stumbled out to the severed head and stared, disbelieving, for a moment. Any hint of celebration in the wake of Thomas's salute was gone.

He swiveled to face Samuel. "Are you mad, man?"

"The head belongs to the man who hung Richard, son of Sacura. We seized him, tried him, and found him guilty. The punishment was death."

Vadal thrust his finger at the head near his feet. "Don't be a fool. You *kill* them and you might as well *be* them. This is your idea?"

"This, you blithering fool, is doing the work of Elyon," Samuel said calmly. "Ridding the world of those who mock him."

"Only to become them?" Vadal shot back.

"Do I look like a Scab to you? Am I—having defiled the love of Elyon himself as you claim—now covered from head to foot with the disease that marks unbelievers? Has he taken away his healing from me?"

Thomas held up his hand to bring some order before the whole thing got out of control. "You've made your point, Samuel. Now take your prize, bury it somewhere far from here, and return to our celebration."

"That's not what I had in mind."

Thomas felt his own patience thinning. "Get off of that horse. Pick up that head. Get back on your horse. And leave us!"

A crooked grin crossed Samuel's face. "Now, there's the father I once knew. Commander of the Forest Guard. The world once quivered at your name."

"And now it quivers at the name of another."

"Does it? Elyon? And just where is Elyon these days?"

"Stop it!" Chelise snapped. She released Thomas's arm and took a step toward Samuel. "How dare you speak of your Maker with such a callous tongue?"

"I'm only stating what is on the mind of us all. Love the Horde? Why? They hate us, they kill us, they strike terror into our camps. They would wipe out this entire gathering with one blow if they could. We are the vomit on the bottom of their boots, and that will never change."

"*You* were once Horde, you insolent pup!" Chelise shot back.

Samuel nudged his horse around the severed head. His posse stood their ground, a group of mind-numb fighters who'd tasted just enough bloodlust to give them a thirst. "Do we not believe that a time will soon come when Elyon will destroy all of this land and the Horde with it, and finally rescue us to bliss?"

Silence.

"Ten years have gone by without one indisputable sign that Elyon still hovers nearby, preparing to rescue us. You're too busy running and hiding from that Horde beast Qurong to ask why."

"That *beast* is my father," Chelise cried. "I would die for him. And you would kill him?"

Samuel paused only a moment. "Kill Qurong, the supreme commander who has sworn to slaughter our children? The Scab who paces deep into the night, poisoned by bitterness against his own daughter because she betrayed him by drowning? *That* Qurong? The one you are obsessed with because he gave birth to you?" He spoke in a soft voice that cut the night silence like a thin blade. "You love your father more than you love any of us, Mother. If it were his head on the ground now, we might finally be free."

Samuel had always been bitter about Chelise's love for her father, but he'd never voiced it so plainly.

Vadal spoke for Chelise, who was swimming in so much fury at the moment that she didn't appear to be able to form words.

"This is heresy! You have no—"

"I took this Scab's head in a canyon twenty miles from here," Samuel announced, ignoring Vadal. "We ambushed him, and my sword cut cleanly through his neck with one swing. It was the most satisfying thing I have done in my life."

"Samuel!" This from Marie, who glared at her brother, red-faced.

Thomas fought a terrible urge to leap upon the boy and whip his hide until he begged for mercy. But he remained rooted to the ground.

Samuel blurted out, "War is permissible. I say we wage it. I've been out there slipping in and around the Horde since I turned fifteen, and I can tell you that with five thousand warriors we could make them regret the day they ever killed one of ours."

"Elyon forbid!" Vadal gasped.

"If Elyon will kindly tell me I'm wrong, then I will step down. We say that evil is on the flesh, that the disease on the Horde's skin is Elyon's curse. So why am I still disease free, having committed this terrible evil by killing this Scab, unless Elyon approves? Until he makes my error clear, my heart will cry for the days when we took them on, twenty to one, and turned the sand red with their blood."

"It's sacrilege!"

"What's sacrilege?" Samuel threw back. "What Elyon tells us himself, or what we have been told he says? Have any of you heard this specific instruction from Elyon lately? Or are you all too drunk on his fruit and water to notice his absence?"

"This . . ." Vadal was trembling with rage. "This is utter nonsense!"

"It used to be that we celebrated the passing of every soul, believing that they had gone on to a better place. Now our celebrations at the passing are filled with mourning. Why? Where is Elyon, and where is this better place?"

None of them could deny the subtle shift in their treatment of the dead.

"We used to long for the day of Elyon, clinging to the hope that any moment he would come swooping over the hills to rescue us once and for all. Now we long only for the day of the Gathering, when we can drink the waters and eat the fruit and dance ourselves silly, deep into the night. The Great Romance has become our elixir, a place to hide from the world."

"You're speaking rubbish."

"I say bring back the days of our glory! Hasten the day of Elyon's return. Fight Qurong the way the Eramites do."

"You'll have to fight me first," Vadal said.

Samuel pulled his horse around on its rear quarter to face the man. His mount snorted in protest. "So be it." Loudly to the whole gathering, he said, "I'm told the followers of Eram also respect the challenge as we once did. I challenge Vadal of Ronin to combat as in the days of old. It is still permitted."

Was it? Thomas felt his gut churn.

"I accept," Vadal snapped.

"To the death."

"Stop it!" Chelise cried. Then, in a softer voice, "I warned you about this, Samuel."

"Did you? Our prevailing doctrine denounces violence against the Horde," Samuel said, "but what does it say of the challenge? We speak all night long about tales of the heroics that preceded us: Elyon this, Thomas that . . . I say let the heroics be seen in the flesh. Elyon will save the one who speaks the truth as he once did."

His argument contained a thread of truth that turned Thomas's blood cold. Before their very eyes they were witnessing the greatest threat to all truth. And from the mouth of his own son. But Thomas was too stunned to form a response. This was his own son, for the love of Elyon!

Chelise whispered his name urgently, and he saw that she was staring at him, begging him to stop Samuel.

Instead, Thomas looked at Ronin and Johan for support. William, Mikil, Jamous—any of them. They all stared at him for guidance. Were they, too, growing tired of waiting for an imminent return that had been imminent for longer than any of them cared to think? Could this be the source of their hesitation?

Samuel wasn't the only one to wonder if Elyon really was coming back for a "bride" anytime soon. After all, he'd allowed them to take beating after beating without so much as lifting a finger. What good was being disease free if you lived in ridicule and on the run?

Thomas caught Ronin's stare. "Ronin?"

The spiritual leader of Thomas's clan frowned, then studied his son Vadal and Samuel.

"No one in the Circle has issued a challenge for a very long time. Never, that I know of. It's utterly foolish."

"But was it outlawed?" Samuel pressed.

Chelise flung both arms wide. "This is so much nonsense, this flexing of the muscle to prove a point. And to the *death*?" She turned to the others. "Come on, Mikil! Johan, surely you can't think this is permissible."

"It's absurd," Mikil said, and Johan agreed, but neither was demanding. The fear in Thomas's gut spread. Why weren't they rushing out and dragging Samuel off his horse in protest? They harbored a small vessel of doubt themselves? Surely not all of them!

Samuel took advantage of their inaction. "Didn't Elyon once condone our use of force? Has he changed his mind? Does Elyon change his mind? *Well, well, by the heavens I've made a dreadful mistake, I will change the way it is done!* Is this a perfect Creator?"

He let that settle.

"No. Elyon knows that it is better to love, that everything rests on the fulfillment of the Great Romance, like the union of bride and groom after a night of dizzying celebration. But sometimes love can be expressed by defending the truth. Vadal has that prerogative. No, Mikil?"

The famed fighter shifted her eyes to Thomas, neither agreeing nor disagreeing with Samuel, but by this very deflection she had endorsed him. Didn't she realize what she was doing? Supporting this ludicrous assertion before the entire Gathering could only bring ruin!

But the fear cascading down Thomas's spine rendered him mute as well. A dozen years ago he would have cut this challenge to the ground with a few well-placed words. Those days were gone, replaced by a wisdom that now seemed to fail him entirely. Smothered by dread.

"Does this Gathering cower from the truth?" Samuel called out. "Let me fight as the Eramites fight!"

Thomas had risked his life on a hundred occasions to love the Horde, to win Chelise, to follow the ways of Elyon, no matter how dangerous or brutal the path. Now that path had doubled back and was running straight down the middle of the Circle itself. The greatest danger was from inside, he always told the others. Tonight it had finally bared its teeth for all to see.

And there was no outcry from the Circle against Samuel's demand.

Thomas looked up at the thousands regarding him. "Who says so?"

No one shouted agreement, as was their right. But after several beats a younger man from another clan—Andres, if Thomas was right—lifted his drink.

"So says I." They looked at him, and he stepped forward into the orange firelight. "There is a time for peace and there is a time for war. Maybe the time for war has come. Didn't Elyon once wage war?"

A hundred *ayes* rumbled through the night.

So then, Samuel *was* tapping the unspoken sentiment of many. This attitude was practically epidemic, a cancer that would eat them alive from the inside.

And this from his own son . . .

Thomas tried to swallow, but the fear now swelling through his head prevented the simple action. He'd faced that devil Teeleh himself and bested him in the blackest forest; he'd hacked his way out of thirty encroaching Scabs with a single broad blade; he'd marched into the city to the cheers of a hundred thousand throats shouting the praises of Thomas of Hunter, the greatest warrior who'd ever lived.

But at the moment, he was only a terrified husk. Useless against this enemy called Samuel, son of Hunter.

It occurred to him that Samuel was speaking again, demanding more from the crowd. "Who else?" he was shouting. And hundreds were agreeing.

"Don't be so thin headed!" William cried over them all. "We've always agreed that we were shown a new way by Elyon, apart from the sword. Now our impatience changes that? Our way is to love our enemies, not wage war on them."

A thousand *ayes* and shrill cries of agreement shook the canyon.

Finally! Finally some sense!

"But I am within my rights to make this challenge, am I not?" Samuel demanded. "And Vadal is in his rights to accept."

"Aye." The agreements peppered the gathering, but all eyes were now back on Ronin and Thomas.

Ronin must have noted the concern that had locked up Thomas, because he addressed the crowd.

"Yes, I suppose it is right what Samuel says. Nothing I know of has outlawed his prerogative to challenge my son. And Vadal has the right to accept that challenge or reject it, which would be the wiser by far. Frankly, I'm appalled that there isn't a protest among you all. Have you decided to feed your bloodlust?"

"He's right," Chelise said. "This is the kind of thing we might do as Horde."

"Or under the old Thomas," a lone voice called.

"All things may be permissible, but not all are beneficial," Ronin said, cutting off any further dialogue that might mire them in their own violent history. To Vadal, his son: "Surely, you see the madness in this."

"I see the madness in what tempts Samuel and half of the Circle," he said.

Samuel slid out of his saddle and landed on the ground with a slap of boots on rock. He slipped his sword from its scabbard, thrust the bronzed tip into the shale, and rested both palms in its handle.

"What is it, O favored one? Shall we test the truth?" The fool wasn't taking any of this seriously! Or worse, he was drunk on his own power and took Vadal's death very seriously.

"I accept," Vadal snapped.

"No!" Marie, Thomas's eldest child and Vadal's betrothed, stepped out, ripped a sword from the mount closest to Samuel's, and twirled it once with a flip of her wrist. "I exercise my right to take the place of any other in a challenge."

"Don't be a fool," Vadal said. "Step back!"

"Shut up. If you have the right to throw away your life, so do I. Those are the rules."

"That was a long time ago. Get back, I'm telling you!"

Marie turned to the elder. "Ronin?"

The spiritual leader nodded. "It is her right."

Samuel grinned, whipped his sword through a backhanded swing, and circled to his right, inviting Marie into an imaginary fighting ring.

"Stop them!" Chelise was glaring at Thomas, whispering harshly. "Do something."

He did nothing. He could hardly think straight, much less trust himself to do something he would not later regret. He could not stop them; they all had the same freedom to make their own choices.

The grin had faded from Samuel's face. Surely he wouldn't use his sword on his own sister. This was Marie's ploy. She knew that Samuel would back down. This was her gamble, and Thomas could see the wisdom in it.

"So, Sister. It's you and me, is it?"

"Looks that way." She walked closer, dragging her sword casually behind her. Not to fool a soul; they all knew she was a devil with that thing.

Samuel glanced at the blade, leaning on his own with confidence. "I'm not the young pup you punished the last time we played this game."

"This isn't a game," Marie said. "You're playing with the fate of our people."

"You'll get hurt," he said.

"Then hurt me, Brother."

3

WHILE THOMAS HUNTER stood in the canyon, unraveling, Billy Rediger paced the atrium of Raison Pharmaceutical in Thailand two thousand years earlier, in our own reality—or the histories, depending on how one looked at it.

Billy took a moment to take in his surroundings: the rich golden marble floor, the huge paintings of a red and yellow flower that looked as though it might be the bug-eating variety, the gilded wallpaper, two heavy crystal chandeliers that could crush a Volkswagen. The drug giant's exotic facade fueled his haunting impression of Raison Pharmaceutical.

This is where it had all started roughly thirty-six years ago, in this very building just outside Bangkok. Seven years before Billy had been born and whisked away to the monastery in Colorado, where he'd been raised and turned into a freak.

This was where Thomas Hunter had stumbled upon the Raison Strain, the deadly virus that turned the world upside down. How many dead was it? Hardly imaginable.

But worse than what had died was what had survived Hunter's discovery.

What would Darcy and Johnny say if they knew of the obsession that had overtaken Billy's mind this last year? He had a pathological need to understand why his life had been profoundly impacted by these books called the Books of History.

If his two confidants knew of his quest, they would leave their safe harbor in Colorado, hunt him down, and lock him in a cage. Because

23

they would assume that Billy was after more, wouldn't they? More than just understanding, more than just connecting with his past, more than chasing down the truth, more than . . .

"They will see you now, sir." The receptionist, a man named Williston, had a heavy French accent.

Billy turned, startled out of his moment of unguarded admissions. *They?* He'd asked to see only Monique de Raison.

He caught his image in a ten-by-ten mirror framed in heavy black ironwork. Still dressed in the same white shirt he'd thrown on just before landing eight hours earlier. The self-applied blond highlights in his red hair looked too obvious, and his head hadn't seen a brush since the take-off from Washington, D.C., a day earlier. *Here stands Billy Rediger, one of the three famed gifted savants who turned Paradise, Colorado into a household name.* The rumpled look would have to do.

He was twenty-nine going on nineteen. If they only knew.

Billy wiped his sweaty palms on his jeans, squirted a dash of cinnamon freshener into his mouth, straightened his collar, and strode for the door as the dark-haired Williston looked on with a deadpan stare.

"Thank you, Williston. Thank you very much, sir. And by all means, ditch the blonde from France. Go for the local girl. It's what you want."

The man blinked with surprise. "Pardon?"

"Ditch Adel. You think she's a whore, and you're probably right. Go for the maid—what's her name? Betty. Yes, Betty."

The man was speechless—probably wasn't every day a stranger told him what he was thinking. This far from home, not many knew of Billy's unique gifting. And if they did, they associated it only with a distant face seen on the Net, not a real, living human being walking before them in three dimensions.

He stepped past the ten-foot doors into a white office with colonial latticed windows that looked out to the thick green jungle beyond. At the room's center sat a large teakwood desk with a cream-colored lamp that shed yellow light over a clean glass top.

The dark-haired woman who stood behind the desk looked younger than her reported sixty years—all those drugs she manufactured, he supposed. After six months of searching out every scrap of information he could harvest from records far and wide, Billy felt as though he already knew Monique de Raison.

She'd accepted full control of Raison Pharmaceutical from her father, Jacques de Raison, after the Raison Strain had all but destroyed the infamous company. Rebuilding the company's shattered image was no small task, but she'd risen to the occasion and delivered with flying colors. The sharp, dark eyes studying him as he walked toward her opened to a mind that missed nothing.

Billy knew, because it was his gift to know what anyone was thinking by looking into their eyes.

This is what Monique was thinking at the moment: *Younger than I expected, dressed like a punk. Is he really reading my thoughts this very moment? Does he know I will turn him away regardless of what he hopes to accomplish? Does he know that he's a freak?*

Billy stretched out his hand. "Yes, I do know that I'm a freak."

Monique stared at him for a moment, then lifted a pair of dark glasses from the desk and put them on, effectively blocking her mind from his probing eyes. She took his hand. "So you *can* do what they say."

"Thanks to Thomas Hunter," he said, and released her hand. Because yes, without Thomas Hunter there never would have been magic books to turn him into the freak he was. But that was all in the past.

Billy was here to change the future.

A blonde woman of about Monique's age sat to his right, one leg crossed over the other, hands folded in her lap. She wore dark glasses already, not wanting to risk any exposure to his prying eyes, but he recognized Kara Hunter immediately. Thomas Hunter's sister, keeper of many secrets regarding the blood Billy was seeking.

Both Kara and Monique in one sitting. He'd struck gold.

Billy crossed to Kara, who rose and offered her hand. "Mr. Rediger."

"And you would be Kara Hunter."

She nodded.

"Please, have a seat," Monique said, motioning to the guest chair in front of her desk.

He did, and they both eased back into their chairs. Eyes on him, he presumed, though he couldn't be certain what their eyes were doing behind those dark glasses.

"It is a bright day, isn't it?" he said, failing to lighten the mood.

"What can we do for you?" Monique asked.

"Just like that, huh? You meet one of the few people alive today whose life was profoundly impacted by the Hunter legacy and that's all you can ask?"

"Every living being on this planet was profoundly impacted by my brother," Kara said. "Not the least, himself. You have this interesting gift because you evidently came in contact—"

"Evidently? Try conclusively."

"Conclusively?" Monique cut in. "And what else have you concluded?"

"That thirty-six years ago Thomas Hunter claimed to have dreamed about another reality. That this other reality was, in fact, real. That the Books of History, magical books that turned words to flesh, came to us from that reality. I should know. I used them. They gave me my gift."

"Evidently."

"Conclusively. Did you know that I wrote about Thomas in the books? Maybe that's why he dreamed what he dreamed and awakened in this other world of his. If I hadn't written it, he wouldn't have gone there, and if he hadn't gone there, he wouldn't have learned how to alter the Raison Vaccine and turn it into an airborne virus that did what it did. You might say I was the one who started it all. That it was all my fault, not yours, Monique."

He knew by their silence that his role in these events was news to them, and he continued while their heads still spun.

"So here I am. Billy, the one who has a gift for seeing more than most people can see, just like Thomas Hunter had a gift for seeing, or in his case dreaming, what most don't dream. That makes me unique, don't you think? You could even say it gives me certain rights."

Kara stood and paced to the window, arms crossed. She turned slowly back and studied him through her dark glasses. "Your case is fascinating, Mr. Rediger—"

"Billy. Please call me Billy."

"Fascinating, Billy. But it's no more than what either of us has faced. I'm sure you can appreciate that. As you obviously know, we both had a singular relationship with Thomas. You came out of your experience with this unique ability to read people's thoughts when you look into their eyes. That sounds like a net gain. I lost a brother. Many people lost their lives."

"Net gain?" he snapped. He tried to remain calm, but he wasn't as adept at controlling his temper as he'd once been. "You call this curse a gain? I'm a freak! My soul haunts me. I can't live in the same happy ignorance that the rest of you can when every lousy thought is opened to me. It's driving me mad, and I have to root out the meaning of all this. End it all."

"We're sorry you've suffered, Billy," Kara said, clasping her hands before her. "But the stakes were always more than feelings, yours or ours. We've all paid a price. I think it's best to leave the past in the past. Don't you?"

"Well, see, that's just the thing, Kara." *A little too much emphasis on her name. Mustn't sound so condescending.* "I don't think the past *is* in the past. For one thing, *I'm* not in the past. I'm here and now, a living consequence of your brother's indiscretions."

"Granted, you're one of the many effects—"

"And then there's the matter of his blood."

He wished for a line of sight into their eyes. But he hardly needed to read their minds to know he'd hit the nerve he'd come to hit.

"Blood?" Monique said, leaning back in her chair.

"Blood. The one remaining vial of Thomas Hunter's blood that you put in safekeeping. Did you think you two were the only ones who knew? The lab technician who withdrew the blood was named Isabella Romain and she lives in Covington, Kentucky, today. Naturally she refused to say what her mind was thinking, but I know with absolute certainty that a vial of Thomas Hunter's blood was taken by you, Dr. Raison, for security."

They did not deny it.

"And these eyes of mine exposed a few other secrets," he said. "Turns out that Thomas's blood allowed anyone who used it to wake up in the reality that the Books of History came from. Is it in fact another reality? Or is it our future? Either way, that makes the vial of blood a potent little vessel of a whole lot of fun, don't you think? Not to mention a path to some pretty powerful books."

Billy couldn't stop the wild grin that twisted his lips. He was sweating, he realized. Profusely. It beaded up on his forehead and ran past his temples. With each passing week he seemed to have more difficulty maintaining control of his nerves. The tics and the sweating were the worst. Thankfully he'd managed to suppress the tics thus far. Wouldn't do to start jerking about like a short-circuiting robot before asking them to trust him with their deepest secrets.

He took a deep breath and made an effort to appear reasonable. "Seriously, friends, I know it all. And I've come to ask you to bring me in."

"In?" Monique asked, one brow raised.

"Trust me. Use me. I'm all yours."

"To what end?"

"To what end?" It was a fair question, no matter how obvious the answer seemed to him. "Sorry, being through what I've been through makes that question sound a bit silly. For the purpose of survival, naturally. To *that* end. So that we can take this messy, crazy world and make sense of it again."

"And just how do you propose to do that?"

"For starters, as I'm sure you realize, some would consider me a fugitive. Have been for over two years, ever since the Tolerance Act in the fabulous United States of America turned people like me into bigots. Wackos at the least. That doesn't sit right with all people. The world is primed for more than simple, regional conflicts. Surely you can see that.

The very laws that are meant to bring peace and love are gonna bring the big boom, baby."

A bit too free with the colloquialism there.

"And?"

"And we may have the one thing that could set things right."

Both stared without showing any reaction.

He stood and paced. "I need to connect with my past. And with the future. Are you catching my drift here?"

"Not really, no."

"I need the blood."

Silence. Dead giveaway.

Monique cleared her throat. "I don't think you understand, Mr. Rediger. Even if we knew where this figment of your imagination was, this so-called vial of blood, what exactly do you think you could do with it?"

"Go into Thomas's dreams! To the place all this began. Please, don't tell me you haven't tried it."

No admission. No denial.

"You have no idea how much work it took to uncover these dark secrets of yours. Only a handful of people know what actually happened: That Thomas Hunter's blood was altered when he crossed into the other reality. That it contained unique properties. That when even a single drop of his blood mixes with a person's while they are dreaming, they, too, can go where he went, which might well be the future. That, my two lovely friends, sounds like a very major trip. You can't possibly go your entire life knowing about such a thing and not try it at least once. Kinda like sex, right?"

They still didn't seem to appreciate the simple honesty he was laying down here.

"No?" he pressed.

"Not really, no," Monique said.

"You haven't tried it?"

"Sex?"

"The blood!"

"We haven't established that this blood you talk about even exists. If it does, perhaps you can tell us where we could find it. The powers you describe sound incredibly valuable."

So, they would play it this way. What he would give to dive into their minds right now.

One way or another, he would have his way with both of their minds.

"Cute," he said. "We're going to pretend, then, is that it?"

Kara walked back to her chair and sat. "Please, Billy, have a seat."

He sat again, aware that his right hand was twitching slightly.

"Tea?"

Tea? A bit late to ask him if he wanted to break bread with them. On the other hand, this represented a sea change in at least Kara's attitude toward him. Yes, indeed. At least a pretention of being sweet.

"No thank you, Kara. No tea at the moment, but thank you for offering."

She smiled. "Perhaps we were a bit too hasty in dismissing you. Let's try a different approach, shall we? After Thomas left, my life never seemed to find its true bearing."

"Careful, Kara," Monique warned in a low voice.

Kara glanced at her friend. "It's okay. He obviously knows at least some of the truth." Back to Billy. "But you must understand how dangerous your knowledge is. I'm not sure you do. In the wrong hands, what you know could bring about more pain and suffering than you can possibly imagine."

"Oh, I think I can imagine it just fine. Why do you think I'm here? I've spent every waking minute for the last year thinking of it, tracking you two down."

"The information you have could end life as we know it," Kara continued.

"It could bring the great dragon down from the sky and fill the oceans with blood," Billy said. "Saint John's Apocalypse."

He could only imagine them blinking behind their shades. Too much, way too much. His imaginations were a thing that he should keep strictly to himself. He should know that by now. Not even these two had the capacity to go where his mind went, which is why he was suited—perhaps even prepared, preordained, chosen, all of that rot—to do what needed doing now.

"As a figure of speech," he said, circling his hand for effect, "the dragon being the symbol of death, virus, nuclear holocaust, Armageddon. Point is, if it's all true, if a person could cross into another world with Thomas's blood, and then return with untold secrets, they might not only unravel the past, but also solve the problems of the future. Of now."

"We get it," Monique said.

He couldn't read her true sentiment by her tone; he'd become too accustomed to reading people by their minds.

"So then. You're going to bring me in?" Billy asked.

"We should lock you up and throw away the key, Billy," Monique said.

"What she means," Kara inserted, "is that none of us is trustworthy with what we know. We both try to stay . . . private. We're not sure you appreciate just how difficult that can be."

"I was raised in a monastery. I think that qualifies me."

"Perhaps. But we don't know where the blood is, Billy. Or if it even still exists. We've removed ourselves from that knowledge."

"For everyone's sake," Monique said.

Nonsense. Billy knew then that they had no intention whatsoever of trusting him with the code to their front gates, much less the most potent secret the world had ever known. And why should they? He'd presented himself as a bit of a loose cannon.

But they didn't know him. He'd danced with the devil himself, and he wouldn't let these two witches stop him from doing it again.

"Well, then we'll have to take this one step at a time," Billy said. "I was wondering if you could recommend suitable accommodations."

The door flew wide and a young woman walked in, dressed in a short black dress with spaghetti straps. Bare feet, petite physique. Her black hair fell loosely past square shoulders, and her soft brown eyes cut sharply through the world.

"Excuse me, Mother. So sorry to interrupt. Henri tells me you've decided to sell our New York research laboratory. One of *my* laboratories the last time I checked. Tell me why Henri has decided to speak lies."

"So nice to see you, Janae," Monique returned in a soothing voice. "How was your trip to France?"

"As expected." No further explanation. Monique's daughter, this stunning creature with a fluid French accent who looked to be in her early twenties, seemed to notice Billy for the first time. She turned her gaze on him and peeled him open with that first look.

And who is this young pip? An American, clearly, dressed to attend a rock concert. What kind of fools is Mother exposing herself to these days? And what are those monstrous glasses doing on Mother's face?

"Mr. Rediger, please meet my daughter, Janae." Billy saw that a thin smile had nudged the corner of Monique's mouth northward. "But then you probably already know all about her, don't you? Perhaps more than I do."

The bold pronouncement left Janae silent for the moment. Billy thought it best to leave the young woman wondering.

"You might want to consider wearing dark glasses, dear Janae. Our visitor from America seems to have the ability to read minds."

Again, silence from the spirited one. Billy decided then that he would out himself fully to the dark-haired beauty. One, because he found her strangely compelling, and two, because he thought it wise to give her a reason to find him just as interesting.

"Young pip?" He stared into her eyes. "This young pip who's dressed to attend a rock concert is inside your mind right now, dear Janae. And what a delicious treat it is, all that hostility and resentment for having never known your father. He vanished when you were a small child, and you're thinking even now that he held secrets that would complete you. Isn't that what all orphans believe?"

She blinked. Her mouth parted slightly but held back the gasp some might utter when so quickly stripped. He liked her already.

"It's okay," he said. "I'm an orphan as well."

"I think we all get the point," Monique said. "He's quite dangerous. I would tread carefully."

But Billy wasn't finished. "I'm here for the vial of blood that your mother harvested from Thomas Hunter three decades ago. Maybe you know where it is. Or you could help me find it."

He might as well have dropped a bomb in the room.

Janae looked at her mother. "What blood?"

"This is completely unacceptable," Kara snapped, rising from her chair.

"On the contrary, this is the only acceptable course," Billy returned. "You need to keep an eye on me. What better way than to keep me close? You know I won't put up with either of you babysitting me."

His implication could hardly be stronger. He took the fact that Janae didn't immediately reject the notion of "babysitting" him as a sign of her interest. A glance into her eyes confirmed this.

On second look, *interest* was a bad word choice to describe her disposition toward him. *Fascination* was better. Billy turned back to the others.

Kara was clearly on rough ground. "Surely you can't—"

"It's okay, Kara," Monique said. "He's right. He can stay in the guest quarters until his curiosity is satisfied. God knows we're all better off with him here than out there where real damage can be done."

Monique de Raison thought she could control him, Billy realized. Anyone else and he would dismiss the possibility outright. But Monique was not anyone else. Neither was Kara.

Nor, for that matter, was Janae, who was still trying to understand him.

"Please give us a moment, Billy," Monique said. "Williston will show you to the guest building. Janae will be right out."

Billy stood and walked for the door. The scent of Janae's musky perfume filled him with a sudden desire as he walked past her. Those deep, dark secrets her father had hidden from her seemed to beckon him. There was something about Janae that pulled at him like a strong tide.

"Take your time," he said, stepping from the room.

4

The Future

CHELISE WATCHED Samuel and Marie stare at each other in the dead silence, seemingly unconcerned by the other's sword, like two roosters facing off, expressionless. Vadal stood to one side, pale. The other leaders looked on, unmoving.

The Circle hung on the unfolding drama as if not quite sure it was all really happening. One moment they'd been awash in Thomas's poetic love for her and for Elyon; the next, the Gathering celebration had been flattened with this insane challenge to the essence of what they held sacred.

The Great Romance was being debated at the end of a sword! Is this what she'd drowned for? They all waited for Thomas.

But Thomas wasn't stopping the lunacy.

Elyon's people had never adopted a hierarchy of government that allowed a few to control the many. Guide, yes. But each person was encouraged to follow his heart. They'd all seen what religion had done when the Horde followed their priests, first Ciphus, then Witch, then Sucrow, and now the worst of the lot, Ba'al.

Thomas had a particular distaste for manipulation through religion, preferring faith and Elyon's Great Romance. But this . . . this was ridiculous.

Chelise glanced at him and saw that his jaw was set. He was going to allow them to fight.

Samuel launched himself at a knee-high boulder, planted his right

35

foot near the top, and threw himself into a backflip high over Marie's head. He brought his sword down as he sailed above her, a devastating swing that took full advantage of not only his well-muscled arms, but his leg strength, transferred now to his downward thrust. Thomas had told her that the splitter, as the move had been dubbed, had been named back in the days of war for its ability to cut a warrior in half, from head to crotch, with one blow.

Marie dropped to one knee, lifted her sword—one hand on the handle, one on the broad blade—and jerked the weapon over her head as a shield. The sound of Samuel's blade crashing into Marie's clanged through the valley, echoing off the cliff walls.

Would Samuel have completed his swing if Marie hadn't reacted in time? The impetuous fool had lost his mind.

Marie's braided hair swirled around her face as she pivoted, still on one knee, then lunged for Samuel's body before he landed and gathered his bearings.

Samuel anticipated her. Somehow he managed to withdraw a gutting knife. With a flip of his wrist he turned the knife back along his forearm and deflected Marie's sword. He landed with a chuckle and used his momentum to throw himself into a back handspring.

But Marie was already swinging around, sword extended for a second blow. This one nicked Samuel's chin as he threw himself out of the way.

Marie snatched her blade back, and Samuel righted himself. He touched his chin, felt the blood flowing over his fingers, and glared, face red. Marie stood on guard, breathing steadily through her nostrils.

A grin slowly twisted Samuel's lips, but this was not the look of humor or the stuff of play. This was a fierce grin, strung with resolve and rage.

"Now," he said. "Now you will see."

"You want to kill me, Samuel?" She circled to her left, opposite him. "Huh? Is that what the love of Elyon has taught you?"

"Was that Elyon who just drew first blood? I could have sworn it was you."

"Only because you challenged to kill my lover," she said.

"One for the sake of many."

"You wouldn't kill me, Samuel."

He responded in a low, guttural voice that could have belonged to an animal, Chelise thought. "Then you don't know me."

Samuel moved so quickly that Marie didn't have time to deflect. She could only jerk to her right as his knife flashed from his left hand, sliced through the night air, and thudded securely into her left shoulder.

Where it quivered, then stilled, buried two inches in her flesh.

Chelise was too stunned to act on the horror that swept through her mind. Thomas looked on, immobilized by outrage or letting history take its own course, she couldn't tell, but she wanted to slap him and tell him to make them stop.

They lived in a brutal world, but the way of the Circle was to avoid this kind of brutality in favor of love, dancing, and feasting deep into the night.

"Stop this." Mikil said, stepping forward. "For the love of Elyon, stop this foolishness."

"Back off." The growl came from Marie now.

Johan joined Mikil. "She's right, this is proving nothing."

Marie jerked the blade from her shoulder and sent it flying in Johan's direction. "Back off!"

He slapped the blade from the air before it reached him and snarled. The general in him hadn't forgotten how to move.

But before any of them could move to interfere, Marie threw herself forward and swung her blade.

Again, Samuel deflected the blow.

Again, Marie swung.

Then they were in close combat, thrusting and parrying, filling the valley with grunts and the clash of metal against metal.

The first sounds from the crowd came in the form of gasps when either Marie or Samuel narrowly escaped the opponent's blade. Then cheers of support or objection rose from a small number when Marie landed a hard blow to Samuel's right leg, severing his leather thigh guard in two.

The crowd is being pulled in, Chelise thought. *They are throwing aside their love for Elyon and blindly following this sickening orgy of violence.* The crowd's cheers of support or opposition swelled. Then one cry rose above them all and sliced through Chelise's mind.

"Silence the Horde lover, Samuel! Gut this child of Qurong!"

Chelise's blood ran cold. The call, a woman's shrill cry rising above the others, had come from the right side.

"They took my child. Take theirs! Vengeance belongs to Elyon, and he will drink their blood as they have become drunk on ours."

Samuel and Marie couldn't possibly have heard the voice amid the cacophony of shouts, the roar of three thousand voices now either crying out in outrage or throwing their support behind one of the combatants.

Chelise's son and daughter by marriage fought on.

There it was again, off to her right. She isolated the voice. "Gut the son of Teeleh. May Qurong and Ba'al, the servant of Teeleh, rot in hell. Qurong is the son of Teeleh, and the Horde who hunt us are Shataiki, who belong in a river of blood." Then even bolder, so that Chelise forgot how to breathe. "May Qurong rot in hell, and all who call themselves loyal to him die under the sword of Elyon!"

"Silence!" Chelise screamed. "Silence!"

But her voice was hardly heard above the clash of swords and cries of outrage on all sides. Many of the people were protesting, she saw. But enough backed Marie or Samuel to spur on their bitter battle.

"Thomas!" She spun back, saw that Thomas had vanished from her side, and quickly searched the crowd. Instead of finding her husband, she was drawn to the sight of a woman who stood on a pile of boulders, fists raised to the sky. She was glaring at Chelise. It could have been the firelight, but the woman's eyes appeared red in the night.

"Death to Qurong and all of his bloodthirsty offspring!"

Chelise took a step back in horror.

Her love for the Horde was a personal love, directed toward her own father, Qurong, and her mother, Patricia, neither of whom she'd seen in ten years. She'd become preoccupied with their rescue from the disease this last year, so much so that Thomas had asked her to stop bringing it up publicly. She needed to curb her incessant, affectionate talk about the leader of the Horde, who had ordered their extermination. Qurong was rumored to walk the halls of his palace, cursing the albinos who'd absconded with his daughter and turned her into an animal. Her love for her father was being met by blank stares, a sure sign that she was testing everyone's limits.

Chelise glared at the woman who ripped her father to shreds in a high-pitched voice. "'Vengeance is mine,' says the maker of all that is pure. He will cut off the impure branch, Qurong and his bloodthirsty priests!"

She knew then that if this one woman challenged her to a fight over the fate of her father, she would accept. She would defend Qurong to her death over the insults of this one witch on the stone.

Marie was doing no less, she realized. Confusion swirled about her.

Marie and Samuel exchanged a round of clashing blows, each effectively deflected by the other. But there was more blood now. Marie's thigh lay open, and the side of Samuel's head was bleeding.

Having sought the right to kill Horde, he was being soundly beaten in a fair fight, Chelise thought. She caught herself and shook the idea from her mind. Had the resentment of their tormentors grown so deep that they could no longer tolerate the abuse? The running and the hiding, the death of a loved one . . .

Just last week one of the camp's finest dancers, Jessica of Northern, had lost her son, Stevie, when he went out to hunt deer with two of his friends. They were young and bold, and their search had taken them into the forest, where Horde assassins called Throaters had fallen on them from the trees and killed Stevie. Jessica had wailed for a day before falling hoarse.

The thoughts spun through Chelise's head at a dizzying pace, punctuated by the cries and clanging of swords. Both combatants were panting, bleeding, caught up in a sole objective now: survival.

She had to stop this. It didn't matter that they had the right to the contest, as Ronin claimed. Thomas had to stop this before one of their children was killed. It would fracture the Circle. It would lead to more death!

But Chelise didn't know what to do.

And then it didn't matter, because in the space of time it took Chelise to blink, Marie was on her back, flailing for a grip. She'd fallen. Tripped on a small ribbon of rock that edged the flat stone.

Samuel, seeing the opening, hurled himself forward. He didn't go for her throat. She would have expected that. Instead, his right foot made contact with the butt of her blade and sent it spinning through the air.

Marie was left without a weapon.

A roar erupted from the crowd.

The woman with red eyes screamed at Chelise.

Samuel dropped one knee on Marie's gut, effectively preventing her from twisting free. His blade slammed against the rock an inch from her neck, spraying her right cheek with shards of stone.

That resounding crash of metal against stone silenced the Gathering. But the night was not quiet. A wail of bitter remorse cut through the air.

Chelise had heard this once, only once, three years ago when twenty-three women and children were beheaded by Throaters while the men were out searching for a lost child. Thomas had heard the news, dropped to his knees, and cried to the sky.

She spun around, crushed by the cry of anguish.

Thomas was on his knees on a twenty-foot cliff behind her, arms spread, sobbing at the night sky. "Elyonnnnnn . . . Elyonnnnnn . . ."

For long seconds he wailed unabashedly, struggling to find breath, trembling like a man who'd just learned that his child had been found dead at the bottom of a cliff. Tears streamed down his cheeks as he wept. For his Maker. For his children. For the Circle. For the Horde.

All around the valley, the Gathering stood rooted to the earth, cowering under this horrible sound. Behind Chelise, Marie and Samuel breathed hard, but there was no sound of swinging blades.

"It's over," Thomas wept. "It's over!"

"No," Chelise said.

He cried to the sky. "You've left us." Then even louder, "You've left us!"

"No," she said again, begging him to hear her. "No, he has not left us."

His chest rose and fell.

"No, Elyon has not left us," she cried. "I did not die for this!"

Thomas lowered his chin and blinked. He looked lost, a shell of the man who'd led the mighty Forest Guard to victory in campaign after campaign before Qurong overtook them. For a moment, Chelise thought he'd lost himself in hopelessness, a man stripped of all he once treasured.

His eyes slowly cleared and he staggered to his feet, looked around at the Gathering. His gaze settled on his son and daughter. Marie still lay on her back, pinned under Samuel's sword.

"Stand up," Thomas said.

Samuel stared up at his father. He made no move to relinquish his hard-won upper hand.

"Get up!" Thomas roared. His voice was heavy with rage, and it seemed to have caught Samuel off guard.

His son slowly removed his sword and stepped back. Marie rolled over and pushed herself to her knees. Then to her feet. They stared up at their father, wounded and bleeding.

"Is this what we have come to?" Thomas demanded. "A band of vagabonds who would return to their own captivity? You want to join the Horde again?"

"We should kill them, not join them," the woman who'd challenged Chelise said in a low voice. She might as well have screamed.

Thomas thrust his hand at the horizon. "Killing is what *they* do. To kill them is to join them!" He paced atop the cliff, and with each footfall, Chelise felt her fear grow. She didn't like the sight of the desperation that possessed him.

"Is it Horde that you want? You've lost your belief in the difference between us and them, is that it?"

"No," Mikil offered. "No, Thomas, that's—"

"You're doubting that Elyon is here, among us? That he cares? That he has any power? You wonder if he loves his bride the way he once did, if the Great Romance has become nothing more than the talk of old men around a campfire? Is that it?" He shouted his challenge.

"Thomas—"

"Enough! You had your chance to defend your hearts. Now it's my turn."

The words turned the night cold. It wasn't often that he was like this, but Chelise knew him well enough to know that he'd made a decision, and no force this side of heaven or hell would change it.

"My own son has challenged the very fabric of our way, and he has drawn my own daughter into a fight to the death. Fine. Then I, Thomas of Hunter, both their father and the supreme commander of this Circle, will issue my own challenge."

He stood above them, legs spread to the width of his shoulders, hands gripped to fists.

"I will settle this business once and for all. I will do it on my terms. We will see if Elyon has left us. The Circle will know to a man, woman, and child if he who woos us, who commands our love, is real or if he is nothing but hot air from the mouths of old men."

"Thomas, are you sure you want to do this?"

But he ignored William. "I hereby exercise my right to take on this challenge from Samuel. Do you accept?"

Samuel offered a cynical grin and looked up through loose locks of hair. "As you wish." Then he added for effect, "Father."

"Good. Then I will go to the Horde and cast my challenge. If Elyon is who I say he is, we will all survive another month. If he is not, then we will all be dead or Horde within the week."

The words echoed through the canyon. The fire was dying, starved of wood. A dog barked from the main camp a hundred yards behind the red pool, where they'd all dipped their cups to celebrate Elyon's love.

Now they were faced with death, and their cups sat heavy in their hands.

"Do I hear any objection?"

"How can you risk our lives like this?" some fool was brave enough to ask.

"There is no risk!" Thomas thundered over their heads. "If Elyon fails us, we *should* be Scabs. We will only be as we should be. If he rescues us, we will finish this celebration in earnest."

A deep breath.

"Anyone else?"

No one dared.

"Send our fastest runners to the other three Gatherings. Tell them to come. We will live or we will die together as one. Is that clear?"

Still no objection. Not even from the council, who surely knew how dangerous this course was. But they just as surely knew that to cross Thomas was futile.

"Good," Thomas said. "I leave tonight. Samuel, Mikil, Jamous, you three and you three alone will come with me. Get our horses."

He was going to the Horde, to her father, without her?

Chelise stepped forward. "Thomas . . . Thomas, you have to take me!"

"No. Your mind isn't clear on this matter."

"How can you say that? I . . . I'm your wife! I've vowed my life—"

"You are the daughter of Qurong." Then, with only a little more tenderness: "Please. Don't question my judgment on this matter."

"Then I should go, Father," Marie said.

"Samuel, Mikil, Jamous." He turned from them. "No more. Chelise, bring me my younger son. Bring me Jake."

Then Thomas of Hunter turned and walked into the night, leaving the three thousand alone by the fire.

5

JANAE DE RAISON stepped out of her mother's office and eased the door closed behind her, satisfied by the soft click of the latch when it engaged. Williston stood near his white desk in the atrium.

"Sit down, Williston," she said. "The answer is no, I won't be needing anything else. Maybe a sandwich, but I would rather fetch that myself if you don't mind."

He dipped his head.

She walked across the travertine floor, cool on her bare feet thanks to the conditioned air. Living in Southeast Asia could be a humid affair without the hum of electricity to suck water and heat from the atmosphere.

"You don't mind me robbing you of that pleasure, do you, Will? I know how much you enjoy it, but I would like to do it." She glided up to him and let her eyes wander over his tie, his black jacket. A handsome man with dark hair, graying at the edges. How many times as a child had she fantasized about having a passionate affair with their butler? Too many to remember.

She put her hand on his cheek and withdrew it slowly, allowing her fingernails to graze his skin. "Is that okay, dear Will? Just this once?"

"Of course, madam. Whatever pleases you." He smiled. It was a game they played often and both managed to take some enjoyment from it, she in tempting, he in pretending to be tempted, though they both knew that he wasn't always pretending.

She drew her hand down his tie, pulled it away from his shirt, then let it fall back into place as she turned away. "Where is he?"

"Where is who, madam?"

"Our fascinating little visitor?"

"In the guest quarters where I left him, I assume." He sounded as if he wanted to say more, so at the twelve-foot arched entry to the hall, she turned back.

"You'd like to add something else?"

"No."

"You don't trust our guest?"

He hesitated. "He is a bit unnerving, madam."

"Hmm. Then perhaps he and I will get along just fine."

Again he dipped his head. "Yes, madam."

Janae made her way to the kitchen, ignoring the servants, who moved like ghosts through the twenty-thousand-square-foot mansion that doubled as the world headquarters for Raison Pharmaceutical. Dusting, always dusting the crystal chandeliers and candle holders, the period paintings, the marble tables, anything that had a smooth surface. They were mostly Filipinos who spoke perfect English, and a few Malaysians. Janae had grown up trilingual, fluent by age eight in French, English, and Thai, but she'd also picked up enough Tagalog and Malay to get by.

She walked through the dining room toward the kitchen, mind on the visitor, on this Billy Rediger who'd waltzed into their home and sent both Monique and Kara into a tailspin, although they would never admit it.

"I'm making a couple sandwiches, Betty," she said, stopping the cook across the kitchen. "Could you get me a tray and two glasses of very cold milk?"

"Yes, madam."

She pulled out a white ceramic plate and made two peanut-butter and strawberry-jam sandwiches, each with a healthy side of Russian caviar.

With each wipe of her knife and dip of her spoon into the caviar jar, her mind went to the man. To Billy. Her mother had been unmistakably direct in her instructions to Janae. Kara had been even more forceful.

"Of course there's no blood!" Kara said, dismissing the whole business with a sweep of her hand. She jabbed at the door. "But there is him.

And as long as there's someone out there with this foolish notion, particularly someone who can read minds, we can't possibly be safe."

"Why?" Janae asked. "If there is no blood?"

"Because there once was," her mother said. "What he said is partially true. We did take a vial of Thomas Hunter's blood and kept it safe for several years. But we feared an event exactly like this, so I sent it to our old lab in Indonesia, where it was destroyed. Neither the lab nor the blood exist today."

"But as long as this fool thinks it exists, he'll be a problem," Kara added.

"So you want me to what? Distract him?" she asked, but she was thinking, *Oh my goodness, what if Billy's right?*

"Is that a problem?"

"No. I think he could be the distractible kind. He really can read minds?"

"Please, Janae. Keep him close, but keep your guard up. He could be a rather dangerous character."

Let's hope so.

Janae picked up the loaded tray, refusing Betty's assistance to carry the lunch. She left the kitchen and wound her way down the hall to the guest quarters.

There were things Mother trusted her with and things she did not. Send Janae de Raison into any plant or laboratory in the world that was slipping, and she would return it to full production within a week. But at times Mother treated her with the same scrutiny she'd showed her enemies. *Keep your friends close; keep your enemies closer.*

Monique and Kara had no intention of trusting Janae with Billy. They intended to keep both as close as needed to monitor every move.

The large white door that led into the guest suite was closed. She thought about knocking but decided against it. Balancing the tray on her left hand, she turned the knob and pushed the door open.

The guest atrium was round, surrounded by windows that overlooked manicured lawns and the jungle beyond. A gilded dome rose at the room's center, supporting a huge iron chandelier. Thick lace drapes swept across the top of each window and hung to the marble floor.

The furniture was mostly old English, wood painted in antiqued creams and browns, nothing too dark. Monique preferred light colors to dark stain here in the tropics, unlike her house in New York, which made ample use of cherrywood and mahogany.

No sign of Billy. He was either in the bathroom to her right, down the hall that led to the bedrooms, or in the parlor that doubled as a library. Janae considered the bedrooms with some interest but quickly decided that he would probably be more interested in books than beds even after a long flight. She angled for the library.

Her bare feet padded lightly across the tile. Giovanni had given her a full manicure and pedicure yesterday in New York, painting her nails a delectable deep ruby red that still looked dripping wet. Her short black dress was formfitting but loose below the waist so it could sway across her thighs.

She'd earned a black belt in jujitsu by age seventeen and had kept it up as a form of exercise over the eight years since. "You can seduce many men with a pretty face," Monique used to say. "You can get them slobbering with a pretty face and a powerful body. But you can turn most men into idiots with a pretty face, a powerful body, and a bank account that earns enough interest to pay for jet fuel."

So far Mother had been right, although she'd missed one: a potent mind was a more powerful aphrodisiac than all of the others combined.

She found Billy in the parlor with his back to her, staring at a bookcase loaded with leather-bound books. His fingers traced their spines slowly, as if he expected to read their contents like he'd read her mind. Her family had always been fascinated by books, and it appeared Billy might also be.

"Hungry?"

He spun around, startled.

She walked to a leather ottoman and set the tray down. "Hope you like peanut butter and jelly with caviar. A taste I picked up in Poland last summer."

Billy held her in his green-eyed gaze. He'd been places, this one. For a few seconds she felt as though she was the lesser here, that he'd come to seduce her, to win his way into whatever prize he sought.

Was he really reading her mind? It seemed preposterous. She couldn't feel anything that suggested his mind was probing hers, peeling back the layers of her thoughts, her deepest secrets.

"No, not yet," he said. "Those I'll save until later."

"What are you talking about?"

"Your secrets."

So it was true, then.

"Of course it is."

Janae turned back to the ottoman and lifted one of the glasses. *And now can you?*

No response.

No, not when my eyes are averted or covered. How fascinating.

She drilled him with a long stare and slowly brought her glass to her lips, allowing him to crawl as deep as he wanted into her mind.

She sipped at the cool liquid, felt it slip down her throat. "And what do you see now, hmm? Anything you like?"

"I see evil," he said.

"Oh?" She suppressed a stab of alarm. "Is that a good thing or a bad thing?"

"Depends."

"On whom, me or you?"

"On us," he said. "It depends on us."

She knew then that she liked this redheaded man named Billy. She liked him very much.

"Sit with me, Billy. Eat with me. Tell me why you've come into my world."

THEY TALKED for an hour, and with each passing minute Janae's anticipation for the next grew. From the moment Billy had climbed inside of her mind and found this so-called evil in her, she knew there would be no hiding from him.

More to the point, she didn't want to hide from him.

They talked about a host of topics, taking their time to slowly unravel each other's lives. He'd spent his childhood in Colorado, though he didn't share many details, before becoming a defense attorney in Atlantic City. He then went on to Washington with an old flame of his named Darcy Lange.

"Darcy Lange, huh? You serious?"

"You know her?"

"She was all over the news a few years back," Janae said, curling her legs back on the Queen Anne chair. She took a teaspoon of caviar and brought it to her mouth. "Stunning creature."

"Yes. Can't deny that. We were . . . you have to understand about Darcy and me. We both started young, in the . . . the . . . you know, the libraries below the monastery."

"Monastery? You met her in a monastery?"

"In a manner of speaking." He was hiding something. "We were kids, and we drifted apart until this whole Tolerance Act thing, when these gifts of ours came out. We had a thing, but it's different now. Our interests have . . . aren't exactly in line."

"Look, my beloved little redhead, if you expect me to open up my mind to you, I expect you to quit hiding yours."

"I'm not."

"You're lying with every other word." She stood up and moved away from the chairs. "Maybe this isn't such a good idea. Honestly, I have enough on my plate. The last thing I need is some guy playing games with me."

"No, it's not like that."

"Whatever. Are you finished? I'll send a maid to collect the tray."

"What?" He stood, spilling some crumbs off the napkin on his lap. "No, that's not what—"

"Why, Mr. Rediger, should I give you even an ounce of my attention?" She knew why, but they had to find a way onto a level field of play.

"It's worth it, trust me."

"I'm not in the mood to trust a man who can glance into my eyes and see things I can't even see myself. You'll have to do better."

"How?"

"For starters, come clean. Tell me how you came to read people's minds."

"I will."

She walked back toward him. "Tell me about Thomas's blood." Even as the words left her mouth, she could taste her desire for whatever Billy might bring her.

She didn't understand the desire herself. As a child she'd always been fascinated by red blood, whether in a movie or from a cut or in the laboratory, vials of blood used for endless tests.

Billy had gone rigid. "You know about the blood?"

"You mentioned it in my mother's office, remember?"

His eyes searched hers. "So that's all you know."

He'd expected more, had searched her mind already and found nothing. But she wasn't finished.

"I have some secrets that not even you can extract, at least not without skills far more seductive than reading a mind. Tell me about this blood."

He slowly sat. Crossed one leg over the other. Janae stood before him, arms folded, challenging.

"You've heard of the Books of History?" he asked, then answered himself after a glance in her eyes. "No, you haven't. They are a set of books that recorded the truth of all happenings, exactly as they happened. Pure history. The books of life, you might call them. But they aren't ordinary books. Whatever is written in blank Books of History will actually happen. The wills of humans can be bent by them, but not forced. Inanimate objects, on the other hand, can be manipulated at will. You could write, 'This room is red,' in one of those books, and the room would instantly become red."

"Now you're—"

"Patronizing me," he finished for her. "Yet it's true. How else do you think I can read your mind?"

What was he saying? Reading minds was one thing, turning a room red with a few words written in a book was another thing.

"Another thing, yes, but true. Sit." Then, "Please, just sit down and let me explain myself to you."

She eased herself into the chair but didn't bother relaxing her arms.

"From what I've been able to piece together, the blank books came from another time, presumably two thousand years in our future. They were brought here by Thomas Hunter and they turned up many years later in a monastery, where I found them and wrote in them. Long story, a kind of showdown that would take a few days to explain. Regardless, one of the things I wrote was that I would have special powers. Twelve years later they began to manifest themselves. So now I can read your mind. It's that simple."

She unfolded her arms and set her hands in her lap. There was a finality to his voice that robbed her of any objection. "You're serious," she managed.

"Dead."

"And you want to know about the blood."

"It was said that Thomas Hunter's blood allowed him to . . . travel, shift, whatever you want to call it, between here and there. Anyone whose blood came in contact with Thomas's blood could make the shift as well, at least in their dreams. And I do believe that both Kara Hunter and your mother know this as fact. I think they've both done it."

"With the blood?" Janae's heart started to beat more deliberately. "They . . . you're saying they used this blood to cross into another reality?"

He eyed her. She was betraying her deep attraction to his suggestions, but she couldn't hide from him, could she? So she didn't try.

"You're saying that's possible?"

"I think it's been done. I know they kept a vial of his blood for just this reason." He stood and walked in a small circle, fingers scratching his cheek. "You have to know, these Books of History are *my* history. I'm who I am because of them. My life is ruined because—"

"Where are these books?"

He looked at her, apparently put off at having been interrupted.

"You're sure the blood is still around, that it exists?" she asked. "I mean, what if they did destroy it like they claim? My mother said she sent it to our lab in Indonesia, where it was incinerated. The lab doesn't even exist today."

"Slow down. Take a deep breath. Do you think I would've come halfway across the world if I wasn't sure?"

Janae stood, unable to hide the desire to know what he knew, to strip this knowledge from his history and to own it. Why? But even as the thoughts whispered through her mind, she was aware that he was also aware of them.

Billy blinked at her. "What are you hiding from me?"

"Nothing. How can I?"

"You can't. So why are you so desperate to know what I know?"

"I . . ." What could she say if she herself didn't know? "I don't know. What would you do if you learned that your mother had a vial of blood that could take you to another world?"

Her pulse was now a steady hammer in her ears.

"You'd think it was preposterous," she answered for him. "But then what?"

"Then you'd want to possess it," he said.

"Assuming it exists."

"It does."

She looked away and tried to still her irrational eagerness to stand here while he reeled her in like a helpless fish.

"Until today I was convinced that I was the only person on this planet who was qualified to find and use that blood," Billy said. "But now I think you may be another."

"Because you need me?"

"Because there's something inside you that I've never seen. And I've probed the minds of a lot of people."

"What's that? Evil?" She walked away from him. "I can't believe I've never heard of any of this before today. She hid it from me all this time?"

"It's not exactly the kind of thing you want anyone to know."

She spun back. "I'm her daughter!"

"Even more reason to protect you."

He really did believe all of this, and the idea was becoming only slightly familiar to her. Familiar, not reasonable, not in the least, because what Billy was suggesting made no sense at all. Who'd ever heard of such a thing?

But it did have a ring of familiarity to it.

"Give me a few hours and I'll tell you a few things that will remove any doubt from your mind," Billy said. "The books exist. There's a journal that talks about them, written by a Saint Thomas hundreds of years ago. They called him the beast hunter. Never saw the book, but I've interviewed two people in Europe who have. I'm telling you there're connections between our worlds that would make your head spin."

"Beast hunter," she repeated.

"Saint Thomas the Beast Hunter," he said. "But it's the blank books that interest me more. Like the ones I wrote in during my life in the monastery. I believe they still exist, probably in the safe keeping of Thomas Hunter. His blood is a sure way to get to him. I want you to help me find the blood."

The notion overtook her with such savagery that she felt compelled to turn her face away. Such raw desire was unbecoming.

"Will you?"

I will, Billy. I will use you to feed my own needs.

The thought surprised her. At least it had been guarded. She cleared her mind and faced him again.

"Maybe."

Janae walked up to him and allowed a smile to caress her face. She placed her hand on his chest and ran it up over his head, through his unkempt hair.

"Might be fun."

"I don't care if you do use me," he said, cutting to the heart of the matter. "I have to do this, with or without you."

Interesting. Her deception didn't bother him. This alone increased her admiration of him.

Janae stood on her toes, leaned forward and touched her lips to his. Then she turned and glided back to the chair.

"Tell me more, Billy. Tell me everything."

6

The Future

QURONG MARCHED the path along the muddy lake in his night-clothes, a white and purple robe woven from silk that swished around his knees with each reach of his leg. The moon was absent from the black sky. Qurongi City, named after himself five years earlier, slept except for the stray dog, the priests in the Thrall, and him.

Well, yes, he had awakened Patricia and Cassak. No king should have to visit the high priest in the dead of night without his wife and general at hand. Ba'al had sent his servant an hour ago, demanding that Qurong rush to the Thrall for a most critical audience.

"Slow down," Patricia snapped, close at his heels.

He planted his foot and swung back. "The first sensible thing you've said all night. Why he insists I leave the palace to join him in the Thrall at this hour is beyond me, but I'm telling you, this had better be the stuff of life and death to every living being or I'll make him pay for this arrogance."

She stopped and glared with gray eyes. Patricia had always been provocative when angry, but in the wake of his latest ailment—this cease-less wrenching in his gut that denied him sleep—he felt only annoyance. She'd taken a moment to apply a dusting of morst to her face and to throw on a hooded black silk robe that covered her body from head to heel. Her stark white face peered from the hood like a ghost. The tattoo of three hooked claws on her forehead had been perfectly placed, red and black against her white skin.

"Watch your tongue, you brute," she cautioned. "We're out in the open here."

"With whom? My general, who'd die for me?" He flung his hand out toward the dark city on the other side of the black lake. "Or with the rest of these rodents under Ba'al's spell?"

"Commander!" Her term when she was beyond despair. "Have you lost your mind?"

"Yes, I've finally misplaced my senses! Ba'al will have a reason to make a play for the throne, and I'll be forced to kill him. Such a tragedy. You're quite sweet to suggest it, my bride."

Qurong swung around and continued his march toward the Thrall, lit by the glow of flaming torches in the temple's towers and doors.

"That's not what I meant," Patricia objected.

"No, of course you don't wish Ba'al dead. You'd likely prefer to kiss his feet."

"You're a double-minded oaf, Q. One minute you wake me, insisting that I offer a sacrifice to Teeleh to heal your ailments, and the next you curse him and his high priest. Which is it? Do you love Teeleh or do you hate him?"

"I serve him. I am his slave. Does that mean that I must drink his blood and have his children?"

"If he demands it."

"Let's just hope this aching in my belly isn't his growing child."

"That would be a sight," his ranking general, Cassak, said behind them.

Patricia wasn't finished. "If you serve Teeleh, you serve Ba'al. One of these days you'll get that through your thick skull."

"Like I served Witch, then Ciphus? Then Sucrow, now this wretch Ba'al?"

"Stop!"

This time when he caught her eye, he saw he'd gone too far. The lines of her ghostly face were etched with fear.

"You will not speak about him that way in my presence!" she said.

"And what am I, your poodle to play with?" Qurong demanded. Then, with a clenched fist, "I am Qurong! The world bows at my feet and cowers under my army! Remember whose bed you share."

"Yes. You are Qurong and I love Qurong, leader of all that is right in this cursed world. I am humbled to have known you, much more to be called your wife."

She was toying with him, he thought, only half-serious, but enough for Cassak to believe it all.

Patricia continued. "And you will show your love for me by keeping me away from danger."

"You're more afraid of that witch than of me?"

"Of course. You love me. Ba'al hates us both, and his hatred would only be aggravated if he heard you speak of Teeleh or him the way you do."

Qurong frowned, but his fight was gone.

A sharp pang of pain cut through his belly, and he resumed his march down the muddy path that led to the Thrall.

They walked in silence until they reached the wide steps that rose to the large gate. It was guarded on either side by bronzed statues of the winged serpent, a likeness of Teeleh that their first high priest, a scheming character named Witch, had supposedly seen in a vision. Few besides the priests had claimed to see the great beast in these last twenty-five years, since the waters had turned to poison. Woref, the general, had once claimed to have seen Teeleh. In Qurong's distant memory, Teeleh was more of a bat than a serpent.

Truth be told, Teeleh was probably a figment of their imagination, a tool the priests used to maintain their hold on power. There had been some sightings of the Shataiki bats that lived in hidden Black Forests, and some of the black bats seemed to have an unexplainable power, but nothing like the power that the priests attributed to them.

When Qurong first defeated Thomas of Hunter and took the Middle Forest, they had just lost Witch in battle. Upon defeating Thomas and left without a priest, Qurong had cautiously accepted the offer of the half-breed, Ciphus, to protect them from evil. Ciphus introduced them to a strange brew of religion that he called the Great Romance, which involved worshipping both Teeleh and Elyon, the pagan god of the Forest People.

Ciphus's time lasted just over a year, until three months after the albinos made off with Chelise, the very same traitor who was now out to poison them all with the red lakes. His daughter had become a she-witch herself.

What started out as lenience toward the albinos became bitter remembrance, and Qurong had fully supported Sucrow's bid to kill Ciphus and return the Horde to the worship of Teeleh, the winged serpent who ruled the powers of the air. In his death, Ciphus became a martyr for all half-breeds to revere, emboldening Eram, who soon after defected with the rest of the half-breeds.

Sucrow's reign as high priest ended on a goose chase for an amulet that reportedly had great power. Following Sucrow's death, a priest had come to them from the desert, stood tall upon the Thrall's highest landing, and declared that Teeleh had chosen him to be high priest of all that was holy and unholy. He claimed to have lived with Teeleh until now, when his time had come. He was the servant of the dragon in the sky. Qurong had seen the people's awe of this skinny sorcerer and agreed to make him high priest.

He told himself a thousand times afterward that it had been a mistake. At best, the balance between Qurong's political power and Ba'al's religious power was delicate. There would come a time soon when Ba'al would have to die. He was altogether too full of himself, drunk on his own power.

"Don't get me wrong, wife," Qurong said as they approached the steps. "I wouldn't be here without a healthy respect for Teeleh. I support all of this . . ." He waved at the Thrall that loomed high above them like a black sentinel with flaming eyes, blocking out half the sky. "I've kissed the feet of Teeleh's vessel, Ba'al, this so-called dragon from the sky, on a hundred occasions. But that doesn't mean he's a god any more than my enemies are gods. He's only human flesh doing the bidding of a god."

"Just keep his knife away from your throat," Patricia said in a low voice.

"Exactly." She could be reasonable when she wanted to be. "I swear, sometimes I don't know who's worse, the albinos, the Eramites, or my own priests. None of them allows me any sleep. My gut is in a knot over all of this."

"Not now," his wife warned.

One of the night watchmen opened the gate for them, and they headed across the stone floor to a large atrium surrounded by more of the bronze serpents.

"This way, my lord."

Qurong faced his right, where a hunched priest hidden beneath a hooded black cloak dipped his head and walked toward the sacrificial sanctum. The priest lifted his spindly arm to a large wooden door charred by fire and gave it a push.

Orange light from a dozen flames spilled out into the hall. He could see the altar on a platform inside, blazing candlesticks on either side. An animal—a black-and-white goat strapped spread-eagle on the altar—sacrificed.

But Ba'al's sacrifices were more like butchery. And although he killed animals with the same regularity that he ate and relieved himself, Qurong didn't know the priest to offer sacrifices in the middle of the night.

Qurong walked into the sanctum, the holy of unholies, as Ba'al called it. Flames crackled from the torches on the room's perimeter. Thick, purple velvet curtains hung from the tall ceiling on each side, framing large gold etchings of the winged serpent. Directly behind the altar, the same material closed off an arched passageway, which led to Ba'al's private library. What kind of plotting and deception was conceived behind that curtain Qurong could only guess, but those guesses were not happy thoughts.

"Where is he?" Patricia whispered.

Qurong hesitated. "Doing the work of Teeleh."

That he, the supreme commander of more than three million souls, had agreed to leave his home in the middle of the night for an audience with Ba'al was offensive enough. That he had to now wait in these ghastly chambers while the witch took his bloody time wiping off his wet blades was infuriating.

But this was not the place to betray his emotions. Qurong knew all too well how revered Ba'al was among the common people, particularly now, during the days of the black moon. During the last lunar eclipse, Ba'al came forth from the sanctum and declared that Teeleh had shown him a vision of the coming red dragon, who would devour the children of all who betrayed him. All those who marked themselves as loyal servants of Teeleh and Ba'al would be spared. Three claws carved on the forehead, the mark of the beast's perfection.

Qurong had received the mark of the beast, naturally, but he doubted that it would truly protect him, assuming the beast existed.

The priest who'd let them in climbed the two steps to the platform, shuffled slowly around the altar, and parted the curtains with a withered hand. The door behind the drapes closed softly, and they were left alone.

"This is asinine," Qurong mumbled.

"Hush."

The curtain parted and Ba'al stepped into the inner sanctum, dressed in his usual black silk robes with a purple sash around his neck. Layers of gold, silver, and black beads hung over his breast. The circular serpent's medallion hung from a silver chain.

Ba'al's narrow white face peered at Qurong from his hood, like a king judging his subject. The expression was enough to make Qurong's blood boil.

The priest carefully navigated the steps down from the platform.

"Thank you for coming to me so late, my lord." His voice was low and wet, the sound of a man who needed to clear his throat.

"This had better be good."

Ba'al lifted his face to the Horde leader, and for the first time Qurong saw that the three claw marks on his forehead had been reopened. Thin trails of blood snaked down his cheeks and the bridge of his nose. The man was a masochist.

"Good?" Ba'al said. "The true child has been born, and now the dragon will wage war on her illegitimate children. That can hardly be good." He walked around a table to the side. The goat's head lay on a silver platter, still bleeding, and Ba'al dipped his long black fingernail into the blood. "Babylon will become drunk on her blood yet."

"Idiots may swoon with your talk of children and dragons and the end of all times," Qurong said, "but I'm a simple man who wields the sword. Let's not forget that here."

"Ah, yes, of course. Your sword, your power, your stranglehold on the Horde. Forgive me if I suggested that the dragon doesn't hold his king in the highest regard. He was the one who made you king, after all."

Qurong had no patience for this. "So what is it that is so urgent to keep me from sleep?"

"The day for your full glory has come, my lord, all in good time. But first I must know who you are and who you serve."

"What glory? Another ritual to this god who has abandoned us?"

"Remember where you are, my lord." Ba'al glanced at the walls without moving his head, then shifted his eyes back to Qurong and brought his wet fingers to his lips. "He has ears everywhere," the high priest whispered around his taste of goat's blood.

Qurong held his tongue.

"Your loyalty hasn't weakened, has it? My king?"

"What are you speaking of?"

"You do still believe that Teeleh is the true god. That the dragon has given you Babylon?"

Ba'al had begun this Babylon business a year earlier; Qurong wouldn't put it past the man to suggest renaming Qurongi City, perhaps calling it Dragoni or something as foolish.

"What have I done to suggest any slackening of my loyalty?" he demanded.

"You still believe that we are the abomination of desolation, the dragon's great Babylon? That we are his instrument to crush the rebellion of those who stand against Teeleh? That it is our prerogative and our privilege, our duty, to drain the blood of every living albino? That there will come from times past an albino with a head of fire, who will rid the world of the poisonous waters and return us unto Paradise?"

Now they were retreading old ground, these prophesies that Ba'al had pulled from his so-called visions.

Still, Qurong would give him the benefit of the doubt. "That is correct."

"That your very own daughter, Chelise—"

"I have no daughter," he interrupted. The priest was egging him on, knowing how the name had haunted his nightmares for so many years.

"That Thomas and the woman at his side lead the rebellion against Teeleh."

"Get on with it, priest. Surely you didn't bring me here to remind me of all I know."

Ba'al stared at him for a few beats, then turned his back and walked toward a desk along one wall. His voice was hardly more than a hoarse whisper.

"Have you ever considered drowning, my lord?"

Qurong couldn't immediately respond. What kind of blasphemy was this?

Patricia stepped up next to him and dipped her head. "Forgive me, my priest, but you go too far." Her voice was strained and high. "An accusation of this kind is dangerous."

"Of course," the priest said, turning back. He'd lifted a small scroll from his desk and held it in his clawed hands. "I make no accusation. You'll understand soon enough. But I do need an answer."

Qurong spat to one side and made no attempt to coat his words with anything other than the sentiment that swelled in his mind.

"If I could do it personally, I would run my sword through every albino who still breathes."

A faint grin crossed Ba'al's face. "And the drowning?"

"It is defiance of my reign and all that we hold sacred. The twisted ways of Thomas would drown all of the Horde and tear down this very Thrall. I would rather drown in a bath of poison."

"How dare you put him through this?" Patricia challenged. His wife's solidarity reminded Qurong why he loved her as he did.

"Just a reminder of who our enemies are. The Eramites, yes, but Thomas and his Circle are the true scourge of our world."

"I don't need your lectures," Qurong said. "And don't underestimate Eram or his army. They are growing faster than we are, and they don't hide like the albinos do. I would think that should concern you."

"I assure you, Teeleh's enemies are albino, not Horde. They will be easily disposed of when the time is right."

Qurong couldn't take this line any farther without casting suspicion on his allegiance. "I bow to Teeleh's judgment." He dipped his head.

"Then drink to him," Ba'al said, picking up a chalice next to the goat's head. "Swallow the goat's blood offered to the dragon, and I will tell you how he will give you your enemies on a butcher block." He glided across the floor and held out the silver goblet, sloshing with red blood.

Qurong took the cup, aware that his hand was still shaking from being accused of such treason, never mind that it was only insinuated. He lifted the vessel to his lips and drank deep. The familiar taste of raw blood flooded his mouth and warmed his belly.

Ba'al had instituted the drinking of blood, claiming that the spirit of Teeleh, indeed the very offspring of Teeleh, came by blood. Indeed, the Shataiki were asexual beings, neither male nor female. They reproduced through blood.

Teeleh was served by twelve queens, it was said, like the queens of beehives. But they and their minions were genderless and passed their seed through blood when they bit the larvae produced by the queens. Ba'al sometimes referred to a queen as a she and sometimes as a he, but to Qurong's way of thinking, all of it was nonsense.

Shataiki were simply beasts.

Regardless, the taste had agreed with most Scabs, including Qurong.

It settled the pain and itching in their flaking skin for several hours and now eased the gnawing in his belly. Unfortunately, there were more than three million Horde now living in seven forests, and there was only so much blood, making it a valuable commodity controlled by the temples.

He drained the cup. "For Teeleh, my lord and my master," he recited, and shoved the goblet back at Ba'al. "Do not test me again, priest."

The dark priest handed him the scroll.

"What is this?"

"A message that came to me an hour ago. Read it."

Qurong unrolled the stained paper and stared at the top. This was a communiqué from . . . the circular emblem at the top bore into his mind. His eyes dropped to the bottom and he saw the name: *Thomas of Hunter.*

"Yes," Ba'al sneered. "He shows his face after all these years."

"Who?" Patricia demanded.

"Thomas of Hunter," the priest said.

The spoken name seemed to rob the room of its energy. Patricia kept silent. Qurong's heart slowly doubled its pace. The last communication with anyone among the albino leadership had come three months after Chelise's departure, when Qurong declared open war on the albinos. Ba'al's Throaters and his elite guard had rounded up over a thousand since, but not one among the original leaders. They'd gone into deep hiding.

He stepped closer to the torches on the wall behind him and read the writing on the paper:

To Qurong, Supreme Commander of the Horde
And Ba'al, Dark Priest of Teeleh, Shataiki from Hell
    Greetings from the Circle, followers of Elyon dead to the disease and risen with hope for the return of Elyon, who will destroy all that is evil and remake all that is good.
    Ten years have passed and still you relentlessly persecute my people, falsely believing that we have meant ill toward the diseased Scabs whom

you rule. We have not waged war on your people, though we have the capacity to do so. We have not burned your crops, nor robbed your caravans, nor harmed you in any way. Still you pursue us deep into the desert and slay us where you find us.

It is in our best interests to end this. I therefore cast before you a challenge:

Take a contingent of your most revered and unholy priests and meet me at the high place with Qurong and his armed guard. I will present myself with three of my most trusted followers. No more. There, at Ba'al Bek, we will know the truth.

If Elyon refuses to show his power over Teeleh, then I, Thomas Hunter, who lead the Circle, will surrender myself and the location of every tribe known to me, and you may be rid of the albinos once and for all. They will either renounce their drowning and become Horde or die by your hand.

If Teeleh refuses to show his power over Elyon, then you, Qurong, and you alone will drown and become albino.

If you betray me and conspire to kill me before the terms of this agreement are met in full, then you will have martyrs in Thomas of Hunter and three of his trusted followers. I await you at Ba'al Bek.

Thomas of Hunter

"What does the traitor want?" his wife demanded.

"He's issued a challenge. A duel of sorts between his god and Ba'al. At Ba'al Bek, the high place."

"For what purpose?"

Qurong turned to Ba'al. "What am I supposed to make of this madness?"

"What madness?" Patricia snapped. She pulled the scroll from his fingers and read.

Qurong ignored her. "Can your god do what he challenges?"

"My god? Teeleh is the only true god, and he's yours as well as mine. Or do you falter so easily after a few words from your nemesis?"

Ba'al clearly saw an opportunity here. That a challenge from a group of scattered vagabonds should be taken seriously was by itself humiliating. But that this simple challenge, however misguided, should unnerve him was unforgivable. Who did Thomas of Hunter think he was, issuing such a foolish challenge?

Qurong's gut clenched with pain and he walked to the table, where a flask of wine sat next to two silver glasses.

"You called me out of my sleepless dreams for this?"

"If you don't mind . . ." Cassak, his general, now held the scroll. "If this is true, if the leader of all albinos is foolish enough to wait for us at Ba'al Bek, we could easily end his life. And the lives of his three followers. Even Chelise, if she is with him."

Patricia glared at him. She still clung to the imprudent belief that she might one day recover a daughter. Cassak was a fool not to understand the way of a woman's heart. He would have to talk with the man.

"Killing Thomas is no easy proposition. Even if he could be taken or killed, he's right; he would be seen as a martyr and replaced by another dozen like him. He's mocking us with this letter."

"Is he?" Ba'al said.

"You suggest we take this seriously?"

"You doubt that I can destroy him in this little game of his?" Ba'al returned.

"I don't know. Can you?"

There was the real question, he realized. He'd betrayed his own doubts in Teeleh's power by asking it.

"Have you seen the evidence of Elyon lately?" Ba'al asked. "No, because there are no angels named Roush nor a god named Elyon. These are the figments of the albinos' imagination. The red waters they drink infect them with a disease that bares their skin and fries their minds. We all know this to be the case."

"And if you're wrong? If Teeleh, who isn't too eager to show his face either, doesn't show up and crush them, then what? I drink their red water? Have you lost your mind?"

"Unlike you, I see Teeleh frequently. Trust me, he is as real as your own scabbing flesh. Don't you see it? Thomas of Hunter is playing into our hands. The red dragon who rules the seven horns will devour this albino child and end the time of the Circle once and for all. Your war on them has had its desired effect. They are begging us, out of desperation." Ba'al bit off each word and squeezed his black nails into a tight fist.

The allure of being handed the whole of the albino insurgency on a platter presented itself to Qurong in full color for the first time.

"Sir." Cassak stepped forward. "Forgive the observation, but there is no guarantee that this isn't a trap to kill both you and the high priest."

"They don't ascribe to violence," Qurong said.

"No, but they could take you and force you to drown. They could—"

"Do the red water's poisons work if one is forced to drown?"

"I don't know," the general said. "The point is, this must not be done on his terms. We should take the army. Even the Eramites take courage from Thomas Hunter's evasion of capture. We look small, unable to kill this one man. Here is our chance. We could then strike at a demoralized Eram and be assured victory."

Qurong regarded Ba'al. He understood now why the priest had summoned him here. This battle would be fought and won in the heavens, not with swords. This was a matter for Ba'al, not Qurong. The dark priest needed only his consent and attendance.

He kept his eyes on the priest as he spoke. "Hunter would see our army and be gone. Those were not his terms."

"Not if I commanded the Throaters," Cassak said.

The temple's military wing consisted of five thousand highly trained assassins commonly referred to as Throaters, named after less-discerning killers among the Forest Guard, before it had been defeated and assimilated by the Horde. Indeed, most of the original Forest Guard had left Qurongi and joined Eram in the northern desert. The Horde's greatest fighters were now Eramites.

But they were vastly outnumbered by his full army, Qurong reminded himself. His own Throaters were gaining strength too. The whole matter was an absurd mess. He hated the albinos with a passion, but he feared the Eramites more, regardless of what Teeleh said. He doubted nearly everything attributed to the bat god, whom none of them had seen for a very long time.

"Perhaps. But our dark priest may be right, this is a war to be waged on a different front. And if he is right and he can summon this red dragon Teeleh to do his bidding, we will be rid of the thorn in our side once and for all."

"And . . ." Cassak hesitated on the next obvious point.

"Go on, say it."

"Teeleh forbid, but I must serve my king." He dipped his head to Ba'al in respect. "But if, however unlikely, this dragon we serve does not devour this albino child, surely no one is suggesting that Qurong do as Thomas has demanded and drink their red poison."

The mention of poison knifed through Qurong's belly, and he wondered if the ailment in his gut over these past thirty days was the result of bad food. Or worse, real poison. Served to him by Ba'al. Or an Eramite spy.

"I have no intention of nearing, much less entering, one of their cursed red lakes," he snapped. "But if Ba'al fails in his promise to summon the beast, I will have permission from him to throw *him* into poisonous waters." He paused, eyes on the priest. "Won't I?"

The three freshly opened wounds on the witch's forehead glistened in the flame light. His thin lips morphed into a grin. The evil man was as much serpent as he was human.

"I've lived in Teeleh's bosom. He will never allow any harm to come to me."

Qurong nodded. "It's a day's march. We will leave in the morning. Bring the Throaters."

7

THOMAS PULLED up his steed and looked out over the Beka Valley, a jagged, stone canyonland. His stallion snorted and sidestepped a blue scorpion that scurried across the sand.

He held the mount steady with a soft cluck of his tongue and lifted his eyes to the high place on the far side. The canyons rose to a plateau that swelled on top, making it look pregnant. With what? Thomas could only assume evil.

This was Ba'al Bek. The highest plateau in this part of the desert. A place claimed by the dark priest. A comet, or perhaps Elyon's fist, looked to have landed at the center of the rise, creating a massive crater the breadth of Qurongi City.

Beside him, Mikil spat to one side. "I don't like this, Thomas. This whole valley stinks of death."

"Sulfur," he said.

Jamous harrumphed on Thomas's left. "Call it what you want. She's right. It smells as if it's rising from Teeleh's hell." He pulled out a kirkuk and bit into the fruit's red flesh. A single bite could keep a man on the move for a day. They each carried a small supply of various fruits taken from the trees near the red pool. Some nourished; others had medicinal value. Without the fruit, the Circle would surely have been wiped out by the Horde long ago. It was their primary advantage, allowing them to heal on the fly and travel for days into the deep desert without any other source of food or water.

Lake fruit. Cherished by albinos, bitter to the Horde.

They had left the Gathering within an hour of Thomas's ultimatum, and the moonless desert night welcomed them in perfect silence. There were no great cheers, none of the customary embraces or wishes for safe travel, no calls for Elyon's blessing on the mission.

Thomas had taken his son Jake out into the desert for a half an hour and assured the boy of his undying love for them all. Whatever happened, Jake must never abandon his love for Elyon, Thomas urged. Never.

"Of course not, Father. Never."

Swinging the child around in an embrace, Thomas had held back tears of gratitude, concerned they might be seen as a sign of fear. The children didn't need more worry.

Then he'd joined Chelise, kissed her passionately, and deflected her insistence that she join them. He'd wiped away her tears, mounted his steed, and rode into the desert with his choice of company: his most seasoned warrior, Mikil, who had laid down her arms with the rest of them years ago; her husband, Jamous; and Samuel, his wayward son, who might be the death of them all.

"Your son should have joined us by now," Mikil said, gazing to the southern desert. "He could be dead."

"Or he's run off," Jamous said.

Thomas had written his challenge on paper, set his seal at the top, rolled it into a scroll, and demanded that Samuel deliver it to the Horde at Qurongi. He arranged to meet them at Hell's Gate, this narrow pass into the Beka Valley. Then, together, they would continue to the high place and wait for Qurong's response.

"It would take a battalion of Scabs to bring Samuel down," Thomas said. "I think he can deliver a message to one guard on the outskirts of Qurongi. He'll be here."

"What makes you so sure?"

"He wants this as much as I do."

Mikil grunted. "Then you've both lost your senses."

"If you hadn't saved my neck a thousand times, I would put you under the sword for that."

"And if you hadn't saved mine as many, I would turn it back on you," she said. Their well-intentioned barbs lightened the mood.

He looked at his most trusted commander, now in her thirties, still childless by choice and still every bit the warrior she'd been when killing Scabs had been an obsession. Her bronzed cheek was marked by a scar, barely visible past strands of dark hair.

"Besides," she said, "we've given up our swords. Remember?" She winked at him.

He had to grin, however thinly. They were all warriors at heart. Given the chance to take up arms against an enemy, they would throw themselves into the task.

But the Horde was no longer their enemy.

The disease was their enemy.

As was Teeleh, who'd cursed mankind with the disease. The way to destroy the disease had nothing to do with the sword and everything to do with the heart. Only by loving the Horde could they hope to persuade any Scab to throw away their diseased life, drown in Elyon's waters, and rise to live again.

"Trust me," he said, facing the high place again, "if the sword could rid the world of Teeleh's curse, I would take sides with Samuel. In his youth he's lost sight of the path and grown impatient for the destination."

"So now you'll risk all of our necks to prove him wrong," Jamous said.

"You think we're risking our lives? So you doubt Elyon will save us? You've proven my point."

"Nonsense. I'm only—"

"You doubt Elyon's power to save us. If even my elders doubt, then I'm only doing my duty. We'll see if your doubt is justified."

"It's not your duty to test the power of Elyon."

"Not him," Thomas said. "I test my own heart. And Samuel's. And now yours and Mikil's. Do you object?"

Jamous looked ahead, silent. He didn't dare object.

But another voice broke the silence.

"I object, Father." Samuel walked his horse from an outcropping of boulders on their left. He'd washed the red war paint off his face and drawn his hair back in a ponytail. His son had reached the pass before them.

"You mean well, but your methods don't work," Samuel said. "Ten years of running and hiding have proven it. So be my guest, prove whatever else you want."

They were the first words spoken by Samuel since their departure, and Thomas wasn't sure if they deserved a response. The time for talk had passed.

He clenched his jaw and turned away from his son.

"Oh, please, you don't think I wouldn't have actually killed my sister, do you?"

"You delivered the message?"

"Naturally. Without bloodshed, just for you."

Samuel pulled up alongside him and stared out over the canyons.

"Don't be such an idealist, Father. This isn't one of your dreams. We aren't in the histories, waging war with some virus. We're in a desert and our enemy uses swords to gut our children. When this little game of yours is over, you'll turn us all over to the Horde and some of us won't go easily. Then we'll have our war."

"Shut your muzzle, boy," Mikil snapped. "Show some respect. This isn't over yet."

"Gladly," Samuel said, then mumbled, "I'm done talking anyway."

The histories. How long had it been since Thomas had given any thought to that time when he'd dreamed of another place? It was rarely spoken about by those he confided in these days. At one time he believed that he'd actually come *from* the histories, where, yes, a virus wreaked havoc on all he held sacred.

The Raison Strain. It seemed so distant now. A dream of a dream. But Samuel had heard it all and forgotten nothing.

Thomas nudged his horse and pointed it into the pass. Samuel was right; they were done talking.

————∞————

CHELISE PACED around the tent, hands on hips. Her son, Jake, raced by, wooden sword in hand, cutting down imaginary Shataiki as they attacked from all sides. Or was his enemy Horde, covered in scabs?

"Enough, Jake! For the last time, put that cursed stick of wood away before you do some real damage."

The five-year-old stopped and looked up at her. His blond curls hung in his round, green eyes. She should take a blade to those locks before he resembled an overgrown tuft of desert wheat.

"Put it away, Jake," Marie said, eyeing her brother. "You know what happens when you get carried away."

Marie's wounds were nearly healed. A day had passed since they'd applied the clear nectar from the green plums. Only the deepest cut across her belly, bared between her halter and her skirt, was still plainly visible. If Samuel had run her through with his sword, she might have perished. There was no rising from the dead, not even with a hundred fruits.

"You're no example," Chelise chided her.

"Please, Mother, we're past that."

"I still can't believe you would subject us all to that display of brutality."

"We've all been subjected to much worse."

"He's your brother, for the love of Elyon. And he"—she glanced at Jake, who was still looking up at them—"is your brother. What kind of foolish notions do you suppose I'll have to pull out of his mind now? Did you think of that?"

"I defended the truth. If that comes at a cost, so be it."

Yes, of course, the truth. Their whole family was going to burn on the funeral pyre in defense of the truth. However noble it might be, Chelise didn't have to like it.

"Leave us, Jake. Find Johnny or Britton and find some mischief that has nothing to do with fighting."

"Yes, Mother."

"Promise me."

"Promise."

He dropped the wooden sword, a gift from Samuel of all people. Jake skipped over the mats and slipped through the canvas flap as if it were made of air.

Most of their industry surrounded desert wheat, which, apart from beds of cactus, was one of the only plentiful food sources in the desert. There was the fruit, of course, but it could only be found near the red pools.

Like the Horde who'd occupied the desert before them, the albinos used the desert wheat for more than its grain. The stalks could be reduced to thread or woven into thick mats. With the help of dye from the rocks, a few Circle tents could turn a small corner of the desert into a colorful flower.

"Sit down, Mother. You're making me crazy," Marie said.

She sat in a rocking chair Thomas had fashioned out of wood, one of the few pieces of furniture they took with them when they fled the Horde. She could understand Samuel's frustration; she could not understand his plan to resolve it.

"The other tribes are on their way?" Marie asked.

"Our runners are probably just reaching them. But they'll be here in record time, you can count on that. I hope your father knows what he's doing. It's a dangerous thing to have so many in one place. He had no right to leave me behind."

"He's also Thomas," Marie said. "Thomas of Hunter. Do you know how many narrow escapes he's survived? How many armies he's defeated? How many times he's been right?"

Chelise stood, no longer willing to sit and rock. "And this time I think he's wrong. He's going to throw everything down on the line, and even if he wins this reckless game, Qurong will never follow through on his end. He'll betray Thomas."

Marie crossed the room and sat in the chair that Chelise had vacated. "Well, you should know."

"That's right." She knew her father. He was as stubborn as a mule. Even more immovable than Thomas.

"That's why you're so upset, isn't it?" Marie said. "This is more about Qurong than Thomas."

"I don't know what you mean. Of course this is about my father, but it isn't a game. It's just . . . it's impossible!" Chelise could feel the heat in her face but felt powerless to stop it.

"I think that's the point," Marie said softly, staring at a bowl of fruit surrounded by a dozen blue pillows on the mat where they reclined to eat. "Impossible for us, impossible for Samuel. Impossible for all except one."

She switched her gaze to Chelise. "What if he's right? What if he wins this challenge against Qurong?"

"My father will never drown. Not like this."

"Then how?"

Chelise turned away, fighting back tears of frustration. For a few moments neither of them spoke. The rocker creaked as Marie stood and stepped up behind her. Her hand rested on Chelise's shoulder, the same hand that had mastered the sword and fended off Samuel just yesterday. But now it was gentle and steady.

"Then let's go," Marie said quietly. "Let's go to your father, Qurong, leader of the Horde, and let's save my father, Thomas of Hunter, leader of the Circle."

"Elyon knows how I want to. How I need to. Saving my father is all I dream about, you know?" Her brow wrinkled in deep thought.

"If what you say is right, if Qurong will double-cross Father, then we have to go."

"Thomas would disagree."

"Of course. He would say that Elyon will protect him," Marie said, removing her hand and stepping around Chelise. "But Samuel's right: no one has actually seen Elyon in ten years."

"Don't tell me you fought your brother with doubt in your heart."

"Honestly? I think I fought Samuel to fight off my own demons of doubt. Does that make me as wrong as he is? Assuming he is wrong?"

So, even Thomas's daughter was harboring doubt. The situation was worse than she'd imagined. Thomas was right in casting this challenge. The Circle was fracturing. It was all breaking apart.

"You don't approve of my honesty?" Marie said, noticing the change in her.

"Honesty? I don't know what is honest anymore. All I know is that we have a problem, Thomas was right about that." She stepped past Marie. "And I know that I fear for his life."

"Where are you going?"

"To speak to the council. Or what's left of it."

"Why?"

"Because you're right. We have to go after him."

8

JANAE SOAKED up Billy's tales, knowing that every syllable he spoke was simple, unaltered fact. She had lived a lie, and this unlikely man from across the seas had found her and brought her the truth.

She listened as he recounted stories of the monastery in Paradise, Colorado, where he first found the Books of History as a boy. And she knew that she, like Billy, had to touch one of these books if it was the last thing she did before dying.

She heard him speak of the large worms in the endless tunnels beneath the monastery, and she fought off the desire to charter a jet on the spot, fly to Paradise, and see for herself if any of these worms still survived. They, like the books, had certainly been spawned by another world. Yet they were here, in this reality?

But what made her mouth dry was Billy's claim that Thomas wasn't the only one who'd crossed the bridge into this other reality or, for that matter, come back *from* the future.

Kara had gone. And returned.

Monique, her very own mother, had gone. And returned.

How? Using Thomas's blood. The idea, once it sank in, was too much to absorb in one sitting.

"You mean, when you fall asleep—"

"While in contact with Thomas's blood," Billy interrupted, making a show of cutting his finger with a fingernail. "More accurately, while your blood is in contact with Thomas's blood."

"And you just wake up in this other place?"

"It sounds crazy, but there's plenty of proof. Me, for starters. The books—"

"Until you fall asleep there, in which case you wake up here," Janae said, on her own track. "As if the whole thing was just a dream. Only it isn't a dream at all."

"Correct. That's what I've pieced together so far."

"And you know, with certainty, that this blood still exists?"

"How many times do you need me to say it, Janae? You think I've done all of this, come all this way, because I saw your picture in *People* magazine and decided I had to have you? As if I said to myself, 'I know, I'll make up stories about books that can transport you between realities and pretend to be able to read her thoughts, that'll impress her'?"

Janae eyed him, captivated by the notion that he was reading her mind this very moment. She stood and brushed by him, smiling coyly. There was more about Billy that attracted her, and it wasn't simply his promise of adventure. He brought out the animal in her. Maybe she should give it to him without pretending.

She reached back for his hand. "Walk with me."

He did so willingly, and they meandered from the suite, still hand in hand.

"From now on this stays between us," she said. "You'll get nothing from my mother, you know that."

"Maybe."

"Not maybe. She hasn't mentioned a word of this to me, which can only mean she's hidden the truth for good reasons."

"Keeping to ourselves won't get us what we need."

"Of course not, darling. I can get us that. But I need to know that I can trust you."

"Trust me? I'm the one sharing secrets here."

She placed her free hand on his chest and gently stopped him. "Look inside me. Tell me I'm not sharing my deepest secrets with you."

Billy's eyes stared into hers. She thought about her father, what she knew, which wasn't much and had been closely guarded. And she told Billy with her mind that she found him exhilarating.

Images of her past skipped through her mind: the first time she'd overseen a board meeting at age twenty-one, her first lover, the time she'd been busted in New York for drug possession and thrown in jail for the night. But her mind finally rested on him. On Billy. On this man who'd fallen from the sky and in a few short hours managed to strip her of her secrets.

She found him stimulating. Enticing. Nearly irresistible. Not only physically, but spiritually. Emotionally. She didn't understand why. She didn't care that she didn't understand.

"You see? You can see into my heart and know that you can trust me. And I have to know that I can trust you as well."

She still held his hand in hers, and she noted that it was clammy. But then, she was accustomed to the effect she had on men.

"Our secret," she said, swallowing.

He cleared his throat. "Our secret."

"I hope I can trust you." She kissed him lightly on his lips and turned to lead him on. But Billy pulled back.

His eyes glanced nervously at the atrium beyond her. "Where are we going?"

Janae turned back. "You don't know? You haven't read my mind?"

"I do know. Learning to live with my abilities has taught me to . . . well, you know . . . go with the flow."

"By pretending not to know. Because you don't want to come off as uppity by showing your superiority over everyone else in the room. Right?"

"Something like that."

"Don't worry, I feel the same way half the time."

"Then you'll understand when I say that I have no interest in wandering around the compound, pretending to be interested in the lay of the land. It's a waste of time."

"A woman needs time—"

"I don't have time."

Her eyes searched his. "That's how you want to play?"

"I don't want to play. This need has been hunting me down for over a year. It's like a presence. I have to know if it's here."

The blood.

Billy turned and walked back toward the guest suite.

"Where are you going?"

"You don't know where it is, I can see that much. And you don't have any idea how to get it."

How rude! Where'd he grown the gall to think he could just waltz away without any regard for his host, a host who'd practically stripped herself bare for him? He was exasperating.

He was . . . like her.

"Slow down," she snapped, heading after him into the rooms. "Just take a deep breath. Fine." She shut the main door to the suite. "I'm as eager as you are, but—"

"You've known about the books for a few hours," he said, spinning back. "Don't talk to me about how eager you are. The idea that these books exist would be a heady thought for anyone, but why are you so . . . crazy about this? I can't see it in your mind, and frankly it's a bit disturbing."

It was a fair question. She told the truth. No use pretending with him. "I don't know."

"No, you don't," he said. "And that's the scariest part. It makes your longing almost . . . inhuman."

She calmed herself. "What do you expect from me? You tell me all of this and expect me to tap my fingers on the table and agree to help you?"

"Pretty much. Yes."

"Please. A hundred dots have connected in my head, and you want me to take a nap?"

"No dots have connected in your head, Janae. That's the problem. It hasn't turned on the lights in your head. I would be able to see that. But when I look inside you, I see something else."

"Is that so? And what do you see?"

"Your heart. Your desires. They're all black."

"Like yours," she said, because she could think of no defense. What he said was preposterous. She was no more evil than the next person.

Billy turned away and walked to one of the windows overlooking the lawn. "I've been here before. Staring down this kind of blackness."

"But your heart is white now?" She walked up behind him and traced the muscles of his back with her fingers. "You're afraid that naughty Janae will bring it all back? Hmm? Is that it?"

He shook his head slowly. "No. It just reminds me that what we're doing—what I'm doing—isn't right." Billy turned around, and she saw that his eyes were misty. "But I can't seem to help it. The power that's in that blood . . . those books . . . you have no idea how much damage it can bring." He looked away, and a tear snaked down his cheek.

For a moment she thought he might be talking himself out of everything he'd just convinced her to do. Panic swarmed her mind. She couldn't let him do that.

Why not, Janae? What is happening to you?

She was certain about one thing: Billy could not leave this place until she knew everything that he knew. And more.

She had to find that blood. Alone, if it had to be that way.

"I know how you feel," she started. Then, "Actually I don't. I don't share your regret. But you're right, I have desires in me that I can't understand. And I believe you share those same desires."

Janae stepped around him, dragging her fingernails delicately over his neck and cheek. She saw light freckles spotting the flesh under his hair when she brushed it away. The vein on his throat stood out, and she touched it gently.

"If your desires are like mine, then you won't be able to resist them," she said. "It's your destiny, to find this blood. To cross over."

Billy looked at her for a moment, then swallowed and cleared his throat.

"You're right. I know. But you're the first person I've met who knows it as well as I do. When I look into your eyes I feel like I'm looking into myself, and it's all a bit disturbing."

Janae felt drawn to his pale neck, so soft and tender, so bare, so full of life. She leaned forward and whispered into his ear, touching his lobe with her lips.

"Then trust me, Billy. We're the same, you and I. We are meant to be together in more ways than one."

She was momentarily distracted by her own audacity, her flagrant attempt at seduction. This wasn't typical.

But another thought eased her concern. Just exactly who was seducing whom here? Billy had swept her off her feet in a matter of hours. Was he playing her?

She pulled away and walked to a crystal decanter. Poured herself a drink and threw it back in one swallow. When she turned back to him, he was staring at her, expressionless. Reading her. His advantage over her was unfair.

It was also part of what made him irresistible.

"So," she said, pouring another drink. "What is it? Are we changing our minds?"

"I wasn't aware we'd made up our minds," he said, crossing to the decanter. He took the glass from her hand and matched her slug. Set it down with a *thunk*.

"Rumor has it that Thomas wasn't the only one to cross over into this world," he said softly, as if what he would tell her now was of greatest importance. He stepped to a large, plum-colored wingback chair, sat down, and crossed his legs. "Several others have come and gone. But I've learned that one came and stayed. A wraith called a Shataiki in that world. His name was Alucard, and he was a creature of the night."

She felt her chest tighten. "Okay, now you've lost me," she said, but that's not what she was thinking. She turned her eyes away so he couldn't see into her mind. "What do you mean, a creature of the night?"

"I don't know much. But I know they spread their seed through blood."

"Through blood?"

"The information is sketchy, but yes. I think so. It's how they reproduce."

She shoved her thoughts out before he could steal them from her mind.

"Unless you think we can tie my mother down and pry her eyes open so you can plunder her mind, there's only one way to find out if she knows where the blood is."

"I've already considered that," Billy said.

"You don't want to try. Trust me. She'll have you dead or behind bars before you can use what you learn."

"Exactly."

"She has to retrieve the blood willingly."

"Clearly."

Janae turned. "I know how to do that." Then she looked into his eyes and let him take her knowledge.

This time she could almost feel his invasive gaze. His eyes widened slowly and he blinked twice.

Billy stood to his feet, face white.

"Seriously?"

"I should know. It's my lab."

"Raison Strain B?"

"A mutation of the virus that turned the world upside down thirty years ago. It's not airborne. But there's no known antivirus. If we inject ourselves with it . . ."

"She'll be forced to try Thomas's blood, because it proved resistant to the original virus," Billy finished. "And if she doesn't have the blood? Or if it fails?"

She reached for the decanter and said what he already knew because a thing like this needed to be said aloud.

"Then we both die."

9

The Future

THE HIGH crater at Ba'al Bek was a good half mile across, ringed by a thick lip of soil and rock. A boulder from the heavens might have created it, or the fist of a giant, or a belch from Teeleh for all Thomas knew.

What he did know was that the whole plateau stank of rotting Scab flesh.

The four albinos had crossed the gorges and now sat on their horses, peering into the high place with a red sun sinking to the west. Behind them, canyons offered cover from any attack.

Ahead, barren ground up to a single row of tall boulders that ringed Ba'al Bek's famed stone altar. This was the first time he'd seen the altar. The Circle had gone deep into the desert for nearly six years after Qurong turned his full wrath on them.

"We have company," Mikil said.

Thomas looked up at the far rim and saw the purple banner sticking over the crest. Then more banners, then heads and horses.

"Qurong's taken up the challenge," Mikil said. "I don't like this, Thomas. This can't be good."

The Horde marched in two columns, each led by a contingent of two dozen Throaters, then the priests. Dozens of priests. They kept coming, two hundred priests or more, by Thomas's reckoning.

Dear Elyon, what have I done?

Ba'al sat in a litter, rocking on the shoulders of eight servants. Qurong rode tall on a black stallion opposite the dark priest, dressed in full battle gear. His own guard, thirty or forty from the Scab cavalry, rode on either side of him. They bore swords, battle axes, sickles, and perhaps the most dreaded weapon in their arsenal, a simple chain with two spiked balls that could be thrown to take down prey from fifty yards. Mace.

The rattling of a thousand bells on the edges of the priests' robes sounded like a desert full of cicadas in the early evening.

"We're mice among lions," Jamous said. "Are you sure about this, Thomas?"

"I thought you said priests only." Mikil had faced her share of long odds, but never this and not for many years. "They've brought half a battalion!"

"It's for their defense, not to take us out," Thomas said.

Samuel's mount stamped its feet. A grin twisted his face. "They still fear us. What did I tell you? We could take them."

"Four against hundreds?" Mikil scoffed. "Even in our 'full glory' as you like to call it, these would have been unfeasible odds."

"Impossible," Jamous mumbled.

Samuel came alive in the presence of his enemies. "The priests are unarmed. We could at least take Qurong and that witch. That would set the Horde far back. Without a head, the snakes crawl into their holes."

Thomas almost pointed out that Samuel's foolishness had brought them here in the first place. Or that a dead high priest would only be replaced by another live one. Or that these were not their true enemies. The real enemy was peering at them from his hidden perch on the crest somewhere. Teeleh and his host from hell, the Shataiki.

But Samuel doubted Teeleh and the Shataiki and even Elyon, for that matter.

Thomas headed his horse down the slope.

"You're sure, Thomas?" Mikil kicked her horse to follow.

Thomas kept his eyes on the entourage snaking over the crest. Bulls pulled six large chests on carts. Then the goats trotted in. He wasn't sure what Ba'al had up his sleeve, but he doubted Teeleh had a taste for goats. This was all for show.

"Thomas." Mikil drew her horse abreast his. "Please tell me you've thought this through."

"You're asking me now? Isn't it a bit late?"

"I didn't believe it would come to this. You've been brooding."

"My mood has just lightened, Mikil. For the first time in far too long I feel like I have nothing to lose."

"Only your faith," Samuel said, pulling abreast.

"If Elyon doesn't show himself tonight, it only means that he wants me dead," Thomas said.

"And the Horde as well."

Thomas gave him that. "If I lose this challenge, then I will assume the way of peace has passed, and I will take down as many Horde as I can before my skin turns."

"Thomas Hunter will kill again?" Samuel said. "Did I hear that right?"

"Thomas Hunter will die. Again."

"You'll tell them where our camps are?"

"As promised."

They headed into Ba'al Bek, four abreast, facing an entourage that dwarfed them.

"And if you succeed in this challenge," Mikil said, "if Elyon shows himself, you actually expect that Qurong will agree to come with us and drown?"

"He's agreed already."

"He'll betray you," Samuel said. "But I don't think you have much worry there; he isn't going to lose this challenge."

Thomas looked at his son. "Maybe not. But if he does lose, I'll have won my own son back, and that for me is worth his betrayal."

Samuel tried to smile. His twisted lips looked stupid on his crimson face.

The tall rocks that circled the altar rose above them now, red in the sunset. The light would be gone within the hour. Thomas would have preferred to confront Ba'al in broad daylight, but it was what it was.

Qurong and his dark priest had reached the high place and waited for the host of priests to take up their position on the altar's left. The Throaters were fanning out on either side as if they expected an attack from the high ground.

"Imagine what we could do with a dozen archers," Samuel said, scanning the crater's rim. "We could make pin cushions out of them in a matter of minutes."

He was right. A dozen years ago, this setup would have provided the perfect ambush for the Forest Guard. Thomas understood Samuel's desires to destroy his enemies. It was the most natural instinct man possessed.

Love the enemy. This was the scandalous teaching of Elyon. It went completely against human nature.

It struck Thomas then that Eram, the half-breed from the north, could just as easily sweep in with his army, surround the crater, and destroy all of his enemies—both the albinos and the leader of the Horde—in one fell swoop.

"Tell us what to do." Mikil spoke quickly, uneasy.

"I will. As soon as I know."

"Elyon help us all."

"Isn't that the idea? To see if those words have any meaning?"

Thomas led the four past the ring of boulders like an arrow into the heart of darkness. It had been a while since Thomas had been so close to Scab flesh. He'd forgotten just how rancid it was. Only as he drew closer did he see the reason: none of the priests had applied the morst paste.

He pulled up and faced Ba'al, who still sat on his cushioned throne under the silk canopy. His servants had set him down. Qurong gazed off to his right, refusing to dignify them with a square look. His general, the one named Cassak if Thomas was right, sat in stoic silence beside him, eyes on Ba'al.

Who led the Horde these days, anyway? Ba'al or Qurong?

Both, he guessed. The thin serpent wielded Teeleh's power over the people, and the muscled warrior wielded the sword.

Ba'al stood and slinked forward. A black silk dress clung to his body from his armpits to his heels. A purple sash wrapped around his neck hung down to his belly. But his shoulders were bare, white, bony.

Three scars marked his forehead. All the others bore the same marks, something Thomas's scouts first reported about a year ago.

"I've come to speak to Qurong," Thomas said. "Not to his servant."

Ba'al made no show of being bothered by this underhanded insult, but Qurong would take note.

"Welcome, pale one," the dark priest said. "The supreme commander, ruler of humans, servant of Teeleh our master has accepted your challenge."

"Then let the master speak for himself. Is he your puppet?"

This time the witch's left eyelid twitched. "Don't assume that all men would stoop to speak to you, albino," Ba'al said.

"But you do. For more than ten years I've evaded the death sentence placed upon me and my wife . . . I think that earns me the right to be acknowledged by the ruler of this earth." Thomas watched Qurong as he spoke.

"Then perhaps you overestimate yourself as much as you overestimate your God."

"That's what we're here to find out," Thomas said. "Don't get your silk dress all hitched up for the dance just yet. I insist on speaking to your leader."

Ba'al stared. His gray eyes betrayed no emotion, no resentment, no sign that Thomas offended him. This was a wicked man, more Shataiki than human, Thomas thought. The night seemed to have turned inordinately cold.

"Can we please dispense with all the fancy footwork?" Qurong said, eyeing Thomas for the first time. "You've cast a challenge, I've accepted. My priest will invoke the power of Teeleh and you will call on your God. We've gone to a lot of trouble to accommodate this game of yours. I suggest we get started. What exactly do you have in mind?"

"Anything your dark priest would like."

None of the three behind Thomas spoke a word or moved. Ba'al kept his haunting, unblinking stare on him. With a little imagination Thomas could see the conniving brain behind those eyes spinning like a beetle tied to a string. For a long time the only sound came from the occasional snorting or shifting of a Throater's horse.

"Is that your son?" Ba'al asked, looking at Samuel.

"I see you've taken to mutilating your foreheads," Thomas said. "The mark of your beast, is that it?"

The white wraith in human form named Ba'al, who was the wickedest of all Horde, raised his hand and extended a thin finger to the horizon. "From the east the pale one will bring peace and command the sky. He will purge the land with a river of blood in the valley of Miggdon. We will offer ourselves to him on that day of reckoning. The question is, will you?"

"No. We will not. We submit to Elyon and to no one else."

The priest eyed him. His mouth was paper thin, scarcely more than flaps of white flesh to keep the bugs from his teeth. He raised one hand by his head and snapped fingers so delicate Thomas wondered how the snap alone didn't break them.

"We shall see, albino."

Two of the priests hurried over to one of the bull-drawn carts. While one unhitched the beast, the other pulled a large, white silk blanket from the chest. Then a silver goblet.

The rest watched, bare of emotion, as the two priests urged the bull forward, tied it to one of four bronze rings on the altar, and draped the white blanket over the beast's back. One of them strapped a ruby-colored cushion on top. A saddle. The priests hurried back to their posts, bells jangling with the shuffle of their feet. The whole operation took two dozen seconds, no more.

What Ba'al could possibly mean to demonstrate by saddling up a bull was beyond Thomas, but the man's continuous, unwavering stare didn't sit well with him.

"Do you like the sight of blood, Thomas?" Ba'al asked.

"Not particularly." *Dear Elyon, do not keep your face hidden now, not now. The whole world is watching, and I'm powerless.* Then, as an afterthought: *Give the word and I will take this man's head from his shoulders for you.*

"I suggest you get used to it, albino. Because our god demands blood. Pools of blood. Rivers of blood. Blood from the necks of our own."

"Your god, Teeleh"—Thomas spat to one side—"may be a blood-thirsty—"

Ba'al moved while Thomas spoke, snatching a hidden sword from his back, slashing down with lightning speed. The blade struck the bull on its spine, just above the shoulder blades, and cut cleanly through its neck.

Samuel's sword scraped its scabbard as he withdrew it.

The bull's head dropped from its torso and landed on the earth with a dull *thump.* For a long moment, the animal stood still, unaware of the blood that pumped from its arteries onto the ground. Then it took a half step and collapsed.

A soft moan broke from the two hundred priests, now swaying in their black robes. The slaying happened so quickly that Thomas didn't think to react.

Ba'al spread his arms wide and spoke to the darkening sky. "Accept my offering, Teeleh, one and true god of all that lives and breathes, dragon of the sky. May your vengeance find fulfillment through my hands."

He lowered his head and glared at Thomas. "Tell your friends to drop their weapons."

The moans ceased.

"Not for you. Not for any Scab," Samuel spat.

Ba'al dropped his own blade. "Tell him."

"Drop it, Samuel."

"Father—"

"All of you, drop your weapons!"

They weren't here for battle or to defend themselves. It took a few seconds, but Thomas heard the blades fall. Qurong sat on his horse, star-ing at the dead bull as two priests hurried in and collected the weapons from the ground. The Throaters closed off any avenue of escape, leaving only their rear unguarded.

"This is only a bull, not enough to satiate the true god," Ba'al said. "The stakes here are far too great for an ordinary display of loyalty." He pointed to his gathered faithful. "I will put the life of Teeleh's loyal subjects up against the life of only one albino. We will see which one the true god delivers."

The implications ran through Thomas's chest like a blade. His own life against these swaying witches. His mind stalled at the thought. What was the priest suggesting, that he lie on the altar and take the blade the way the bull had?

But he'd come here to either die or be saved. Any further hesitation would only make a mockery of all he stood for.

"Against your witches," Thomas said, "and you. Agreed."

Ba'al's eyes shifted over Thomas's right shoulder. "We will all bleed and trust our master to show his power as he has in the past. All of them. And then your son. And then me."

Thomas froze. "Never! Myself, not my son."

"You don't trust your god to deliver even this one albino? Is your son beyond Elyon's reach?"

"I decide for me, not for my son." Thomas spoke the words, but his mind was crying out to Elyon already. He had been tricked. Pushed into a corner. He saw the trap, but failing to see a way to break free, his mind cried out. Then his lips, in a barely audible whisper. "Elyon . . . Elyon, I beg you . . ."

"I haven't asked your son about his faith in this God you serve," Ba'al said. "I'm asking if *you* have the faith to put his life in your God's hands."

Thomas felt his lifelines slipping. He'd expected any scenario but this. How could he offer up his own son?

"Do you believe Elyon will save your son?"

The cool night air had gone frigid.

"Elyon has no limits."

"Father—"

"And if your son doesn't agree?" Ba'al cut in. "Would that weaken your faith? Would you be frightened that Teeleh would steal your child the way you stole Qurong's child?"

Chelise. Qurong sat with jaw fixed.

"Listen to me, you skinny little witch," Thomas bit off. "My son, like Chelise, decides for himself whether he lives or dies. He's not your bull to slaughter."

"I thought Elyon and Teeleh were to decide who would live or die. I'm only asking if you, not your son, will give Elyon the opportunity to decide."

Thomas's face flushed with indignation. But he truly was ensnared by this pathetic wretch's challenge. If he delayed in giving his consent, it would only show his doubt. He'd come to prove his faith in Elyon, and already he was flapping around like a wounded chicken.

But he couldn't bring himself to say it. He couldn't stand here and—

Do you want to swim with me?

Thomas's pulse spiked.

Swim in my waters, Thomas.

The distant voice whispered. The same voice he'd heard on occasion in the deepest part of Elyon's waters. A boy's voice, so tender, full of mischief and life. Elyon . . .

"What did I tell you, my lord?" Ba'al said to Qurong. "I've handed you a victory with the slaying of one bull. The great Thomas of Hunter doesn't have—"

"I accept your challenge," Thomas snapped. "I would offer my son. But I can't speak for him."

"No. But I can." Ba'al nodded.

Thomas twisted on his horse and felt the blood drain from his face. The Throaters had closed the gaps between the boulders fifty yards behind Mikil, Jamous, and Samuel. None of them had any weapons.

There was no escape, not even for a fighter of Samuel's caliber.

Ba'al was going to bleed his son.

"Come, my master," Ba'al whispered in a trembling voice. "Enter your servant."

Six Throaters rode in from the left, swords drawn. They didn't hesitate as they would have if facing an armed warrior of the Guard, but stormed straight toward Samuel, slamming into his horse. One of them whipped a long chain around his son's throat and tugged.

"Father . . ."

"Let him go! Release him!" Thomas spurred his horse into the fray, took the butt of a sword on his chin and blindly struck out with a fist. He felt his knuckles sink into spongy Scab flesh. The warrior he'd hit grunted and swung his spear like a stick. It glanced off Thomas's shoulder.

Panic joined his desperation. Even if there was a chance to overpower the Throaters, he would betray his own challenge by attempting anything so foolish.

The sound of a brutal blow to Samuel's flesh made him recoil. A grunt. Then silence. They'd dragged Samuel to the ground and knocked him out.

Thomas spun back to Ba'al, swallowing against the dread rising in his gut. "This wasn't my challenge!"

The dark priest was staring at the dusk sky, hands raised and trembling. He jerked his head down. "It is mine."

Whimpers and murmuring spread through Ba'al's priests, their eyes on the darkening sky. Thomas looked up.

At first glance it appeared as if a huge black cloud had drifted over the high place and was slowly rotating—a hurricane forming several miles over their heads.

But this wasn't a cloud, Thomas saw. For the first time in many years, the Shataiki were showing themselves. Hundreds of thousands of the black beasts peered down with red eyes, having gathered to watch the butchery.

Elyon . . . Dear Elyon, help us . . .

10

CHELISE PULLED her mount up with a sharp tug, digging her heels into the leather stirrups. She threw her weight back to compensate for the sudden stop. The pale mare, bred to blend into the desert, snorted and tossed its head, protesting the bronze bit that dug into its flesh.

The sky . . . there was something wrong in the sky.

"What?" Marie cried, whipping her head around as she shot past. She forced her horse to a tramping halt. "What is it?"

"I . . ." Chelise stared at the black cloud on the distant darkening horizon. Something about the sight spread a chill over her skull. "I . . ."

Marie followed her eyes and gazed with her. "What is it? A cloud?"

"It's moving."

"So clouds move. What's gotten into you?"

"Over the high place, as if—"

"Shataiki," Marie whispered.

The horses were breathing hard from their run, but this one word uttered by Marie felt like a kick to Chelise's gut. She hadn't put her finger on it, but now that Marie had labeled the huge, swirling vortex, the dreadful certainty that her daughter was right wrapped its claws around her throat.

Shataiki.

"That's impossible," she finally managed.

Marie twisted in her saddle. "It's over the high place, Ba'al Bek."

"But . . . so Qurong accepted Thomas's challenge?"

Marie turned her jittery mount back to Chelise, casting an eye at the Shataiki. "Unless they've gathered in defiance of Thomas's presence on

94

their sacred turf. He would be the first albino to enter the cursed place of worship."

"But no one's seen the Shataiki for years. Have you ever seen one?"

"I may have. At one time I thought I had, but it could just as easily have been a shadow. This is . . ." Marie couldn't seem to form her thoughts around the idea that they were actually seeing Shataiki. But there could be no doubt. It was a massive cloud of black bats, each the size of a bloodhound if the legends were correct, packed so closely together that they looked from this distance like a solid mass. "So many . . ."

Chelise had finally convinced the council that Qurong and Ba'al would accept Thomas's challenge only if they intended to double-cross him. She argued that Qurong would never stoop so low in his mind to go with Thomas if he lost the challenge. The only person remotely capable of winning Qurong's heart was his very own daughter. Chelise.

Marie earned the right to go because she had defended Thomas's honor by fighting Samuel in Vadal's place.

They left Jake with Susan, who complained bitterly that a fighter of her caliber should go with them.

After eight hard hours of riding they were less than halfway there. But they had the fruit; they would not stop.

"We're not going to make it," Chelise said. Her heart pounded in her ears. "If they've already started this ill-advised game, we're going to be too late."

"I'm not sure there's anything we could do if—"

"Then go home," Chelise snapped. "It wasn't my idea that you come."

"Easy. I'm not second-guessing our decision. I'm just stating the obvious. We don't stand a chance against that." She nodded at the cloud of Shataiki, slowly rotating in the dusky sky.

"You're forgetting about Elyon. You nearly killed your brother for his honor—"

"I would never kill Samuel."

"—yet you doubt Elyon's power?"

"If it's up to Elyon, then why does he need us? He's got Thomas out there. What good will two more be?"

"Qurong—"

"Can be won by Elyon much more easily than by you," Marie cut in. Then with less bite: "So it would seem to me."

"You're far too much like your father," Chelise said. "Everyone should take care of themselves, is that it? Your independence is only cute when there's no real danger." She kicked her horse, and the beast surged forward. "If Elyon could snap his fingers and win anyone's heart, the Horde would have flocked to the red lakes long ago," she cried. "That's obviously not the way it works."

Marie urged her mount into a full run and pulled abreast. "I'm not suggesting we don't go, Mother, but Thomas and I aren't the only ones who are stubborn. Father knew that your love for Qurong might jeopardize his mission, not to mention your life. I think that cloud only raises the stakes. Don't do anything rash."

"Now the youth are giving the advice?"

"I'm not a child! I'm the one who's here to keep your backside out of trouble."

"I'm not a fool."

"No, but love is blind. And you, Mother, are blind when it comes to your father."

There was some truth to what Marie said. Chelise would give her life to save Qurong, if Elyon required it. But her love for Qurong didn't make her stupid.

Chelise pushed her mare into a full gallop. "Fine, save my backside. At this rate you're not going to be given that opportunity, because it'll all be over by the time we get there."

She breathed a quick prayer, begging Elyon to keep them all alive until she could show up and make things right. She immediately chided herself for such arrogance.

"How far?" she breathed.

"We can't push the horses like this all night. Daybreak. At best."

Thank Elyon they'd brought the healing fruit.

11

THE PRIVATE laboratory had been constructed underground and fortified with reinforced concrete, halfway between Raison Pharmaceutical's Bangkok laboratories and the mansion on the south lawn. Monique's reasoning for choosing the location was simple: Any attack on the compound would focus on the buildings, not the grass between them. All critical samples would be stored in the five-thousand-square-foot facility where the most sensitive research was conducted.

They called it Ground Zero, home of some of the world's most potentially destructive biological materials. Raison Strain B for starters.

Janae swiped her security card through the reader, heard the magnetic locking mechanism disengage, and looked back at Billy. Sweat beaded his forehead. His eyes darted to hers, then back to the metal door.

She pushed it open and walked into the hall. "Close the door behind you. And hurry. Just because it's midnight doesn't mean security doesn't already know my card was used to gain access. I wouldn't put it past my mother to have instructed them to alert her every time I enter."

"She's that distrusting of you?"

"No. Not normally. But you're here, aren't you? The redheaded bloodhound who can climb into people's minds."

"With the bloodhound who uses her tongue to steal the minds of men," he said.

"Whatever." But he was right.

He followed her down the hall, past several doors where supplies were kept. The passage ended at another steel door that again required her card for access. She could hear Billy's steady breathing behind her.

He'd questioned her no fewer than a dozen times since she first suggested they call Monique's bluff by infecting themselves, though his obsession with reaching the Books of History was reason enough for him to follow through. After all, he explained, he'd grown up with them, used them. He might even be *responsible* for them. He'd been pushed to the outer limits of himself and found nothing more than the blackness he'd come to recognize in his heart.

The fear and horror of a dozen years had turned him into a rag doll at the mercy of that blackness, he'd said, pacing with both hands in his hair. The chance of finally understanding what had turned him into the person he was, however dangerous, was worth the risk of Monique hanging them out to dry. For that matter, maybe he'd only find what he was looking for in death.

But what drove Janae to the same desperation? Nothing Billy could see in her mind. So what was it? He wanted to know. What?

She guessed. "Maybe because I have that same blackness in me. I always have. From the time my father vanished, I've hated my life. That same blackness is calling me. You can't see it in my mind because it's beyond my mind. I don't even understand it, but today, for the first time, hearing about the blood and the Books of History, and my own mother's involvement—I feel alive, Billy. I've come back from the dead."

"And so now you're willing to risk death again?" he'd challenged.

She turned away. "Mother won't allow that."

"But if she does."

"Then she does. But she won't. On occasion I may be the child she wishes she never had, but my mother loves me."

She unlocked the metal door and led Billy into the heart of the facility: a white laboratory blinking with a hundred monitoring lights. The door closed softly behind them, and she gave him a moment to study the room.

A dozen workstations were positioned under fluorescent lights, perfectly ordered with flat touch-screen monitors. Not a pen or piece of paper out of place. Not a single paperclip or piece of lint on the shiny-mirror black floor.

Her mother was obsessive compulsive when it came to research. Two large liquid-cooled servers provided the room with enough computing power to run the Pentagon, but Mother controlled the real brains behind what happened here. Her own.

Then again, there was little her mother knew that Janae did not.

"This is it," she said.

"Impressive. What are all those machines?" His eyes were on a wall lined with high-voltage equipment.

"Nothing you and I need. Magnetometers, electron microscopes, cryogenics, homogenizers . . . too much to explain now. What we need is in the subzero refrigeration system."

She walked to a small room with a skull-and-crossbones symbol under a sign that read *Quarantine*, punched a code into a small pad, and pushed the glass door wide. Inside lay four gurneys with restraining straps. Each had its own life-support system, now disconnected.

"So this is it," Billy said, stepping into the room beside her.

"We won't need all the technology. A syringe will do the trick. But yes, we do need to seal ourselves in. Can't risk additional contamination, right?" She forced a grin.

"Right."

"Please try to relax, Billy. You do realize the real risk here, don't you?"

"I think I do, yes."

"It's not my mother. It's that what *you've* told me isn't the truth. Frankly, seeing you sweat like this makes me wonder."

"It's the truth," he insisted. "Your mother may love you, but how do we know the blood exists? That's the real risk."

"The blood exists. I saw it in my mother's eyes. Like I said earlier, you're not the only one who can read minds. My intuition has never failed me."

"Then you should know that I've told you nothing but the truth," Billy said.

She frowned. Her hands were tingling with energy and the fact that Billy seemed reticent only added to her eagerness. She turned from the quarantine room, crossed to a panel in the wall, and entered a ten-digit code she'd written on her palm: 786947494D. Motors hummed to life as the retrieval mechanism went for the sample in question.

"It's in the wall?"

"The ground, actually. Twenty feet under us. All of the sensitive stuff is."

He looked a little lost, standing there in his jeans and T-shirt. She stepped over to him, stood on her tiptoes, and gave him a light peck on the lips.

"Ready to commit suicide, darling?"

He reached his right hand behind her head, pulled her close, and kissed her long. When he pulled back, his green eyes sparkled. "I am. More than you know."

Interesting. Not the reaction she had expected. Perhaps she'd underestimated him.

A small beep indicated that the sample had been delivered. Janae slid the door of the caddie open and withdrew a Plexiglas tube that contained a glass vial of amber liquid. She habitually flicked the tube with her nail.

"Raison Strain B. No known antivirus."

"How's it different from the original Raison Strain?"

"Well, for starters, it kills in about a day, not thirty days. Never mind the details, let's just say this one is much harder on the body. We'll be bleeding internally within an hour. The only saving grace is that like most viruses, this strain isn't airborne. It requires an exchange of bodily fluid. So even though strain B is stronger, it doesn't present the same threat as the first strain."

"How much do we need?" he asked, eyeing the vial in her fingers.

"Need? The smallest drop. But I don't want to play around. One cc should do the trick. We won't feel anything anyway, not after the sedatives we take kick in. We'll be out."

"May I?"

She handed him the sample, struck again by the fire burning in his bright eyes. He was like a kid next in line at an amusement-park ride.

She plucked the sample from his hand and walked toward the quarantine room. "Why don't you let me do this? I doubt my mother would take any terrible risk to save you. It's me she'll move heaven and earth to keep alive."

"No," he said. "It doesn't work like that. The point is to get Thomas's blood into our own bloodstream. His blood is what should allow us to cross into his world."

"Thomas's world, even though he originally came from Denver, Colorado."

"I mean the Black Forest. The future, where I sent him by writing in the Book of History. Call it whatever you want, that's not the point. Your own mother was able to follow him by injecting herself with some of his blood. That's the point. If you're infected and she injects you with his blood, you'll cross over, at least in your dreams. I didn't come all this way to stand by your bed and watch you cross without me. If Monique uses the blood on you, she'll use it on me as well, assuming we're both infected."

"Don't say I didn't offer."

"How will she know?"

"That we've infected ourselves? When the resident technician does his rounds in the morning, he'll call her. Assuming she isn't alerted earlier that I've been in here all night."

Janae retrieved a syringe from the cupboard, slipped on a needle, and set it in a three-foot glass chamber with a bottle of sedative and the vial of Raison Strain B. She closed the chamber and inserted both arms into the sleeves that gave her access to the airtight compartment. Billy stood by her, watching.

The vial was sealed with a soft, nonpermeable glue, which broke free with a firm twist. "There it is, Billy. Nasty, nasty stuff." She set the vial in a tray that held it upright. "The wonder drug that's going to take us to a whole new world."

"Actually, the virus is the killer. Thomas's blood is the drug."

Blood. Even now, faced by death, the thought of the blood made her pulse quicken.

Janae inserted the needle into the vial of Raison Strain B, withdrew two ccs of the fluid, and repeated a similar operation with the sedative. She capped the syringe with a rubber sleeve and rotated the glass, giving the two fluids time to mix. She could have done it all without the isolation chamber, but habit compelled her. There was always a chance of spilling and contaminating the room.

She pulled the syringe out of the chamber and faced him. "So, darling. Are you ready for this?"

He glanced at the white-sheeted gurneys. "Just lie down?"

"Go ahead." She winked at him. "I'll be gentle."

Billy gazed into her eyes. "I still can't figure you out. Why aren't you afraid?"

"Thomas found my mother, and his life changed forever. Now you've found her daughter, and your life is about to change. Maybe Thomas isn't the only one with something in his blood."

"Right."

"Lie down," she said.

Billy walked to the nearest gurney, rolled onto the mattress, and looked up. He looked so disarming with his big green eyes and disheveled red hair. A jeans-and-T-shirt guy with worn Skechers and fair skin. It occurred to her that she might be staring the fate of the world in the face. Isn't that what they'd said about Thomas Hunter?

Janae leaned over Billy and touched her lips to his. She impulsively bit his lower lip, and when he didn't pull away, she bit it harder.

The fresh taste of his blood sent a faint tingle through her tongue. She was surprised that he still didn't jerk away. Instead he pressed up into her mouth, then calmly settled back down.

"Let's do this."

"Turn your arm over."

She formed a tourniquet of surgical tubing above his elbow, gently traced the median cubital vein on the inside of his arm, and brought the needle to the skin. Billy stared into her eyes.

Then she inserted the needle into his vein and shot one cc of Raison Strain B into his bloodstream.

Damage done.

She withdrew the needle and released the tourniquet. "Lie still." But she wasn't thinking of him lying still as much as she was her own need to follow him.

Janae had drawn her own blood more times than she could count and now decided to dispense with the tourniquet. Disinfectant was a bit of a joke considering what they were putting into their arms. And it seemed proper now to share the same needle, however unclean.

She opened her arm, found the faint line of her vein, plunged the needle through her white skin, and pushed the rest of the amber liquid into herself.

Damage done.

A sting, nothing more.

She set the syringe back into the isolation chamber, sealed it, and took her place on the gurney next to Billy's. Her black dress had ridden up, and she pulled it down so that it covered most of her thighs.

"Now what?" Billy asked.

Janae turned her head and faced him. "Now we fall asleep and slowly die."

"Twenty-four hours."

"More or less." She could feel the deadening effects of the sedative already. "See you on the other side, Billy."

12

THOMAS PACED twenty yards from the altar, trying to remember why he'd allowed the scene before him to unfold as it had. Beside him, Mikil and Jamous were muttering their horror, demanding under their breath that he do something, that this was intolerable, that he'd mistaken Elyon's intentions.

But there was nothing left to do. Except beg.

Beg Elyon to show mercy. To provide a way of escape. To save his son. To stop Teeleh's servant, whose sickness knew no bounds.

He'd watched helplessly as they hauled Samuel down with hardly a fight. His son seemed to know that resistance without a weapon was hopeless. His green eyes held Thomas in a bitter stare as they hauled him to the altar, stripped him, and strapped him spread-eagle to the rings at each corner.

All the while, those red eyes in the sky watched him. Thomas had turned away so they wouldn't see his weak resolve in the face of such a tragedy.

But it would be a tragedy only if Elyon failed them, right? And if Elyon failed them, there was no reason to live. He could only beg Elyon, and so he did, without a pause.

Ba'al stood before the stone slab in perfect stillness as his priests carefully stacked wood in a tower ten feet from the altar. When they'd doused the wood in oil, they took up their places with the others, swaying. Qurong and his general still sat atop their horses, watching from thirty yards back. The Throaters held their posts at the boulders.

All was prepared.

"You're going to get him killed," Mikil said in a low, unsteady voice.

How dare she doubt his love for his son at a time like this? "If Ba'al was going to kill Samuel, he would have done it already. He can't afford a martyr in front of his people. He needs his devil to show his face."

"He *has* shown himself!" she whispered, glancing at the Shataiki circling high above. "I can't watch this."

"Then I suggest you join me and demand that Elyon show himself as well."

Ba'al shrugged out of his robe and stepped forward, naked. His body was threaded with sinewy muscle that looked more like roots than flesh. The man was even thinner than Thomas had imagined. In his right hand he held a long dagger shaped like a claw.

The dark priest lifted the blade high.

"Dark Master, hear our cry!" Ba'al wailed. His eyes, glistening with tears, searched the sky. "Rescue your servant from this body of death! I who am your captive, locked in your embrace, implore you. Show me your mercy."

Thomas's breathing slowed, then stilled. It sounded almost as if Ba'al was praying to Elyon, as if Ba'al had learned his own ways from the Forest Guard. As if he were a half-breed.

"Hear my voice, great dragon," Ba'al cried. "I once knew your enemy as you did, was betrayed by my own and left to die. But you, Teeleh, and your lover Marsuuv showed me mercy." He wept at the sky like a prodigal begging to be allowed back in his father's palace. "I beg you, imprison me once again. Show your great power. Don't allow them to make a mockery out of me."

Thomas hung on his twisted words. The gathering of priests had taken up a soft moan to accompany their swaying. One of them walked out and placed a torch on the wood. Flame leaped up, licking at the sky.

Samuel lay on the altar, chest rising and falling like a blacksmith's bellows. The priest who'd lit the fire gathered up Samuel's clothes and threw them into the flames, putting an exclamation mark on their intention. Samuel would not need any clothes where he was going.

Ba'al's voice rose to a scream. "Kill me now, or send me back to the other world where you sent the chosen one through the lost books. But do not betray me!" He shook where he stood, gasping for air. "Let the land of the living know that you live with power to consume all who will not bow at your feet."

Ba'al's cry cut through the pain ravaging Thomas's mind. *The chosen one.* The words carried the sound of secret knowledge. What did the dark priest know of the chosen one, and what were these lost books? Whispers about seven lost books had been heard around late-night fires, but they were only talk.

Samuel was on the altar, chest heaving with terror.

"We offer our blood to you. Drink and taste our waters of life, lord of the night. Devour our gift to you, the son of this idolater, who serves the one who cast you into the pit."

The priests' moaning rose to a dull roar. On some unseen cue, the front row stepped out and approached Ba'al in single file. The first took the dagger from Ba'al's lifted hand, kissed his high priest's fingers, then nicked his own wrist.

They were bleeding themselves.

The priest stepped to the altar and let some of his blood drip onto Samuel's heaving chest, then walked past as the second priest took up Ba'al's dagger. Cut himself.

"I won't watch this," Mikil said, turning her back. But Jamous and Thomas watched without wavering. And after a moment, Mikil turned back and spit to one side. "Elyon has abandoned us."

Ba'al was begging Teeleh to take Samuel.

And Thomas was begging Elyon to save his firstborn son, covered by the priests' blood on Ba'al's altar.

Mikil grunted. "This is the end."

"So be it," Thomas said, glaring. "But if this is the end, then it's by Elyon's design. Have you forgotten who once turned the world inside out? Who saved us from the Horde more times than you can hold in your sliver of a memory? Unless you have a prayer, keep your mouth closed."

"That was then . . ."

"And this," he shouted at her, "is now! Pray!"

He faced the altar and saw that seven priests had spilled their blood on Samuel. Dark trails ran off his son's chest and pooled on the stone.

Qurong had backed away with his general and vanished from the circle of Throaters. Now it was Thomas and Elyon against Ba'al and Teeleh, a contest of spilled blood against . . .

Against what? What would it take to get Elyon's attention? He'd left them with some fruit and some red pools and then seemed to have vanished. They could rid their bodies of the scabbing disease by drowning; they could heal their bodies with the fruit; they could dance and sing deep into the night, remembering his love.

But where was Elyon to rescue them from the Horde who pressed in relentlessly? What would it take? Samuel's blood?

No. There was no more need for blood. This would come down to the very essence of the challenge he'd first cast. The stage was set. Either Teeleh would take Samuel's life and prove that he could destroy Elyon's own, or Elyon would show his might.

Still the moaning priests filed past the altar, slashing their skin and wetting his son. Still Ba'al stood over the scene, white arms spread wide, gloating over Samuel's bloody body. His eyes glistened, round, unblinking, like those of the Shataiki circling overhead.

The mangy black beasts had descended, and he could make out their triangular heads. They looked like flying wolves, emboldened by the constant moan begging them to come. By the priests' shuffling dance, shaking the bells on their robes. By the sight of the albino's smooth skin covered in blood.

The priests' self-inflicted wounds dribbled slowly. They'd undoubtedly cut themselves before for the beast whose mark they bore on their foreheads.

Thomas let the scene wash over him, allowing his anger to boil beneath his good reason. This display of evil was not Horde. This wasn't the making of Qurong or Eram and his half-breeds. The blood sacrifice before them was the creation of Teeleh and this wraith named Ba'al, who had lived in his bosom. Thomas would be in his rights to take a sword and slaughter the man where he stood.

Instead, he pulled at his hair and begged Elyon to come to his senses.

But the night only grew darker, and the Shataiki thicker, and the raging fire consumed more and more wood. Samuel lay still, by all appearances resigned to his fate, but Thomas knew better. If Samuel lived, his bitterness would know no bounds. This challenge would cost him dearly no matter what happened.

It was too much! It was far too much!

Thomas could no longer hold himself in check. He stepped forward and shouted his bitterness. "Is that all you have, Ba'al? This is all the blood you can spill on my son?"

Ba'al showed no indication he'd heard the mockery. Mikil started to offer some advice, but Thomas cut her off.

"Your dragon-god needs to feed his bloodlust with more than just a bucket of blood," he cried. "He drinks from the jugular! He's drunk on the blood of Elyon's faithful. A little dribble from your sick, wounded animals won't do. Is that it?"

The moaning grew louder, joined by the rush of flapping wings overhead. The Shataiki hovered half a mile above them now, an organic river of rotting flesh, silent except for the *whoosh* of their wings.

"The beast requires a pool of blood to fool himself into believing he, too, has a lake, like Elyon's red lakes," Thomas shouted. "Cut yourself, Ba'al. Drain your blood, you betrayer of all that is holy. You half-breed."

At that last word, Ba'al seemed to be pulled out of his trance. He slowly turned his head to look at Thomas, as if trying to decide what to make of the accusation that he'd been one of the Forest Dwellers when the Horde overtook the forests, and, like all half-breeds, had only then become Scab.

He grinned, faced the roiling black bats, and cried to the sky. "Take me home, Marsuuv! Fill me once again with your glory. Take this first-born son as an offering to ease your wrath."

"Louder!" Thomas cried.

"It is written," Ba'al cried. "I am your chosen one, and the books will be yours. By blood you will enter the secret place and reclaim all that was once yours!"

"Louder, you pathetic worm! More blood. Drain yourself!"

Tears were now streaming down Ba'al's face as he screamed his petition to his god and his lover, Teeleh, and this Shataiki named Marsuuv.

"Save me!" The high priest gulped at the night air. His eyes were closed and his body shook from head to foot, like a boy trapped in a dungeon, crying out for mercy. "Save me. Save me, please save me!"

"Dear Elyon," Jamous muttered under his breath. "He's a tortured beast."

For the briefest of moments, Thomas felt pity for the dark priest. If he was a half-breed, then he'd once known the truth and rejected it to become Horde. But if Qurong guessed his high priest was a half-breed, the leader would surely execute him outright. Any possible connection between the priest and his enemy Eram was far too great a risk to be tolerated.

Then again, Qurong was easily deceived by Teeleh. And whatever else Ba'al might be, he was a handmaiden of the beast. Or of Marsuuv, who was likely some queen who supped at Teeleh's bloody table.

The two hundred priests had all cut themselves and deposited their blood on Samuel once. Now they were halfway through the second round. Their swaying had yielded to jerking as they joined Ba'al and cried with greater frenzy. They didn't merely dribble their blood on their sacrifice now; they leaned over his body or leaped onto the altar to express streams of blood from their veins before staggering off in a weakened state.

How long could they keep this up? The cuts merely seeped when the priests weren't wringing their arms over Samuel's body, but it was only a matter of time before they collapsed. For now they lurched on, accompanying Ba'al's flagrant call for salvation.

"He can't hear you!" Thomas screamed.

Ba'al flung his arm toward Thomas and pointed an accusing finger.

"My lord has shown himself through his servants, but there is no sign of your feeble God. The dragon from the sky will devour the child. The tribulation you have suffered all these years, running from the ruler of this world, has now come to an end. You will bow or be consumed!"

The authority with which Ba'al thundered his announcement made Thomas's gut turn. His last reserve of patience melted like ice under a flame. But rather than shout over the cacophony, he chose his words carefully and bit each off so there could be no misunderstanding.

"Elyon shows himself now, to all who have the eyes to see. He lives through me and through the one you seek to kill on your bloody altar. The dragon tried to kill the Creator once, but Elyon lives still, in his servants, free of disease. You've made a mistake, half-breed. You're serving the wrong god."

Ba'al whirled back to his priests. "More! Empty yourselves. Die for your master, you unclean worms. Shed your blood on this son before Teeleh consumes you himself."

Thomas watched with dread as the priests each leaped on the altar a third time, slashing their arms and chests in a frenzy. Blood poured from their wounds, spilled over Samuel, and ran into a three-foot-wide trough at the base.

Samuel lay still, breathing steadily. His hair and his loincloth were both soaked red. If one didn't know better, he would surely assume Samuel's skin had been stripped off his muscles.

Jamous and Mikil had turned away and clung to each other, muttering protests or prayers or both.

But Thomas could not turn from his son. He could only stare through his teary eyes and beg Elyon for mercy.

The first priest to die collapsed while he was still on the altar, trying to bleed on Samuel. Nothing would come; he hadn't practiced enough restraint earlier. Grunting, he milked his left arm with his right hand, but failed to produce more blood.

Ba'al shrieked and swung his sword. The blade severed the man's arm cleanly at his elbow. Blood dribbled out.

The man stared at his arm silently, tried to stand, then toppled sideways, bounced off the corner of the altar, and lay still on the ground.

"Bleed!" Ba'al screamed. "Bleed or I will bleed you all!"

The priests clambered onto the altar and gave their blood to satiate the beast.

Yes, this was his son, but he could no longer stand to watch. The Circle's code demanded that no man, woman, or child who suffered should be left to suffer alone. They would mourn with those who mourned, weep with those who wept, and above all, they would never hide their eyes to protect their own hearts when another suffered pain or death.

Yet this . . . *Elyon, dear Elyon* . . .

Thomas settled to one knee and steadied himself. He no longer had words for Elyon.

Thomas lowered his head. With the first flood of tears, his resolve vanished and he felt himself slumping to the earth. Pain spread from his heart, robbed him of breath. He pulled his knees closer and lay on his side, and he wept.

The priests' wails cut through the night as they stood upon the altar, offering themselves to Teeleh. Then Thomas pressed his face into the dirt and cut himself off from the world.

If he could retreat as he once had, he would. He'd sleep here and wake in another world where he'd changed history. New York. Bangkok. France.

He'd never been able to confirm with certainty that the world of his dreams was real, but it had served him well when all seemed utterly lost here.

But now, dreaming only delivered him into a world filled with imaginations. There was another way, he was sure of it. Another path into history. If he could only leap onto the altar, take up his son, and vanish there now . . .

Thomas stopped himself. He was here in the real world, in Ba'al Bek with the dark priest and two hundred of his pagan worshippers. His son was strapped to an altar, waiting to see if Teeleh would swoop out from the sea of swarming Shataiki and consume him.

This was the world that Thomas of Hunter was in, and it was a world totally beyond his control. He pushed his face against the sand, clenched his watering eyes, and pushed everything but Elyon from his mind.

13

"HOW FAR?" Chelise cried, slapping her horse as they thundered over the canyon's lip. The steed slid down the steep incline, snorting in protest. But their mounts were no strangers to the roughest terrain, and she let it have its head, leaning back so that her shoulders rested on its rear quarters.

The horse took to the air ten paces from the bottom, launching itself parallel to the ground to ease their landing. Marie rode three strides ahead, whipping her mare with a short strap of leather.

The Shataiki had to be blind not to notice the two albinos racing through the canyons that rose to Ba'al Bek, where Thomas was either dead or about to be dead. The black beasts had settled over the plateau like a hovering lid, so close and low that Chelise could see their red, empty eyes.

"How long?" she demanded.

"Have I been here before? Just ride."

Just ride. Straight into the pit. What two lone albinos with nothing but fruit could hope to accomplish against a throng of Shataiki and Throaters was still a mystery to her. But there was zero chance of changing course.

This challenge Thomas had cast was about more than the fracturing Circle. It was about each of them. About her. About her father. Here, in Ba'al Bek, her worlds past and present were converging. Her father must join her and the Circle before it was too late!

If she could accomplish this, her life would be complete.

Every bone in her body betrayed her single-minded focus as she slashed her mare on, ignoring the threat circling above them. Her fingers latched onto the reigns, her muscles strained her toned arms, her neck stretched forward as her hair whipped behind her head. There was no denying her obsession now.

"Chelise—"

"Ride, Marie! Keep your mouth shut and ride."

———⦿———

THE WAILS were fading.

Thomas snapped his eyes wide and stared at the sand, listening.

This was not his mind playing tricks on him; the cries had nearly ceased. Conspicuously absent was Ba'al's cry. Had he given up and retreated into his pain? How long had it been?

Thomas jerked his head up and pushed himself off the dirt. The scene robbed him of breath. Bodies were strewn about the ground, still. Only Ba'al and four priests still stood. The rest had bled to death.

His son lay on his back, facing the Shataiki who still circled, silent except for the rush of wind on their wings. Blood covered the stone altar and filled the trough that ran around its base.

Ba'al stood with both arms elevated, eyes closed, lips moving.

One of the priests sank to his knees beside the altar, held his hand over an open wound on his chest, then fell sideways with a hard crash. Ba'al didn't react. He was waiting for them all to die. This was the price that he believed Teeleh required.

Two more of the priests settled to the earth to die. Then the last sat back on his rump and watched Ba'al.

Thomas stood, surrounded by the two hundred priests who'd died for their dark priest and his demon, Teeleh. An eerie stillness settled over Ba'al Bek. He scanned the lip of the depression. No sign of Elyon, but neither was there any sign that Teeleh had accepted Ba'al's sacrifice.

Qurong and his general were approaching from the southern lip on their mounts as if they, too, understood that a turning point had been reached. Soon it would be Qurong's turn to meet Thomas's demands.

The challenge had come down to this moment. It was Thomas's turn. The hair on his neck bristled. And if Elyon did not show himself?

He faced Ba'al, who was still moving his lips inaudibly. "You've failed," Thomas called in a strong voice.

The dark priest opened his eyes and stared at Samuel's bloody body. The sight of his son lying there . . . Thomas pushed back a wave of nausea.

"You've offered your priests as a blood sacrifice, but your dragon isn't impressed."

Ba'al was still fixated on Samuel. He took three steps, sprang into the air with an agility that surprised Thomas, and straddled Samuel.

"You have lost!" Thomas cried, stepping forward.

Ba'al lifted his right arm to the sky and pressed his clawed blade to his wrist. "Now!" he cried. "Now accept the fullness of what you demand, my lord and savior, Marsuuv." He jerked his blade across his wrist.

Ba'al's blood flowed from the cut, wetting Samuel's belly. He was adding his own blood to his priests'. To what end? This was what this Shataiki queen named Marsuuv demanded?

Ba'al's naked body began to tremble. He gripped the dagger, the tendons of his hand drawn tight like bowstrings. His lips peeled back over clenched teeth, fighting not to cry out.

He leaned his head back, yawned wide at the sky, and let loose a toe-curling scream that started higher than was humanly possible. His cry hung high, then fell through the register, lower, lower, until it was a throaty roar that shook the ground.

The Shataiki above began to shriek.

"It's him!" Mikil gasped. "It's Teeleh! We have to get out!"

"Father!" Samuel cried. "Father?"

"Hold still, Samuel. Hold!"

Ba'al's mouth snapped shut. He lowered his head and looked at Thomas with haunting eyes, one purple, the other blue, possessed. His voice came in a low guttural growl that couldn't possibly be human.

"Hello, Thomasssssss . . . Such a treat to finally make your acquaintance. I've heard so much about you." A wicked grin slowly distorted his mouth. "Welcome to Paradise. It's time for black to come out of its box"—his head jerked spastically once—"and for Samuel to go into his."

This was Teeleh who'd possessed Ba'al? No, not Teeleh, but the queen Ba'al had spoken about. Marsuuv.

"We loathe boys named Samuel," Ba'al said, looking down at the bloody body under him. "I accept this offering."

Samuel looked like he was hyperventilating. His resolve had finally shattered. "Father?"

Ba'al, who was possessed by Marsuuv, slashed so quickly that Thomas hardly knew he was moving before the blade cut through Samuel's chest, through the muscle, through the bone, into the lung chambers.

Samuel's back arched and he cried out. It had taken a moment for the full pain of the sudden cut to reach his mind, but now that it had, his son could not hold back his screams.

Thomas could not move. Through Ba'al, Teeleh had answered the challenge and taken Samuel. This could not be! Elyon would not allow his son to be ravaged and mocked. Samuel . . .

What if Samuel is no longer Elyon's son? What if he betrayed Elyon and is no longer his son?

The world seemed to spin, and Thomas fell to one knee. Beside him, Mikil and Jamous were immobilized.

But where reason failed Thomas, passion raged. "Elyon." It was barely more than a whimper, because his throat was frozen, but Thomas was screaming.

Ba'al threw back his head, straddling his victim, and roared to the sky. "Come! Come and feed!"

"Elyon . . ."

A section of the Shataiki swarm broke from the main flock and dove. Several hundred fell like rocks, the privileged few, shrieking, ravenous vampire bats with bloodlust in their hearts. Thomas watched in horror as the black, mangy beasts slammed into the bleeding bodies of two hundred priests and began clawing open their flesh. They bared their fangs like dogs and tore at the skin, sucking at the exposed blood, too consumed by their feast to pay Thomas any mind.

Ba'al stood above them all, arms spread wide, gloating.

"Elyon!" Thomas shoved himself up, numb.

"Elyon . . . Elyon!" He stepped forward and screamed. Begging, protesting, raging. "Elyon!"

"Elyon is dead," Ba'al snarled, stabbing Thomas with his blue and purple glare. "I killed him."

Surrounded by a thousand Shataiki fighting over the remains of the fallen priests, Thomas considered this possibility for the first time in a decade. What if it were true? What if everything he'd fought to preserve—the Great Romance, the love of Horde, the embrace of peace, the drowning—what if it were all wrong?

Panic battered him as the thoughts glanced off his mind. And there, because of his own stubbornness, lay Samuel. Dead.

Thomas stumbled forward, succumbing to panic. He had to get to his son, to hold him, to take him away before these animals tore at his body.

A dozen Shataiki spun and snarled, blocking his path.

Thomas pulled up, panting. Samuel lay still. Ba'al stood gloating.

He'd lost? He'd lost both the challenge and his son.

He sank to both knees and sat back on his heels, blinded by hopelessness. Sense fell away, like shackles. He clenched his eyes, sobbing. When he screamed out, his heart, not his mind, hurled the words from his mouth.

"Elyon . . . Elyon, do not turn your back on me! Save us." He held his fist in the air and wept at the sky. "Do not allow them to take your son into hell! Save us!"

Thomas was hauling in breath, mind shot, when he noticed that his eyes were red. Or the lids that protected his eyes were red.

He snapped them open, saw the blinding light above, and threw himself back on his seat. As one, the Shataiki recognized the imminent danger. Shrieking, they scattered in every direction, like a flock of black birds reacting to a predator. Those on the ground clawed at the air for purchase, shrieking with each flap of their wings. Those circling above streaked for every horizon.

The light descended from the night sky like a shaft of sunlight, but thick and cloudy and fluorescent green.

Water. Water? This was a shaft of luminescent mist descending from the sky?

An image of a lake filled with Elyon's green water flooded Thomas's mind. Before Teeleh had brought the scabbing disease, when the Gathering had taken place on the shores of a green lake. No words could approximate the intoxication of those beautiful waters.

The color of Elyon, green. It was why all albinos had green eyes. Why the lakes had once been green. Why the forests broke the harsh desert landscape with this beautiful color. The color of life.

Green.

The radiant, green light descended toward the altar. Ba'al cowered with his neck arched back, gawking at the sudden shift in power.

This . . . this was Elyon. Not Elyon himself, not any more than Ba'al was Teeleh, but this was his power. And Thomas could feel the power on his own skin because all of the air in Ba'al Bek was charged by it.

Ba'al whirled and leaped off the altar like a cat. He bounded over the stripped carcasses of his priests toward Qurong, whose horse was rearing. The Throaters who'd circled the high place were having difficulty controlling their mounts. Some of the assassins were racing back to protect Qurong at the south side of the plateau.

Thomas spun back to the watery green light. The shaft settled over the altar and stopped, silent, but the air was heavy and charged. Fingers of light and a shade of darker green curled and twisted inside the shaft.

He heard the soft song of a child, faint, as if it were buried deep in the water. He knew this song. And his need to be in the water again brought a quake to his bones.

The coaxing fingers of light coiled around Samuel and slowly lifted him off the stone surface so that his back arched, and his heels and head draped down. He hung suspended about two feet in the air, surrounded by the translucent green presence, this raw power of Elyon holding his son.

Thomas wanted to run up to the light, which he knew couldn't be anything as simple as water, and push his hand inside. He wanted to feel the power he'd known when Elyon revealed himself to them like this every day.

Samuel's arms jerked and his chest expanded. He was alive.

"I always did like you, Thomas," a voice whispered. In his head or aloud so they could all hear, he couldn't tell. "You make my head spin."

The words of approval echoed through his mind.

"The end is near, much sooner than you've guessed. Find your way back. Take the diseased one with you. Use the books that were lost." The voice paused. "Here is your son." Samuel's body was released by the tendrils in the green light and landed on the stone surface with a dull thump. "Let him have his heart."

And then the green shaft withdrew to the night sky, slowly at first, then faster. It pulled up in a slight arc to the west, then vanished in a blink. After hours of chanting and ringing bells under a rushing wind caused by so much rotting Shataiki flesh, the night was pristine and quiet.

Then Samuel's bloody body sat upright and sucked in a lungful of air.

A gasp rippled through the Throaters, who remained to guard Qurong and Ba'al, stunned by the sudden reversal of fortunes.

Thomas lifted his arm and lined his finger up with Qurong. "You, father of my bride, tell us all what has happened here!"

———— ⚬∞⚬ ————

QURONG SAT on his steed, unable to respond to the infidel's command. He was to explain what had just happened? He was supposed to interpret these signs from the heavens and suggest the next course of action? Was he a priest? Had he ever pretended to know the ways of Teeleh or Elyon or these cursed creatures of the night?

No. He was a simple man who knew two things only: One, that the ways of the gods were trickery, always trickery, so that no man could truly know the ways of the gods. And two, that although no man could know the ways of the gods, they all could and did understand another way.

The way of the sword.

Where was his wife when he needed her? She was better versed in these never-ending deceptions, not because she herself employed them, but because he didn't, preferring a straight up-and-down fight over clever talk and deception. He'd been down that road and was still paying the price.

"My lord, you must—"

"Quiet, priest." He raised the back of his hand to Ba'al. "You've failed."

"No." The man trembled. "My master has delivered Thomas to you. I heard his voice. He spoke to my belly. You have to take him."

"Leave me! And for the love of all gods, put some clothes on."

"My lord, I cannot express the price we will pay if—"

"Leave!"

Ba'al jettisoned a stream of black spittle, glared at the infidel Thomas, and spun away from the altar. One of the twenty-four priests who hadn't bled themselves approached him and threw a purple cloak over his skinny body. Ba'al was dismissed.

But what he said wasn't lost. Qurong had seen enough in the last few minutes alone to know that the powers behind both Ba'al and Thomas were not only real, but life-threatening.

More to the point, the power behind Ba'al was life-threatening. The other, the green magic, however impressive and disturbing, didn't strike him as . . . fatal.

Qurong walked his horse closer to Thomas and the boy, who'd crawled off the altar, stripped the robes off a dead priest, and was joining the other albinos. To think that Thomas was the husband of the daughter he'd once held precious . . . there was no end to injustice in this cursed world.

He pulled up, ten yards from the man. The mighty Thomas of Hunter, leader of all albinos, poisoned by the red pools, enemy of Teeleh. He didn't look so threatening without a sword. No battle dress. The tunic he wore was made of tanned leather, perhaps sewn by Chelise's own hand. His brown hair was tossed by a long ride. What had happened to cause Thomas to issue such a challenge? Was he losing control over the Circle?

His son hadn't appeared too eager to submit.

"Our agreement was clear," Thomas said. "And now the outcome is as clear. Your daughter awaits."

Qurong didn't turn the tables yet. "You want me to go with you and drown?"

"That was our agreement."

"So what is that like? Sucking in water and dying?"

"Do I look dead to you? It's life, not death."

"Because you don't drown, and you don't come back to life. The red poison strips your skin bare and clouds your minds. So you have a few thousand followers who are gullible enough to believe they've somehow drowned and been brought back to life. Well, I can imagine offering that kind of immortality would make you a bit of a legend. Religious nonsense."

"Thomas . . ." It was the albino woman warning him. But Thomas didn't seem interested.

"You will soon know, won't you?" Thomas said.

"Yes. Yes, of course, that was the agreement."

"Do you doubt that Elyon has brought my son back to life here on your altar?"

"Is that what you saw?" Qurong glanced at the carnage. "Clearly there are powers at work here that none of us understand. But I saw more. Much more."

"You saw the life-giving power of Elyon scatter a hundred thousand Shataiki and embrace my son with new life."

"I saw the power of Teeleh. And I see that two hundred of his servants have been slain. Now that you've killed two hundred priests, if I were to take you into captivity, you would no longer be seen as a martyr."

"Father . . ." Now it was Samuel who warned.

"Your daughter cries for you every day," Thomas said quietly, unfazed by Qurong's direct threat. "I've never seen a daughter love a father the way she loves you."

The words cut like a dagger, and for a moment Qurong lost his bearings. Then rage flooded his heart.

"I have no daughter."

"Go!"

The woman and the albino next to her had issued the command together, unexpectedly, as if the word were an arranged signal. Thomas whirled and sprinted just behind Samuel and the others, picking their way over dead bones, directly for the horses. The speed with which albinos could move never ceased to amaze him.

"Stop them!"

"You saw the power of the one we serve," the woman cried, leaping to one of the four albino horses they'd tethered to a stake.

Even Cassak hesitated. The albinos were already leaning over the necks of their mounts, whipping the animals' rumps, hair flowing behind as they galloped toward the far ring of boulders. It had been years since Qurong had engaged albino warriors in the open, and watching them flee brought the reason into clear focus. They could move at two, maybe three times the speed of his Throaters. His men could match them in strength, but this swift movement was a skill that made him cringe. A beautiful thing.

He thundered at his general. "After them, you fool!"

The man seemed to snap out of a trance. "Close the gap. After them!"

"I want them back, dead or alive," Qurong shouted. "Either you or Thomas, Cassak! I didn't come all this way to watch magicians play tricks!"

"Understood, sir." Then to the warriors behind them: "Markus, Ceril, drop behind and cut off the Mirrado Pass west. Keep to the high ground. If they escape, Ba'al will have your head."

The albinos reached the boulders a good twenty paces before the closest Throaters did, and they flew past the perimeter at twice the assassins' speed. They rose to the depression's lip and vanished into the dark horizon.

Qurong swore and spun his horse back. His personal guard, a dozen strong, waited in a line. Ba'al had already fled the high place, leaving the vultures or the Shataiki, whichever dared return sooner, to feed on the remains of the two hundred bodies. The high priest would rage like a wounded tiger and become more dangerous than he was before.

But it wasn't fear of Ba'al that pounded through Qurong's head as he galloped south to Qurongi City. Nor was it the desire to seize Thomas and lock him in a deep hole until he died of starvation. Nor was it the half-breed Eramites who undoubtedly plotted his overthrow even now.

All of these problems spoke to him, pulling for attention. But none shouted so loudly as the seven words spoken by Thomas before he'd fled.

Your daughter cries for you every day.

14

KARA HUNTER hurried down the hall, hot, not because Bangkok was a humid city regardless of the time of year, but because a bomb had just exploded in her chest.

Blood. More to the point, Thomas's blood.

Why did life always come down to blood? The blood of a sacrificial lamb to atone for sin. The blood of Christ to drink in remembrance. The blood of the innocent to feed the bloodlust of creatures in the night. The Raison Strain, plundering its host through the bloodstream.

Blood had taken her brother, Thomas, into a reality that changed everything. She knew because she had followed him, using that same blood, and what she found took her breath away.

When it was all over and the world set about the business of picking up the pieces, she and Monique had hidden away one vial of that precious blood. Just one vial, ten ccs to be exact. All for understandable, even noble, reasons. They'd planned on every conceivable threat.

But they'd never factored in a maniacal redhead named Billy who could read minds. Worse, they'd never imagined that Janae, Monique's own daughter, would willingly throw herself into a pit of vipers with this stranger from Paradise, Colorado.

What could she possibly have been thinking?

Kara flashed her ID badge at the white-suited security guard, who used his own pass card to open the heavy steel door into the secure lab. The hall ended at a second door, also under guard.

"'Morning, Miss Hunter. She wants you to suit up."

Kara wanted to object. Raison Strain B could only be contracted through direct contact. Instead, she nodded and stepped through the glass side door into a room equipped with white biohazard suits and a chemical-mist shower. She shrugged into the suit and slipped on black gloves, but didn't bother with the head gear or with sealing the suit. A barrier against accidental contact was wise, but going in like a polar bear didn't make any sense.

She stepped though a narrow passage and walked through a second glass door that slid open with a loud buzz. Seven lab techs were at work, three at their stations, four standing with folded arms, deep in discussion that hushed as Kara crossed the room.

Monique stood outside the quarantine room, hands on hips, suited like Kara, staring at the gurneys inside through one of the glass panels. Kara saw the reclining forms, dressed in street clothes rather than in typical lab attire. Janae in a short black dress, par for the course. Billy wore what he'd waltzed into their world wearing: jeans and a T-shirt.

The egotistical little snot-nose.

"How long ago?" she demanded, stopping beside Monique.

Other than Thomas, Monique had been more complicit in the creation of the first virus than any other living person. She sighed. "Based on the culture we're looking at"—she nodded at the clean room opposite this one—"I'd estimate eight hours ago."

"So we have time."

"Some. Not much. She shot them each with a full cc."

"What? Has she lost her marbles?"

Monique just looked at her, deadpan.

"Dumb question, sorry."

"Is it?" Monique said, looking back at her daughter lying parallel to Billy Rediger. They lay on their backs, hands folded over their chests, which rose and fell together. Lost to this world.

"Thing is, I don't think Janae *has* lost her mind," Monique said. "She knew exactly what she was doing." She clenched her jaw, closed her eyes, then opened them again, still deadpan. This was Monique expressing contempt for herself. "I can't believe we allowed this to happen."

"We didn't. She did."

"I should have known the moment that punk entered our compound that he was bad news."

"You did."

"I should have known he was the devil himself, able to bring to life the worst in Janae."

She was referring to the nonsense about Janae having bad blood from her father. Monique had never opened up about her affair with the man who'd fathered Janae and then vanished, but whenever Janae did something irrational or particularly unhanded, Monique blamed it on her father's side. Bad blood.

"She knew what she was doing all right," Monique said, jaw bunching again. "At this rate they'll both be dead within twenty-four hours. Maybe sooner."

Kara felt like she should object, turn to her friend and express her horror at such a prospect. Demand they use the blood immediately.

Instead, she felt only confusion, so she said nothing.

Monique came to her rescue. "They took a strong sedative to ensure that they would be asleep the moment Thomas's blood made contact with theirs. She knew that I wouldn't be able to resist."

What was Monique saying? That she would use the blood?

"And why should she assume anything different? Have I ever not showed her all of my love? She's the only one I have now. She means everything to me."

Tears settled in Monique's eyes. Kara wanted to put her hand on Monique's shoulder, but she was still torn by the conflicting emotions that hammered her own mind.

"There's no guarantee that the blood will work," Kara said.

"No."

"What are the risks?"

"The same as they were the last time a gateway was opened to the other world," Monique said.

Speaking of it so stoically in the face of such a tragedy required a measure of self-possession, Kara thought. The world had barely survived the last such crossing.

"Or worse," Kara said. "That was Thomas. This is a crazed psychic named Billy." *And Janae*, she thought but did not say.

Monique nodded slowly, keeping her eyes on her daughter. "Billy and Janae. They could do a lot of damage in either reality."

"If they did make it to the other world and back . . . only God knows what magic they could bring back to upset the balance of powers. They could destroy a world."

"They can't possibly be trusted."

"No."

Simple. But not so simple at all. This was Monique's daughter on the table, slowly drawing breath.

"She knew exactly what she was doing!" Monique whispered, barely able to control herself. "Maybe we should have discussed it with her. She's doing this out of bitterness." She wiped a tear that had spilled over her lower lid.

"You know we couldn't risk her knowing that we had the blood. She might have tried something like this a long time ago."

"Not if we didn't tell her where it was hidden. Indonesia's a long way from here."

"Monique." Kara did put her hand on her friend's shoulder now. "You can't blame yourself. Janae is a grown woman who decides for herself. Thousands, millions of lives could be at stake. Sometimes . . . the risk has to be weighed."

Monique glared at her. "Please, Kara, I don't need a lecture."

She felt horrible. What if it were Thomas on that gurney? What would Kara say then? *Let him die, let the fool die.* But she'd already crossed that road once. They both knew that the moment Janae had injected herself with the virus, she'd signed her own death certificate.

At sixty years of age, Kara could live with that. She'd seen so many come and go in this life. And she'd spent some time in that other world.

"Do you think it would work?" Monique asked, staring at her daughter's calm form.

"It didn't work in the test—"

"We didn't inject his blood into a living body," Monique interrupted. "We couldn't risk the possibility of the subject crossing over. I'm talking about crossing over, not killing the virus."

"Would a person whose blood comes in contact with Thomas's blood wake up in the other place?"

"Surely you still wonder what it would be like to go again." Monique spoke as if lost. "What Thomas is doing. If he's even alive. The Horde . . . the lakes . . . what's become of everyone?"

"How old is he? Is he married? Children? Everything was happening very quickly over there," Kara said. "Maybe it's all over. I think about it every day."

Monique nodded and wiped another tear, then turned away. "We'll never know."

Which was as good as stating that she wasn't going to use the blood on Janae. It was the right decision, of course. Janae and Billy were only two lives. Opening a way into the other reality could be disastrous. And they'd done this to themselves. She pitied Billy, felt sick that Janae, who in so many ways reminded Kara of herself thirty years earlier, had taken her life like this. She'd liked the girl very much. Such a spirited woman, so beautiful, so intelligent. Such a waste.

However difficult, this was the best way.

"Do you think letting them die is murder?" Monique asked.

15

THE HORSES clawed up the incline at dawn, struggling for breath after the brutal ride through hidden canyonland that rose to the Ba'al Bek plateau. Marie had let Chelise lead but pulled alongside as they approached the huge rim.

Chelise was out of breath, not from riding, but from her own state of unrelenting anxiety. They were too late. Every fiber in her being warned that they'd come too late.

They'd plunged into a deep canyon an hour earlier and lost sight of the Shataiki mass that winged over the plateau like a cloud of giant locusts. When they emerged, the sky was empty of all but stars.

Which could only mean that the reason for their coming was also gone.

But that didn't mean Thomas was gone. He might still be there, clinging to life, waiting for her to rescue him from certain death, the way he'd rescued her once. Or maybe the challenge hadn't started yet. The Shataiki could have been drawn by Thomas's presence on their sacred ground. He could be seated with the others around a campfire, biding his time while Qurong considered his challenge. A dozen scenarios could explain what they'd seen on their approach.

"Careful, Chelise," Marie breathed. "They might see us if we stumble over the top."

She was right, but Chelise didn't let the horse slow until she was nearly over the rim.

The sight that greeted her nearly stopped her heart. Marie was whispering harshly, throwing herself and her horse to the ground, but Chelise couldn't do the same.

The depression was at least half a mile across, sinking twenty or thirty feet to dusty earth. A large ring of boulders circled the center, where a rectangular cube of stone stood in the graying dawn.

An altar. Wet with fresh blood.

But it was the bodies that struck terror into Chelise's chest. Hundreds of dead bodies strewn about the altar. The putrid stench of the scabbing disease washed over her, crowding her taxed lungs.

No sign of Thomas. Nor of Samuel. Nor of her father.

"Down! For the love of Elyon—"

"They're gone," Chelise said. Then again, as if to convince herself, "They're gone. We're too late."

"It could be a trap. There could be Throaters down there."

"No." Few knew the Horde's ways like she did. None knew Qurong's ways as well as Chelise. "No, Marie. No, but I see something more disturbing."

She slapped her mare and rode the beast down the slope, into the depression, picking up speed as she approached the ring of boulders. Marie followed far to the rear. Only when she passed the long stones that reached for the sky did Chelise let the horse slow.

Here the smell was almost too much, a thick fog of invisible scabbing disease that covered her face like a muzzle. She held her breath and pushed on, scanning the scene for any trace of evidence that might give her hope.

The dark priest, Ba'al, dead. Charred stones or burned corpses, anything.

But no sign indicated that Elyon had had his way with these priests, and none of the bodies looked to be dressed in purple, the color that Ba'al would likely be wearing.

And no sign of Thomas or Samuel.

"Elyon have mercy on their souls," Marie said, pulling her horse into a walk beside her. "They look like they've been through a meat grinder."

Chelise stopped her horse five feet from a corpse and studied the carnage. "Suicide," she said.

"They did this to themselves?"

"They cut their wrists and bled to appease Teeleh."

"Their bodies are torn apart!"

"By Shataiki. You can see the claw marks on the flesh."

Where are you, Thomas?

Chelise sat on the horse, struggling to remain calm in the face of her failure to reach them in time. She lifted her eyes to the far rim.

What have you done, Father?

"Then I would say this is a good sign," Marie said.

"Good? The only thing good about this is that we don't know for certain that my lover is dead. Nothing else is good."

"This is my father we're talking about," Marie snapped. "If he's not here, then he's alive! And if he's alive, then he's doing what he thinks is right."

"I don't need you to tell me that he's safe. The man he's up against is *my* father, and you know nothing about him. Qurong may not be the craftiest fox in the forest, but he's as stubborn as a bull and he follows his heart. I can promise you his heart despises my husband."

Marie stared at the bloody altar. "Then why don't you enlighten me? What happened here? Where is my father? And what do we do now?"

"A challenge happened here. Qurong agreed to Thomas's terms, and Ba'al, that snake of his, brought two hundred priests as a gift for Teeleh. The Shataiki came, and Ba'al no doubt went mad for the beast. He either won the challenge and took Thomas with him, back to Qurongi, or . . ."

"Or he failed, and your father took my father anyway, as you predicted. Or Father won and fled when Qurong refused to keep his end."

"Thomas would never kill Horde."

"Did I say *kill*?"

"If my father planned to betray Thomas, he would have set a trap," Chelise said. "Without the use of weapons, not even Thomas would be able to escape."

"Unless there was a distraction."

"Such as?"

"Such as Elyon."

"Do you see any sign that Elyon was here?"

"What do we know about what evidence Elyon leaves behind?"

Either way, Thomas was gone. Qurong was gone. Chelise wasn't eager to debate the comings and goings of Elyon.

She grunted and nudged her horse forward, dug her heels into its flank when it resisted her. She drove the mare over the bodies, slapping its rear hard to urge it closer to the altar. She became sick at the sight of so much blood, enough to feed a thousand of the beasts for a month. The trough around the base was full and overflowing.

At this very moment, Thomas could be in a spirited debate with Qurong, in chains headed for his dungeons. The thought was enough to fray her nerves. Not only was the man she loved more than her own life in terrible danger, but he was in the hands of Qurong, the only other grown man she would move heaven and earth to save.

"Thomas is with my father," she announced. "And I belong with them. He needs me."

"Who does, Thomas or Qurong?"

"Both. Johan should look for me in the dungeons if I don't return in three days."

"What are you talking about? We can't go to Qurongi under these circumstances."

"We're not going. I am. You're going back to the Gathering."

"No. No, that is not acceptable! If you insist on going, I'm coming with you. This whole mission was my idea!"

"They need to know, Marie. The three thousand are gathered, waiting since Thomas dropped this hot coal in their laps. The rest are on the way."

"Going in alone is suicide."

"I know the Horde, child. You're a half-breed who drowned before she knew what it felt like to be Horde. If anyone can get into Qurongi, I can."

"You haven't been with them for ten years."

"Don't argue with me! Turn your horse around and head back before the Shataiki decide to come back for the rotting flesh!"

They glared at each other for a full ten seconds before Marie broke her line of sight, but her face was still red. The thought of the long trek home alone was no doubt a factor.

"I have to do this, Marie." Chelise was surprised to feel the strength of the knot that rose in her throat. How could she put this delicately? "Jake. He's so young, so innocent . . ." Her eyes watered and she looked away. "Promise me."

Marie didn't answer immediately, and when she did, her voice was calm. "Don't worry about Jake. He's my brother, isn't he? If anything happens, I'll take care of him as if he were my own son."

"Thank you."

Chelise jerked her horse around and struck its flank with such force that it bolted away from the altar, over the dead carcasses. Headed south.

Headed directly toward Qurongi City.

16

THEY'D LOST the Throaters in the canyons to the north of Ba'al Bek, but not easily. This general, Cassak, seemed particularly adept at anticipating their moves. The Circle had always enjoyed the advantage of speed in the Horde's constant game of seek-and-destroy. This edge was somewhat mitigated by the Horde's dogged persistence and overwhelming size. Still, the Circle survived. But this general had eerily strong instincts.

Much like Ba'al, who had demonstrated an uncanny familiarity with parts of their legends. The horror Thomas felt at seeing his son on the altar had been replaced by curiosity about the dark priest's prayer to Teeleh. His words about the books demanded more explanation.

They pounded through the sand, twisted through canyons, and urged their horses up steep inclines only to plunge down a cliff fifty yards farther, mindless of where they were going except to safety, away from the two dozen armed warriors who gave pursuit.

Still, the sound of hammering hooves followed them.

Still, the cries of Ba'al echoed through Thomas's mind.

Then Samuel pulled his stallion to a standstill at the intersection of two large ravines, each cluttered with boulders the size of horses. He held his hand up to stop them all.

"What?" Mikil demanded. "Which way?"

He motioned silence with his finger and listened to the faint sounds of hooves. Scabbing disease stench clung to the dried blood that still covered Samuel's hair, face, and body. The cloak he'd borrowed from a fallen Horde priest, along with the Scab sword he'd snatched from another, made him look Horde. Thomas preferred him half-naked and unarmed to this.

Ba'al's cry whispered through his mind again. *Send me back to the other world where you sent the chosen one through the lost books . . .*

What could this possibly mean? Surely not back to the other world, as in back to the histories. How would Ba'al know of the other world?

The lost books must be the ones spoken about in legend. Could they be real? The mere thought that there was still a way back to the histories was enough to make Thomas's blood run cold. Dreaming had long ago failed to take him anywhere but to a fantasy.

"They're splitting," Samuel said, lowering his hand. "Cutting us off to the west where the canyon opens to the desert. That would be our way back."

"North would take us into Eramite country," Mikil said, eyeing the long canyon to their right.

"And the Horde fear the Eramites."

Thomas followed his son's gaze. "Then north. You know this land?"

Samuel turned his horse without responding and spurred it into the long canyon. He hadn't looked Thomas in the eyes once since he'd crawled off the altar. Thomas slapped his horse and followed with the others.

Samuel led them for fifteen minutes at a steady run before cutting right into a small ravine, climbing to the crest of a plateau, and stopping to listen again.

"We've lost them," Mikil announced.

Samuel jerked his horse around in a tight circle. "For now. They know we will head west—there are only two routes through the canyons west."

"So, they'll lie and wait."

Samuel shrugged. "This is Cassak, not just any Scab. Not since Martyn or Woref has there been a full-breed as crafty as this general."

"Martyn was a half-breed," Thomas corrected. Not that it mattered.

"Was he?" Samuel stared north. For the first time he turned his eyes on his father, and the look chilled Thomas. "And what would that make me?"

"My son," Thomas said. "Purebred albino."

"I don't think so. I don't think we even know how this so-called scabbing disease works. Do you?"

"Now isn't the time to discuss doctrine."

"No? This from a man who just put his son's head on the chopping block to prove his doctrine."

Thomas wanted to lash out at the boy, but he stayed in control of his words. "Samuel, I know what just happened doesn't make sense to you now, but it will, and when it does, your life will never be the same."

"You almost had me killed back there!"

"Elyon *saved* you back there!" So much for calm. "You have the audacity to sit here and challenge me after the one you doubt breathed new life into you?"

"I only know what I know, Father, and that isn't much. I'm sick of all this guessing. Elyon did this, Elyon did that. Everything good is credited to this unseen God of yours, and everything remotely evil is blamed on Teeleh."

"You didn't see the Shataiki? You didn't watch two hundred priests pour their blood on you in worship of that devil? You didn't feel the green light lift you from the altar? What was that, my imagination?"

"Of course I saw something. But I no more understand it than you do. So Shataiki exist; did anyone say they didn't? So there is power in the heavens to affect us all; does that mean we understand it? If it was so plain, then why put your son on an altar to prove your point?" His accusations cut deeply, in part because they carried so much truth. "If the truth is so obvious, wouldn't the whole world easily see it?"

"Seal that loose mouth, boy!" Mikil snapped.

Thomas held up his hand. "Let him speak. He's owed at least that much."

Samuel walked his horse closer to Thomas, glaring. "That's right,

Father. After you refused to lift a hand to save me from their blades, the least you can do is let me say my piece. Well, I will."

"This is not—"

"Mikil! He's right."

"Sir—"

"Speak, boy. Tell us all how little we know."

Samuel hardly needed Thomas's encouragement. "I'm not the one challenging you, Father. This Circle of yours is falling apart, not on account of me or the Horde. It's splitting apart inside. The rumors and speculations have spawned a dozen different groups that claim to know the full truth, and you don't even know what the truth is, isn't that right?"

Yes, it was right.

Samuel thrust a finger into the air for emphasis. "Some say Elyon will arrive in the clouds before a time of great suffering." He snapped a second finger into the air. "Others say he will only come after the time of great suffering." Another finger. "Still others say in the middle. Some say Elyon doesn't show his face the way he once did because the time of the super-natural is past. Others say he refuses to show himself to cold hearts."

The splintering had been growing over the past several years, but not until now had it alarmed Thomas, thanks to Samuel and his severed Horde head.

Samuel dispensed with the finger counting and threw his arm wide in exasperation. "Then there are those who claim to have *seen* Elyon. Behind every bush, it would seem. But they call him out into the open and he never shows. Never. They're a fanciful lot lost in delusional hope."

"And what of you, Samuel? Where is your hope?"

Samuel plowed on. "Do you even know where the disease comes from, Father? Do you know how the red waters work? How do you know they're anything more than plain old disease and natural medici-nal water?"

The questions bordered on blasphemy, but they were at the very core of Samuel's struggle for meaning. Had Thomas known . . .

But the past was gone. The fact was, Samuel wasn't simply confused about which doctrinal path to take when it came to the Horde; he had lost his way entirely.

"Are you done?" Thomas asked.

"Not even close. But I won't waste my breath. You don't have the answers."

"The disease comes from Teeleh. His worms, evil incarnate, like a virus, infiltrate the skin and muscle and mind, making one stupid to the truth."

"That's your version."

"But Teeleh despises Elyon's waters," Thomas continued. "They kept his disease away when we bathed every day. The virus of Teeleh was killed by the waters. And when the Horde drowned Elyon, those waters turned red. Now we drown as Elyon drowned, and our flesh becomes new, resistant to Teeleh's virus, so that we don't have to bathe every day as we once did. Is this too much for your mind to hold?"

"I don't know, Father. Maybe my mind's full of worms. Like the half-breeds."

He snorted through his nostrils and stilled his stamping horse.

"What I do know is that I can no longer follow a man who feels justified in putting his own son on the block for the sake of his Circle."

"And yet Elyon did the same."

"Then Elyon should go back into the sky where he belongs!"

"Stop it!" Jamous glared at them. "Both of you. We're in enemy territory. The Horde is out there. And Eram. For all we know, our enemy is watching us at this very moment."

"Enemy to whom?" Samuel said, drilling Thomas with a hard stare. "It seems that my own people think of me as their enemy. The half-breeds would welcome a warrior like me."

"Don't be ridiculous," Thomas said. "Your ego is bruised, but I will raise you up as a hero when we return. The Circle will embrace you like a long-lost son."

But Samuel was already stripping off the priest's robes. "For how long? Until I dare speak the truth again?" He cast them aside, then turned his horse away.

"You can't be serious," Mikil challenged. "What fool albino would join the Eramites?"

Samuel twisted back in his saddle. "The fool albino who knows that all half-breeds were once albinos, Forest Guard, despised by the Horde as much as you are. The son of Thomas Hunter will join the Forest Guard once again."

Thomas was so taken aback by what his son was suggesting that words failed him. Elyon had just saved the boy, and now Samuel, covered in Horde blood, would turn his back on the Circle and join forces with Eram? Samuel had thought this through. A naked man would be less threatening to the Eramites than one dressed like a Horde priest.

He must have planned this. He and his band. They were waiting for him.

"Samuel! They wait for you?"

Without turning, his son kicked his horse into a full run, plunged into the canyon they'd just climbed out of, and galloped north, toward the land of the Eramites.

Mikil and Jamous seemed as much at a loss as Thomas. This . . . this had to be a show. Elyon's green waters had just saved the boy, for the love of Elyon! He was toying with them to make a point.

No, Thomas. You've seen this coming.

No, not this. Rebellion, yes. A strong spirit like his own father's, predisposed to stumble into danger, yes. But to betray his own blood? Never!

"He means it," Mikil said.

And Thomas knew that she was right. He sat on his horse and stared at the empty horizon, trying to disbelieve. His son was gone.

For a few moments his mind spun around empty thoughts. Had he been alone he might have fallen from his horse and wept into the sand. But the Horde was in pursuit and the Circle waited and . . .

Thomas released his reins, closed his eyes, and struggled to breathe calmly. What was happening? He'd faced his son's death through the night, and they'd survived only to face this?

"He's bluffing," Mikil said, reversing her earlier position.

She was only saying it to give him hope, and she was failing miserably.

Samuel was right; everything was falling apart. The end was coming. Ba'al knew something that they did not. He'd called the Shataiki out of hiding and fed their lust with more than just his own blood.

Send me back to the other world where you sent the chosen one through the lost books . . .

Thomas opened his eyes. What did Ba'al know about this other world?

The chosen one. Could the rumors of the seven original Books of History be true? Had they truly been lost? Was there a way to the other world through those books? And what if Ba'al or Qurong possessed the books at this very moment?

"Whatever you're thinking, I'm not sure I like it," Mikil said. "I've seen that look before."

"I've lost my son to the half-breeds. Do you expect me to laugh?"

"I wasn't talking about anger or sorrow."

No one but Chelise could read him like Mikil. They'd been through the gates of hell together.

"Then what?" Thomas demanded.

"That far-off look," Mikil said.

Thomas looked away and tried to think through any reasonable course of action. None came to mind.

"I'm at a loss," he said. "I feel like I've been battering my head against a stone wall."

"Then you might want to try something else," Jamous said.

"In the past . . ." He let the thought trail off, baiting Mikil.

She took it. "Please, not that again."

"You have a better idea? All I'm saying is that when I came to the utter end of myself then, the answer always waited for me."

"In your dreams," Mikil said.

"Something like that."

"But your dreams no longer work. Not like that."

Jamous exhaled. "Shouldn't we be plotting a course to safety?"

Thomas ignored him. Mikil knew far more about Thomas's dreams than Jamous did. She'd met one of the women from his dreams once. Monique. Monique de Raison of the Raison Strain. Dear Elyon, to even think about those days when he could travel back and forth with the ease of sleep . . . it felt scandalous now. Perfectly absurd.

Send me back to the other world . . . Thomas's pulse rode a steady pace.

"That doesn't mean the other world doesn't exist. Or that I'm not uniquely chosen to bridge the gap."

Mikil stared at him with wide green eyes. But she didn't protest. And she would protest if she wasn't at least considering the idea.

"Now *you're* the chosen one?" she asked.

Thomas shrugged. "My son was right about one thing: there's much we don't understand."

He looked north. Samuel was gone. He'd left with rage in his heart and bitterness on his tongue. There was no way to undo that here. The answers he sought lay elsewhere. Perhaps in the histories.

The urge to recover this last decade, during which he hadn't found a way to return to the other world even once, ballooned in Thomas's mind. He faced Mikil.

"You can't deny it, Mikil. Monique came to you. You know the other world is real."

No response.

"If there was a way back . . ."

"Don't do this."

"Do I have a choice?"

"There *is* no way back. And yes, unless you've stopped breathing, you always have a choice."

"I think there could be a way. And I think I have an obligation to find out if there is a way."

"This is madness."

"It's who I am!" he insisted. "This is my path." Thomas pointed to the south. "You saw Ba'al! He's in touch with the dark world. He'll ride this dragon's back and devour Elyon's bride. This is only the beginning."

"Then the Circle needs you."

"And you saw the look in Qurong's eyes. Ba'al is his enemy as much as Eram is. I'm telling you, Mikil, the world is headed for a showdown unlike any we've seen."

"We've always known that."

"But it's *now*!" His horse shifted at the sound of his cry.

"We're not alone," Jamous said, scanning the cliffs. "Check your passions."

Thomas took a breath. "Tell me I have no business doing this."

Mikil kept her silence.

Jamous turned back, confused. "What exactly are you talking about doing? Going to another world?"

Mikil kept her eyes on Thomas. "Going to Qurongi City," she said.

"You can't be serious."

Thomas regarded Mikil steadily. "Then you heard Ba'al as well."

"Of course I heard." Mikil set her jaw and looked south, toward the Horde stronghold. "So Ba'al knows a thing or two. What are we to do, rush into his temple and demand he share what he knows?"

"Not we," Thomas said. "Me."

She scowled. "Over my dead body."

"No, over my dead body. I'm dead already. My son's left me. I lead a people who are falling apart after a decade of running and dying. Qurong may have a hard heart, but his enemies are pressing in, and if Samuel joins the half-breeds, his problems are about to get worse. Qurong is desperate for an ally."

"The Circle? Albinos may never slaughter Horde again, but we can never be the ally of the one who hunts us!"

"No, not the Circle. Me. I will make Qurong my ally."

"And die."

Thomas nodded. "Or die trying."

17

THE GREAT library ran off the main atrium, just down the hall from Monique de Raison's office at Raison Pharmaceutical. It contained more than ten thousand volumes, nearly half of which were collector's editions of old books, each worth a small fortune as books go. They lined mahogany bookcases that rose to the twelve-foot ceilings. The room's temperature and humidity were controlled by twenty-four digital thermostats, one at each case. The whole room could be counted as the world's largest humidor.

Kara often came here with Monique, mostly to reflect on the unique connection they shared. Thirty-five years ago, just after the incident, Monique had commissioned two identical green journals embossed with the same title: *My Book of History*. They'd both written of their experiences, recalling even the minute details, then compared their writings late into the evening, expanding and embellishing as they saw fit, perhaps hoping that these diaries, like the blank Books of History from the other reality, would magically transform their own reality.

Normally the journals were in a safe behind a painting of the Capitol building in Washington, D.C. The painting was significant because, for one, it was a fairly innocuous painting of little value, unlikely to be removed by any thief, and for another, much of Thomas's past was linked to that building.

It had all started thirty-six years ago in Denver, Colorado, when Thomas had claimed that he lived in a different reality, in the future, and that this one was a figment of his dreams. He was asleep, dreaming of history in the other, real reality.

None of Kara's world was real, he said.

She'd quickly convinced him that this was real. They had both grown up as army brats in the Philippines and spoke Tagalog to prove it. Their father, a chaplain, had left their mother for a Filipino woman half her age after twenty years of marriage.

Kara had thrown herself into higher education and studied to become a nurse, which she did successfully. Thomas hadn't fared quite so well. He left the Philippines a well-known and respected street fighter with a wicked scoring foot on the soccer field, and landed in New York as a lost soul who didn't quite fit. When his life finally came apart, he fled New York, moved in with Kara in Denver, and took a job at the Java Hut while he put things back together.

The dreaming had started then, late one night in Denver, with a single silenced bullet out of nowhere. Loan sharks from New York were chasing him, he claimed. But soon after Thomas left her for the final time, Kara had sought out said loan sharks, eager to avoid any lingering bad blood, only to discover that they weren't the ones in the alley that night.

The identity of the men who had been chasing Thomas thirty-six years earlier remained a mystery to this day.

As for his dreams, well, that was the question, wasn't it? Just how real were those dreams of his? At one time she'd been sure they were real. But three decades later, it all seemed a bit fuzzy.

Real or not, Thomas's dreams of another world had forever altered Kara's life. Monique's as well, but on many levels Monique was still the same bioengineer she'd been when Thomas first met her.

Kara, on the other hand, had found living in the United States nearly impossible. She had been inexorably drawn back to Southeast Asia. Back to the land and people who'd birthed her.

Back to Thomas's own history.

She'd never married as Monique had, fearful that any relationship might suffer the same fate as Monique's, a passionate and all-consuming but short-lived flame. A rocket rather than a candle.

Kara was no Mother Teresa, but she'd given the last three decades of her life to serving the young, broken girls of Bangkok's sex industry.

And she'd dreamed. Dreamed of what it would be like to dream with Thomas's blood once again. Of what it would be like to vanish from this world and wake in another, if only until she fell asleep again.

But it wasn't that simple. Greatness was never that simple.

Monique had asked Kara to join her here while she decided what to do about Janae. She stood and crossed to the towering bookcase that housed part of the collection from Turkey, in which the scholar David Abraham had first discovered the Books of History. Of course, Monique had never been able to secure even a single volume of the books, and the other titles on the shelf, however valuable and ancient, couldn't remotely compare.

Her gaunt face betrayed the anguish that had flogged her for the last eight hours. She tried to interest herself in the books but, unable to do so, returned to her seat where she settled and crossed her legs.

"What would he do?" she asked. She turned her face to Kara, who clasped her hands behind her back and paced on the round handwoven rug under the crystal chandelier. "Tell me that, Kara, and I swear I'll leave the whole thing alone. I'll let her die . . ." Her voiced trailed off.

"You mean Thomas?"

"Because she'll die. They'll both die in the next eight hours if I don't administer the blood. They might die anyway. We hold their lives in our hands, you and I. But what would Thomas have done?"

"My brother didn't always do the most logical thing."

"Maybe because the most logical thing isn't always what it's cracked up to be."

"Listen to you," Kara chided. "You were always the strong one, demanding we follow the strictest policy."

Monique nodded. Dabbed at a tear that broke from her right eye before it smeared her mascara. "All I want to know is whether you think Thomas Hunter would ever sacrifice his son or daughter for the good of others."

Kara considered the question.

"Listen to me, Monique. You're every bit as much a sister to me as Thomas was a brother. He and I share the same mother, but you and Thomas share the same heart. And blood, if you consider the fact that you entered his dream world."

"It was more than a dream, you—"

"Okay, it was. My point is that you're as qualified as I am to answer your question."

But Monique didn't. In this reality anyway, Monique wasn't capable of killing her own daughter.

"Okay." Kara walked to the overstuffed chair next to Monique and eased down. She held her hands in her lap and leaned back. Blew some air. "We both know that Thomas would probably break every rule to save his son or daughter. So let's break this down. Assuming—just assuming—we give Billy and Janae a small dose of the blood, what's the worst that could happen?"

Monique looked up. "They enter the other reality, get their hands on the Books of History. Only God knows how much damage they might do with the power to write anything into existence. Please don't tell me you don't see the danger."

"Just making sure we're on the same page. It is all a bit mind-bending. Back on point, I think Thomas would save his daughter regardless of consequence."

Monique held her gaze, neither accepting nor rejecting the notion outwardly.

She continued. "What steps could we take to mitigate any danger? We have considerable resources at our disposal. Maybe we're thinking about this all wrong."

Monique averted her eyes and stared into space. For a few moments she seemed lost, but the haze that enveloped her gave way to the faintest sparkle. "We could lock them up," she said, turning back to Kara. "Assuming the blood keeps them alive."

"There's no guarantee of that. It's never been attempted. We're only guessing that his blood will have an effect on the virus."

"It saved you and me from the virus once before."

"Yes, it did."

"Janae and Billy clearly think it would work."

"Okay, assuming the blood works, which is the hope, they go into the other reality and return to find themselves locked up until we can determine what to do."

"For all we know they won't enter the other reality. Their eyes to that reality can only be opened if they believe . . ."

"Clearly, they believe. They're risking their lives for the chance to travel."

Monique smoothed her skirt with nervous hands, rubbed her palms on the arms of the chair. Unable to sit still, she pushed herself up, then quickly walked to the door and back.

"You're saying we should actually do this?"

"I'm saying Thomas would," Kara said.

"And if we were to keep them restrained, we would reduce the risk to our world considerably."

"Well, no, I didn't say that. We would mitigate the immediate threat they might pose. If they do get a taste of the other world, they won't forget it because we slap their hands when they awaken here."

"Then we keep them in chains," Monique said. The prospect of saving her daughter at any cost was asserting itself. "Better alive and in chains than dead."

"Maybe. We still have no control over what they might do in the other reality. For all we know, they might find a way to blow open the passage between our worlds."

"We could destroy the rest of the blood. A return trip would be impossible."

"Unless they find another way."

"Assuming they even go," Monique shot back. "Even then they would only be over there until they sleep. Hours, maybe a day, no more."

"More than enough time to—"

"Are you for this or aren't you?" Monique snapped. "Make up your mind. First you say Thomas would save his daughter, now you go to great lengths to make sure I understand what a terrible decision it is? I can't play these games!"

Kara acquiesced. If Janae or Billy were the child she never had, she'd be crawling the walls. "Just want to be clear." She stood. "How long will it take?"

That settled Monique. "I could have the blood here in five hours."

"Well, then. Make the call."

They faced each other, aware of the momentous decision they were making. The blood was their forbidden drug as much as it was Janae and Billy's. They probably should have incinerated it a long time ago.

"Save your daughter, Monique. Make the call now, before it's too late."

18

SAMUEL PULLED up on his reins and grabbed a fistful of air to signal a full stop. His comrades Petrus, Jacob, and Herum held back at horse length. A lone, stubborn buzzard peered at them from the cliff top ahead and then flapped for the sky to join two that had just vacated their perch.

It was something else, not they, who'd sent the birds away.

"Easy, boys," Samuel said quietly. "No sudden movements. We've come as friends, let's make sure they know that."

The cliffs rose vertically on three sides, leaving only a thin trail ahead up the steep face, or a retreat behind. Samuel had met up with his men, who'd shadowed him as planned, then led them into the canyon, knowing it was a dead end. Only a fool would venture so deep into Eramite territory. The half-breeds' tracks were nearly covered by the sand, only visible to the trained eye, perhaps. But to Jacob, who could spot the trail of a Shataiki ghost on a field of rocks, the sign screamed danger. Any Eramites patrolling this far from their main city would be warriors, surely perplexed over what kind of fool albinos would set themselves up so easily.

And why their leader wore only a cloak of dried blood.

"I don't like it," Jacob mumbled. "They have skilled archers. We're mice in a pit."

"They're Horde, not cats. Open your arms." Samuel released his reins and spread his arms wide in a sign of nonaggression.

Three hours had passed since he left Thomas and the others at the edge of Eramite territory. What his father would do now was anyone's guess. The man was given to rashness matched only by his courage.

But that bravery was now misaligned with an old, dead philosophy that clung to fading hopes. Only three years ago Samuel would have challenged any man or woman who spoke back to his father. He'd been younger and naive, a blind follower like the rest. So much of what they experienced could be explained as the working of Elyon.

But the realities of life cast doubt on that interpretation. Samuel's experience had slowly but thoroughly crushed his wholehearted acceptance of all he'd been taught. He awoke from a fitful sleep a year ago and realized he didn't know what he believed any longer.

Who could say that Elyon wasn't just another force in their world, like gravity or muscle or the sword, manipulated by his users?

Who was to say that the scabbing disease was a disease at all? What if it was just another condition of man, cleansed by the medicinal red waters?

Who was to say that the fruit was a gift from Elyon? Why not just a product of the land with powerful properties?

Who was to say that Teeleh was more than another force, counterbalancing the force called Elyon? Absolute good and evil were nothing more than constructs fashioned by humans who needed to understand and order their everyday lives.

Who was to say that the force that had made his body whole after Ba'al slashed him was any different from the force that grew the fruit? He'd been aware of the power, but only as a distant abstraction, a light that had vanished into the sky as he regained consciousness. And the Shataiki, though unnerving, didn't seem so terrifying to those who worshipped them. Loving them would be like loving the Horde, those scabbed vermin who proved far more dangerous than Shataiki on any day.

One thing was clear: the Horde had vowed to kill every living albino—man, woman, or child. That made them enemy, a force that did not agree with him or his desire to live in peace. He'd faced enough blood, but it was time to speak the only language the Horde understood with absolute clarity.

War.

It was time for the Horde to bleed, and the fact that two hundred priests in Ba'al's service had bled and died on his account was as good a sign as any that the time had come.

I will show you, Father. You'll see that I am right in the end.

"Take us to Eram!" Samuel shouted. His voice echoed through the canyon. "We come for the benefit of Eram!"

Nothing.

"I hope you know what you're doing," Petrus muttered.

"We're past the time for second-guessing."

"I'm hoping, not second-guessing." Petrus drew a deep breath and chased Samuel's call with his own. "We're unarmed, you goats! Come out and meet us. We have words for Eram!"

"That's endearing," Jacob said.

The first Horde warrior to rise into view stood on the cliff to their left. He was a tall Scab warrior dressed in tan battle gear, a cross between the old Horde robes and the Forest Guard armor, with leather guards strapped to thighs, arms, and chest. No helmet covered his clean, thick black hair. No dreadlocks on this one.

The others rose into view along the ridge, a hundred at least, two dozen of whom were armed with unstrung bows. They clearly didn't see the four albinos as a credible threat. More like trapped animals for their amusement.

It occurred to Samuel that he'd never addressed a Horde warrior with anything other than his backside in flight—except more recently, with the edge of his sword.

"Greetings."

The leader stared down at him for a long moment, then twisted in his saddle and spoke to someone behind him. The line parted and their leader slowly moved into view, mounted on a large brown stallion that wagged its head against the bit in its mouth.

No helmet. No leather guards. He wore only a calm, almost casual disposition that spoke of supreme confidence, but he was still as much a Horde as any Horde Samuel had seen.

This could be Eram himself. Samuel felt his pulse quicken. The scene could easily be taken from one of a hundred tales of the old days, when the Forest Guard was led by the great warrior, Thomas of Hunter.

Only this wasn't Thomas. This was a half-breed who had embraced the scabbing disease and waged war on Qurong.

"Greetings," Samuel called again.

"You're naked," the leader said. "I would have expected more from the son of the great warrior."

The man knew who he was?

"My name is Samuel of Hunter," he called. "These are my men, and we come in peace."

"Peace? Do you have any choice?"

A light chuckle mocked them.

"Give me a sword and you'll find me less interested in peace," Samuel said.

"Then you would be a fool."

"If I'm a fool, it's because I've left my father to join you for war."

"Is that right? Even a bigger fool than I thought." Again, laughter from the cliff. "You go from being the sacrificial lamb to the traitor so quickly."

They'd seen?

"These are my lands, boy. My men have been watching you from the moment the first black bird circled overhead."

"Then why didn't you kill Qurong and Ba'al while you had them?"

"Because, unlike you, I'm not a fool. Our time hasn't come. When it does, the whole world will know."

So the rumors that Eram was up to something were true.

"I've come to speak to Eram, the half-breed feared by all Horde. Tell Eram that his time *has* come. And the whole world knows."

The leader watched Samuel for a few seconds, silenced by the bold insinuation. Then the warrior turned his horse around and spoke gently, like a commander accustomed to watching a thousand of his men run with the mere flip of his wrist.

"Bring them."

19

NIGHT WAS falling. Thomas Hunter balanced near the top of a massive oak, studying the glimmering fires in Qurongi City. It had taken him most of the day to snake his way south, careful to avoid any Horde patrols, which were few thanks to the Dark Moon celebration.

How long had it been since he'd laid eyes on the forest once proudly inhabited by the Forest Dwellers? Ten years. So much had changed since he fled this city.

He pulled back the hood of the Scab robe Samuel had discarded, which he'd exchanged for his own tunic. Before the Horde's time, the crystalline lake's southern shore had been white sand, reserved for the nightly celebrations. His people had defended the forests against Qurong's encroaching armies, always returning victorious to this safe haven. It was a place where flower-crowned children and youths too inexperienced for war had run through the streets, welcoming them home. The homes were simple but colorful. They often danced late into the night to the sounds of guitars and flutes and drums.

They'd bathed in the lake together, washing away all traces of the dreaded scabbing disease.

To think that he'd once brought his people bits and pieces of advanced technology from his dreams of another world—it was hardly conceivable now. He'd lived in two worlds at once, awake here while dreaming in the other, and awake there when dreaming here. There he'd loved a sister named Kara and a woman named Monique.

If the lost books, as Ba'al had called them, did indeed exist . . .

He brought his mind back to the city. Except for the palace on the far side, and the Thrall, which stood alone on the near side, Qurongi City was practically colorless. Gray blocks of mud and stone topped by straw roofs leaked smoke from the dinner fires inside. The Horde still subsisted on wheat cakes, but instead of harvesting desert wheat as they once had, they grew green wheat in the large cleared fields of the forests to the south. Meat was a delicacy, reserved primarily for the upper class, the priests, and royalty.

The Thrall stood tall by the muddy lake's shore, lit by orange flames that illuminated a spire rising to the height of three buildings. They said that Ba'al had erected this new addition, topped by a brass image of the winged serpent. The new wing that looked large enough to house hundreds of priests stretched out from the western wall.

The lost books would be either in this temple, under Ba'al's watchful eye, or in Qurong's care. If the dark priest had access to them, he would surely have used them.

The thought had clawed at Thomas's mind for the last eight hours as he pushed his horse south. If a man like Ba'al were to find his way into the other world . . . The thought made him shiver.

But Ba'al apparently hadn't used the books. His lament to Teeleh made it clear that he hadn't been sent like the others. This could only mean that Ba'al didn't have the books.

Qurong must have them. Assuming they existed, of course, which was anything but certain.

Either way, Thomas's need to know had grown like a monster inside him. He felt sure that his fate was somehow dependent on what happened in the other world, which also meant that the Circle's fate was tied to the other world. To the books. It had always been about the Books of History, he could see that now.

"Hello, old friend."

Thomas twisted to his right, lost his grip on the tree trunk for a moment, and grabbed a handful of branches to steady himself. He looked into the large, green eyes of a Roush perhaps two feet in height.

The fuzzy white creature's huge eyes stared unblinking. "Sorry."

Thomas couldn't find his voice. This . . . a Roush!

It had been so long since he'd seen one, even he was beginning to wonder whether he'd only dreamed of the legendary creatures that did Elyon's bidding. Yet here one was, perched not five feet away, looking at Thomas as if he might be an idiot.

"You're real," Thomas finally managed.

"And so are you. Unless it's now my turn to dream."

Then he recognized the Roush. Could it be?

"Michal?"

"Thomas?"

"So . . . so it's you?"

"In the flesh."

"Seriously?"

"Now you're beginning to worry me. We have considerable history together, and yet you sound as if you doubt my existence."

"No. Just . . . we haven't seen one of you for an eternity."

"Actually, that's a long time and yet to come. It's been ten years, I believe." He clucked with his tongue. "You humans do have such a short memory."

"Dear Elyon, if the others could only see."

"Your eyes were opened to the Shataiki?" Michal asked. "Yes?"

"Yes. Yes."

"Well, then. Now you see me. But it doesn't mean I haven't been around."

"No, of course not." Thomas wanted to hug the creature. Wrap him up in his arms and bury his face in that fuzzy neck. But then he wasn't a boy any longer. Or was he? What was it Elyon used to say?

Am I a lion, a lamb, or a boy?

He swung to a lower branch and dropped twenty feet to the soft forest floor. The Roush stared down at him, unmoving, then made a soft humphing sound and hopped into the air. He floated to the ground, spreading wide his wings of thin white skin.

"You've developed a fear of heights?" Michal asked. "I would . . ."

It was as far as the Roush got. Driven by a desperate need to know, to touch, to feel, Thomas fell to his knees, threw his arms around the creature's neck, which was hardly a neck at all, and pulled the soft torso tight against his chest.

The feeling of this warm body, so real in his arms, flooded him with a brew of emotion that pushed tears into his eyes. Joy. Love. Relief. Vindication and power.

Samuel was wrong, so very wrong.

"Easy, easy. Phew, the stench of that robe . . . please, you're going to suffocate me!"

"Sorry." Thomas pushed himself back and stared at the round face. "Sorry."

"Understood. Apology unnecessary but accepted. They told me you'd disguised yourself in this dreadful garb, but I didn't expect to have to wear it myself." Michal hopped to his right and glanced back. "Good thinking, by the way. It should get you into the city easily enough. It's getting out that I worry about."

"Then you approve of what I'm doing."

"Not mine to approve or disapprove. I'm simply here with a message. But while I'm here, I could be talked into parting with some advice. That is, if you still value the advice of Elyon's Roush."

"I would be a fool not to. Has your opinion of humans fallen so low?"

The Roush lifted one eyebrow.

"Okay, so we've made a few mistakes along the way."

"Will," Michal said. "We *will* make some mistakes along the way."

"Okay, will. But surely this will all come to an end before we all drop dead of old age."

The Roush gazed off into the forest. "Is that what you think? That there's an end? That when you die it all ends?"

"No, but not everything is forever." That seemed to satisfy the Roush. "You have a message?"

Michal stared at Thomas, nodded once, and spoke as if he was reciting poetry. "The colored forests, like Elyon, Maker of all that is good, will come again. This is the beginning and it is the end, and yet still the beginning. The first will be last and the last will be first. What was once black will be green. And what was once green will be consumed by darkness. Follow your heart, Thomas, because the time has come. Weep with the mourners; beg with beggars; knock and knock again, because he will give you what you ask in that hour when all is lost."

The Roush took a deep breath and looked off again. "Go to the place you came from. Make a way for the Circle to fulfill its hope."

The night grew still. A night bird cawed far off, and the breeze rustled leaves overhead.

"That's it?"

"It's not enough?"

"No. Well, yes, it is, but it's not exactly clear."

"For him who has ears to hear, it's perfectly clear."

"Then explain it to me."

"I can't."

"Why not?"

"It'll become clear in time."

"You don't understand it?"

The Roush threw him a side glance. "I understand what I'm meant to understand."

Thomas scratched his skull and paced. "Then at least tell me what you understand. I'm out on a limb here. I've just lost a son to the half-breeds, the Circle is fractured, the Shataiki have gathered at Ba'al's call . . . my world is falling apart! At least tell me how to save my son."

The Roush sighed and waddled a few steps, steadying himself with a flutter of wings.

"You've heard of the lost books?"

So he was right. "I've heard rumors . . ."

"They are true. The seven original Books of History went missing, three of them into history."

Into history? He was about to demand the furry creature continue when Michal spoke.

"It's a long story, more than you need to know. But what might be useful is the knowledge that these seven books aren't like the other Books of History. With all seven, one could rewrite the rules that control the blank books."

"Like a key."

"If you like. The Books of History reflect the truth of all that has occurred in history. Write in one of the numerous blank books with the faith of a child, and create history. But with all seven of the original books, one can actually change the rules that govern the rest of the books."

"And these seven original books are no longer lost, I take it."

"They were found by four warriors—"

"Johnis and—"

"Another story altogether. But they ended up here, hidden in Qurong's private library. Fortunately Ba'al"—Michal paused as if considering what to say, then continued—"doesn't know that Qurong has them, or he would have used them a long time ago."

"Used them? To rewrite the rules of the books?"

"No, you need all seven to do that. Qurong has six. But with only four of them, a person can unlock time that binds history and travel into it."

Thomas's heart pounded. The suggestion was immediately clear. "So . . . I can use the four books to return to ancient Earth?"

Michal raised an eyebrow and offered a coy smile. His words whispered through Thomas's mind. *Go to the place you came from. Make a way for the Circle to fulfill its hope.*

"How? How do you use these four books?"

"As I was saying . . ." Michal cleared his throat. "A person can travel into history if he touches four books together with his blood."

"Four books," Thomas said, holding up four fingers.

"Yes, four books."

"Which Qurong has."

"Yes, which Qurong has."

"Qurong has them, but only Ba'al knows of their power."

"Correct, Qurong has them, but Ba'al wouldn't dream of telling what he knows about the Books of History."

"And if I cut myself and touch four of these books, I will enter history, so to speak. Like I could once do in my dreams."

"Not quite the same. You would go physically, along with anything in your possession."

"Physically? You mean actually, *poof*, go?"

"Yes. *Poof.*"

Thomas blinked. "And return the same way? *Poof*?" He snapped his fingers.

"Yes. *Poof.*" Michal made an inaudible snapping motion with his small fingers.

"And this is what I'm meant to do?" Thomas asked.

"That is up to you. I'm only a messenger, and I can't say that the message was so clear."

"And how is this supposed to get me my son back? Without Samuel, I have no hope."

"Did I say the books would help you find your son?"

Thomas's reasoning stalled. "You're saying he's lost?" He paced, frantic. "I won't have it! There has to be a way to save Samuel."

"And I didn't say there wasn't. Go. And return quickly before it's too late. Do that and you might save your son."

Thomas ran his hands through his hair and tried to think clearly. The prospect of returning to history pulled at his mind like a powerful magnet tugging at a steel ball. They were inexplicably linked, he and the histories. Perhaps because he really had come from Denver, Colorado. From Bangkok. The histories where his sister, Kara, waited.

"Be careful, Thomas," Michal was saying behind him. "Where there is great hope, there is also great evil. Teeleh's time has also come. The blood will flow like a river."

"Yes," he said absently. "Of course." Was Kara still alive? Monique? The books were in Qurong's possession. He'd been right in coming for them, regardless of the risk to himself. If he could get his blood on the four books and return to history, a new hope would present itself.

And then the end would come.

"Whose time has come?" He turned back. "What evil are you . . ."

But there was no furry white Roush to hear him. He looked up, saw only empty branches, and turned around, scanning the forest.

Michal was gone.

The Roush had made himself seen after ten years and said what he'd come to say. It was indeed the beginning of the end.

Thomas faced Qurongi City, where the lost books waited. He took a deep breath, flipped the hood of the priest's robe back over his head, and ran.

20

THOMAS WALKED down the road leading to the palace as he imagined a priest with urgent business would walk; his head was bowed to hide his face, hands folded under his long sleeves, feet taking quick short steps. The sooner he passed any curious onlookers the better.

His urgency came from the books. More specifically from the need to return to the histories, where he would find a way for them all.

Once again, the world hung in the balance of every choice he made.

Michal's words haunted him as he strode by a Scab warrior who mistook him for a priest and gave him a wide berth. *What was once black will be green. And what was once green will be consumed by darkness.* So, after all these years the great pursuit of mankind's heart would finally end. Either Teeleh or Elyon would win them all.

Follow your heart, Thomas, because the time has come . . . he will give you what you ask in that hour when all is lost. What this meant, Thomas could not know. Only that an hour was fast approaching when all would appear lost, a prospect that certainly justified some urgency. The Roush's next words could hardly be mistaken.

Go to the place you came from. Make a way for the Circle to fulfill its hope.

He approached two guards at the palace gate. The dried blood that covered the dead priest's garment couldn't hurt his chances.

"Open!" he hissed, snatching up a hand, careful to keep his flesh hidden beneath the sleeve. "I have urgent business from Ba'al."

The guard on the left made for the latch, but the other stepped up. "Does his Excellency expect—"

"Open or I turn back and bring the dark priest to answer your questions!"

"No, my lord," the first one said, pulling the gate open. "Ba'al's word is Teeleh's word."

Thomas rushed past, giving them no time to peer beneath the hood. Six Throaters were positioned on each side of the path ahead.

"Let Ba'al's servant pass," the guard called. The mere prospect of answering to Ba'al had the desired effect. None of the warriors questioned the order. Even better, the guard at the next wooden entrance had heard the call and opened the door with a bow.

Thomas hurried inside the large atrium and pulled up, pulse pounding. Two large torches lapped at the walls on either side, filling the room with orange light. To his right, a bowl of morst powder sat beside some fruit. A round table made of stone centered the room, adorned with a tall statue of the black beast, Teeleh.

He considered powdering his face with the sweet-smelling morst to cover his albino skin, but he hadn't come to hide. Instead, he threw back his hood, took several calming breaths, and introduced himself at the top of his lungs.

"Patricia, wife of Qurong, the servant of Ba'al calls you to hear him in the most urgent matter!"

His voice rang through the stone atrium and beyond. A servant appeared in the archway and looked at him curiously. Her eyes went wide, and she uttered a short cry before running off, yelling in a high pitch.

Thomas strode forward. "Patricia, wife of Qurong, Ba'al demands your presence."

"Then come," a woman called back impatiently. "What's the ruckus? For the love of Teeleh don't stand out there, come in and speak."

Thomas entered the receiving room. A long table sat under three brass torches suspended by leather thongs. The walls were decorated with a dozen skulls of bulls and goats, either painted in reds and purples or plastered with morst paste. Chairs made of bone supporting leather seats ran around the table.

He recognized Patricia immediately. She had a large yellow melon in one hand and a black candle in the other, a woman not too elevated in her own eyes to help where she saw the need, despite having dozens of servants at her disposal. Her pale green dress ran to the floor, a long-sleeved garment with a brown belt. Her hair was braided and smothered in the white morst, as were her face and hands. Odd how the Horde claimed to prefer the smell of their own skin over the stench of albino flesh, yet they went to such great lengths to moderate their own stink.

"Well, then, speak." Patricia glanced up as she set the candle in a stand on the table's far side. "You know I honor the word of . . ."

Her mouth dropped open and she froze.

"The husband of your daughter," Thomas said. "Thomas of Hunter, leader of all albinos. I come in peace."

She still didn't find her voice. Two Throaters with drawn swords rushed into the room, no doubt alerted by the servant.

Thomas shrugged out of the robe and let it fall around his feet. He spread his hands.

"I'm unarmed. Hold them back."

Patricia hesitated, then waved them back. "Leave us."

Neither moved. The cries of others came down the halls now, yelling a general alarm. Two of them burst into the room from a side hall and pulled up sharply at the door.

"Leave us!" Patricia snapped.

"My lady . . ."

"I said leave us. Or I'll have your head! All of you. Stand down."

They glanced at one another, then backed away slowly, muttering something about Qurong. Thomas kept his eyes on Patricia, knowing now that he'd chosen the right introduction. As the husband of her daughter, he held a place of importance to Patricia. She might relish the prospect of torturing him for tearing their family apart, but not before gaining some understanding about her daughter.

"I've come from Ba'al Bek, where Elyon made a mockery of your dark priest," he said. "Now I'm here to appeal to Qurong without that snake's knowledge. But I fear he may not hear what I have to say."

She plopped the melon on the table and put a hand on her hip. "And what makes you think I'm interested in what my enemy has to say?"

"Because you were sent packing from Ba'al Bek with your tail between your legs." Thomas said. Too strong?

"Is that what happened? Perspectives shape how we see mystical matters. I heard of a great victory."

"Two hundred priests died. They didn't tell you?"

"You mean Ba'al's offering? I heard that Teeleh and his black beasts showed themselves to the world. The streets are teeming with fear already."

"But in the end, my son climbed off the altar, alive." He didn't have the time to persuade her of what she hadn't seen with her own eyes. Ba'al had already put his spin on the whole mess.

"Never mind," he said. "I have a new proposal for Qurong. One that will help him destroy the enemy he fears."

Patricia walked around the end of the table. "You're mistaken if you think Qurong is threatened by the albinos. Just because you managed to steal Chelise doesn't mean we fear you."

"I'm not your enemy," Thomas said. "You should fear the Eramites and Ba'al."

He saw the quick movement in her eyes. He continued before she could form a response.

"My wife weeps for her mother and her father. No one has a more tender heart toward the Horde than she. What I have to say could save you all. I beg you, take me to Qurong and convince him to listen to me before he disposes of me."

She stared at him, flat-footed. For long seconds neither moved nor spoke.

"And how is my daughter?" she finally asked.

A voice spoke from the darkened hall on Thomas's right. "We *have* no daughter." Qurong walked in, dressed in a leather tunic with long pants and soft-soled boots. No guards, no weapons. He stood nearly a foot taller than his wife, and his bare arms were maybe one and a half times the diameter of Thomas's. His legs, thick like trunks without an ounce of fat. The man might not have Thomas's speed, but he could likely drop a bull with one blow to its skull.

The supreme commander of the Horde snatched up a chalice of red wine and splashed some into a glass goblet. This he threw back in one long drink before turning his eyes to Thomas. He studied him for several long beats.

"I see Cassak failed to prove his worth," he finally said.

"On the contrary, your general proved better than most. But it was an unfair race. My son knows Eramite territory too well."

To this Qurong said nothing.

"You're wondering why the man who just fled you at Ba'al Bek now stands before you," Thomas said.

"You'll have to forgive us." Qurong spat to one side. "It's not every day a smelly salamander snakes its way into our courts."

"How about a drink? It's been a while since I've had a good drink of Horde wine."

The leader hesitated, then nodded at his wife, who poured half a glass and stepped back. Thomas stepped up to the table and took a sip of the bitter liquid, grateful to hydrate his parched throat despite the nasty taste.

"He's earned his right to speak," Patricia said.

"Quiet, woman. I'll decide who has what rights in my own house." Qurong looked at Thomas. "So taking my daughter wasn't enough? Now you come back and try to seduce my wife?"

Patricia glared at him. "Don't be—"

"Silence!" he thundered.

"Her beauty and charm notwithstanding, I have no intention of seducing your wife any more than I seduced your daughter," Thomas said. "I simply loved her, as I now love all people—albino, Horde, half-breed—they are all one. But if you don't let me talk, you may not learn how Samuel, my son, whom Ba'al allowed to escape, is conspiring your death. Kill this albino salamander who stinks up your palace, and my knowledge will die with me."

The man surely wasn't foolish enough to dismiss this claim, not considering the source. Qurong frowned, then looked at his wife.

"Leave us. Seal the doors. I want no one within earshot."

Her eyes didn't leave Thomas. "How is she?"

Qurong held up his hand to stop them. But when Thomas spoke, he didn't silence him.

"Good. Excellent. Healthy and as spirited as ever." Thomas offered her a thin smile. "She speaks of her mother and father every evening, making you both heroes in Jake's mind. Sometimes I wonder why she ever left you for Elyon."

When he didn't offer more, Patricia spoke very softly. "Jake?"

"Forgive me, I thought you'd heard. Jake is your grandson."

He might as well have told them that they'd just swallowed poison and had only minutes to live.

"Leave us," Qurong repeated in a low voice.

"I—"

"Leave us!"

This time she bowed at his raised hand, turned, and walked from the room, issuing orders to those beyond. The door slammed, leaving Thomas and Qurong to face off alone.

"Listen to me, albino. Your pleas for sympathy may melt the hearts of mothers, but all of this talk falls on deaf ears now. Never speak to me of this woman and her child again. Do we understand each other?"

"Yes, I think we do."

"I need you to be certain."

"Then yes."

"If it's war you speak of, I'll give you one minute to explain yourself."

"It's all I need," Thomas said.

Qurong finally let out a breath, poured himself more wine, and sat. "I'll never figure out you albino ghosts. Any other enemy and I would feel compelled to put you in chains the moment you enter our city. But you've all forgotten how to fight. You're hardly a man."

"I can see how you might think that."

"Well, you've earned this right to speak"—Qurong waved his hand—"so speak."

"It's simple. The only reason the Eramites haven't annihilated you is because they don't have the numbers. But that's about to change. My son has turned against me and will take half of all albinos with him to join Eram for the sole purpose of waging war against you."

He let that sink in. It was a bold-faced exaggeration, but he was here for the books, not to help Qurong. His only ally was Qurong's fear.

Thomas pressed his point. "Your high priest would like nothing more than to see you dead."

"What would you know of Ba'al?"

"He let Samuel live. Why? Because he has conspired to bring you to ruin, and Samuel is his greatest ally. Once your body has fed a dozen Shataiki, he will step in and control all of the land, Horde, albino, and Eramite."

"Absurd!" But Qurong stood and walked around the end of the table, clearly concerned.

"You're deceived about some things, Qurong, but otherwise you're a wise man. You surely know most of this already. Tell me that Ba'al isn't your enemy."

The leader glanced at the door.

"Or that Eram doesn't lead a growing army that can no longer be discounted. Or that Samuel wouldn't try to slit your throat if he were standing here."

"Your minute is up."

"I haven't told you how to end this threat, once and for all."

Qurong glowered. "There's no end to your disrespect. This young woman who used to be my daughter may have drowned, but I . . ." He seemed to shudder. "I'm not such a fool."

"You misunderstand me. I'm not here to tell you how to drown. I'm here to tell you how to defeat Eram, Ba'al, and Samuel."

"Is that so?"

"It is."

The man cast another glance at the doors to be sure they were secure. He lowered his voice. "Well, then. Speak."

"My minute is up."

"Then I give you another."

"Did you ever wonder how I've been able to stay a step ahead of you at every turn for so long? How the Forest Dwellers were always the innovators, sprouting technology as if it grew in our closets? The forging of metals, the use of wheels, weapons—all of it, first to the Forest Guard and then to the Horde through your spies?"

The man frowned. "Hurry it up."

"It was me. I came across the secrets to these advances personally."

Qurong waited for more. "And how will this deal with Eram?"

"We can do it again," Thomas said.

"Do what again?"

"Go into the Books of History and retrieve what we need to defeat Ba'al and his hideous god, Teeleh."

"Go into the books?" Qurong was incredulous.

Thomas slipped into a chair and folded his hands on the table. "Not any books, naturally. One of the lost books."

Qurong nodded slowly. "I see. You've come to enter the lost books. Have you lost your mind? This is worse than Ba'al's antics. I know nothing of any lost books or this magic you're trying to seduce me with."

Here it was, then. Either Qurong had the books or he didn't.

"No." Thomas leaned forward and spoke softly. "You may not know of them as the lost books. There were initially seven, the number of perfection. But a great power can come from only four of them."

Qurong wasn't blinking. His whole face had stilled like a mask.

Thomas continued. "The lost books can open a window into a world of great power and magic, Qurong."

Now Qurong blinked.

Thomas put his fleece out. "Does Ba'al know that you have the books?"

The commander's eyes scanned the room.

"Don't tell me you don't know what I'm talking about," Thomas pushed.

"There are six books that I've kept from him," Qurong said in a low, quick voice. "When he first came to us from the desert, he turned the city inside out looking for any sign of them. He claimed he needed these books for ceremonial purposes. These could be the books . . ."

"Six? We need only four."

"We?"

"You have them, I know how to use them. We."

The prospect of returning to the other world was now so realistic, so palpable, so close, that Thomas had difficulty calming a tremor in his voice.

"Don't be a fool," the leader said. "We are Qurong and Thomas. There are no two greater enemies."

"You're sadly mistaken, my lord. The lust of Teeleh and the wrath of Elyon will make our differences sound like whispers in the night. But even here, in your own palace, Ba'al is a greater enemy than I am. As is Eram and now Samuel. Next to all of them, I just might be your closest friend."

"This is blasphemy."

"Show me the books."

"How can I trust you, the greatest deceiver of them all?"

Thomas took a deep breath and tried to sound calm. "Because if you don't, you will die."

Qurong remained silent. Suspicious, but no longer defiant.

Thomas made it clear. "We will all die."

21

BILLY REDIGER was aware of several things in his state of dreaming. He knew that he'd thrown himself off a cliff of some kind, but the exact nature of that cliff kept shifting in his mind. At times he was falling into a black hole, clawing at the air to stop his never-ending descent and thinking that if he could just grow wings, like those of a huge bat, he would be fine.

Then he was being chased through a Black Forest by that very bat. It hounded him, snapping at his heels until it hauled him down and went for his neck with a ferocious snarl.

But Billy knew that he was dreaming. And dreaming was good, because dreaming meant that he was still alive. Or was he?

Then he remembered for the hundredth time: He'd lost all sense of himself, and despite Johnny's and Darcy's best efforts, he fled Colorado in search of himself.

In search of the beginning. The truth behind how his own fall from grace had begun. Before Marsuvees Black. Before the showdown in Paradise. Before he'd learned that he was the chief of all sinners.

Before he'd written that first word in the Book of History so long ago.

The truth came down to a man named Thomas Hunter and what remained of him: one vial of his blood.

He had to find the truth about himself, but having met Janae de Raison, he knew that her truth was a part of his truth. She was his soul mate. And he knew he would follow her to hell and back. Which is exactly what he was doing, lying on this gurney: following her to hell.

And hopefully back.

The murmur of voices interrupted Billy's reverie. "It doesn't take that much . . ." The voice sounded as if it came from the edge of a distant canyon.

"We don't know that. We don't know anything about how this will work."

Then Billy knew. The sting on his arm wasn't Janae. Her mother, Monique, was injecting his arm with a new needle. They were doing it.

Janae, dear Janae . . . your gamble has paid off. At this very moment they were shooting his arm with Thomas's blood.

"Pulse rising!"

Of course, his pulse was rising.

And what if you wake up, Billy? What if you're not dreaming when the blood hits your blood? What if Janae goes but you don't?

He began to panic.

"Pulse 158 and rising . . ."

Billy jumped off a dark cliff and thought about black bats chasing him through darkness. Down, down. Deeper, still deeper, into the swirling blackness below.

The darkness suffocated him. Swallowed him with pain. He cried out and he knew that they could hear him.

KARA HUNTER instinctively jerked her hands to her ears when the scream came from Billy. His back arched. Like Janae, his body had begun to bruise as the capillaries near the skin hemorrhaged, ravaged by the Raison Strain B. Their deterioration hadn't progressed as quickly as Kara feared, but they were now both dying at a breakneck pace.

Billy dropped back down on the gurney and went silent except for the ragged sound of his heavy breathing.

"Pulse 168," Monique said calmly. They'd already injected a half cc of Thomas's blood into Janae's vein, and although she, too, was panting, she hadn't reacted as violently.

"Dear God, it's working," Kara said. "He's . . ."

Monique jerked the needle out and did not blot the insertion point with a gauze pad, as she had for her own daughter. Blood oozed from the tiny wound.

"It's too early to tell," she said.

"No, I mean he's there." Kara's voice cracked and she continued in a whisper. "Billy's in Thomas's world!"

"We can't possibly know that," Monique shot back.

"He's there! Look at him."

Billy had turned as white as the walls, mouth stretched open, neck veins protruding like ropes. His eyes were wide, staring at the ceiling, but Kara knew better. Billy wasn't seeing the ceiling.

He was seeing either himself or someone like himself in another world.

AN ORANGE GLOW grew in the darkness, and Billy snapped his mouth shut. Held his breath.

But he was breathing still, staring at a stone wall with two black candles blazing on either side of a crude, black-veined mirror. He . . .

This was it? He'd made it?

An image of a hollow man, dead perhaps, stared at him from the mirror. He spun around to see who was standing behind him.

No one.

He stood alone in a room, its walls hewn from stone lit by two large torches. Ancient books lined a case along one wall, overlooking an altar that was stained by the blood of both man and beast. It was an ark of covenants, guarded on both ends by the winged serpent, Teeleh.

Billy knew all of this because he was in his own library.

To his left stood his desk, carved from a single stump taken from the Black Forest. Marsuuv, the Shataiki queen who'd caged him, had allowed him to take the tree.

This he knew as well, as if it were his own history. But that was impossible because he also knew that he was Billy Rediger, from Colorado, the United States.

You're both. Billy and Ba'al.

Ba'al. I am Ba'al. He relished the name.

Then his mind flooded with the full truth, and he had to reach out and steady himself on the desk chair to stay upright.

He knew who he was, what he'd done here in this world. Why he was who he was. "I am yours," Ba'al whispered—Billy, who was in Ba'al's body, whispered.

"My queen, Marsuuv, I am your only lover, and I will die to prove my worth." Ba'al's voice was scratchy and thin, barely more than a whisper, but here in the subterranean library, it vibrated like the hiss of a snake. Billy's mind blossomed with the nature of the Shataiki queens. Teeleh and his queens longed to be loved, as Elyon was loved. They were incapable of sexuality but commanded absolute loyalty and servitude. To be the lover of a queen meant throwing your life at his feet.

Billy turned to face the room. Two books sat on the desk. Books of History. These were a fraction of all the volumes that told the stories of history, a recording of all that had ever happened in human history. These two were filled with facts already. They didn't have the power of a blank book, which could be used to create history, but the sight of them eased his fear.

He had come home. This, more than Colorado or Bangkok or anywhere in the other reality, was home. It was exhilaration, not fear, that he felt. After so many years wondering who he was and why his battle with evil was so monumental, he finally knew. He hadn't just created evil, he was possessed by it. The only time he'd really embraced redemption had been in a dream. He'd never fully pushed evil from his heart. Not like Darcy and Johnny had.

Another book lay open on its spine next to an ink jar and quill. Ba'al's blood book, another term for *journal.*

He stepped up to the desk and reached for the blood book. Then, for the first time since awakening in Ba'al's library, he saw the flesh that encased his wrist and fingers. He stared at the flaking, cracking skin, and his first thought was that he'd been consumed by a severe case of scabies.

But the thought was immediately displaced by Ba'al's knowledge. This was the scabbing condition caused by the Shataiki, a badge of honor to be worn by all who refused to drown in the albinos' red water.

Billy turned to the mirror, pulled off his hood, and stared at himself. His cheekbones were pronounced beneath his gaunt, white face. Gray eyes, like clay dimes. White morst paste coated long dreadlocks. The image was at once terrifying and beautiful.

He reached up and touched his cheeks, but the sensation in his fingertips was deadened by the scabbing disease.

This is me, Billy. Ba'al. He pulled his robe aside and looked at his chest. *And I still have the blood of my priests on my flesh.*

The memory of Marsuuv's power flowing through his tall, thin frame as he stood over the son's corpse flooded him now, and he trembled with pleasure. He was greater than anyone could possibly imagine, in either world.

Then again, he'd seen the power of the light in both worlds. Thinking of it now, fear crept back into his bowels. A light so bright that no wraith from hell could stand in its presence without screaming in pain.

You are weak . . .

The thought was Ba'al's, not Billy's, and it was laced with such hatred that Billy froze. He realized then that he wasn't wholly Ba'al or Billy now, but a strange breed of both.

A half-breed.

But he had been a half-breed before, in the worst of ways.

Ba'al impulsively walked to the desk, picked up a knife, cut his wrist, and let his blood dribble into a bowl. "Rid me of this weak parasite, my lover, Marsuuv. Cleanse me and make me whole."

Billy blinked at the audacity of the wraith called Ba'al. Didn't they share the same history? Weren't they of the same blood?

"I'm you, you fool!" He squeezed his wrist and wrapped a strip of cloth around the cut to stem the flow of blood.

Billy stared at the blood book on the desk. Here, in this one secret volume, Ba'al had collected all that he knew about the world. He lifted the book and slowly turned the pages, which contained drawings and explanations of everything from the Roush to the Shataiki, excerpts from other scribes pasted in, memories from the time before . . . all here, carefully pieced together.

And who better to write of this world's deepest, darkest secrets than Ba'al? Because Ba'al had once been Forest Guard. A follower of Elyon.

The thought nauseated Billy.

"Hello, my love."

Desire bit deeply into his mind at the sound of the soft voice behind him. He turned around and looked at the priestess who'd entered. This was Jezreal. His lover, as humans loved.

"Haven't I told you not to disturb me in my sanctuary?" Ba'al spat.

"Yes." Jezreal moved forward, smiling. Her ruby fingernails toyed with a golden cord that hung from her long gown's plunging neckline. "And has that ever stopped you from ravaging me before?"

The connection between them was far beyond anything so banal as the mere copulation of animals. She was the only human who understood Ba'al's dependence on Marsuuv, who had first let him drink Shataiki blood. One drop, and any mere human was forever locked in the embrace of evil.

Indeed, Shataiki reproduced through blood, Billy realized. They were asexual, neither male nor female. They wanted slaves, not partners.

Jezreal, on the other hand, was human. Human urges raged behind those glassy gray eyes, and unless Billy was mistaken, Janae and Jezreal were one.

She stepped up to him, close, so that he could smell her sick breath. Her tongue toyed with the tips of her front teeth. "Billy . . ." she breathed. "Or should I call you Billos?"

He didn't respond, in part because the knowledge that he had once been an elite fighter named Billos, sworn to protect Elyon's forests from the Horde, was one of his most closely guarded secrets. He'd once bathed in Elyon's lakes and sat around fires late at night, speaking of his greatness. He was a Judas who'd gone in search of the lost books—the books of blood—found them, used them, and then lost them.

He had been Billos of Southern, and if the people knew that he was not full-breed Horde, doubt would be cast over his loyalty.

More than this, he despised even the name Billos. Marsuuv had given him a new name, and he'd embraced the full embodiment of Ba'al, the god who required blood sacrifice.

"Billosssss . . ."

Ba'al slapped her face with enough force to cut her cheek with his fingernail. How many times had he insisted she not use the name that she alone knew? Jezreal smiled, then winked. She wiped some of the blood from her cheek, looked at her fingertips, and licked it off. "I've told you before, my love. I don't require warming up. And yet you insist."

She slowly stretched her hand out to his lips, offering him a taste of her blood. He turned away, not because of the blood, but because she was mocking him, reducing him to his former self. To this Billy that had haunted him. To Billos, whom he despised.

He was Ba'al, lover of Marsuuv, the twelfth of Teeleh's twelve queens.

"You're not Billy?" she demanded. "You're Ba'al, of course, my master and my savior. And that's all."

His anger fell away as Ba'al's presence was appeased.

Billy reasserted himself and swallowed.

"Right?" she pressed, eyes skittering over his face. "You're not Billy?"

"Janae."

Her eyes widened, and the look of concern faded to a smile. Her voice shook when she spoke. "We made it, Billy. We're here." She turned, drinking in the library, the torches, the books, the altar with its winged serpents. "It's the most beautiful thing I've ever seen."

"We're not alone."

Janae, who was also the priestess Jezreal, didn't seem bothered by this fact. She touched the altar. Ran her fingers over the dried blood. "I feel like I've come home. The smells, the feel of the air . . . it's as though I've gone back into the womb and have been born again, baptized in blood."

He couldn't help but be seduced by her awe. Billy loved this woman. Janae, not Jezreal, though they were one and the same, and he suddenly needed to tell her what he knew.

His breathing thickened. "Janae . . ."

She looked into his eyes, reacting to the tenderness in his voice.

"There's more you should know if we're going to do this together," he said.

She stepped around the altar, and this time he didn't pull back when she touched his lips with her fingers. "Tell me."

He took her hand in his and kissed it. "We're home, but not truly home, not as long as we are parasites in these wretched bodies."

The Ba'al in him boiled with rage, and Billy felt his face contort.

Janae hushed him, smoothing his knotting lips. "It's okay, ignore him. Tell me."

He wrested control away. So . . . Ba'al was the weaker one. He continued in a whisper but with more confidence now.

"There are four lost books. If all four are gathered and touched with blood, time is unlocked."

"Time?"

"It's how we can return here. You and I."

"In the flesh?"

"In the flesh."

Her eyes frantically searched his. "How is that possible?"

"How is *this* possible? But I've done it. When I was Billos."

She stepped back and paced to her right. "Then we have to do it! We have to wake up and return!"

"We don't have the books."

Janae spun back. "What? You tell me this, but we don't have the books? Where are they?"

"We don't know. But we can't risk waking up until we find out."

Ba'al's outrage at the suggestion that the books were for Billy, not for him, threatened to send him into a fit. Billy noted that he shared the body of a viper that would strike him down without hesitation.

Could he kill Ba'al now? What would happen if he committed suicide? No, he couldn't risk death. But he could draw the battle lines clearly.

"It's okay, Janae. I'm going to get the books. It's my destiny."

"And it's my destiny to be here, Billy, so I hope you know what you're talking about."

"I do."

Her look of uncertainty slowly changed to interest.

"Oh?"

"Ba'al has just made it clear to me," he said, smothering the weaker Scab. "He's assumed that the saying was about him, but he's wrong. It's about me."

Then he quoted the prophecy given to Ba'al by Marsuuv. "*There will come from times past an albino with a head of fire, who will rid the world of the poisonous waters and return us unto Paradise.*"

Meaning ignited her eyes. She stared at him for a long time and then spoke in barely more than a whisper. "An antichrist."

Billy didn't respond. But in that moment, all of his own turmoil and angst made more sense than it ever had. This was the demon in him, that evil nature that refused to be extricated, haunted by Marsuvees Black in one world and held captive by the Shataiki queen Marsuuv in this world. He, Billy, was destined to crush this world. And to usher in Paradise in the other.

Janae approached again, dripping with desire. "And I will be by your side. Your queen."

Billy wasn't sure why he was suddenly compelled to remove the strip of cloth from his wrist, but he pulled it free and let her see the fresh cut.

Her eyes dropped and she smiled coyly. Touched the blood and playfully brought her finger to her tongue. But the moment she tasted his blood, her face registered shock.

"What's this? This is Teeleh's blood?"

"Marsuuv's blood." Because Marsuuv had bitten Ba'al and allowed him to take some of her blood. It's where his own thirst had come from.

"Marsuuv," she whispered, staring at his wrist with a craving he'd not yet seen in her. "May I?"

"Yes, you may."

She brought his wrist to her mouth, smothered the bloody cut with her lips, and sucked. Her whole body trembled with desire.

Then Billy knew the truth: Janae, like Billos, had Shataiki blood in her veins.

And Ba'al despised them both.

22

"NO ONE knows of this room?" Thomas asked, leading the way down the flight of steps.

"None," Qurong said gruffly. "Keep your eyes ahead."

"I've had ample opportunity to take you out, if I had any intention of doing so."

"Don't think so highly of yourself."

"You've let your guard down a dozen times. You know I have no desire to see you harmed. It's not only against my nature, it's against Chelise's."

Silence.

"She knows," Qurong said.

"Of this place?"

"I showed it to her when she took such an interest in the books. But that was before I came into these lost books you speak of."

The light from Thomas's torch cast a flickering glow over the stone stairs. They came to a small atrium shut off by a wooden gate.

"Inside."

"How did you manage to build this without anyone's knowledge?" Thomas asked, pushing the gate wide.

"It was here."

"It was?"

"The tunnels and caves were here. A nest of some kind—Shataiki, for all I know. Ba'al tells me they have a wicked appetite for the books."

"Naturally. They seek to make their own history by bending the will of all men in the same way they've bent yours."

Qurong grunted and steered him to his right, into one of five tunnels beyond the gate. The hollowed passage looked as old as the world, carved through the rock but straight enough. They walked twenty paces before making another right through another wooden gate and into what appeared to be a library.

Old books lay on a round table at the center. Bookcases along the right wall. A writing desk to his left. He was about to ask if this was it, when a glow flooded the room. Qurong had lit a second torch on the wall.

Four chairs sat around the table, and beyond it, a couch with stuffed silk pillows. There was everything a reader intent on studying could want down here, including a pitcher of water, a bowl of fruit, even a fireplace.

"This was here?"

"As I said, the cave was here. It's my only escape from the dark priest's prying eyes. He has servants in the walls."

At least one of the shelves was stuffed with volumes from the Books of History. But the Horde could not read the books; Thomas had established that much long ago. To the albino, the words read perfectly clear, but the scabbing disease turned this truth to nonsense in the Hordes' minds. Their scribes were obsessed with writing their own history in plain bound books, a way of legitimizing their own failure to read the Books of History.

Everyone wanted to create his own history. There was nothing as powerful as the written word; history had taught them all that much.

"You can read the Books of History?" Thomas asked to be sure.

"No one can."

"Albinos can."

"That is a lie," Qurong said simply.

There was no way to prove otherwise. He could just as easily pretend to read from the books and Qurong would never know the difference. Such was the nature of religion, plied by man to control the masses.

"But we didn't come down here so you could admire my library." Qurong crossed to the desk. "You say you can give me what I need to destroy my enemies through these books."

He opened a drawer and pulled out a canvas bag bound by rope. He untied the bundle and withdrew colored Books of History, one by one, setting them on the desk. Six of them. The binding of each one a different color.

Qurong faced him. "So show me."

Thomas walked up to the desk and reached for the books. "May I?"

"One. And only one."

"Of course."

He picked up the green book. They were all bound by old leather embossed with the same concentric rings, the symbol for completeness. Elyon's stamp.

The Circle.

Thomas traced the symbol. "Have you opened these?"

"They're empty."

Blank! But Michal said these were a key to both time and the rules that governed the other blank books.

He pulled the cover back. The page was smothered by blood. It had been used. Thomas's heart pounded at the prospect of entering.

"Let me have your knife."

"Don't be a fool."

"Do you want to do this or not?" Thomas snapped. Then he considered a possibility that made him second-guess himself. What if he vanished into the other world without the books? How would he ever make it back? He couldn't conceive of going without knowing he would return to Chelise and the Circle. To Samuel. To Jake.

Michal had all but demanded he use them. So he would.

"Do you have any rope?"

"What for?"

"Trust me. Rope."

Qurong eyed him, then plucked a length of twine from a stand beside the desk and tossed it. "I'm now relegated to trusting my gravest enemy," he said.

"Don't be thick, old man. I don't have any harm in mind. We are in this together."

"And just what are we in for?"

Thomas bound four of the books together with the top cover held back to reveal the first page stained with blood. He then tied the bundle of books to his arm. "I need your knife. Trust me, if this works you're going to love—"

"No!" Qurong slammed his hand down on the books, pinning them to the desk. "Enough trust!"

Perhaps he had been too hasty. Thomas lifted both hands to calm the man.

"Easy. I thought I'd already explained. These books unlock time. You and I can vanish"—he snapped his fingers—"and wake in another world where it will all become clear to you."

"Assuming this nonsense is true, what truth do you speak of? How will this save the Horde?"

"I can't explain it. You'll have to . . . to trust me. The world will become clear in ways you've never imagined. Think of it as a gift, one that will save far more than you—"

"Just that?" Qurong snarled. "Just 'trust me'? I am the supreme commander of the Horde kingdom, and I rule all of the known world. I am not a servant for you or for Ba'al or for any other living creature to toy with!"

Thomas's eagerness was partly to blame for Qurong's frustration.

"Listen to me, you old crustacean!" He was shouting. "My son Samuel has just joined the half-breeds! They will rain rage and fire down on you for the torment you've caused them all. The Horde will be drained of blood, and the Shataiki will *feed* on your precious kingdom! Now give me your knife!"

CHELISE PULLED up sharply at the sound of Thomas's voice murmuring urgently down the tunnel.

She'd entered the city from the south, through the familiar gardens that she once frequented. The journey took longer than she'd hoped, for the simple reason that unlike most albinos, her face, even without the scabbing disease, would surely be recognized by any who caught a glimpse of her.

But she knew a secret way in, behind the stables, via an alley that she'd used numerous times as a girl. Then through a low basement window that she was glad to find had not been boarded up.

She'd donned a cloak from a closet behind the kitchen, then crept through the servants' quarters with one objective on her mind.

Find her father.

Find Qurong, who would know what had happened to Thomas. She would make sure he knew of her love for him after ten years without a word.

Naturally, she could live without Qurong. Had lived without Qurong. But without Thomas, she wasn't so sure. He'd been her lover since the day she learned how to love, really love. He'd shown her the Great Romance. She'd begged Elyon for Thomas's life with every step she'd taken.

The palace was buzzing, and she'd hidden behind a pile of barrels in the pantry. Still, she could hear whispers of an albino who'd come, and that could only be Thomas. No one seemed to know where Qurong had vanished to.

Her first thought was of his library. She'd slipped into the root cellar that led to the tunnel, found the door into the secret passage open, and descended on light feet.

And now . . . her breath hung in her chest. He was alive! Thomas was alive and with her father, whose voice reached her now.

"Just 'trust me'? I am the supreme commander of the Horde kingdom, and I rule all of the known world. I am not a servant for you or for Ba'al or for any other living creature to toy with!"

"Listen to me, you old crustacean!" She was astounded that Thomas would use such language with her father.

"My son Samuel has just joined the half-breeds! They will rain rage and fire down on you for the torment you've caused them all. The Horde will be drained of blood, and the Shataiki will feed on your precious kingdom! Now give me your knife!"

It took a moment for the words to form meaning in Chelise's mind. They claimed that Samuel had joined Eram and intended to wage war on the Horde, but that was . . .

How could Samuel consider such a thing?

"Thomas?" She started to run. "Father!"

THOMAS REALIZED he'd pushed too far. Panic began to set in. Once angered, Qurong wouldn't be easily overcome. A woman's voice yelled down the tunnel.

They both spun toward the gate. They were discovered! Patricia?

Now! While Qurong was off balance. He had to move now!

Thomas whirled and snatched Qurong's knife from his belt. Slashed his own palm, barely aware of the pain.

Qurong swung his arm to retrieve his weapon, raging like a bull. Thomas ducked under the blow and grabbed his other hand. Tugged it toward him, blade ready.

For an absurd moment they each pulled at the hand, Qurong desperate to be free, Thomas knowing that his plan to win Qurong by taking him now threatened his own mission to return.

"Father!"

The woman was behind them, at the gate, screaming. Not just any woman, not Patricia, not Horde.

Chelise.

Qurong faced her. As he flinched, Thomas seized his last hope. He yanked the man's hand, sliced his fingers, and thrust both his hand and Qurong's hand onto the blood-smeared page.

Immediately the world began to spin, and his heart stopped.

It was working.

He twisted back, saw Chelise fading at the gate, eyes wide.

"Save the Circle, Chelise! Save them from Samuel! I'll be back!"

But everything had gone black.

CHELISE'S BLOOD ran cold. They were there inside the library, in a tug-of-war over her father's hand, when she cried out. Her father looked up, stunned by her appearance.

Thomas had moved like a man possessed, slashing Qurong's hand with a knife, slamming their bleeding fingers onto a stack of bound books.

Thomas twisted his head; she knew with one look into his wide, green eyes that he was the same man she'd always loved.

"Save the Circle, Chelise! Save them from Samuel! I'll be . . ."

Before he could finish, he vanished. They both disappeared—knife, books, and all—before Thomas could utter another syllable.

There one moment, grappling and bleeding, gone the next.

She stood in the gate, stunned. It had happened. This other world Thomas had talked to her about so often as they lay next to each other under the stars was real. Not that she'd doubted . . .

But she had.

She walked in. Stepped through the space her father and lover had occupied just seconds earlier. His world was not only real, but it had taken him again. She cried out, fists tight. How could he do this? Both of them! Gone! She could kill them both.

Save the Circle, Chelise! Save them from Samuel! I'll be . . . Back. He meant back. *I'll be back.*

Samuel . . . What had the boy done? Dear Elyon! She had to get back to Marie and the council.

Chelise turned and ran from Qurong's library.

She had to get back to her only son. To Jake.

23

"HOW LONG since we injected them?" Kara demanded. "We have to bring them back."

"Twenty-three minutes," Monique replied, peering through a microscope at a sample of Janae's blood. "It's working. Thomas's blood is destroying the virus."

"Already?" The pace of its effectiveness was alarming. "You're sure?"

"Take a look." Monique straightened and looked at the isolation room where Billy and Janae still dreamed in fits and moans. Whatever was happening in their minds, they had to stop it.

Kara bent over the eyepiece and acquired the virus, a microscopic organism she'd always thought looked like a lunar lander. "How can you . . ."

"Dear God, help us," Monique breathed in such a dreadful tone that Kara thought one of the two might have just died.

"What?" She jerked back from the microscope. "What is it?" They were too late, she knew it! Too late for what, she didn't know, but this whole thing had been a bad idea from the start.

Monique stared, pale faced, at the isolation chamber. Two techs stood inside with their backs to the observation windows, fixated on the two gurneys. Only they weren't any ordinary techs in white lab coats.

One was a man dressed in a long black cloak, like a gothic priest. The other . . .

Kara's pulse went from heavy to a dead stop. She recognized the clothing worn by the second man, and his morst-coated dreadlocks.

She hadn't seen anything similar in three decades, but this image had haunted a hundred nightmares in that time.

Horde.

The one dressed in black turned around and stared out at her.

Kara felt faint. This was her brother looking at her. He was older, not much, and his face appeared hardened by time, but there was no mistaking Thomas, not in a thousand years.

"Thomas?" Monique breathed beside her.

"It's . . ." Kara didn't know what it was. Thomas—yes, Thomas!— or a vision of Thomas. The man with dreadlocks turned around. Gray eyes. Most definitely Horde, covered by the scabbing disease.

"We're dreaming," Kara said. She glanced at two lab techs to her right and saw that if she was dreaming, so were they. One had dropped his clipboard and left it by his feet as he gawked.

When she turned back to the room, Thomas was walking toward the door. He opened it. Stepped out.

Spoke.

"Kara . . . forgive me, I know this is a shock." He gripped four books with bleeding fingers, the top book open and smudged with fresh blood. "I . . . I made it back," he said.

She could hardly breathe. "Thomas?" A stupid thing to say, but nothing else would come.

His green eyes darted around, as wide as she'd seen them. He was as shocked as she. His lips slowly twisted into a quirky grin. "Wow."

The emotion of seeing Thomas, who had been lost to this world, crashed over her like a pounding wave, and she made no attempt to stop the tears that flooded her eyes. She uttered one halting sob and stumbled forward.

She rushed the last three steps and hugged him awkwardly. There was so much to say. Endless questions. But at the moment her mind was blank. She could only cry.

The Scab crept from the isolation room in a crouch. "What magic is this?" he demanded loudly. "You've cursed me!"

Thomas eased away from Kara and addressed him. "It will be clear. I told you to trust me; now you have no choice. We've arrived."

The door swung open and two guards burst in, saw the Scab, and leveled their handguns. "Steady . . . no sudden moves."

"Lower your weapons," Monique said, motioning the guards to stand down.

The laboratory adviser, a biological engineer named Bruno, spoke in an urgent voice from behind them. "Miss Hunter, I urge you to step back. The chance of contamination is unknown."

The smell, Kara thought.

"Ma'am, I urge isolation immediately."

The sulfuric stink of the Scab's rotting flesh had filled the room. There was no telling if or how the scabbing disease would spread in this world.

"No," Thomas said. "If the disease spread easily, I would have brought it back with me years ago, when I shifted realities."

But Monique shook her head. "You were only dreaming then. And this . . . You've brought one of the Scabs with you?" But rather than backing off, she walked up to him, eyes fixed on his. "Seal the laboratory's perimeter, Bruno. Leave us."

"Ma'am—"

"Now, Bruno." Eyes still on Thomas. "Out, all of you."

They backed off and headed to the decontamination chamber like scurrying mice. The Scab was dressed in a leather tunic, not battle dress. Cracks on his face ran with sweat that marked the morst paste with long jagged streaks. His eyes, though gray, looked bright with panic.

"End this!" he thundered.

"I don't think you understand, Qurong," Thomas said. "This isn't just a vision that I or you can end. We've unlocked time with the books and are now in . . ." He stopped and glanced around. "Where exactly are we?"

"Raison Pharmaceutical," Monique said. "Bangkok. Hello, Thomas."

His eyes settled on her. "Monique."

"In the flesh," she said. "As, it seems, are you."

"Why did we come to this location?"

"I don't know."

"How long has it been?"

"Over thirty-five years here," she said. "And there?"

"Ten years since I last came. But why would I return *here*, to this exact spot?"

Qurong wasn't following them in the least. "How can this be? We were just in my library. I've awakened in a land of albinos."

"Listen to me, Qurong!" Thomas seemed downright perturbed by the Horde leader. "What have I been saying all along? There's more to the world than your little city and gray water. In this world you'll find no Horde. We're all albinos, as you call us. Not albinos, but human, without your skin disease."

"How is that poss—"

"You've had a thick skull to deny Elyon, but now you'll face the truth. Am I delusional or is this really happening?"

Qurong stared about, but it was impossible to know what he was thinking.

Kara stepped up to Thomas and touched his cheek. "It's really you. You're alive." Her mind was still spinning, trying to make sense of what was happening. Dreaming was one thing, but this . . . he'd just appeared out of thin air!

"Your blood," Monique said.

"What about my blood?"

"Maybe you returned here, and now, because of your blood." She glanced at the room behind them, and Thomas followed her eyes.

"You . . ." He spun back. "They have my blood in them?"

"Yes. They . . ."

But he was moving already, flying past a startled Qurong, into the room, up to Billy's gurney. He slapped the redhead's face with his open palm. *Crack!*

"Wake up! Wake up, get out of there!"

He bounded over to Janae and slapped her cheek hard. "Up, up, up!"

"What are you doing?" Monique demanded. But they knew.

"Wake them! You can't let anyone into my world. The books . . . it's far too dangerous!"

"We did it once."

"Never again."

"They're dying!"

"Then let them die," Thomas snapped, spinning back. "Who are they?"

"My daughter," Monique said. "And Billy, the one who first wrote in the Books of History."

"What is this madness?" Qurong raged.

As if in answer, Billy's eyes opened and he groaned. He pushed himself up and looked around groggily.

"What . . . what's happening?"

"Billy?"

They turned to Janae, who was trying to sit up.

Monique rushed to her daughter's side. "Lie down, both of you. You're in no condition to get out of bed."

Recognition slowly dawned in Janae's expression. Like a deflating balloon, her face wrinkled with scorn and bitterness.

"No!" she cried. She yanked the IV needle from her arm, pushed her mother away, and staggered from the gurney. "You have no right! Where is it?"

"You woke us up?" Billy shouted, red-faced. "You meddling—!"

"What on earth?" Monique looked from one to the other. "We saved your lives, you ungrateful little beasts!"

"Where's the blood?" Janae was by the counter, trembling like a drug addict, searching for the vial of Thomas's blood. "Where is it?"

"Janae!"

She whirled to face Monique. "I was there, Mother. What have you hidden from me?"

"I don't know what you're talking about."

"Tell them who I am, Billos. Tell them!"

And he did, blinking. "She's Jezreal, lover of Ba'al, who is also Billos of Southern. Me."

Qurong grabbed the IV pole, jabbed the air as if it were a spear, and backed out the door. "Stay! Stay or I swear by Teeleh's blood I will kill the first one who comes for me."

Thomas walked toward him, unfazed. "Then kill me. And your way back home will die with me."

The threat gave the diseased man some pause.

"Put the weapon down."

"Tell me what's happening to me. And by the gods, don't tell me I've traveled to another world. No one's heard of such a thing."

"What would you like to hear? That this is a nightmare? That your greatest enemies, Eram and Ba'al, don't really exist? That your daughter, Chelise, really isn't your daughter?"

"Silence!"

"I've told you the truth and in time you will accept it. Now put the weapon down!"

But Qurong didn't appear interested. "Enough magic. Wake me up or I swear I'll kill you all in my dreams!"

"Who is this brute?" Janae demanded. "The old fool Qurong himself. You see, Mother"—she pointed at Qurong—"this is who I am. I belong in his world. Give me the blood, send me back, and kill my body here."

"Stop this!" Monique's face had gone white. "You don't know what you're talking about, Janae; you can't just die in one world and live in another!"

"We don't need to die," Billy said. They turned to him and saw that his eyes were glued to the books in Thomas's hand. "Give us the books."

But Thomas was more interested in Qurong at the moment. "Step back in here. Lower the weapon. Let's be reasonable about this." After a moment's hesitation he added, "Please. My lord, please."

The Scab leader said nothing, but he seemed to be considering a different course. Kara's mind spun with the shocking reality of a very real future to which Thomas had gone and returned.

"He has the lost books, Janae," Billy said, slipping from the gurney. To Thomas: "If you want to be reasonable, let us use them. You'll be rid of us forever."

"Qurong?" Thomas was still fixated on the leader, who finally drew a deep breath and set the pole down.

"Thank you." Free of concern about Qurong, Thomas stared the red-head down. "You have no right to enter our world. We have one Ba'al, we hardly need another."

"And you, Thomas Hunter, have no right to deny me anything. You're here because of me."

"Now you're barking mad."

"I was the first to write in a blank Book of History when they were discovered under the monastery in Paradise, Colorado. More important, I was the one who wrote into history the fact that you traveled to the other world. You went because of me."

Thomas looked shell-shocked.

"You could even call me Father. Now be a good son and give me the books."

"That's not possible. I went long before the books were found in the Paradise monastery."

"No, Thomas," Kara said in an apologetic tone. "I mean, yes, you did go before, but the books reside outside of time. Whatever is written in the books is fact: past, present, and future. At least as far as we've been able to learn."

He seemed to soak that in.

"So then, you're the one who started all of this. Bill. You've been to the Black Forest?"

Billy shrugged. "All I can tell you is that I belong there. I have a purpose there."

"And I have a purpose here," Thomas said. "It does not include sending even more wickedness back to my world. I'm here to find a

way for a land that's lost all hope. Unless you have a message of profound
hope, I doubt you qualify."

"You don't know us," Janae said. She walked toward Thomas, wearing a faint smile of seduction. "Good or evil, it doesn't matter. We belong
there, Thomas. It's Billy's world as much as it's yours. And now it's mine."

"Get back from him," Monique snapped.

Janae had other things in mind. "Is that what you want, Thomas?
You prefer the old mother over the daughter?"

"Back!" Monique grabbed Janae's black dress between her shoulder
blades and jerked her back as if she were a feather. She shoved her onto
the gurney and aimed a long finger at her nose. "Sit!"

"You tell me to trust you, Thomas," Qurong muttered, "but I'm
telling you I can't trust my own eyes. If the magic is in the books, then
we should use them."

Thomas backed away from them all, untying the rope that tethered
the books to his arm. "Kara, if you don't mind."

She walked up to him and accepted the books.

"Step through the door."

The isolation room was only twenty feet square, and the doorway
was open, five feet beyond Thomas. Kara retreated from the room and
faced them through the doorway.

"Monique, help Kara."

"I—"

"Now! Please."

She glanced at her daughter, who stood by the gurney, then hurried
past Thomas, who had his eyes on Billy.

The redhead pieced it together first. "So what, you're just going to
lock—"

"No!" Janae threw herself forward, possessed by a desperation that
was quite literally of another world.

But Thomas moved like a cat, slammed the door shut, and shoved
the outside bolt down. That he'd had the presence of mind to notice
the outside lock was testament to refined instincts, but the way he'd

moved . . . Kara wasn't sure it was entirely human. Long ago he'd displayed some astonishing fighting skills that he claimed to have learned from his dreams, but this speed and strength was new, maybe because he had lived it rather than dreamed it.

Janae slammed into the glass with little effect, mouth wide in a scream Kara could not hear. See, Janae had only gone to the other world in her dreams. As for Qurong . . . now, there was a man who must have the power of a bull in both realities.

Qurong peered out, mystified. This was undoubtedly the first time he'd seen such strong, clear glass.

"Is there any way out of the room?" Thomas demanded.

"You're going to keep them locked up?"

"What would you have me do?"

Monique looked at the three, caged like animals. "I guess it'll hold them until we figure something out."

Thomas took the books from Kara. "Then let's be rid of this place. I need space to think without monkeys peering at me. We don't have much time."

Kara felt a grin tug at her mouth. Thirty years had changed the way Thomas spoke, but he was the same brother. Thomas Hunter was most definitely back. And to her it was like the second coming.

24

"TEN YEARS," Kara said. "So that would make you how old over there?"

"The same as I am here," Thomas said, pacing beside the towering shelves of bound books in Monique's library. "Forty-nine. Amazing." He rubbed his face with his hand, a habit he'd developed—to check if his skin was turning Horde, Chelise used to joke.

"But it's been thirty-six years since you left us. You were twenty-four at the time. You should be sixty, like me. Instead, you're under fifty and you hardly look forty."

"All I know is that I was twenty-four—or was it twenty-five?—when I first woke in the Black Forest, and nearly twenty-six years have passed since then." He scanned the ceiling. "Utterly amazing."

They'd left the laboratory, taken an elevator to the ground level, and retreated to Monique's library, issuing strict instructions to be left alone.

"A lot's changed since you left us," Monique said.

"It's not the change. It's being back in civilization. Elyon knows how much I love the desert, but this . . . this is fantastic."

"So you're married? In the desert?"

Thomas looked into her bright eyes, recalling what they'd shared. Was that only a dream? The relationship between the two worlds still confused him. What was less confusing was the fact that he was physically here, now. There was only one Thomas Hunter, and he stood in a city called Bangkok, looking at an older woman who, at sixty, was stunning.

"Married? Yes. Happily. No, *happily* is a silly word for it. My wife is the jewel of the desert, the light that guides my heart through the darkness when I grow tired of waiting for the end."

Monique grinned. "Wow. Sounds like I missed out."

"Sorry, I didn't mean it like that. You're married?"

"Once."

"Janae's father?"

"Yes. It was a torrid affair that lasted a year. His name was Philippe, and he raged into my life like a tornado when I was feeling sorry for my loss. I knew it was bad, but he gave me what I longed for and then disappeared. He knew about you, naturally. You were still quite famous then."

Philippe. Thomas wondered what connection he had to the other world. They were all connected, it seemed. The only real question was, in what way? Albino, Horde, Eramite half-breed, Shataiki? Roush?

Kara walked up to him with a roll of gauze and some tape she'd grabbed on the way out of the lab. She took his hand and rubbed his skin, studying the cut on his palm. Then she wrapped his hand in the bandage.

Her hair smelled like soap. Perfume. Flowers. He still wore the Horde robe, which carried the faint odor of scabbing disease—to them he likely smelled like a skunk.

"I still can't believe you're here," Kara said, tapping the bandage. She lifted misty eyes. "Really here."

He slid his hand behind her neck, pulled her close and kissed her forehead. "Trust me, to know that all of this exists . . . it certifies me sane. So many times I believed I might be losing my mind."

"You're here to stay?"

Her question took him off guard. He dropped his hand and walked away. "I was told to come, find a way, and return to the Circle. My son is lost without me. I don't have much time."

"So, how long?"

"He didn't say. Quickly, that's all. You don't understand . . . there's trouble brewing. My son has betrayed the Circle and joined Eram." Saying it renewed his sense of urgency, never mind that it all sounded a bit preposterous. "I fear the worst. War. The unraveling of all good in the land."

Kara studied him, eyes fixed. "Take me back with you."

"Back? No, no."

"Yes," she said. "Take me back."

"This world needs you!"

"This world needs Monique. I don't have anyone left. Mom and Dad are long gone. I've been alone for thirty years."

"You never married?"

"Never."

He considered the notion.

"You can't be serious about this," Monique said, standing from her chair. She crossed to a bar and poured a drink from a bottle of amber liquid. "We don't even know what the true connection between the worlds is. It's far too dangerous."

She was grasping.

"We do know!" Kara snapped. "It's obvious."

"Then tell us."

"Thomas's world is the future of this world, thousands of years from now, remade, a kind of new earth. The essentials of history are being replayed; everything spiritual here has become physical there. It's like take two. Isn't that what you said once, Thomas?"

"I'm not sure I understand," Monique said.

"In the other world, words become flesh through the Books of History. And vice versa: reality becomes words recorded in the same books. The spiritual has physical manifestation. When those books came into our reality, they still had the same power to turn words into flesh." She motioned at the stack of four books on the desk where Thomas had laid them. "The books are the bridge between the worlds. Literally, a bridge."

She'd put it so simply.

"And the blood?" Thomas asked. "My blood, Teeleh's blood, Elyon's blood. Why always blood?"

Kara joined Monique and poured a drink. "I don't know. In both realities, blood is life. Disease here and evil there are both carried by blood. And they're wiped out by blood. You'll have to tell us the rest."

The connections hadn't escaped Thomas all these years, but he'd never put it so plainly in his head. "The red lakes," he said.

"What lakes?"

"They came later. The lakes were turned red by Elyon's blood. By drowning in them we stay free of the disease."

"Drowning? Really drowning?"

"Yes, we die. But it's life, really, because Elyon paid that price so we can escape it."

"Price for what?"

"The cost of our embracing evil—death. Elyon cannot live with evil; it must die. Or so we say."

"So it's like a baptism?"

Thomas nodded. "Perhaps. Only Elyon knows the full extent of these connections."

"Unfortunately, like you say, Elyon seems to have gone quiet," Monique said. "In both realities. And you may have brought the worst to us."

"How so?"

"Qurong." Monique set down her glass and crossed to the window. "There's another connection that I'd like to consider."

"The Raison Strain?" Kara said. "You can't think the scabbing disease is the same as the Raison Strain."

Monique turned back. "Would it surprise you?"

The room fell silent, and Thomas began to feel oddly misplaced here in the world of medicine and machines. What if he couldn't go back? He eyed the books, still bound and smeared with his and Qurong's blood. What did he really know about the rules that guided these lost books?

"Please, Thomas." He turned to Kara, who was watching him in earnest. "Take me with you."

He felt his face slowly offer up a soft smile. "You never were one to capitulate, were you?"

But he couldn't promise her anything, not without knowing more.

"I could never go," Monique said in a thin voice cut by sorrow. She was staring out the window again, lost in thought. Thomas understood a small part of what she must be feeling.

She could never enter the world where Chelise lived. They both knew that Thomas had given his heart and soul to another woman who waited now, braving any danger for him.

The memory of Chelise rushing into Qurong's underground library swallowed him for a moment, and he had to push back the compulsion to rush over to the books and use them again. While he stood in safety, Chelise was . . . was what?

See, that was just it. He wouldn't put anything past his desert bride. Her spirit more often than not pulled her into the most dangerous path. She could be rushing toward Eram to retrieve Samuel or returning to the Circle to warn them. Assuming she'd escaped Qurongi City.

Meanwhile, he'd stumbled back into a love affair that had never quite died.

Monique turned. "But that's my cross to bear. And to be honest, it's not an impossibly heavy one." She took one deep breath and let a smile toy with her mouth. "Although I must say, you do look like a scrumptious dessert. The desert air must agree with you."

"It's the fruit," he said sheepishly, then realized that he might be coming off as pretentious. "And I'm younger. Honestly I was just thinking how beautiful you look."

They stared at each other, and the air grew stuffy.

Monique rescued him. "This is rather awkward." She crossed to him, kissed his cheek, then turned away. "The fact is, however fantastic this turn of events might seem to us, we all know that we're playing a role on a grand stage that determines the lives of millions. I owe this world my work and my life. And Thomas"—she faced them both— "your world is waiting for you. So, what can we do to help you?"

There was still Kara, Thomas thought. Where did she belong?

He nodded. "I will always remember your graciousness."

Monique dipped her head.

Thomas sighed. "As I said, what I know is this: One"—he stuck out a finger—"the Circle has been pulled apart by arguments in doctrine. We still hold to the same basic tenets, but now even those are being challenged. What was once sacred is slipping into obscurity. And the greatest of all guiding imperatives—that we love the Horde—has been abandoned by more than even I probably know."

"Sounds familiar," Kara said.

"How so?"

"You think this world is any different?"

Thomas hadn't considered it; his mind was on the desert. He ran his fingers through his long locks of hair and continued.

"It's as if another kind of disease, this forgetfulness, has been eating away at their hearts for years like a cancer. Now it's too late to reverse it. We never used to live for the desert, because we knew that it was just a transition. A better world was just around the corner. We endured terrible persecution and death, driven by hope. But now that hope of a better world is losing its appeal. Forgotten."

"Again, familiar."

"That doesn't help me."

"So you need what, Thomas?" Monique asked.

"A way for the Circle to fulfill its hope."

They just looked at him.

"Maybe a few guns would do the trick." Still those empty stares. "But I couldn't, of course. I didn't come for a way to kill."

"And what else?" Monique pressed.

"Qurong. I brought the supreme commander of our greatest enemy in the hope of helping him put to rest the impossible stubbornness that's badgered him all these years."

"You shouldn't have brought him," she said.

"Why not?"

"He's death."

25

QURONG STANK of dead fish, Billy thought. The thick, sulfuric scent was inexplicably appealing, and this realization sickened him slightly. Janae paced like a caged animal, seemingly oblivious to Qurong, who was so far out of his comfort zone that he could do little but stand and sweat.

Billy leaned against the gurney, running through their options, which were clearly limited. The Raison Strain B virus had been stopped by the blood; this was good. He had finally, after over a decade of wondering, found himself—his inner demons, his purpose, all that made him tick. This was even better.

But the only way to reconnect with who he really was required the lost books. Right now, he was in the wrong world.

"There has to be a way out of this prison," he said.

Janae whirled, furious. "It's built to keep people in, you idiot! We're stuck!"

Billy stood up. "So now I'm your enemy too?"

She closed her eyes, drew long breaths through her nostrils, and finally pushed air back out through pursed lips. Sweat matted her long black hair to her cheeks, and her mascara had run, but even so she looked as alluring as she had when she was Jezreal.

"Okay. Sorry. Sorry, I'm just . . ." Her eyes opened, misty. "This is all happening too quickly. I don't know who I am anymore, Billy. I don't know why I feel this way."

His ability to read minds hadn't been affected by the disease, but he didn't need to look past her face to see that Janae was hopelessly lost.

Like a newborn child seeing the light but not understanding where the womb had gone.

Thomas was lost as well. As were Kara and Monique. His mind-reading powers hadn't been present while he was in Ba'al's body, and they'd taken a few minutes to reassert themselves after waking, but in the short time he'd stared into Thomas's mind, Billy had learned a few things.

He learned that the Circle was fracturing and might very well shatter with just a little more pressure.

He learned that Samuel, Thomas's son, had betrayed him and gone to Eram.

And he learned the location of the three thousand who waited for the rest of the Circle to join them. All of the Circle in one canyon.

None of that helped him now, locked in this isolation room. He focused on Janae. She'd gone from a lost but spirited young woman to Jezreal in minutes. There could be no doubt: she was somehow tied to the Shataiki. But exactly how, and why *she*, of all people, he didn't know yet.

Then again, her mother, Monique, had been at the center of Thomas Hunter's life. Perhaps Janae's father had approached Monique because of this.

Billy stepped in front of Janae and brushed her hair off her cheeks. "I know. You're conflicted and it's tearing you apart. Trust me, I've been there. When we get back, you won't feel divided. We belong there, Janae. It'll all be okay when we go home."

She lunged forward and kissed him on the lips, drawing desperately on his breath. She wrapped her arms around him and held him close, trembling.

"Don't leave me behind," she whispered. "Promise me, Billy. Never leave me."

He pulled back, feeling awkward. She was like a woman possessed by a spirit that had awakened from the dead.

"I won't leave you."

"Swear it!"

"I swear."

Qurong grunted, and Billy saw that he wore a scowl. Looking into his eyes, Billy saw more. Much more. And he felt compelled to set the record straight.

"Your forehead may bear Ba'al's three claw marks, old man, but you hate him. On the other hand, you love your daughter, though you deny it. You fear Thomas more than you fear Teeleh. And deep down inside, you suspect that Elyon is real, but the Shataiki larvae have invaded your mind and made you stupid."

Which is why I, not you, am the chosen one, he didn't say. "How do I know? Because I also know you were eating blueberries with sago paste when Thomas burst into your house and tricked you into this journey."

Qurong's gray eyes were round. What if the answer to how they might return somehow rested with this man?

"Be careful what you think, Qurong." Let him stew on that for a minute.

Billy kissed Janae on the hair. "It'll be okay, we'll get back. Let's take a deep breath and think this through. Starting with this beast."

"I can tell you, there's no way I would allow you to enter my world," Qurong said, spitting on the clean floor. "You're witches. Albinos who have an alliance with Ba'al. If you think you belong anywhere but hell, you're mistaken."

"This coming from an overgrown lizard who smells like hell," Billy said.

Janae wiped her eyes and breathed out again. "Blood," she said.

Billy frowned. "Blood?"

"Yes. I was drawn to the blood. When I was in Jezreal and you let me taste your blood . . . there was something about the blood that captivated me."

"The blood books." Having been with Ba'al even for an hour, Billy still had many of his memories, and he dipped into them now. "Thomas's blood. Marsuuv gave Ba'al her blood when Ba'al was Billos. Ba'al became part of the Shataiki. How does that help us now?"

Janae studied Qurong. "Well . . ." She hurried to a closet, pulled the door wide, and withdrew a microscope. She tossed Billy a small, clear plastic box.

"Take a blood and skin sample from him. Apply them both to the slides."

Billy looked at Qurong. "From him?"

"From him, yes. Hurry, we don't have all day."

"What's the meaning of this?" Qurong demanded.

"It means that you're going to let us look at your blood under this machine." Billy walked up and handed him a glass slide. "Smear some of the blood from your wound on this piece of glass."

Qurong looked at the slide as if it might be a weapon of great significance.

"Hurry!"

"This means nothing to me."

"Do you want to go home before Ba'al takes your throne?"

The man grunted and plucked the slide from his hand. He awkwardly rubbed some of the blood from his finger onto the glass, then handed it back.

"And his skin," Janae said, handing Billy a small scalpel.

"Now your skin." Billy handed him another slide and the knife.

"You expect me to cut my skin off?"

"Just scrape some off." Janae looked over from the eyepiece. "The thinner the better."

"You heard her," Billy snapped.

"Whatever for? This is preposterous!"

Janae spoke as she focused the microscope. "Call it grasping at straws, I don't know, just do it. Has anyone ever studied your blood before? I doubt it. I'm a scientist, it's what I do."

Qurong scraped some skin off his forearm, then dragged the blade across the slide, depositing a layer of morst and dead flesh on the clear glass. "Albino fools."

Billy set the slide on the counter next to Janae. "Anything?"

"This is . . . I think . . ." But she didn't elaborate.

"What?"

Janae quickly pulled out the slide with blood and slipped in the sample of Qurong's skin.

"What?" Billy demanded again.

"I . . . if I'm not mistaken, he has what looks to me—although I can't be sure without more tests, this microscope isn't the most powerful—"

"Just say it."

She adjusted the focus. "He has something similar to the Raison Strain in his blood. Looks like a slightly different strain, but . . ." She adjusted her view of the skin sample.

Made sense. In a twisted kind of way.

Janae gasped and left her mouth agape.

"What?"

She straightened, eyes on Qurong.

"What?"

"That's it," she said, approaching the man. She reached for him. "Can I have a closer look?"

He hesitantly held out his arm. Janae took his wrist in one hand and rubbed her thumb on his skin. "Horde are a little stronger than albino. Isn't that correct?"

"Yes," Qurong and Billy said in unison.

"But albino are much quicker," she said. "They don't have the same pain and their joints are free to move with ease."

"So some claim."

"For heaven's sake, Janae, just—"

"I know why they're stronger," she said, looking at Billy with some wonder. "It's the Shataiki."

"They have Shataiki blood?"

"No. Maybe, I don't know. But their skin is infested with millions of microscopic larvae."

"Shataiki larvae," Billy said, mind overflowing with Ba'al's knowledge. "The twelve queens spawned by Teeleh reproduce by laying eggs that form unfertilized larvae. They can live for centuries in this state until another Shataiki fertilizes them with blood."

"How?"

"They bite. Pass blood through their fangs."

"Vampires."

"No, Shataiki," Billy said, then shrugged. "Same difference."

Qurong was staring at his arm. "Worms?"

"Tiny larvae," Janae said, hurrying back to the microscope and peering in. "In this world we have scabies, a skin disease caused by a tiny mite called *Sarcoptes scabiei*, invisible to the naked eye. They burrow into the skin and lay eggs that produce larvae and more mites. The rash on the skin is a reaction to the mites. Similar to what we have here."

She looked up again. "The Horde are covered by Teeleh's larvae. They evidently infect Horde blood with something similar to the first Raison Strain. But rather than kill them, the virus passes on some Shataiki properties, like strength."

"Walking breeding grounds."

"This is complete and utter foolishness," Qurong said, dismissing them with a wave of his arm.

Billy suddenly knew how they might get out. "Janae, if we could get out of this isolation room, could you get us out of the laboratory?"

"I don't know." She looked at the main door, where two guards were normally posted.

"Surely there's another way out of here. Ventilation, a passage, something."

"Ventilation?" She blinked. "We're underground, the vents are huge." She brushed past him. "I was a kid when they built this place, and I crawled through some of them then. The main return shaft runs over the rooms down the hall, opening to each one." She was staring at the two-foot-by-two-foot grille near the top of the wall, five feet to the left of the main door. "That would get us out. Maybe."

"Maybe? Why wouldn't it?"

"For starters, we're boxed behind reinforced glass. And even if we followed the ventilation to the end of the hall without getting the guard's attention, the shaft turns straight up, twenty feet. There's no way—"

"We don't need to go up," Billy said. He tore the sheet off the nearest gurney and tossed it to Qurong. "Wrap this around your fists. The glass is made to withstand human force, but they didn't have Horde in mind. You can break it."

Qurong looked at the glass, the sheet in his hands, and then back at Billy. He tossed the sheet back. "I'll take my chances here."

"Whatever for? You heard Thomas! He has no intention of letting you jump back now that he has you under his thumb. He knew that kidnapping you would immobilize the Horde, perhaps giving the Eramites and Samuel the advantage they need to mount a crushing blow."

The thought had just presented itself to Billy, and it made sense, maybe more than they knew. "But Thomas doesn't know Ba'al the way you and I do. There's no telling what the dark priest will do in your absence. We have to get back. Now!"

"Not like this. I go back with no advantage. I would just as soon trust Thomas as you." Qurong was settling into his normative, crafty self.

"I can give you an advantage," Janae said. She looked at Billy, gave him her thoughts, and then addressed Qurong when Billy nodded.

"I could give you a weapon. One that you could use to wipe out all of the Eramites, the albinos—any army that came against you."

Qurong's face twitched. "That's not possible."

"You know nothing of this world! What I have is small enough to take through the books, and believe me, it could end life in your world."

"What is it?"

"A virus. A disease that will only affect those you want it to."

"You're bluffing. Whoever heard of such a thing?"

"You're saying that a lot these days, I'll bet," she snapped, then motioned to their surroundings. "Whoever heard of *this*? Whoever heard of the reading of thoughts and the unlocking of time and space with a *book*? In reality the whole world is one big whoever-heard-of-it!"

"She's got a point, you buffoon," Billy said. It occurred to him that he was talking to the most powerful man in a world where he might soon need allies. He would have to curb the insults.

"You're an intelligent man, Qurong. I saw this when I shared Ba'al's mind, and frankly it scared me. You're also the most powerful man on the planet. Your subjects tremble when you walk by. But we both know that everyone at the top is a target. What we're offering you will ensure your survival. And we can be your greatest allies."

The Horde was sweating again, but he wasn't arguing.

"Every minute we stand here doubting puts distance between us and the lost books," Janae scolded. "We have to move."

"How will you get out?" Qurong asked. "Where is this weapon?"

"Not in here." She shoved her finger at the reinforced glass. "Break it! At least try, for heaven's sake."

Qurong grunted and began to wrap the sheet around his elbow. "I don't like this. You put me at your mercy. I have no reason to believe you'll take me with you."

"You have no choice but to trust us."

The man kept his eyes on them as he stood by the large window, roughly eight by five. Qurong nodded, gripped his fist with his left hand, and slammed his elbow back against the glass without removing his eyes from Billy.

The room shook as the window fractured into a hundred thousand hairline cracks. Qurong pushed the broken glass, and it fell to the ground like rain.

Janae uttered something that made no sense, then scrambled over the sill into the main laboratory. She spun, motioning silence with a finger to her lips, and ran to the same electronically operated storage cabinet from which she'd withdrawn the Raison Strain B.

Working like a mouse over a crumb, she began punching in access numbers. She motioned to a closet and issued whispered orders. "A ladder and tools; remove the grate; wait for me. Just get it off."

"You're getting the virus?"

"Hurry!"

Billy paused. What if the Raison Strain didn't have the same effects in the other world?

"You have other viruses, right? Ebola?"

She caught his eye and glanced at Qurong. "Please, trust me. I need a moment. Alone."

Billy understood immediately. She didn't want Qurong to know what she was up to. Perhaps where on her body she hid the viruses.

He pulled the door to the closet open, grabbed the ladder and a small tool kit. Hurrying to the wall under the return air grate, he shoved the ladder at Qurong. "Keep it quiet." The main door was sealed tight and would offer a good sound barrier, but there was no telling what other security measures had been put in place.

Qurong tried to unfold the ladder as Billy pulled out a Phillips-head screwdriver. "Here, back off." Billy grabbed the ladder, set it on the floor in proper position, and hurried to the top. Four screws secured the grate, and they all came out without a hitch. He hung the panel on a hook that protruded from the ladder, then peered into the return duct.

Large enough for both Janae and him, but the Horde oaf would never make it.

"Get down."

He twisted back and saw that Janae stood beside Qurong, looking up at him.

"Hurry! Get down here."

Billy dropped down beside them. "We can't all—"

"Wait with him by the door," she interrupted, mounting the ladder.

"Me? Wait a minute, I'm coming with you!"

Janae glared back at him. "Shut up, Billy." Then, noting his shock, "I didn't mean it like that. But I'm the only one who can do this. I know where I'm going. Two doors down into a large storage room that has survival equipment and fresh lab coats. Flare guns."

"That's how you're going to get the books, with a lab coat and a flare gun?"

"No, that's how I'm going to walk up to the guards before I disable them and open this door."

"They'll kill you!"

"They know me! I've been giving them orders for years. Trust me, they won't shoot, not before sorting through their confusion. By then it'll be too late for them."

"You're going to overpower them with a flare gun?"

Her jaw muscles bunched with impatience; he was struck by her beauty, standing up on the ladder in her short black dress, dark hair twisted around her face, eyes fired with passion.

"This is Bangkok, the home of kickboxing. Little girls like me learn to take care of themselves at an early age. Stay here."

Then she scurried up the ladder, slipped into the return air duct like a cat, and was gone.

26

THEY SPENT nearly an hour bouncing between their own shared history and the fantastical nature of Thomas's appearance in Bangkok. Although more than ten years had passed since he'd made the last trip in his dreams, the feeling of being here with Kara and Monique was familiar. It wasn't what he'd imagined a ten-year class reunion might be like.

Then again, these women were not mere classmates.

For them, his appearance was more staggering. In the past, his reality jumping had occurred in his mind while his body remained, making it no less real to him, but far less real to those who watched him sleep.

The four lost books still sat on the lamp table by the door. The cut on his palm was wrapped.

He wondered briefly if they would return him to the future. But he thought so—they seemed to follow a path consistent with the traveler's heart.

"So it's basically true, then," Kara said. "You're saying that Earth's history has essentially replayed itself there and been compressed into twenty-six years?"

"Something like that."

Monique had fallen silent over the past ten minutes, seated with one leg draped over the other, still dressed in her laboratory smock. She cleared her throat.

"All of our history," she said.

"So it seems. Not the particulars, of course. But the similarities are inescapable."

"Think of the implications for our world," she muttered. "So this

212

battle between good and evil is as real here as there. Religion may be misguided on most fronts, but it's sniffing around the right notion."

He nodded. "Exactly." Funny how he'd once been so confused about the whole purpose of history. His understanding of the coming and passing of life had all been so egocentric. Looking beyond oneself to a greater purpose was always so difficult for the average person who lived and died before that purpose found its full meaning.

Now, having lived through so much in such a short span, the purpose of life seemed obvious to him. It was nearly impossible to understand how someone could not believe.

And yet, here he was, two thousand years in the past, searching for a way for the Circle precisely because the Circle had begun to lose sight of the true way. What was once obvious to them was no longer quite as obvious. Why was it that humans lost sight of truth so quickly?

They were like a married couple who celebrated in passionate bliss through the honeymoon, yet found themselves estranged only a few years later. It was no wonder the Roush questioned Elyon's wisdom in creating such fickle beings.

This was the essence of the Books of History: human free will. And it always seemed to lead to disaster.

Monique was speaking again. ". . . a real person. Not just an idea."

"I'm sorry, what was that?"

"Elyon. He's a real person. A real being, not just a symbol for an idea."

He regarded her, not quite sure why she would ask such a basic question. "You were there, you should know."

"Trust me, a lot grows hazy in three decades."

And that was the crux of it, he thought.

Thomas sat down, crossed his legs, and faced them both. He looked out the window behind Monique. It overlooked a jungle, teeming with unseen life, but if he took one step into the brush, that life would become very real.

"So." Eyes back on Monique. "What hope is there in this world that would change the course of the other world?"

"Maybe that's not the right question," Kara said.

"No? Then what?"

"Why is everything always about your world? I realize it's where your mind's at, but look at it from my perspective. Until you left us, you were always from this world. Who's to say what you're going through isn't all for us, not for them?"

"Them? You mean Chelise. And Jake and Samuel and all those that I hold dear?"

"And what am I? A figment of your imagination?"

"No." Dear Elyon, she could be obtuse. He leaned forward. "I'm forever in your debt. But you've lived your life here, and I've found mine there."

"Promise me," she said.

She was demanding to go with him again.

He sat back. "Maybe you're right. So what do you have in mind? Besides going with me."

"The present sounds very similar to the future. Yes, I know, the surfaces are very different. There's no Horde, no Shataiki, no Roush, no Circle . . . at least not by those names. But what we do have is a world in which the faithful have forgotten hope. What if your coming is for them, as a part of our history?"

"I'm not here long enough to give your fools hope."

They just looked at him.

"Okay, that was harsh, but please, my own people are desperate! I'm here only to find what I came for and return. An hour or two. A day at the most. This isn't like before. I have to return quickly!"

Kara took a deep breath and eased back in her chair. "Did you know there's a statue of you on the east side of the White House lawn? White granite. Can you imagine what Washington would think if you walked up that lawn and greeted the president after all these years?"

He stood abruptly. "Out of the question."

"Maybe," Monique joined in. "But trust me, the world would come unglued if you walked out of here, Thomas Hunter, returned from the dead. And the world could use a little hope right now."

"That has nothing to do with me. My son has just joined the Eramites, for the love of Elyon! Let's stay focused."

"In giving you shall receive."

"You're manipulating the situation."

"Are we?" Kara said. "Think about it, Thomas. There's a link between the present and the future, and it isn't just you. It's as real for us as for you. Maybe if you find the answer here, you'll find it for your world."

He had no desire to take one step outside of this room, but maybe there was some truth to what Kara said.

What happened in the histories had always been uniquely tied to what happened in his world. If he could find a way to *alter* this history, he might find the answer for the other.

Then again, that didn't feel right. He sat again, sweating now. "I don't like it," he said.

"Since when did what you like have anything to do with truth?" Monique said. "I haven't liked *it* since you left."

Her words felt like a deserved slap.

"And maybe we're wrong," Kara offered. "But the way I see it, you're here, and as long as you're—"

"I'm not here for long," he insisted. "Just keep that in mind."

"Help us, Thomas," she said. "You changed the world once; do it again."

"That was a long time ago."

The door flew wide and a robed servant rushed in.

A robed servant?

It took Thomas only a moment to see that this was Billy, and that Billy held a nine-millimeter sidearm.

Thomas watched, stunned, as Janae, then Qurong, lumbered in behind, scanning the room.

Billy waved the gun at them. "Back! Stay back!"

Janae's eyes rested on the lost books.

The pieces fell into Thomas's mind and formed a complete picture. Their hands were already cut and bleeding. They'd come for one reason only: to use the lost books.

"Don't move!" Janae snapped again, stepping closer to the stack of books. If they touched the books, they would vanish—with the books.

Thomas held up his hand. "Please . . ."

Janae was the first to dive for the books, followed closely in near frenzy by both Billy and Qurong. Her bloody hand slammed onto the top book and the whole table began to topple, sending the lamp crashing to the floor. Thomas was screaming at his legs to move. *Move! Follow them through; move!* But his legs were frozen.

Janae's hand disappeared, followed by her arm. She was vanishing before their eyes!

But not before Billy and Qurong got their hands on her, clambering to join her in the passage momentarily opened by the books.

It all happened in the space of three—no more than five—beats of Thomas's heart. Janae, then Billy, then Qurong, were swallowed by thin air.

And then they were gone. The space they had just occupied was empty. And the books . . .

The books had vanished with them.

Leaving Thomas stranded in this world, while Billy, this redheaded version of Ba'al, and Janae, the bloodthirsty vampire, and Qurong, enemy of all albinos, returned to ravage Thomas's world.

The blood drained from his face. "Elyon help us," he managed in a thin voice. His whole body shuddered. "Elyon help us all."

27

SAMUEL OF Hunter sat cross-legged on a straw-stuffed cushion before a low table strewn with dates, walnuts, and wheat cakes. Hot tea steamed in small, crudely fashioned glass cups. A servant offered a brown crystalline powdered substance that didn't look familiar to him. He lifted his questioning eyes at Eram, who was watching Samuel and his companions from a reclined position across the table.

"Dried from the sugarcane up north. It makes the tea sweet, much like the blano fruit that the Circle uses."

Samuel dipped his head, and the servant scooped some of the dried sugarcane into his cup using a wooden spoon.

"Go on, taste it."

He sipped on the liquid. Found it entirely pleasant, like much of what he'd seen since coming with his men. They'd ridden in silence with the Eramites deep into northeastern canyonlands, through a massive valley spotted with miggdon figs, to a wide desert plateau that boasted a view in all directions. It was no wonder the Horde had never attempted to take their army against the half-breeds. The Eramites held the high ground.

Samuel raised the cup. "Good."

Eram smiled. "We spare no comforts, boy. None. The Horde may be rich, but we're no worse off. Certainly better than your poor tribes, eh? We have it all here: the prettiest women, the sweetest teas, the most meat, more space than we can use, and above all, freedom. What else could a man want?"

"That's how you view the Circle? Poor?"

"Don't be thick, boy. You're villains on the run, vagabonds who wear scraps for clothing and dance the night away like fools to cover your pain."

The man had a point. Everyone knew albinos were poor, but Samuel had never realized the enemy saw it as a defining characteristic.

Samuel looked around the canvas tent, a semipermanent structure built against a mud-and-straw wall, a combination of Horde and Forest Guard construction. Four women, among them Eram's daughter, leaned against posts or sat on cushions watching them, likely the only albinos who'd ever set foot in the city.

Six warriors stood behind Eram, and another dozen waited outside. Like all Eramites, they were covered in the scabbing disease and wore tunics woven from the same light thread the Horde fashioned from stalks of desert wheat. They ate like the Horde and stank like the Horde.

But that's where the similarities ended. Rather than dreadlocks, their hair was washed and styled in a variety of fashions, both straight and curled. Strange. And strangely pleasant if you looked long enough, particularly the women.

The armor they wore was straight from the traditions of the Forest Guard, lighter than most Horde leathers to prioritize ease of movement over protection. On the trek through the canyons, Samuel saw that many of the warriors chewed a nut of some kind, then spat red into the sand. Seeing his curiosity, one of the soldiers had offered him one and called it a beetle nut. Eaten with lime, it eased muscle pain. The man said it was used only by warriors and only out of the city. Samuel refused a sample.

Their religion paid no homage to Teeleh and in fact used a kind of Circle emblem taken from the Great Romance. The only real difference between Eramite and albino was the Eramites' rejection of the drowning, Elyon's greatest gift. Then again, Samuel sometimes doubted the drowning as well, at least as it pertained to anything more than a hallucinogenic state induced by whatever made the waters red.

"I'm impressed," he said, taking another sip. "You've done well for yourselves out here."

"We've done even better than you can imagine," Eram said.

"And who were you? Before . . ."

"Before the Horde invaded the forests?" Eram exchanged a look with a gray-haired man who stood by a green tapestry on the far wall. "You don't recognize any of us, young Samuel? I guess you were only a boy when we had the seven green lakes to wash away this blasted skin disease, weren't you?"

"So you were part of the Forest Guard."

"That's no secret. We lived with your father before he lost his mind to the red waters. Many of our friends gave their lives for him. Not all have abandoned the struggle, but we've never had an albino among us. Certainly not one of our former leader's own children."

"We're not here to join you," Jacob said.

"No? You wouldn't quite fit in, would you?" Eram turned his eyes to Samuel. "So why are you here?"

Samuel's mind buzzed with a hundred conflicts, but he set them behind the one overriding belief that had brought him to this place. Peace with the Horde would not come by any naive expression of love. They were an enemy who understood only force.

He set his cup down. "Jacob is right. Albinos can't join half-breeds. What kind of children would we make? Half-Horde?"

Someone behind him chuckled and Eram's gray eyes twinkled.

"But we can strike an alliance."

"An alliance?" Eram smiled at his general. "Just what we've been waiting for, eh, Judah? The brilliance we lack found in the minds of four albinos. We should celebrate with a fatted calf."

"Not four," Samuel said.

"No? How many?"

Samuel needed a better understanding of Eram's interest before he divulged that information. Otherwise it could be used against them. "I wouldn't underestimate the skill of albinos in battle. We might be the poor who dance away our troubles around open fires, but we can also dance circles around the Horde."

"Yes, I forgot, you don't have the disease. You're superhumans in battle."

More chuckles.

"Something like that."

The room stilled, and Eram's smile took on a mischievous quality. For a moment Samuel wondered if the man was mad, as some claimed. But what other kind of person would put a death sentence on his head by openly defying Qurong?

"Show Marsal just how superhuman you are."

Samuel heard the faint shuffle of boots on dirt behind him before fully realizing what Eram was asking, but his instincts kicked in at the last moment.

He jerked to his left and brought his right elbow up sharply. It connected with an arm, warding off a blow.

In one smooth motion Samuel grabbed the arm, hefted his shoulder into his assailant's armpit, and pulled down and forward, using the man's own momentum against him.

The body rolled over Samuel's shoulder, and he slipped the man's knife from his belt while the body was above him, then slammed the man onto the table, smashing glass and scattering food.

Samuel leaped to his feet, knife in hand. "Should this superhuman kill your man?"

Before an amused Eram could respond, Samuel flicked the knife to his right. It spun through the air and embedded itself in a post, six inches from the general, who watched with wide gray eyes.

The half-breed named Marsal sprang off the table, ready to go at it again, but Eram held up his hand. "You've made your point."

"I told you we should have slit their throats in the desert," Marsal spat.

"Why?" Eram countered. "So he couldn't make you look like a wounded possum? Back off."

The man turned and walked out of the tent with a grunt.

"Are all albinos so violent?"

Samuel shrugged. "Not all. But not because they aren't capable. You forget—like you, most of them were once warriors. They haven't grown soft in the desert. Some would say the fruit we eat makes us even stronger than the Forest Guard once was. Certainly quicker. You be the judge."

"Sit."

Samuel glanced behind, then sat.

"So." The Eramite leader put his elbow on the table, picked up a spilled miggdon fig, and bit into its dry flesh. "I'm listening."

"The Circle isn't as united as it once was," Samuel said. "Many have grown weary of running from an unrelenting enemy while they wait for a day that never comes. There are those ready to join me if I could give them a new hope. It may be the same for you."

Eram spat out some unwanted skin. "Go on."

"We may not have the strength to mount our own offensive against the Horde, but can make life difficult for them."

"Guerrilla warfare," Eram said. "This is your ingenious thought?"

"Ambushes may not excite half-breeds—you don't have the skills for it. You may be faster than the Horde, but you don't have the same advantage that even a few dozen albinos under my command would have. Imagine what I could do with a few hundred. Twenty or thirty well-placed teams to hit them from every side, every other day. Like hornets turning a bull's skin raw."

The leader said nothing, and that was enough encouragement for Samuel to lean into his convictions.

"Think about it. The Forest Guard has always assumed a defensive posture against the Horde's attacks. The Horde has never faced a direct attack. It would force them into a defensive posture that would keep their Throaters home and cripple their efforts to pursue the enemy, both albino and Eramite."

The tent had gone silent. Eram chewed slowly on his fig.

"What he says has merit," the general said.

"How many men will follow you?"

"I don't know. What we don't get at first will come after word of our success spreads."

"A new Hunter comes out of the desert," Eram said. "The new generation with a new answer. Is that it?"

"Something like that."

The leader pushed himself to his feet, wiped his hand on his pants, and walked toward the tent wall behind him. "Let me show you something."

Samuel followed him as he walked to a window and pulled up the canvas flap. He stepped aside and invited Samuel to take a look.

The tent sat on the edge of a large canyon cut from the plateau, a formation easy to miss from most vantage points. The floor ran at least several miles before opening to the northern desert, and as far as Samuel could see, the valley was covered by tents, not the domestic homes that filled the city. These were the tents the Forest Guard had once used in battle.

This was Eram's army.

Then Samuel saw movement. A sea of what he'd first thought to be rocks shifted several miles downwind. Horses in formation. More than could be counted.

"Do you think we've been sitting on our hands all of these years?" Eram asked.

Samuel was taken off guard by the sheer size of the army.

"How many?" Petrus asked.

"All told, one hundred fifty. Thousand."

"So many," Samuel said.

"More than the Forest Guard at its strongest, gathered from all seven forests. They are men, women, anyone of fighting age who is half-breed and possesses the will to retake our homeland."

Samuel's pulse pounded. "Why haven't you?"

"Gone against Qurong's army? All in good time, my friend. We're still vastly outnumbered. Qurong's army is greater than five hundred thousand. We go when there will be no chance of failure." He drew a breath. "Zero," he said.

"That time could be sooner than you think," Samuel said.

"Why wake the sleeping bear before its time?"

"Don't underestimate what we can do for each other."

"How so?"

Samuel no longer had anything to lose.

"What if I could bring you elite fighters able to defeat ten Horde with a single blade? I'm talking about a new kind of Forest Guard capable of holding the flank or ravaging an army's backside as you take it head-on."

"Yes, so you've said—"

"I'm not talking about four. Or forty."

No response.

"What if I could bring you four hundred?"

This time Eram stared over the massive canyon filled with his army in serene silence. When he spoke there was a new respect in his voice.

"Then you will be a legend among the Eramites."

28

THE FIRST thing Billy noticed when he opened his eyes in the other earth—the future earth—was that he was exactly the same person as he'd been a moment ago, before diving into the book behind Janae. Same jeans, same T-shirt, same hands, same pounding heart.

The second thing he noticed in this future was that he, Janae, and Qurong had followed the books into the same location as Janae's last journey here, the visit she had paid in her dreams. They were in Ba'al's study, staring in wonder at the ease with which they had crossed realities.

Of course. The books take you where you think you belong. In some strange way, I am Ba'al. Or at least someone who identifies with Ba'al.

But in other ways, he was nothing like Ba'al.

Ba'al's journal, his blood book, lay on the desk beside him. This one book held the secrets to more than he could recall from his short time in the dark priest's mind. He picked up the ancient book.

"It worked," Qurong said, looking at his hands. "We . . . we're back."

"You doubted us?" Billy asked.

"I think you meant to leave me," the leader said, heading for the door.

"Where are you going?"

"Where I belong as the ruler of this world," Qurong replied, turning back.

"Is that what you think? Teeleh is the ruler of this world."

It struck Billy then that he couldn't read the man's mind. Or the mind of Janae, who was staring at the bloodstained altar upon which sat the lost books. Now that he was here in the flesh, his gift no longer worked? But the vials of virus had come through, surely. And the gun?

"I mean no offense," he said. "But we have to regroup here and think through what just happened."

"Nothing happened," Qurong said. He resumed his march for the door. "Nightmares are not for me to understand."

"It wasn't a nightmare," Janae snapped. She'd come to herself, and he saw that she'd had the presence of mind to shove the gun into the pocket of her lab coat. But where were the vials?

"There's more at stake here than your little kingdom, you fool."

"Easy, Janae," Billy breathed. This wasn't their world, not yet.

She blinked, then visibly relaxed. "All I'm saying is that the world you were just in is real. Everything you heard was true."

Qurong held his hand on the door latch. "Such as?"

"Such as the fact that you're surrounded by enemies. The Eramites, the albinos, Ba'al . . ."

"And two albino witches from another world are here to save me, is that it?"

"We have a few tricks up our sleeves, yes," Billy said. "You've already forgotten?"

"The weapons," Qurong said. "Am I blind, or do I see nothing? Show me."

Janae glanced at Billy, then pulled out the gun.

"Of course," Qurong said. "The blunt knife you claim can throw steel. I'm quaking in my boots. This is what I'm supposed to slaughter the Eramites with?"

"No. The virus is for that."

"And it didn't come through," Billy finished.

Janae glanced at him. Surely she would take his cue, knowing that turning anything over to Qurong now only stripped them of their leverage.

"But that means nothing," Janae said. "The point is, we are of tremendous value to you."

"How?"

"We can use the books, go back, retrieve whatever we like."

"I'm not impressed." Qurong opened the door and left the room, leaving them alone in Ba'al's study.

Interesting that he left the books behind. Surely the man wasn't as dense as he appeared. Billy shoved Ba'al's journal behind his belt, pulled his T-shirt over the cover, and scooped up the four volumes. "Just go easy. We have to figure things out."

"What we have to do is get out of this place. We don't belong with these people."

"And go where?"

Her eyes shifted, and he suspected she knew as well as he did. If so, she wasn't admitting it. "I don't know yet," she said. "But I didn't come here to hang out with these fools."

"Did you think they would be gone? That this was Paradise?"

"Why the hostility? The last thing we need now is to start at each other. The fact of the matter is, we have more power than they can possibly imagine. We just have to figure out how to use it."

"The virus came through," he guessed.

She felt the side of her bra. "Unless they insist on an intrusive strip search, it's safe enough. This, on the other hand"—she put the gun back into her coat pocket—"doesn't scare anyone."

"It will once they know what it can do."

"That's right, Billy. Knowledge." She stabbed her temple with a pointed finger. "What we *know* is our greatest weapon."

Fair enough.

"Why did you come here, Janae?"

She stared at him, peeling back the layers. "You can't read my mind?"

"Not in this place."

She sighed as if this was to be expected, and headed into the dark hallway Qurong had entered. "For the same reason as you, Billy. I came to find myself."

Billy followed her, thinking she was right: they didn't belong here. Not in the temple, not in the city. His destiny rested with another, a Shataiki named Marsuuv, who lived in the Black Forest. The memories he'd taken from Ba'al while in his body were now faint, but three crucial elements drummed through his mind without reprieve:

There was a part of him that wasn't of the natural world.

His destiny was irrevocably linked to a queen named Marsuuv.

Everything that had happened, from the birth of evil to the Raison Strain to the coming apocalypse, was all his doing, because he'd not only started it all, he was going to finish it all.

Billy, the redhead from Paradise, Colorado, was the first and the last. The beginning and the end.

He was ground zero.

No, a small voice suggested somewhere in his brain, *Thomas is ground zero. You're just trying to catch up.*

But he knew that wasn't the truth. At the very least, they were both ground zero. Two sides of humanity. Take your pick.

Billy and Janae walked down a dark hall and peered into a large sanctuary filled with images of the winged serpent, Teeleh. Another altar, like the one in Ba'al's study, sat at the center of the room, still glistening with blood.

Billy stepped past Janae, overwhelmed by awe and the full impact of the room's icons: The black candles, spewing smoke into the air. The brass images of Teeleh on the altar. Long velvet curtains on all the walls, emblazoned with the same three claw marks that they all wore on their foreheads, this mark of the beast.

Familiarity hit Billy with the force of a punch to his chest. He'd found his way home.

He looked over his shoulder and saw that Janae's jaw was parted. She felt it too, didn't she? She knew more than she was saying. Or at least felt more.

He walked into the room on light feet, as though the stone floor was holy ground easily defiled. They'd crossed the centuries and were standing in the sanctuary of an exotic religion that worshipped the same being who'd made him Billy.

He touched the altar, impressed by the silky surface of the stone— was it granite? Perhaps marble?

Ba'al had been in the presence of Marsuuv, Teeleh's queen, and the memory played at the edge of Billy's mind like a pied piper.

"We made it, Billy," Janae breathed.

"Put the books on the altar," a voice rasped behind them.

Ba'al.

Billy turned slowly, having no intention of setting the books anywhere. Then he saw Qurong, standing with arms crossed behind Ba'al, who'd evidently been waiting for them, and he knew they had made a terrible mistake.

"Back off," Janae snapped. She waved the gun at them. "Stay where you are or I swear I'll blow both of your heads off."

Ba'al had tasted Billy's own thoughts, but clearly nothing about guns had surfaced during his short visit. He walked forward, fearlessly. "She said, back off!"

"Then blow my head off!" Ba'al snapped. "Use your toy and kill me if it be Teeleh's will. But know that I am his servant. Marsuuv is a jealous beast who has no patience for albinos who threaten holy men with toys."

His argument wasn't lost on Janae, whose aim faltered.

"Good to see you again, Ba'al," Billy said. "Or should I call you Billos?"

"Call me what you like. I am who I am."

"And so are we, two lovers of Teeleh. Show us how to find him and we'll leave you."

"These two are liars who could lure a snake into bed and bite its head off," Qurong said. "Don't listen to them."

Ba'al walked around them, smiling. "Snakes, are you?"

"No," Billy said. "But we belong to one, and his name is Teeleh."

"So you keep saying. We'll find out soon enough. In this very room. Set the books on the altar and step away."

"I can't do that."

"No? You, of all people, should know why you must do it. You've been inside of my mind and know that I've searched for those books for a very long time. Marsuuv compels me to take them to Teeleh. You would stand in the way of his queen?"

A quandary.

"Give me the books and I will let Teeleh have you," Ba'al said.

"Shoot him, Janae. Kill this weasel now. Put a bullet between his eyes and end his miserable life before . . ."

Click.

Billy blinked. Was that what it sounded like?

Click, click, click.

"It doesn't work," Janae cried. She pulled the trigger again with no better results.

"Why should it work?" Ba'al asked. "If your eyes were opened you might see Shataiki claws at work this very moment, protecting Marsuuv's lover. Please, throw down this useless tool. Lay the books on the altar. It is my last invitation."

Billy hesitated only a moment, then set the books down carefully. If Ba'al was telling the truth, he would take them to Teeleh rather than use them. Perhaps it was best for all of them.

"Tell us how to find him."

"You don't find Teeleh, he finds you. Go out into the forest and call his name. Trust me, he's always there, watching." Ba'al lifted the books and stepped to one side. "Thank you." He headed for the door that led to his study. "Dispose of them as you like."

"What of this virus they speak about?" Qurong asked.

"Yes, of course." Ba'al turned, but his mind was clearly on the books in his hands, Billy thought. "Strip them, search them. I'll instruct my priests to sacrifice them tonight when the moon wanes."

"I would be more comfortable if you were to oversee their execution."

"I won't be here. My master compels me. It is the end, my lord. The great dragon's time has come."

Billy's breathing had stalled.

"They are crafty," Qurong said, frowning.

"They'll be dead tonight, my lord. I swear it."

29

QURONG WALKED down the hall, stormed into the atrium at the front of his home, and shrugged out of his robe before he passed into the dining room. "Get me my general!" he boomed. "Now."

The robe dropped to the floor, where one of the servants would retrieve and wash it of the stink that came from his nightmare. Thomas's reputation as a wizard was well-known. Even as the commander of the Forest Guard, he'd possessed an uncanny ability to appear and vanish at will, along with his army on occasion.

But this! Deceiving Qurong with the illusion that he was in another reality was a talent surely no other man had.

"Where's Cassak? Get him now. In my quarters!"

He didn't care who heard him, only that he was heard. A shuffling of feet preceded the fleeting image of a servant fleeing the dining room.

"Hello, my love." He turned to Patricia, who leaned against the hall entryway to his left, still dressed in her night robe. She crossed her arms and ran her eyes down his body. "You're either feeling frisky this morning or you've lost your mind."

He glanced down at his half-naked body and swore. "I should have killed that albino ten years ago when I had the chance."

Patricia walked to the table and picked up a piece of yellow nanka. "He's escaped?"

"Of course not." But Qurong suspected that Thomas had indeed given him the slip. He'd taken Thomas to his private library, where the witch had somehow put him under with a spell. The next thing he knew, he was popping out of the vision in the Thrall with two equally evil albinos, whom he'd turned over to Ba'al.

"I've released him," Qurong said.

"You've released Thomas," she repeated scornfully. "You have no right to make these kinds of unilateral decisions!"

What on earth was she talking about? How dare she question his authority.

"She's my daughter too," Patricia snapped.

"Daughter? I've been tricked by a conniving witch and all you can think about is a daughter you haven't seen for ten years?"

"I waited up for you all night, you thickheaded bull! Who am I, your servant?"

"Silence!"

"Don't you silence me, Tanis."

He felt his veins run cold. She knew how he loathed his ancient name.

"I spent the night alone in the darkness, alone because both my husband and my daughter have left me," she said. "Fine, Qurong. Be the big, strong hero for all your people to see. But don't toy with my heart."

"*Now* what have I done?" he demanded. Only a woman could make so much out of so little. Give them a single fact and they'd fashion it into a story before taking a single breath. "I've just spent the night in a hellacious trance. My kingdom's falling down around my ears, and you scold me?"

"Don't try to distract me with more tales of how close we all are to the day of doom, Husband." She took a deep breath and gripped both hands tightly, a very bad sign indeed. "I want you to find my daughter," she said. "I want to speak to Chelise."

She turned and strode toward the kitchen hallway. "The next person I speak to with Qurong's blood will be my daughter." At the door, she shot him a daggered stare. "And don't bother coming to my bed." Then she was gone.

Qurong stood rooted in complete befuddlement. Surely she had to know his heart, that he was as bothered by Chelise's absence as she, that he'd lived in misery since her departure. He tried to inoculate himself with bitterness and denial, and that had helped for a while, but even his obsession with finding and eliminating the Circle was for her sake. He would slaughter this cult of fanatics who'd brainwashed her.

He talked about not having a daughter, but only to protect Patricia and himself. This was required of a strong leader forced to make hard choices in times of war.

"Cassak!" he roared.

"Here, sir."

Qurong spun to see his general standing in the doorway. How much had he heard? It didn't matter. Qurong had more pressing matters to tend to. So he told himself, but he'd learned long ago that nothing was as pressing as his wife's peace of mind. He would rather go to war with Eram than face down Patricia.

He spat to one side and marched into the hall that led to his bedroom. "Follow me."

He couldn't think about bringing Chelise here now. He didn't even know how to find her! And what would he say? *Your father has finally come to his senses—please, let's be a family again?*

She was *albino*, for the love of Teeleh!

Meanwhile, Ba'al was conspiring to overthrow him. Qurong couldn't be sure of everything about Thomas's magic, but it had revealed a thing or two, and he wouldn't ignore the warnings.

"My lord?" Cassak was hurrying to keep pace behind him.

Qurong entered his room and stripped out of his undergarments. He needed to cleanse himself of the albino stench before leaving the palace. This time he would welcome the pain of bathing.

"Sir."

"Yes, Cassak. Close the door." Qurong grabbed a fresh tunic from the end of the bed. He pulled it on and faced the general.

"Tell me how much I can trust you."

Cassak hesitated. "I am your servant, my lord, not Ba'al's. If you were to order me to kill him, I would."

So then, Cassak was aware of the threat as well. Was it so obvious?

"I wouldn't issue such an order, but I accept your loyalty. What I am about to tell you cannot leave this room."

"Of course not, my lord."

Qurong walked to the window overlooking the western city. More than two million Horde lived in Qurongi City; of those, over a quarter were males of fighting age, trained in combat as required of all adult men. But no sign of impending war was evident in the sprawling city with its mud huts and smoky chimneys.

His subjects had grown fat off the forests; rich, even. Little did they know the mounting threat from the desert.

"Prepare the army." He swung around. "Send word that we will march north to the Torun Valley for training exercises."

"Consider it done. It will be good to take our third division out; they've grown fat."

"Take everyone," Qurong said. "Including the temple guard."

Cassak blinked. "I'm not sure I understand. A training mission that size has never been attempted."

"All of them! North. Within the week." He glanced at the door, then back. "I want them well fed, hydrated, armed, and ready for a full-scale assault at my command."

Understanding filtered into Cassak's eyes. "Then it's not a training mission."

"Recall our scouts from the northern desert and debrief them. Send out six teams of Throaters with orders to infiltrate the Eramite city and report back by week's end." He paced. "I want to know numbers, strengths, weaknesses. How many children, how many women. Weapons. Morale. Anything that has changed in the last few months."

"A week isn't enough time—"

"It's all we have."

"You're saying you plan on invading within the week?"

"I'm saying I want to be ready to crush the infidels within a week. Sooner if I decide."

Now Cassak was quiet. The order was unprecedented. Not since the invasion of the forests had the Horde fought a full-scale war, and even then they'd never committed all of their assets to one front.

Qurong kept his voice low. "The war drums are beating, Cassak. Samuel, son of Hunter, is uniting Eramite and albino forces with the intention of undercutting us."

"I didn't know the albinos had a force."

"They don't, but it's not for lack of strength. Their will is weak, but that could change. I don't intend to give them that chance."

Cassak nodded and joined him by the window. "I agree. Eram is a thorn to be rooted out. But one week? What's the rush?"

"Ba'al's the rush. He's on his way to some cursed Black Forest now, and if I'm not mistaken, he has ambitions of his own."

"So we move before he can get his prickly fingers into our business."

"And we take his own little army with us."

His general regarded him with a crooked smile. "I was going to say that the dark priest is a snake, but now I should say that about you."

"I never claimed to be a serpent. And I don't think Teeleh would be too upset if Ba'al were his only loss in a war that destroyed the half-breeds and the albinos together."

"Agreed, sir."

Qurong nodded. "I also want you to send out three of our best scouts into the west with flags of truce." He sighed, not eager to pass on the order. "Tell them to find Chelise."

Cassak stared as if he'd heard wrong. "Impossible. We can't just *find* the Circle."

"No, but they can pass word for Chelise to meet her mother in the Torun Valley in four days. She will come."

"They could ambush the queen, my lord. This isn't safe!"

"I thought you said they're a peaceful bunch." Qurong grabbed a bowl of morst for his skin and headed toward the door. "Just do it. And there're two albinos in Ba'al's dungeon, scheduled for execution tonight. See to it that they both stay dead."

"Sir?"

Qurong turned back. "Dead, Cassak. I want them both dead."

∞

THE ONLY reason the search didn't leave them naked was the guard's ignorance that anything so small as a vial hidden under the band of Janae's undergarments could do any damage. This and the Horde's general disgust for albino flesh. Maybe if Qurong had overseen the search, Ba'al's journal in Billy's underwear and the precious vials would have been found.

Their situation was simple and dire. Billy and Janae's advantage was worthless in the dungeon below the Thrall where they awaited execution at nightfall. The ten cells ran along a tunnel lit only by a single torch near the heavy wooden door to freedom. All were empty except for the one they occupied, but the stench of urine and sweat crowded the small space.

"Still there?" Janae demanded, bunched up in one corner.

Billy pressed his face between two bars and peered down the passage where two priests stood guard. He pulled back and paced the straw floor.

"Well?"

"Yes," he whispered.

"Don't these animals ever use the bathroom?"

They couldn't tell what time of day it was, but nightfall had to be fast approaching.

Billy bent down and uncovered the items he'd hidden under straw in the corner. A vial of Raison Strain B. A vial of one of the most potent, nonbiogenetically engineered viruses, Asian Ebola, responsible for over a million deaths the decade before a vaccine was developed. A third vial contained Thomas's blood. Janae had lined her bra with all three in Bangkok.

The last item was Ba'al's journal. The blood book.

They considered calling the guards over and trying both viruses on them. But Billy and Janae didn't know what the results would be and would surely tip their hand. Regardless, the guards had refused to come after repeated calls.

Still, within half an hour of exploring their cell, they landed on a simple means of escape. The lock.

A brief examination of the crude metal lock revealed it to be an archaic thing with a rudimentary mechanism. She was convinced that she could pick it using nothing more than the underwire from her bra, which she'd already removed.

They would still have to contend with the two guards at the end of the hall. And once out of the dungeon, they had to escape the Thrall and then the city.

Billy had pored over Ba'al's writings in the dim light, filling in the numerous blanks between the memories he'd taken from Ba'al earlier. The collection of writings carefully outlined hundreds of details from numerous sources about this world, but the sections that Billy read and reread as the hours passed related to the Thrall and Marsuuv's Black Forest.

Ba'al had sketched the Thrall's basic blueprint, which showed a back door just beyond the dungeon's entry. If they could get past the guards and climb the steps to the atrium unnoticed, he was sure they could escape the Thrall.

And once out of the Thrall, their course was clear.

"That's it," Janae snapped, rising. "We have to go now, before they come for us."

"Slow down, we only get one shot at this! Keep your voice down."

Her face wrinkled as if she was going to cry. "We have to go, Billy," she begged. "We're going to run out of time! Do you hear me? This is going to get us killed!"

She looked to be on the edge of her own sanity. He had no shortage of urgency himself, but Janae looked like she was on the verge of a breakdown.

She scratched at a rash that had sprung up on her right arm. Only then did it occur to him that his lower back had begun to itch as well. *Rash.* Surely, it had to do with lice or something in this cursed place.

He imagined larvae crawling through their skin. Worms. He'd had his fill of them already.

Billy shivered and snatched up the artifacts. "Okay. Try to spring the lock, but keep it quiet." She was already at the gate, her frantic hands fiddling. "But wait until I say; just try to get the lock open."

She spun back, and held up the sprung lock. "Simple."

So fast? She'd obviously messed with locks in her time. He hurried forward and handed her the vials. "Hide these."

Janae grabbed the small glass containers and stuffed them back into the sides of her bra. Her skin was milky white, and he saw now that the rash wasn't only on her arm but on her belly and neck.

An unreasonable fear slammed into his mind. Déjà vu. He'd been in this situation before, far below a monastery. The worms there had been much larger, but he was now certain that they'd come from Shataiki. He and Janae should wait—they should proceed with extreme caution, but he wanted nothing more than to be out of this cage, guards or no guards.

Billy brushed past her, pulled open the gate, and slipped into the dark hall. His recklessness was an impulsive, irrational reaction to the fear, and he knew it even as he faced the guards down the tunnel, but by then it was too late.

They stared back at him as if he were a ghost.

"I appeal to the power of Marsuuv, queen of the twelfth forest," Billy said, marching forward. Never mind that he was a bare-chested albino; he had knowledge that no ordinary man, Horde or albino, should have, and he intended to use it now. Janae was breathing hard behind him.

Billy lifted the blood journal. "My maker, Marsuuv, with the blackest heart compels you—bring Ba'al and I will speak for my lord."

Ba'al was gone, Billy knew that. The guards yanked out their daggers and crouched, but they didn't sound an alarm. "Back," one cried in a hoarse voice.

Billy stopped no more than six feet from the guards and spread both arms wide. A surge of power swept over him with surprising force. More then adrenaline. There was a power in the air.

He tilted his chin up and spoke with as much authority as he could muster. When his voice came, it sounded like that of an old man, but it carried a power that shook his bones.

"I am born of Black; I am eaten with worms. My place is with my lover and my master, who waits for me in the twelfth forest with Teeleh. Any man who touches my servant will die."

He could barely breathe, so powerful were his words. A wave of power rolled down his spine, and he knew, as he'd never known before, that he was close, so close to being home. The fact that home resembled hell more than any utopia hardly mattered.

He belonged. This was his destiny.

A cry and a *whoosh* of air startled him out of his reverie. Janae had taken the dagger from one guard and slashed his neck. She was now thrusting that same blade at the second guard, moving with unnatural speed. She, too, seemed empowered beyond herself.

She thrust the long dagger straight through his belly, pinning him to a beam. Janae held his body there for a moment, then released it and stepped back, panting.

"Okay, then," Billy breathed. And for a long moment neither said anything else.

Janae absently wiped her mouth with the back of her hand, smearing it with blood. She licked her lips and swallowed, eyes still on her handiwork, perhaps unaware of what she'd just tasted.

She finally faced him, eyes wide. "The twelfth forest?"

Billy swallowed. "Marsuuv's forest. My forest. It's where the dark priest has taken the lost books."

Janae spun and started up the steps. "Then we have to go."

"Wait."

She didn't wait. "We have to go now!"

"Wait!" he spat. "You need to cover up. We'll dress in these priests' clothes first."

She turned and stared down at the bodies. After a moment she began to strip the clothes off the first guard she'd killed. The bloodier of the two.

They both dressed quickly and slid the daggers into their belts. With any luck they would pass through the city under cover of darkness and be free.

"How far?" she asked.

The Black Forest. "Three days. Maybe two if we don't stop."

"Then we can't stop."

He thought about objecting, thinking he should be rational. Better to be cautious and live than die rushing over a cliff. But he couldn't deny his own desire.

"Agreed," he said.

Janae suddenly turned to him, wrapped her arms around his body, pulled him tight, and kissed him on the lips. "Billy . . ." She kissed him hungrily, smearing the guard's blood on his mouth, breathing through her nose. "Thank you, Billy."

Her teeth bit into his lip, drawing blood. Strangely, he found it natural. This was how Shataiki mated, wasn't it? He wasn't sure of the mechanics, but he knew it had to do with the passing of blood. And this . . .

This small expression of affection was merely foreplay, he thought.

Then Janae pulled away and hurried up the steps, hiking her robe so as not to trip on the long garment, like a maiden rushing up the tower stairs to meet her prince.

30

A FULL DAY had passed since the books vanished with Billy, Janae, and Qurong. Thomas spent half of it wearing the carpet thin.

His first reaction had been to deny what his eyes told him. The books were there on the table by the door, and the redheaded witch, who was one with Ba'al, was securely locked up. But then Billy was in the library, and in the books, and gone.

The lost books, vanished. He'd rushed to the table and slammed his hand down, as if by force he could bring them back. Slowly the bitter truth dried his mouth. His only way back was gone.

Following an urgent discussion, Kara and Monique appeared eager to reassure him. He was here for a purpose, Monique kept saying. It would work out, Kara agreed, but she wasn't disappointed that they were together. He should embrace this turn of events for his own sake, she suggested. For the sake of the world.

Their words fell on deaf ears, because Thomas could only think about Chelise now. An hour later, unable to shake the haunting of her face, he'd asked to be alone so that he could clear his head.

He'd been separated from his lover many times, and though he always missed her, he'd never been cut off from her. There was always a path home into the arms of the one woman he'd come to depend on more than anything else in his world.

In fact, it wasn't until now, stranded, that he realized just how much he needed her. He glanced at the empty table again, dropped his head into both hands, and held back his emotion.

He'd once lost those he held closest, and the notion of suffering through it again was too much. What if he never saw her again? What if he'd been returned to this world to finish whatever business awaited him here? What if this was the end of the other world for him?

Panic crowded his mind.

The white bat's order whispered to him. *Go to the place you came from. Make a way for the Circle to fulfill its hope. And return quickly before it's too late. Do that and you might save your son.*

The same could surely be said for Chelise. Images of his bride swelled in his mind's eye.

He recalled the time she'd rushed out to meet him with Jake thrown over her shoulder like a bundle of firewood. "Look, Thomas!" She dropped their son onto his seat and stood back. "Show him, Jake. Show him what you can do." Jake wobbled to his feet and began to walk. How the boy managed to stay upright was a mystery still, bobbing and weaving and crossing his feet like a drunken stork.

They'd danced late that night and exhausted themselves in passionate expressions of love. Thomas had always been the impulsive one, given to zeal over reason, but next to Chelise he was the calm leader. After all, he was more than ten years older and had commanded armies. It only made sense that he would begin to settle down.

He remembered the time he'd tasked his elder daughter, Marie, with teaching Chelise everything there was to know about hand-to-hand combat. Like in the days of old, their fighting arts resembled a choreographed dance, thrusting and sparring with ferocity, but always for the precision and beauty of it, not with Horde in mind.

After only a month, Chelise and Marie performed by the fire for the whole tribe to see. Marie's skills were finely tuned, unmatched at the time. But Chelise . . .

His throat knotted, remembering: Her toned legs cutting through the air in an airborne roundhouse kick that showed her stunning grace. Landing nimbly on her feet, like a cat, then flipping into three consecutive back handsprings. The way her hair swirled around her face, her fiery green eyes, the cries from her throat. She reminded him of his first wife, and lying in bed that night, he'd wept.

Chelise had asked him what was wrong, and when he'd finally confessed, she'd wept with him. For him. He'd never thought of another woman, dead or alive, since.

How many times had Thomas walked through the meadow with Chelise, hand in hand, listening to her enthusiasm on whatever subject had ignited her that day? She'd never been shy of her passion, and if her aim was ever off, she would eventually acknowledge her overexuberance on the matter, though usually in soft, mumbled words.

"But don't be mad," she would say before kissing him. "I'm just learning."

She'd been learning how to be the wife of Thomas of Hunter, supreme commander of the Forest Guard, for ten years now, but as he often told whoever was gathered about the fire, it was he, Thomas of Hunter, servant of Elyon, who was learning from Chelise.

Not that she wasn't also teaching him other things, he would say with a grin. Who could light up a tent like Chelise? Who could lighten a load with a single giggle? Who else could master fighting techniques in only one month? Was there a more perfect vision of a bride in the whole of the Great Romance?

Then he would excuse himself to find his bride. They had unfinished business. Thomas and Chelise *always* had unfinished business. And at no time had he been so aware of just how unfinished their business was as now.

He remained alone in the library for an hour, allowing his self-pity to numb his mind. When no amount of focus presented an immediate solution, he headed out and found both Kara and Monique seated in the hall, waiting for him.

It was Kara's idea to help settle him by taking him into the city. He rejected the idea of leaving the library, where the books would hopefully return. But after a moment of argument, he saw that Kara was right.

He had to clear his mind. Bathe. Get into some clean clothes.

He'd forgotten how luxurious hot running water could feel on the skin, and he let it wash away the lingering Horde stench until the water turned cold. To his surprise, Monique had held on to some of his clothes, among other memories. The jeans weren't as loose as a tunic, but both Kara and Monique insisted they fit him perfectly.

The shirt fit tightly over his chest muscles; too tight, they agreed with sly smiles. Much too tight. Had he been doing pushups? No, hefting boulders.

He sat in the back of a Mercedes with Kara and Monique, and the driver drove them through Bangkok. They made five stops; at each one, more memories flooded his mind. The smells of frying pork rolls; the sound of a thousand cars diving for the same intersection, with blaring horns; the taste of a Cadbury milk-chocolate bar.

And albinos. Everywhere he looked, hundreds, thousands of albinos of every imaginable race. The world had truly become a melting pot in his absence. The word *albino* meant something entirely different here, but he'd embraced the meaning used in his world.

As he saw the city, however, the realization that he was a stranger here became more and more obvious to him. The sights and smells and sounds were familiar, but they no longer felt welcoming.

He belonged in a desert spotted by forests under Horde rule. He belonged in the Circle, rallying the followers of Elyon when the clarity of their purpose waned.

He belonged in the arms of Chelise.

"Take me back," Thomas finally begged. "It's too much."

Monique ordered the driver home. Thomas fell into bed without bothering to change, begged Elyon to save him, and dropped into the embrace of his second lover. Dreams.

But even as he dreamed of his true home, he knew the visions were only imaginations of the mind. Fanciful thinking liberated by REM sleep. Not the reality-shifting dreams that had first taken him to the future so many years ago.

He rose with the new day, showered long again, dressed in the black

slacks and white shirt Monique had laid out, pulled on what he'd been
told were a pair of fashionable black shoes, and emerged from his guest
quarters with a determination to embrace the reality handed to him.

Monique and Kara assured him that he was looking a thousand per-
cent better. The comment only made him think of Chelise. What would
she say to these ridiculous duds? Then again, she might find them alluring and insist he wear them at the celebration that very night.

"We have something you should see," Monique said as the servants
cleared the table of breakfast. "It might give you new insight."

Half an hour later, he peered into the microscope in the underground lab. "Larvae?" His breathing thickened at the sight of microscopic worms. "This is incredible."

"They cause the scabbing disease. Any ideas where they come from?"

Thomas straightened. "Teeleh. It's said that the Shataiki come from
larvae, or some say worms. But . . ." He bowed for another look. Tiny
white larvae wiggled in and out of the flesh sample, feeding on it. This
was the root cause of the Horde's skin disease.

"Elyon's water must kill them," he said.

Kara cleared her throat. "So Qurong, who was just here, was covered
in these things?"

"Being covered in microscopic organisms is nothing new," Monique
said. "We all live with constant, unseen companions."

"But this . . ." Kara said, "these worms are evil incarnate. Evil made
visible, not unseen, like here."

She might as well have hit him with a hammer. He'd been overlooking the most obvious connection between the present and the future, but
here under the microscope it became as clear as spring water.

"The difference between our worlds is plain," he said, grappling
with how to make what was plain also understandable—a monumental
task at times. "It's right here in front of us all!"

"What is?"

"Evil! The worms! Teeleh."

"And?"

"And?" Thomas absently turned his hands into fists and shook them as if to seize the point. "You see how obvious the truth is when you see it with your own eyes? So many people doubt evil exists as a force beyond just the mind!"

"Not all, but—"

"'Out of sight, out of mind,' isn't that what we once said? You forget about evil until it visits your doorstep."

"Yes. What are you driving at?"

Wasn't it obvious? No. Which only reinforced his point.

"The primary difference between my world and yours is the nature of the spiritual reality, yes? There, the spiritual has a physical form, so we can actually see it. The scabbing disease is actually Shataiki larvae, infesting the skin and the mind. I'm sure you'll find these in the Scabs' brains as well. Elyon has placed his power in his waters—again, that's a physical incarnation. Do you follow?"

"Yes. We've already talked about all that."

"But my point is the converse: Just because you don't see something doesn't mean it's not there. It takes certain instruments to see what is real." He motioned to the microscope. "We become so used to the familiar that we begin to doubt the unfamiliar, until our eyes are opened and we *see*. One second it's Horde flesh, the next a breeding ground for Shataiki larvae."

"Makes sense," Kara said. "It's not a new idea."

"Nothing is new," he said. "But it's a reminder. Just because you can't see something doesn't mean it's not real."

They stared at each other, and Kara finally nodded. "So then maybe this is it. This is your message to your world."

31

THE JOURNEY back to Paradose Valley, where the Circle waited, was taking too long. Not longer than ordinary, but far too long to relieve Chelise's growing desperation.

Thomas had vanished, for the love of Elyon, just vanished! She couldn't shake the image of his and her father's sudden disappearance. And she had no word of Samuel except Thomas's plea, echoing through her mind: *Save the Circle, Chelise! Save them from Samuel!*

But she felt powerless to save herself, much less the Circle. To say she was despondent understated the sickness now eating away at her soul. Tears brought no relief.

She whipped her horse and drove it through the dark forest, ducking branches that crowded her passage. *Elyon, please, if you're there . . .* She hardly knew what to say any longer. The Circle had been crying at the skies for so many years and had what to show for it? More death. More running. And now this, betrayal of the most unnerving kind.

Maybe Samuel was right.

She caught herself and cursed her own weakness. How could she, who'd drowned and found new life, question the reality of Elyon now just because the world was dark?

Because it is dark, she thought. *All hope seems lost! My lover Thomas is gone. And my lover Elyon is quiet.*

Where was the light now? Where was even a hint of hope? How could Elyon allow them to enter such a wasteland? She was alone on this steed, blind in a world sinking into despair.

Chelise broke into a clearing and urged the horse to run faster through the grass. Tall dark trees loomed ahead, reaching for a black—

She started. A bundle of white sat perched high upon one of the trees. A living bundle of fur. With wings.

In her shock, Chelise failed to pull the horse to a halt. This was a Roush, one of the legendary creatures. It had been ten years since she'd seen one, so long she'd given up hope of ever seeing one again in the flesh. Yet here was one!

She yanked back on the reins, brought the horse to a heaving stand-still, and stared. The creature stared back, unaffected. Its green eyes were bright despite the darkness. Resolute. Absolute.

It's true. They've been here the whole time, she thought, and hope flamed deep in her chest.

She tried to speak, to say something, anything, but emotion stopped her up, and she had to swallow to keep from crying out with relief.

The Roush dropped from the branch, spread its wings, and swept around, gliding west just above the treetops. Toward the desert.

Toward the Gathering.

"Wait!" She cried out, afraid it might be leaving, and spurred her horse after the furry creature. But it wasn't leaving her; it was circling back. Then it faced west again, satisfied she was following.

She was not alone. The light was there, begging her to follow.

JANAE PULLED her horse to a halt next to Billy's and stared at the massive canyon. The sun was hot, and sweat exacerbated the rash that now covered the skin around her joints—the crooks of her elbows and knees, her neck, armpits, and groin. The growth had slowed after an initial outbreak, and in the last twenty-four hours it hadn't pro-gressed at all.

She swatted at a fly that buzzed by her ear. "I don't see anything but more rocks and sand. This isn't right."

Billy was studying the journal again. Always the journal, as if it was his new lover. "Yes . . ." He glanced up at the stars, then consulted the page again. "Yes, this is it."

"Where?"

He motioned to the dark canyon below them. "There."

"Fantastic," she said bitterly. "I've crossed the desert with a redhead from Colorado who's so twisted up that he's seeing black bats in the shadows. If they're there, why can't I smell them?"

He dismissed her with a turn of his head and urged his horse forward. That was Billy: forward, always forward, into the desert, as if following a bright star to the birthplace of some new king. It was a book that guided him, though, and even more, some inner homing device seemed to keep him trudging forward. Always forward.

He had the rash as well. They decided it was from the air. The atmosphere was filled with microscopic Shataiki, and the two of them were reacting to it. Clearly, their skin didn't react to the disease like the Horde's skin, or they would be covered in the sores by now. Or perhaps Thomas's blood was in them still, fighting against the virus.

They'd escaped the city, taking four horses from the temple stables for the hard journey north. Billy had cut loose the two mounts they'd exhausted after a day, and Janae was certain the two they now rode would give out before the end of the night.

"Billy!" She got her mount moving again and plunged down the slope after him. He didn't turn back. He didn't even acknowledge her presence. She was following her own internal guide, sniffing out the scent of something that pushed her inexorably toward her destiny, whatever that might be. But Billy . . .

Billy was on autopilot. He was so lost, so completely swallowed by his mission that he could no longer articulate exactly what he had in mind.

"Billy!" She kicked her horse, and it bolted forward with a snort of protest. "Tell me why I can't smell their blood. Stop. Just stop this idiocy!" She pulled her horse across the nose of his to force sense into him. "Don't ignore me!"

Billy's glazed eyes studied her. "What?"

"What? What's your problem? We've been running for two days straight, and we haven't seen a hint of Shataiki. Or Horde or albino, for that matter."

"I know where I'm going."

"Maybe you do. But I can't do this anymore!"

His jaw muscles bunched with impatience. "You think we have options here?"

That was just it: they didn't. The sum of her own predicament swelled in her mind, and the world spun. Less than a week ago she'd been in a position of power at Raison Pharmaceutical, tolerating a deep-seated knowledge that she didn't belong, at odds with her mother and the rest, but at least stable. She'd learned how to cope with her dreaded desire to smash everything around her.

Then Billy had turned her world on end. In hindsight, she'd always known that she would eventually meet another like herself, a soul mate with the same insatiable longing for more, far beyond the limitations of flesh and blood. She didn't understand her feeling of emptiness, but she'd known it couldn't last forever.

The moment Janae had awakened in the body of Ba'al's priestess, Jezreal, she knew she'd found herself. Almost. Her identity was entwined with the blood Ba'al loved. With the sacrifices to his master.

To Teeleh.

It was the beast's blood more than his name that called to her.

And Billy was right. They had no options except to find Teeleh. An overwhelming desperation settled over Janae as she stared into Billy's distant eyes. She swallowed past the tightness in her throat, but the emotion rose like a fist, and she felt despair strain her face.

"I need it, Billy!" she whispered. The longing for the blood swallowed her whole, and tears welled in her eyes. "I can't wait for it."

"You need what?" He maintained his hard edge.

She looked away and wiped her cheeks with the back of her hand. "I . . . I don't know." A long silence settled over them. "I'm scared."

Billy uttered a harsh laugh. "Yeah, well it's a bit late for that. You follow me across the universe into hell and now you decide you're afraid?"

"No." She faced him, furious at his insolence. But she depended on him even more now than before. So she closed her eyes and tried to compose herself. More to the point, she loved him—the way a drug addict might love the needle. She *needed* Billy.

Janae opened her eyes and watched him by moonlight. He couldn't read minds in this reality, a small consolation that leveled the playing field somewhat. But Billy was no less extraordinary. Not because of what he *did*, although the fact that he'd been the first to write in the magical Books of History was no small feat.

Still, it was Billy's identity that made him extraordinary, she thought. He was the one responsible for Thomas Hunter's entry into this world. He was the one who'd given birth to evil in those books.

In a sense, Billy was all of humanity bundled into one boy who'd been besieged by evil. Unable to rid his mind of the evil, he embarked on a quest to face it. Only then could he embrace it fully, or reject it, never to return. He'd said as much, but looking at him now, she understood it.

Janae eased her horse next to his, facing the opposite direction. She rested her hand on his thigh and leaned forward slowly until her lips were an inch from his.

"I love you, Billy," she whispered.

He didn't move. She kissed him lightly on his mouth.

"I don't know what's happening to me." The taste of his saliva made her head spin. "I can't . . . I don't know why I'm feeling like this."

Billy returned the kiss, and she had to suppress the impulse to bite his lip as she had before. She moved her hand from his thigh to his back and pulled herself closer.

"I'm not afraid to be here with you, I'm afraid of this feeling." Tears came again. "I don't know what's wrong with me, Billy. I need it."

His breath was hot through his nostrils, and he pulled back so that their mouths were separated only by the moisture between them. "You need what?"

"The blood," she breathed without thinking.

It was the first time she'd admitted it so plainly, even to herself, but doing so brought a flood of adrenaline. Her heartbeat surged, and she crushed his lips with her own.

Billy didn't speak, not with words. He was breathing hard, and he returned the kiss with as much passion. They were locked in an embrace, eyes closed and lost to the world. Images of black trees and large black bats slid through her mind. But instead of being repulsed or frightened, she now felt a wholeness that only fueled her desire.

Billy was her Adam, and she was his Eve, embracing the forbidden world. His lips were fruit to her, the sweet nectar of an apple.

She groaned and bit down deeply, then felt warmth flood her mouth. Like a drug, the blood flooded her with desire and peace. Complete wellness and security. Billy wasn't a mere man; he was a god. Her own to consume.

She knew that she'd regressed to a form of herself that knew only darkness. But there in the darkness of that womb she felt one with herself. She . . .

Her mount snorted and shifted under her. Billy's hand was squeezing her shoulder like a vise. Pushing her away.

She opened her eyes, confused and hurt, but before she could speak she was stopped by darkness.

Not just darkness. Blackness, like ink. So black she could feel the night as if it were a living organism that meant to smother her.

Janae jerked her head away from Billy and saw the circle of red eyes peering at them from the edge of a blackened forest twenty feet away. Where had the trees come from? They surrounded Billy and Janae. She gasped and spun around.

The red eyes were attached to mangy black creatures standing several feet tall, loosely resembling the images she'd seen in the temple.

Shataiki.

Her heart bolted, and she turned to look in the direction that had captivated Billy. A beast twice the size of the others perched on an angular branch above and behind the ring of Shataiki. He watched them with piercing red eyes.

Not a sound. Not a movement. Janae's heart pounded in her ears. The moon had been cut off by a thick tangle of leafless branches, draped in long strings of dark moss. Where only moments earlier sand and rocks had covered the canyon floor, now mud and shale lay on the ground. A single path tunneled into the dense foliage.

Their eyes had been opened to the Black Forest. The twelfth of twelve forests, Billy had said. The queen Marsuuv's domain. And Janae had little doubt that the beast staring at them from his higher perch was none other than Marsuuv himself.

Billy dropped to the ground and went down on one knee, head bowed to the queen. Before Janae could decide what her reaction should be, the large beast sprang into the air with astonishing agility, shot above the canopy, and was gone from their sight in the direction of the path.

As one, the ring of Shataiki flapped noisily off the branches, squawking and hissing. Half flew after the queen, and the others swept in, jaws snapping. Janae crouched as a set of fangs clamped shut close enough for her to feel the creature's hot, sulfuric breath on her neck.

Billy stood slowly, eyes on the path, ignoring the vicious cacophony of the beasts. He calmly mounted and turned his horse into the path. Satisfied, the Shataiki pulled up and fluttered about the canopy.

The air smelled like an open wound rotting with gangrene, but it was laced with another scent that drew Janae like the sweet smell of water drawing herds after a long, parched season.

"Billy . . ."

He pushed his snorting mount onto the path, then into the forest.

"Billy?"

He smacked his horse's rump and it bolted. Janae ducked low and raced after him. The darkness made the path nearly invisible, but the horses followed their own guide, hauling Billy and her into the jungle at breakneck speed.

Two thoughts drummed through her mind. The first was that they were rushing toward their deaths. The second was that she didn't care, because she could smell life in the air, and this was the life she needed as much as breath itself.

The scent grew stronger, and with it her certainty that she had to reach the end of this path, if for no other reason than to find the source of the smell.

She called out his name later, in a moment of unexpected fear. "Billy." But her voice was weak, and even if Billy was listening, his silence seemed appropriate. The fear lifted, and she hugged her horse's neck as she rode it into the night.

Into this hell.

How long they rode or where the twisting path went, she neither knew nor cared. She kept telling herself she was going home. All secrets would be laid bare with her queen.

My queen. She whispered it aloud. "My queen. My queen."

Her horse stopped suddenly and she jerked up in her saddle, eyes peeled. They had come to the bank of a large black pond surrounded by a thick forest. The Shataiki covered the canopy, their millions of red eyes staring in silence, casting a dim glow over the waters.

Janae pulled up next to Billy and followed his gaze. A single wooden platform stood on pylons over the water like a pier. And on the platform, three thick inverted crosses, black against the night.

Crosses. Why crosses?

Janae saw that five or six Shataiki carcasses had been nailed to the crosses and hung like huge dead rats. "Upside-down crucifixions."

Billy kept his eyes on the ancient symbols of execution.

"Where is Marsuuv?" Janae asked.

"In the grave."

They were whispering, and even then, Janae wondered what did or did not offend Shataiki. She felt her skin quiver, like the flesh of the mount beneath her. Something was wrong here. All of it was wrong, terribly wrong. All except the scent. And now her body quivered with desire.

"Where's the grave?"

"In hell," he said. "Below the crosses."

"Under the lake?"

Billy directed his horse to a rotting wooden door into a large mound beside the lake. Like a bunker or a root cellar. For long seconds he sat on his horse and stared in silence. The throng overhead watched like a jury, perfectly still, as if what they were witnessing had been anticipated for a very long time.

History was being written before their eyes. But it wasn't her they were staring at, she realized. It was Billy.

She looked over at him and saw that he was crying. Streams of tears wet his cheeks, and his face was wrinkled in anguish.

"My lover . . ." His voice was raspy, barely more than a whisper. "I've made it. I've come back to you."

A knot rose in Janae's throat. In this moment, she felt such a solidarity with him that she couldn't hold back her own sentiment. "I love you, Billy."

But the moment she said it, she knew she meant Marsuuv. She, like Billy, had found her lover. Certainly not in a way humans found lovers. No, this was far more basic, like finding water in a desert. Or blood after being drained.

Life.

Billy slowly gathered himself, then turned to her. "Do you have the strength?"

"Yes."

"He'll take everything."

And give me his power, she thought.

"He'll take your soul."

She looked at the door, a rudimentary door bound together with vines in a criss-crossing pattern. "He already has it."

Billy dipped his head, then reached for her hand. His fingers were ice-cold, but the gesture filled her with a new warmth.

"Thank you, Janae," he said. "Thank you for sharing this with me."

"Of course."

He looked up at the three crosses on their right. "You know, I once thought I had defeated the evil in my heart. I learned something: We can face our demons, burn them up, stomp them into the ground. I turned mine to ashes. But even if you destroy the evidence of evil, you can't heal your heart. Not by yourself. Only he can do that."

Billy was staring up at the crosses when he said it, and for a moment Janae thought he was capitulating.

He looked at her again. Smiled. "Call me Judas, Janae. We all have our roles to play. I love him too much."

Even if she wanted to, there was no way to turn back now. The scent pulled at her like an airborne intoxicant that beckoned her to come and taste. "I want to love him too."

"He's waiting," Billy said. "Marsuuv is waiting."

Then Billy and Janae slid from their saddles, walked up to the door, and descended into hell.

32

CHELISE LOST track of time as she followed the Roush through the forest, flooded with renewed energy and desire. Even the horse seemed to have gained strength, an almost unnatural stamina to chase this angel of mercy who flew above the branches, in and out of sight.

She knew that the desert would be upon them soon, and then it would be lighter and the path to the Circle more certain.

They are showing themselves again, she told herself. *Something is happening. The world is flooded with darkness because it knows something is happening. It's going to change.* The thoughts repeated themselves over and over, and she clung to them as if they were a tether to Elyon himself.

She lost sight of the Roush in a thick section of forest, and with some panic wondered if he'd left her. Then she burst out of the trees and faced the open desert.

The white creature sat atop a small dune not fifty yards from the tree line, watching her.

Chelise walked the horse closer. Up the slope. She stopped twenty feet from the Roush.

"Come closer, my dear," he said.

Oh, dear. Oh, dear, the Roush was speaking. Chelise couldn't move.

"It's okay, I know I must frighten you to no end. Like a ghost in the night."

"No," she blurted. "No, I . . ."

She couldn't find the words to express her gratitude at seeing this Roush after so much fear and doubt.

The Roush looked at her a moment longer, then wobbled forward on spindly legs hardly made for walking. He stopped ten feet from her and spoke in a soft, comforting voice.

"I am Michal, and I'm here to give you courage. I come . . ."

Chelise heard nothing more because she was dropping to the sand, stumbling forward, craving to know, really know that this was no figment of her imagination, but a real, furry, white Roush.

She managed to come to her senses before running him over, feeling suddenly foolish. But instead of backing away, the Roush stuck out its wing.

"Go ahead. Everybody seems to want to make sure by touching these days."

She touched his leathery skin. Ran her fingers over the fur along the wing's spine. Then settled to her knees with a sob and gripped both of his wings.

Michal stepped closer, and she embraced his furry body. It was real, so very real. And soft, like downy cotton. Only when he coughed did it occur to her that she might be squeezing the air out of him. She let go and backed off.

"Sorry. Sorry."

"Don't worry," he said, waddling to her right. "It happens." He faced her. "Yes, dear, yes. It is all very real, don't lose sight of that. The world is darker now than it has ever been. If you only knew the treachery being plotted in the Black Forest, you would tremble."

"I already am trembling."

He arched his brow. "Then take courage. If I'm real, so is Elyon. And if he is, so is his purpose."

"So Thomas will be okay? Samuel, my father . . . all of them will be okay?"

"I didn't say that. Darkness demands its price—"

"What price?"

"I can't tell you what will happen. Frankly, I don't know. But Thomas is no fool. Trust him. Do what you must do. Go with courage; the light is brimming behind all of this darkness. You'll have to trust me."

"But why?" She knew she was bordering on sacrilege, being so bold, but after days of fearing the worst without a hint of hope, she couldn't help herself. "Why would Elyon force us to face such darkness and tragedy? For ten years now we run and die and, yes, we dance at night to forget it all, but still the horror haunts us. Why?"

Michal frowned. His mouth slowly formed a gentle, empathetic smile. "I'm sorry for your trouble, my dear. But aren't lovers always tempted to find another? You humans are lovers, yes? So you have this awful tendency to reject him who first loved you and follow after intoxicating scents. Evil is a jealous lover who will try to destroy what it cannot possess, so now evil is having its say. But don't discount the power of a loyal heart. You'll see. Have hope."

"How can I hope when evil will charge its price?"

Michal eyed her for a few moments, then, without any answer, he began to turn.

"Hurry, Chelise. The world waits for you."

To do what?

"They will come for you in the desert. Wait for them." And then he leaped into the air and glided into the night.

"Wait!"

"Courage, Chelise!" he called back. "The world awaits you!"

Who would come for her?

STANDING BEFORE the queen Marsuuv was like standing in the presence of God.

The vast underground library was lit by three torches that illuminated thousands of ancient books along the walls; the ceiling was covered by a black moss. But Janae felt only intrigue at these observations.

Marsuuv put out another scent, stronger even than the mucus, and it drew her like clover draws a bee.

They'd descended a long flight of stone steps in silence, then entered one of several tunnels cut horizontally under the lake. Flames illuminated the passage's well-worn walls, interrupted by iron gates that closed off smaller rooms: a storage room filled with artifacts that Janae couldn't place, a smaller study with a writing desk overgrown by roots, an atrium leading into another tunnel.

But Billy took them deeper still, seemingly drawn by a force beyond him. Perhaps his connection to Ba'al.

In the library, the four lost books sat on a large stone platform, a desk of sorts, flanked by two tarnished silver candlesticks fashioned to look like upside-down crosses.

Marsuuv sat on a large bed of red vines beyond the stone desk. The carving in the mossy rock wall behind him explained the crosses on the lake platform. Three hooked claws dug into the cross's inverted beam— a display of dominance. The talons were so long and hooked that they resembled sixes. Their tips looked to have pierced the wall, coaxing forth small rivulets of a dark fluid.

The queen Marsuuv sat at the edge of the bed with his own long talons hanging nearly to the ground. His black fur looked manicured, not bare in spots like the other Shataiki they'd seen. Quite beautiful, actually.

His head was large, like a wolf's or a fruit bat's, with pink lips loosely covering sharp fangs. Red eyes stared like marbles, shiny, without pupils. You could look at this creature and find it magnificent, Janae thought. Absolutely stunning.

She stood next to Billy before the beast, aware that she was trembling. The mix of emotions coursing through her mind made her legs feel weak. The queen was wonderful, but not even someone as enchanted as Janae could look at this sight and not fight off waves of terror. She was unsure which she should pay more attention to, her longing or her fear.

"Hello, Billy." The queen's voice purred, soft and seductive. "Welcome home."

Billy lowered himself to one knee and bowed his head, speechless. It struck Janae that Marsuuv was fixated on Billy, not her. His eyes had been on Billy from the start.

Billy found his voice. "I am your servant. Your lover."

"Are you sure?" a voice rasped. The dark priest Ba'al stood in a doorway to their right, arms folded into a loose black cloak. He walked in and stood before them all, looking even more emaciated than Janae remembered. "Are you sure you know what you're getting into, feeble human?"

"He's mine, Billosssssss," Marsuuv said.

The priest stared at Billy for a long time. Slowly his face contorted into an expression of pain and sorrow. A tear glistened on his left cheek, and he buried his face in his hands, weeping now.

The sight was so unexpected that Janae felt a tremendous flood of empathy for the poor soul.

Ba'al lowered his trembling hands and stumbled forward. "Please, I beg you to reconsider. What did I ever do to deserve this? You're throwing me away for this albino?"

Marsuuv just looked at him.

"I defied you once, I know, but look in his history and you'll see the same. We all defy you once before embracing the darkness." Ba'al words came out in a breath-starved flood. "You bound me and you whipped me, and I still learned to love you! You gave me reason to live as your only lover. 'Bring me the books, bring me the books,' you said. Now I've brought you the books and you'll throw me away? I cannot live with it."

"Billossss," Marsuuv said. "Always so impetuous."

"I am not Billos!" Ba'al screamed. His face was a mess of mucus and tears. "I am Ba'al."

"What life you have as Ba'al came from me. You have my blood. You are mine."

Janae's belly tightened.

"Please . . ." Ba'al leaned against one of the pillars for support. He lowered his voice. "Please don't throw me away. I'll . . . I'll do anything."

"Will you join me in hell?"

Ba'al rushed around the table, grabbed one of Marsuuv's talons, and fell to his knees. "Just say the word, my lover. Say the word so that we can be together in eternal hell."

The queen uttered a soft chuckle. Then purred. He lifted his claw, pulling the man to his feet. Ba'al clambered onto the bed, clinging to the beast's talon with both hands now. Casting a glance up to be sure he was being accepted, not rejected, Ba'al settled against the beast's furry underside and curled up, weeping softly.

Billy was still on his knees, weeping with Ba'al as Marsuuv watched him. Janae believed he understood Ba'al's pain more than she could know. Billos had been held and tortured until he'd slowly become the wretched man named Ba'al. Billy had felt that pain when the two were one.

And what of her? Was she here on a fool's errand, stranded in a foreign dimension, another victim of this hideous beast's insatiable appetite? Heat washed down her neck. She'd made a mistake? She'd willingly entered this hell and would now pay for it like Ba'al had?

And Billy . . .

The sap was just kneeling there, weeping like a baby.

"What?" Billy groaned "What do you want? I can't live like this. I can't! I've seen the light; I've tasted the good; I don't deserve to live."

Marsuuv absently ran his claws over Ba'al's body. "Such a tormented soul. But you've come to me. I will ease your pain and fill you with a new pleasure that you'll crave. Nothing will be the same now, Billy."

Billy gripped his hands to fists, leaned his head back, and cried at the ceiling in anguish. His voice echoed around the room. Janae wanted to tell him to stop this embarrassing display of weakness, but she knew her advice meant little here.

She was the disposable one in the room.

Billy finally ran out of breath and calmed. Marsuuv nudged Ba'al, then pushed him away. "Leave us."

"My lord?" Ba'al was aghast. He began to cry again. "Please!"

"Leave us!" Marsuuv's snarl shook the room, and Janae took a step back. Her pulse quickened. There was something about his jaw, his pink tongue, his fangs that excited her. The scent of blood . . . Could it be coming from his mouth?

Ba'al spun, hiked up his cloak, and hurried from the room, trying to hold back his cries of regret.

Marsuuv watched Billy. "Come here, Son of Adam," he purred.

For a moment, Billy did nothing. She could imagine the fear pounding through his veins.

"Let me take away the pain, Billy. Let me give you pleasure."

Billy pushed himself up and then walked slowly around the stone desk where the four books were stacked. He stepped in front of the beast.

Marsuuv lifted his claws and stroked Billy's wet cheeks. "Why do you cry, my love? You've been chosen for a task that is the envy of the world."

"What?" Billy breathed.

"Teeleh will tell you. You'll be going back soon. We only have a short time together. We should treasure every moment."

Billy was shaking from head to foot, and Marsuuv seemed pleased. His talons touched Billy's head and arms and neck as if they were made of a delicate membrane that would break with the slightest pressure.

She knew Billy and Marsuuv shared a special bond that she did not. This was the devil, and Billy had welcomed him into his head a long time ago.

The truth of this began to eat away at Janae like a flaming cancer, and she began to fear for herself. How could she stand before such a terrifying sight and feel such jealousy? She should be on her knees, showing respect. Her anger would end badly. She would say or do something that triggered this beast's fury.

But he hadn't so much as acknowledged her yet. In fact, now that she thought about it, even back in the clearing, Marsuuv's eyes had been on Billy, not her. She was sure of it.

She was nothing more than a rat caged for the next meal. She'd crossed into this nightmare to be food for this dreadful beast!

And yet, there was nowhere else in the world, or in her mind, that Janae wanted to be but here, facing the truth, the scent, the source of her own desire.

"What about me?" she said.

The beast ignored her. His long tongue snaked out and licked tears from Billy's cheeks. This display of affection combined with the scent of blood on Marsuuv's breath proved to be too much.

Janae stepped forward, enraged. "Am I just a piece of meat here?" she cried.

Marsuuv jerked his head to face her for the first time, issuing a crackling snarl as he snapped the air. "Patience, human!"

The Shataiki's breath washed over her, and with it his scent, so strong now that tears stung her eyes again.

"The desire is so strong, is that it, daughter of Eve? Just one taste?"

Her voice cracked. "Yes."

He shifted on the bed of vines so that his whole body now faced her. "Do you know how we reproduce, Janae? We carry blood in our fangs."

Of course. Yes, of course.

"You are now in my nest, where I lay unfertilized eggs that become larvae. Any Shataiki but a queen can bring the young ones to life; all it requires is a single drop of blood. A single bite."

Janae found the words irresistibly seductive. She wasn't sure why; what he said surpassed all she yet knew about her own existence.

"You wonder why you long for this blood, don't you, daughter?"

"Yes," she whimpered, stepping closer.

"Once there were twelve of our forests, each a nest for a queen. One forest was burned, and the queen Alucard left us. And when Alucard left our world, he entered yours, two thousand years before you were born, at the turn of your calendars. There were no Shataiki to fertilize his own larvae. But he found a way to satisfy his need for offspring by injecting his own blood into a human woman. We know this from one of the blood books, the journal of Saint Thomas the Beast Hunter, where it is recorded that a race of half-breeds came into existence and spread their seed on earth. He called the descendants Vampirum. Offspring."

She knew where he was going, and it terrified her.

"You, Janae, crave the blood because your father many generations removed was a half-breed. Shataiki blood runs in your veins still. You are offspring." He paused. "Does that excite you?" Marsuuv was speaking softly, drawing her in with his eyes and the gentle movement of his talons.

"Yes," she breathed. She could taste a hint of blood on her own tongue, and she gave herself to the desire for it. Even Billy . . . his blood had hints of the same irresistible taste.

Shataiki blood.

As she stepped closer, a distant voice whispered a warning: *It's evil, Janae. Raw, unfiltered evil, like the larvae. You have entered hell, and you are begging to drink evil.*

"Come, my sweet," Marsuuv purred. "Come, taste and see that I am evil." He sprang from the bed and swept the lost books from the stone desk. An altar, she now saw. It was his altar.

Janae walked around to his side of the altar and reached for his claw. He leaned close so that she could feel his breath; the power in that hot blast of air robbed the last threads of resistance from her. She understood Ba'al's desire to be with this magnificent beast.

She instinctively leaned forward and took his fur in her fingers, longing to be closer. He reacted like a sprung animal, plucking her from the ground and slamming her down on the stone. Pain flashed down her back.

The beast leaped upon the altar, gripping the deeply scarred edge with his long claws. He hunched over her and glared.

"You want more," the beast growled. "More. This is why he chose you."

Janae began to cry with gratitude. She'd always known that there was something wrong with her. Something different. Her own appetites for adventure, for pleasure, for more, always more, were far more pronounced than others'. Now she understood.

It was the blood. Shataiki blood. Her own father had passed this desire to her.

"Please . . ." She grabbed the creature's hair and pulled. "Please . . ."

"You long for it. To be Teeleh's daughter?"

"Yes!"

"To curse Elyon and embrace evil for eternity?"

"Yes!"

His jaw came down slowly, and she stretched her neck for him. Felt his fangs touch her skin.

Then Marsuuv, queen of the twelfth forest, bit into Janae's flesh and injected his blood into her veins. And the power that flooded her body made it shake like a dying rat.

Her jaw snapped wide and she screamed. With pain, with pleasure, with the terror of raw evil.

Marsuuv pulled his fangs free, still dripping with her blood, dug three claws into her forehead to mark her as his own, offered a satisfied shudder, and slowly climbed off the table, leaving her to jerk alone.

Billy was saying something, protesting, but she couldn't focus on him because her nerves had turned to fire. Not with pain, necessarily, but with sensitivity. She could sense everything, the cool stone beneath her, the movement of air around her, the pinpricks of pain on her neck. The scent of the flames, the blood, the sweat, the mucus, everything. Her pain had turned to pleasure, and she was having a hard time containing it all.

"In good time, my love," Marsuuv was saying. "All in good time. Get her up."

The sensations softened, leaving her exhausted and content. Hands pulled on her cloak, and she opened her eyes. Billy leaned over her, shaking her. She smiled. "Billy."

"Get up."

She looked up at him, lost in the moment.

"Get up!" he snapped.

She sat up, forgiving his jealous outburst. She hopped off the altar, feeling more alive and energized than she'd ever felt. An image of Ba'al's shriveled husk of a body crossed her mind, but she dismissed it without a second thought. She was no Ba'al.

Janae glanced at Billy, aware of how little she cared for this human now. He seemed small and pitiful to her, a feeble man who'd succumbed to the thirst for evil, not unlike herself, except that she had been bred for it. What was his excuse?

Billy was the author, her inner voice whispered. *He's now your master.*

She turned away, refusing to indulge the notion, and faced Marsuuv, who sat on his bed of vines once again.

"You wish to prove yourself?" he asked. Somehow he must know. Perhaps his mind had joined hers while he fed on her blood.

She pulled the three vials from the side of her bra and set them on the altar. He reached for the tiny bottles and touched them with the tip of his talon.

"Tell me," he said.

"The one marked with the white tape is Raison Strain B. It has the power to destroy all life. Billy and I are immune to it now."

"It cannot kill albinos or half-breeds," he said. "None who have bathed in the lakes."

He knew about the virus?

"The virus originates with Teeleh's blood," Marsuuv said, seeing her raised brow. "It will only worsen the disease the Horde already have."

Her mind spun.

"And the other sicknesses?" he demanded.

"The one marked with the black tape is Asian Ebola. Terminal to all but Billy and me. We've been inoculated with a vaccine like everyone in our world. The last vial is as labeled, a sample of Thomas's blood, which we both have in our systems as well."

The beast reacted to the mention of Thomas with a jerk of his head.

"He's in Bangkok," Janae said, wondering how much the Shataiki knew.

Marsuuv pulled back slowly. "So, the time has come. The humans will decide. We can destroy the land, we can pluck their eyes out, we can whisper evil into their minds, we can rape and pillage and burn, but in the end only humans can unlock their destiny."

"And now we bring you the keys to that destiny," Billy said.

"Not you, Billy. My master has another task for you. As soon as you and I become better acquainted."

Billy glanced at Janae with furtive eyes.

"But Janae," Marsuuv said, purring again, "you will be our new Eve. Together we will destroy them all, and the world will know that Teeleh owns the humans."

She had a craving for his blood.

"You will find Samuel. Seduce him. Seduce the half-breeds." His voice popped with phlegm. "Seduce the albinos. The time has come for the dragon to consume his young."

He plucked the vial of Asian Ebola from the altar and set it by his side, leaving Thomas's blood untouched. "You have no need for this. The Raison Strain will give you the power you need."

"What about the half-breeds?" she asked. "The albinos."

"They will die."

"How, if my poison only affects full-breed Horde?"

Marsuuv glared. "Do I look like a fool? Do as I say."

"And me? Will I die?"

"You, too, are his lover," he said slowly, enunciating each word. Teeleh's desire was to destroy them all and begin over with Billy and Janae, his new lovers in his own twisted garden.

It all fit. The only reason the Shataiki hadn't already destroyed humanity was because only humans could destroy humanity. As such, people were more powerful than Shataiki. Unable to complete their revenge on the world, the Shataiki had hidden themselves, biding their time.

Now that time had come. Janae held the virus that would destroy the Horde and leave the destruction of the Eramites and the albinos to Teeleh.

Marsuuv gazed at her. "Go and do what you must do quickly."

33

TORUN VALLEY, to the northwest of Qurongi City, had been turned black with the swarming masses of the Horde army. Chelise stared at the sight, amazed that she was alive, much less here. If not for the Roush, Michal, she would surely be at the Gathering now, safe, but still lost.

She'd wandered into the desert with the Roush's words swimming around her: *They will come for you in the desert. Wait for them.*

Wait for who, the Horde? The Circle? Thomas and her father? Could it be that Elyon was coming for her? Or the Shataiki . . .

The sun rose after Michal left her, and she had slowly worked her way home toward Paradose Valley and the Circle, waiting to be over-taken any moment by whomever she was to wait for. The sun rose. The day passed.

And as she drew nearer to home, she began to see signs of albinos arriving in response to Thomas's call. They were coming from far and wide, eager to flood Paradose Valley. Perhaps she should leave the desert and return to the Gathering rather than wait. She wanted to kiss her Jake and make sure that all was well. But of course all was *not* well. Thousands would be pouring into the valley. Samuel was in danger or was a danger. Thomas had vanished.

Besides, how would she know she'd been found by whomever she was waiting for?

And then she had crested a tall dune, seen the Scab patrol under a lone tree, waiting for her, and she knew. She'd been found as she was meant to be found.

Still, it took her five full minutes to work up the courage to approach

the two men, who seemed content to watch her. She approached with
dread and determination.

"My name is Stephen," the young Horde scout had said. "Your
mother, Lady Patricia, has requested that you join her in the Torun
Valley immediately."

Immediately. Chelise knew that the worst had happened. Qurong
and Thomas had fallen into terrible trouble. Why else would a plea
come from her mother?

"Stephen?" It was the first word she'd spoken to a Scab since her
drowning.

"Yes, my lady. We will keep you safe, but you must not leave our
sides."

It wasn't until much later, after the first long day's ride, that she realized he wasn't protecting her from other Horde warriors. He was on the
sharp lookout for the new breed of albino fighters. "We all know they
are much faster, far more skilled than even the Eramites."

His companion had chuckled. "And everyone knows the Eramites
are superior to most Horde."

"Really?"

"How does an army that has no war stay in fighting shape?" the man
named Reeslar demanded. "Our Throaters and scouts are the only ones
who have the skills that once made the Horde proud."

"And even then the Forest Guard used to beat us up pretty badly,"
Chelise said.

Her use of the inclusive "us" silenced them for a moment. But it had
been "us" back then, and it should be again, she thought. Their smell
didn't bother her as much as it bothered other albinos. In fact, the only
difference between them and many albinos was the fact that albinos had
drowned in a red lake.

Stephen had broken the silence. "Teeleh save us if the albinos ever
decide to take up arms."

The other grunted his agreement, and for the smallest amount of
time, Chelise understood Samuel's desire to fight. Until now, she hadn't

understood the superiority of the average albino's fighting skill and strength. The absence of disease and their constant running from scouting parties had kept them fresh and hardened, ready to engage any enemy.

After crossing the desert for the second time in a day, she sat on her mare between the two Throaters and studied the armies in the Torun Valley. She'd seen dozens of patrols as a youth, but always from a distance. Before they'd overtaken the forests, the Horde went to great lengths to blend into the sand, breeding horses with tan hides and keeping to the valleys. Afterward, they'd reversed their strategy, preferring to be seen in all their dominant glory rather than hide as fugitives like the Circle.

A small army of Horde had once made it to the edge of Chelise and Thomas's camp before the tribe of albinos had escaped. She'd watched the Horde with Thomas from the nearby hills, wondering if she could talk reason into them.

That was at the beginning, before her father unleashed the full force of his rage against them. The Horde butchered several camps and captured hundreds of albinos in the months that followed. She'd once helplessly watched from a cliff as Throaters hung three albinos she knew well: Ismael, Judin, and Chrystin.

Chelise wept that day, and Thomas made the decision to go deeper into the desert. The Circle learned to adapt, and the Horde grew impatient with the meager pickings. But life in the deep desert was harsh, and the red pools were scarce. They had to move every two or three weeks to find food and wood, and long trips were made to harvest the desert wheat. A hunting party might take a week to kill two or three deer for a feast.

This, and the fact that Elyon had left his red pools in and near the forests, persuaded Thomas that they should move closer to the forests once again. The danger was higher, but so was the reward.

Besides, the elders often agreed, Elyon would be returning soon anyway. Any day. Any week. Not even a few months. Surely not more than a year.

That was seven years ago. And now more than a few albinos wanted to retake the forests.

This Horde army crawling through the Torun Valley might be slower and weaker than any albino army, but they were as numerous as the sands! A massive blanket of men and horses and tents stretched out to the horizon, then was swallowed in a dusty haze.

"There must be a million," she said.

"Many," Stephen said.

"The whole army?"

Again, silence, though Stephen had already let the fact slip. At times, she was certain he forgot she was albino and regarded her only as royalty. He was taking her home, after all.

"All this for a training exercise?" she asked in wonder.

"It's never been done, but it makes sense. The army needs training."

"Yes, but the logistics. It must be a nightmare to move so many men."

Reeslar scoffed. "We did it all the time in the desert! This . . . this is nothing."

"You're sure my father isn't with them?"

Stephen ignored the question. "They're waiting. We shouldn't wait."

"They?"

The scout turned his horse from the crest of the hill and trotted toward the trees. "Your mother awaits you, daughter of Qurong."

"Where?" She kicked her mount into a run, flanked by the other two.

"Close. Just over the hill."

They rode hard, passing by several patrols and guards stationed in the trees. She wore a hooded robe at Stephen's insistence. His orders were to deliver her in secrecy. They could either go in with her bound in chains or looking like Horde, and he recommended the latter. She was, after all, Qurong's daughter.

The royal camp was erected on a plateau above Torun Valley, surrounded by a company of Throaters who'd formed a perimeter several hundred yards out. A dozen flags bearing the winged serpent image flapped over a large canvas tent that was bordered by four smaller tents. Around this grouping sat several dozen smaller tents belonging to the royal entourage and the guard.

Temple guard, if she wasn't mistaken. Then Ba'al was out here as well?

"It has been a pleasure escorting you, daughter of Qurong," Stephen said. "I pray that Teeleh will favor you from the many evil spirits who seek to kill the less fortunate."

How long had it been since she'd heard such a blessing? "Thank you," she said.

He slowed as they passed the main guard, then saluted another, who glared and took her reins.

"You're a good man, Stephen. I pray Elyon will smile on you."

The scout hesitated, then dipped his head.

Her new guard dismounted and delivered her to the main tent's flap before stepping aside. "Inside," he said gruffly. Chelise took a deep breath, pulled the flap open, and stepped back into her past.

The first thing that stood out to her was the bowl of morst by the entrance. She wasn't sure why this would take her attention from the lavish furnishings inside or from the three people who stood across the room. Maybe because the morst represented all that was wrong with her old way of life.

To think that a paste the consistency of soft flour could cover up a disease was ludicrous. It was a beautiful lie.

She released the flap and peered into the dimly lit room. Patricia, whom she had not seen in ten years, stood by the center pole ten yards away, hands clasped in front of her. She wore a red robe, and her hair was drawn back in ceremonial fashion.

"Chelise?"

She felt her knees weaken. To hear her mother call her name . . . She'd missed the woman more than even she'd realized.

"Is that you?"

Her hood! She was standing in the shadows with her hood pulled up. Chelise stepped forward into the light cast by two lamp stands and slipped her hood off.

"Hello, Mother."

Patricia's face slowly wrinkled as emotion swallowed her. Her hands lifted as if to embrace her daughter, but then lowered. She glanced to her right, where the two men stood. The first was the general she'd known years earlier when he was only a captain. Cassak. The second . . .

Chelise felt every nerve in her body shut down as she stared at the large form and gray eyes belonging to Qurong, supreme commander of the Horde. Her own father, whom she loved as much as her own life.

She couldn't speak. She wanted to rush toward him and throw her arms around his thick neck, and she wanted to tell him how often she thought about him: every night, every day. Every time she drank the red waters and ate Elyon's fruit, she saw his face in her mind's eye. She dreamed he would follow her into the red pool and drown his pitiful self—never mind how powerful he was—and find a new life that would make him dance through the night!

But she couldn't. She couldn't even move after imagining this moment for so long.

Qurong's eyes were soft. Even sad. But he turned his face away.

Chelise looked at Patricia, whose sharp glare softened. "Welcome into our home, Daughter."

She dipped her head. "It's my honor, Mother."

Silence.

"Hello, Father."

He glanced over and dipped his head politely.

Then her mother was rushing forward. They embraced, mother and daughter, Horde and albino.

"It's so good to see you, Chelise," her mother whispered, struggling not to cry. "I've been so worried."

She kissed Patricia's cheek. "It's good to see you in good health."

"And your son?" her mother asked, pulling back.

"Jake. He's a bundle of energy."

"Of course." Her mother laughed. "He would be, with Qurong's blood."

"He already handles a wooden sword as if he was born with it."

Patricia laughed, as did Cassak. But Qurong stared ahead and asked a most natural question, all things considered. "And is this an albino sword or one crafted by the Horde?"

"Oh, stop it, Qurong!" Patricia scolded. "Albino or not, he's your grandson. Stop being a baby."

Chelise wanted to reassure him but didn't know what to say to cut through all the deceptions that guided him. All of this was his fault, after all. From the very beginning, her own father had expanded the divide between albino and Horde.

She had this one chance to persuade him, but all the speeches she'd rehearsed lying under the stars in the desert fled her mind.

"Where is Thomas?" she asked.

"I have no clue. Gone."

"Tell us about Jake," Patricia said. "Come and sit. Are you thirsty? Cassak, please bring us some fruit."

Chelise sat at the table and politely accepted an orange from her mother. She told her about Jake, a little rascal who was as stubborn as both his father and grandfather. But as cute as a young Roush, with his fluffy blond hair.

She kept glancing at her father, who remained standing—under orders from Mother, no doubt. It was her idea, not his, that they meet.

They talked for a few minutes, and Chelise tried her best not to answer her mother's questions in a way that might offend their way of life, but the challenge quickly became impossible.

"He sounds precious," Patricia said, returning to Jake. "And healthy."

"From his baptism on, he's been as healthy as a horse."

"Baptism? What is a baptism?"

"The drowning. All of our children drown in the red pools. It keeps the disease away."

That robbed the tent of air.

"Barbaric," Qurong said. "You actually kill your children?"

"Do I look dead to you, Father?" Chelise stood. "I know that none of you can appreciate the drowning or you would have chosen it long ago. But you must know from your very own daughter, it is life-giving.

The dark priests tell you it's poison. Do I look poisoned? Is that why we are so much stronger than even your best warriors?"

"Nonsense!"

"Please," Patricia whispered, "don't speak of such things here."

But Chelise had waited ten years to speak of precisely such things here. She stepped around the table and approached her father.

General Cassak moved to intercept her. "Stay back."

She ignored him. "My father isn't afraid of women, particularly not his own daughter."

That stopped the general, who looked at Qurong but got no instructions. Chelise stood several paces from her father and searched his eyes.

"I saw you vanish into the books with my husband, Father. Can you tell me where he is?"

"He's escaped."

"Into this world? Or another?"

Qurong shifted his eyes. "I know nothing of another world beyond the nightmares that plague me every time I close my eyes."

"Please tell me that he was well the last time you saw him," she begged. "I deserve that much."

"How should I know? He's a witch who changes what men can see with their natural eyes. Beyond that I know nothing."

He was in complete denial about what she'd seen in his secret library. But she hardly blamed him. Who'd ever heard of vanishing into books? He'd categorized it as a nightmare.

"Father, I beg you to reconsider your ways. Albinos are a peaceful people who mean no harm to the Horde. They long only to be reunited with Elyon as was always intended. Everything that has happened from the beginning of time points to that end."

"Death and destruction are part of that plan? Don't be naive."

"No, those were man's choosing. But the evil was allowed so that we might all choose our lover. This is the meaning of the Great Romance— to choose to return the great love Elyon has shown us."

She paused, then spoke softly, knowing he must understand her.

"Do you remember what it was like before the Shataiki were set free, Father?"

"All of this is nonsense."

"To you who don't believe! Even to *me* before I believed. But to those who believe, it is the power of rescue. If you drown, Father, you will know what I know. Good and evil are not playing games to alleviate their boredom. The stakes are devastating! Our very lives are in the balance, all of ours—albino, Horde, and Eramite."

Qurong stared at her for a long time before turning and walking to a pitcher of ale. He poured some of the amber drink into a pewter mug.

"Please, Father. I'm begging you." She spoke in a soft, breaking voice because her emotions prevented her from screaming the words. "Drown with me!"

He took a long drink, refusing to look in her direction. Controlling his own emotions, she thought. She was getting through. How could anyone resist such simple truth?

"You speak of albinos who are peaceful, yet at this very moment they conspire to destroy the Horde," he said.

"That's just not true."

He faced her. "Samuel has joined Eram and is conspiring to pull the albinos into alliance with the half-breeds."

The moment he said it, Chelise knew it was true. This was what Thomas had meant!

And with such a show of power, more than a few albinos would be drawn into a war that promised to finish the Horde once and for all. Chelise's belly turned. Thomas was right, the world was crumbling!

"Thomas . . ." she said. "We need Thomas! He can stop them."

"Is that what he was doing when he offered his son up to Elyon at the high place? Stopping a war?"

"Yes! And you betrayed your word, Father." She stepped up to him and placed her hand on his arm, desperate to gain his trust. "I beg you, Father. You can stop this senselessness. For my sake, I beg you. For the sake of your grandson."

"Do not patronize me. There will be no war!" He pulled back, gripped his hand into a fist, and shook it. "But if there is, I will crush any force that comes against me."

"Qurong!" Patricia crossed the floor to them. "Remember our agreement. Watch your tone!"

"I am Qurong!" he shouted. "My women do not tell me what to do!"

Chelise felt smothered by a sudden urgency to return to the albinos. Samuel had to be stopped!

"If she'd never fallen for Thomas's lies, we wouldn't be in such a predicament," Qurong snapped.

"Oh, please, you can't possibly blame this on her," Patricia said. "You should look no further than your own priest."

"He is not my priest."

Qurong glanced at the door flap. It wasn't in good form to say such things about Ba'al aloud. Not all was at peace in the Horde camp. But none of this mattered to Chelise at the moment. She was without Thomas. And Samuel might be heading to the Gathering this very moment, intent on taking albinos with him to wage war on the Horde.

If he did, the Horde's days might be numbered.

"Cassak, see that she leaves her enemy camp without danger," Qurong said, heading for the door. "I have business."

"Qurong!" Patricia cried.

"You're not my enemy, Father," Chelise said. "I love you as much as my own life."

But her father marched out without another word.

All is lost, Chelise thought. *I've lost my husband, my son, and now my father, who is going to wage war on my people.*

The world waits for you, Chelise.

34

FOUR DAYS advising the Eramite army had proved to Samuel that he not only made a good choice in coming to Eram, but a choice that would reshape history. A choice that would soon be heralded as the definitive turning point in the era of Horde supremacy. Thomas of Hunter had become a legend because of a choice like this one, and now his son, Samuel of Hunter, would follow in his footsteps and be praised among the Circle as the one who liberated albinos from the scourge called Horde.

The children would engrave his name on bracelets, and men would sit around fires exaggerating his deeds until he was nothing less than a god in their eyes. And women . . . he'd never married, because deep down inside he knew that he was destined for greatness. While others his age spent day and night trying to impress demanding women, he'd spent his days refining his crafts of war. Now the young maidens would keep their hopeful eyes on him wherever he went.

But he hadn't counted on this particular woman, who found her way into Eram's inner circle twelve hours earlier. Her name was Janae, she said. She was an albino, she was disturbingly intelligent, and she was more beautiful than any woman he'd ever seen. Which gave him pause, because he'd seen all albinos and would certainly have noticed this one among the rest.

"No, my lord," he said, glancing back at the woman who studied them from her horse, twenty yards behind. "I don't think you should follow her advice. I think you should follow mine."

He and Eram sat on horses flanked by Eram's personal four-man guard, overlooking the eastern valley where Samuel's men were working with Forest Guard turned Horde. They'd agreed to place four thousand men under Samuel's command, an elite force of the best fighters Eram could offer. They would be led by as many as four hundred albino fighters, assuming Samuel could come through on his end of the bargain. They'd know soon enough. Tomorrow Samuel would take his small army west, announce his intentions to the Gathering, and challenge any who sought justice to join him in leading a guerrilla warfare campaign against Qurong.

Samuel would take his army, divide them into ten tightly knit, elite units, and station them on all sides of Qurongi City. Their first attack would be surgical and brutal, leaving Qurong's army with deep wounds to lick.

The second, third, and fourth attacks would follow immediately from three sides before the Horde could properly reassemble. Even if they did manage to form up, they would be confused without a clear campaign to execute or an army to engage. Within a matter of months, Samuel would soften Qurong's massive army, and then Eram would bring the full weight of his own one hundred fifty thousand to crush the Horde.

It was a reasonable plan, with almost no chance for failure, assuming Samuel could persuade enough of the Circle to join them. Assuming Eram didn't change his mind for fear of betrayal.

Assuming this woman named Janae didn't bring the whole thing down with her ridiculous talk of an immediate full-scale war on the authority of a Shataiki queen named Marsuuv.

"Please, just look at her. Have you ever seen a witch in service of a queen Shataiki? Not until now."

Eram followed his eyes and twisted his lips into a sly smile. "An albino witch? That's a new one. Where have you been hiding these stunning creatures?"

One thing was certain: Eram loved the ladies. Samuel had never known a man with such a voracious appetite for women. The Eramite leader made no attempt to hide his displays of affection whenever or wherever the impulse struck him, and yet he did it with tact, like a gentleman, despite the fact that his intentions were well-known. His people seemed to love him for it. Their leader was a passionate, virile man who had the backbone to lead them out into the desert. Who would castrate such a man?

"Forgive me for pointing it out," Samuel said, "but this isn't about a woman, however seductive."

Eram's grin softened, and the moment he shifted his eyes Samuel knew he'd spoken out of turn. "Are you looking for a knife in your throat?"

"No, my lord. Forgive me. But surely you can't be bowing to her nonsense."

"Bowing? You beg forgiveness for one jab and follow it with a slice to my head?"

"Forgive—"

"You're a dangerous man, Samuel of Hunter. I served under your father when you were a pup, and I see you have his audacity."

Samuel was glad for the shift in subject. "Like father, like son, they say."

"No, lad. Don't make the mistake of assuming you will ever be even half the man your father is. I would have laid my life down for him on the worst of days, and I'm not sure I wouldn't do the same today. He's a legend without peer and always will be."

"And yet you don't follow him."

"I don't follow his ideas. But I bow to the man. And him alone." The leader took a deep breath and cracked his neck with a jerk of his head. "To the matter at hand . . ." A crazed look lit his eyes. "I think the woman has more than seduction to offer us."

"Yes, danger. Take the whole army to the Gathering? Now? It's a huge gamble."

"I see no danger to me. If she's wrong, I lose nothing but some time and effort. If she's right, on the other hand, she'd replace your lofty status as the hero, isn't that it?"

The Eramite leader was a brilliant tactician in political matters;

he'd pegged Samuel's fear even before Samuel had fully formed his own understanding of it.

"But I'm not one to change with the wind," Eram said. "I've given my word to you, so now I leave this matter in your hands. You decide. Come." He turned his horse from the valley and walked it toward Janae, who still watched them from her perch under a tree.

She wore a red cape with a short black cloak that covered fighting leathers. Odd, this red cape. The breeze lifted long black strands of hair from her shoulders and wrapped them around a porcelain white neck. He'd noticed a light rash on the skin at the base of her neck and on her wrists. Similar to a rash he'd noticed on his own skin yesterday.

Rash or no rash, this woman who'd come to them bearing a challenge from the Shataiki was truly stunning. It was her eyes, Samuel thought. They watched above perpetually curved lips, cutting deeply into his mind. Honestly, she frightened him, not only for her potential threat to his stature among new friends, but for her effect on him personally. Unlike Eram, he resented the notion of seduction now.

The guard held back as Eram and Samuel approached her under the tree. "So, the mistress of a Shataiki queen has brought the poor Eramites salvation, is that it?" Eram said, his smile matching hers.

Janae shifted her eyes back to Samuel. Her longing stares had favored him above Eram since the patrol first deposited her in Eram's court. For now she seemed satisfied to simply look into his eyes.

"How is it that an albino mates with a Shataiki?" Eram asked. "Hmmm?"

"How is it that an albino becomes a half-breed?" she returned, eyes still on Samuel.

"Indeed. The world has changed. Now the most beautiful come from the Black Forest."

"Your flattery means nothing to me, Eram, old boy. I'm fascinated with this stallion."

He chuckled, genuinely amused, Samuel thought.

"And for the record," the woman said, now exchanging a smile with the leader, "I am not the mistress of any queen. Marsuuv, the queen who sent me, has another for his lover. Billy. Perhaps you know him as Billos. As for me, I don't come from the Black Forest. I'm from another world, where my kind are better known as vampires. But you can call me the messiah. And I am mistress to no one but Teeleh, my lord and savior."

She spoke as one reciting poetry, a minstrel from the dark side who captivated even jaded men like Eram with her every word. A wicked woman who melted hearts. Surely Eram saw that much.

"A witch from another world," Eram said, "who comes to tell us that she can deliver the albinos if only we follow her. That if we take our full army to the Circle, they will join us for war. In three days' time, no less."

"I am here to serve, my lord. Not to lead. And unless my aim was to seduce the bravest leader in the land, I would be a fool to come with words alone."

Janae slipped her hand into her cloak and withdrew a small glass bottle, perfectly formed, perhaps three inches tall. She held it between her thumb and forefinger and twirled it.

"This, my lovelies, is the answer to all of your prayers."

Samuel cleared his throat. "A bottle filled with Teeleh's urine will save us? Tell me why a half-breed who still follows Elyon in the ways of old, and an albino who rejects Teeleh, should entertain the mistress of Teeleh himself?"

She ignored his second question, as if it were too silly to take seriously.

"You might be surprised to know what a single drop of Teeleh's blood can do. But for now, we'll have to do with the Raison Strain, a brutal, incurable virus that destroys the body from the inside in a matter of hours."

"We have our poisons," Eram said. "So you have another. What of it?"

"Oh, that's right, I forgot, neither of you has a PhD in biochemistry."

Samuel didn't know what she meant, but he heard the mockery in her tone.

"Let me put it to you this way: if I could deliver what I hold in my hand to the Horde army, the condition that afflicts them already would become worse. Much worse. It would immobilize them in minutes. A strong army could wipe them out."

"And how do you propose to get such a small amount to the entire Horde army without also infecting us?" Eram asked, intrigued.

"Every witch has her secrets," she said. Her eyes turned to Samuel. "Do as I suggest and I will prove my power in front of the entire Gathering."

So, she had more than words and beauty. Or so she claimed. Eram chuckled and faced Samuel. "As I said, young Hunter, the decision's yours." He turned his stallion around and winked. "I'll give you some time to . . . consider this alone."

Eram galloped away, motioned his guard to follow him, and rode over the hill, leaving Samuel alone with Janae. The conniving rogue likely thought Samuel too weak to fend off the advances of this witch, but he didn't know the backbone of Thomas Hunter's son, now, did he?

When he turned back, the woman was staring to her right, into nothing but the horizon from what he could see. Her sly grin was gone, her sultry eyes now harsh. Finally, the real woman stripped of ulterior motives.

"You may have our brave leader by the loins, witch, but I have no intention of handing control of his army over to you."

"That's funny. He said you would be the most difficult."

"Who did?"

She faced him. "Marsuuv. The son of the mighty Thomas Hunter has a backbone of steel like his father. Stubborn to the heels."

"Then the old bat knows more than I would have given him credit for."

Janae dismounted and walked toward the trees. "Let me show you something."

He hesitated, then followed her into the small grove. She let him catch up and took his hand without it being offered.

"To be perfectly honest, the disease these filthy beasts have disgusts me. It's good to touch the flesh of a normal human." She rubbed her thumb on the back of his hand as she led him through the trees. "What

I said about me coming from another reality wasn't meant to make me look foolish, Samuel. It's the truth. I come from the same place your own father once came from. This very planet, actually. Two thousand years ago. The world was much more advanced then. Evil wasn't as plain. Good was even less plain. I do believe it all ended badly, judging by what I see here. All the cities and cars, the roadways, the concrete jungles . . . gone."

They stepped out of the trees on the far side and gazed out at lowlands that stretched as far as the eye could see. "You see this world? It's a simple place compared to what was once here. Manageable. And whether or not you like it, dear Samuel, you and I have been chosen to manage it." She released his hand and slipped her arm around his waist, eyes still on the lowlands. "At the very least, we will manage it the next few days."

He wasn't sure what to say to that. She'd changed her tone.

"You may not like the Shataiki, but they share one thing in common with you."

He was meant to ask what, so he did, but his mind was on her hand, which now softly rubbed his back in an unapologetic show of tenderness. Did she think him a child to be so easily manipulated?

"The Shataiki, like you, despise the Horde."

"Along with the rest of humanity," he said.

"Granted. But also like you, they mean to destroy the Horde, and they have empowered me to help you do it."

He didn't know what to make of this claim.

"I have no interest in taking your place, Samuel. I'll help you, only if that's what you want." She turned into him and pulled him close, staring up into his eyes. "And I won't lie; I wouldn't mind some companionship in the process."

Her approach was so direct, so transparent, that he lost track of her motivation for trickery. He should pry her hands off him and call her out! But he didn't, not yet. What if she meant what she said?

"Our goals are the same, Samuel," she said, searching his eyes in that way. "We are one at heart. Both albinos, both with the same hatred of the Horde, both called by powers beyond our understanding. We were meant to be together."

She's a witch, Samuel. She'll use you and leave you for dead. Still, his breathing thickened.

"I hate the Horde because they've waged war on my people for as long as I can remember," he said. "If you've come from the histories, why do you harbor such hatred for those who've done you no wrong?"

His mind was swimming in her eyes. Her soft lips, her perfect jawline. But above these, her words. So perfectly placed, so knowing. Enough to make his belly rise into his throat.

"Don't be silly, Samuel," she said, coming closer to his face. She spoke in a low, purring voice, but her eyes flashed with passion. "We all want the same thing. Hmm? The contentment, the pleasure, the power we were born for. Love life or die trying, isn't that a fighter's motto?"

Was it?

He broke into a sweat, knowing full well that she was manipulating him. But he couldn't remember what part of her suggestions didn't align with his own desires.

She touched his lips with her own, not so much a kiss as a peck, but it made his mind go completely blank.

"Say yes, Samuel," she whispered. "This is what you want. What you need as much as I do. Tell Eram that he shouldn't wait another day."

"Take the army today." He meant it as a question, but it came out as a statement.

"If you march all night, you could be in the western canyons when the sun goes down tomorrow."

"The others have gone to the Gathering. I would speak to them."

"You would speak to them," she whispered. "Samuel, son of Hunter."

"Some would follow us."

"No, Samuel. Many would follow you. I've been assured."

The party doing the assuring could only be Shataiki, his greatest enemy, but at the moment this minute detail seemed strangely inconsequential. He placed his arms around her waist and pulled her against him. Her lips were softer than he had imagined, and for a few moments he felt like a boy discovering love for the first time. She kissed him hungrily, and he knew that he could not say no to the woman in his arms.

Worse, he didn't want to. How things had changed in just a few short minutes. Eram was right. Janae was right.

The time to change the world would not wait.

"Say yes, Samuel. Tell me yes. I want to hear it."

Stripped of any reason to deny her, he said it softly but without reluctance.

"Yes."

35

QURONG DISMOUNTED the sweating black stallion, threw the reins to one of the Throaters who'd accompanied him on the long ride back to Qurongi City, and marched up the Thrall steps, still furious for having left his army in the dead of night. But the situation had become complicated and he was forced to abandon his good sense for the sake of a woman and a priest.

His wife had emerged after spending hours eating a meal with Chelise and demanded to be taken back to the city immediately. Qurong would have sent her with an escort, but then word came from one of the temple priests: Ba'al had returned from the Black Forest with a message that was a matter of life and death for the Horde. Qurong must come immediately. No, Ba'al could not come out because certain rituals were required.

So Qurong endured the silent four-hour trek, during which he and his wife ignored each other in protest over the other's behavior regarding their daughter.

What did she want? He had principles. Chelise might be his daughter, but she had joined his greatest enemy, for the breath of Teeleh! He spat on the temple steps. She'd *wed* his greatest enemy. Borne a son by him. Now Patricia wanted him, Qurong, leader of the world, to throw away decades of conflict so that she could cuddle her little albino grandson? She'd likely catch his disease!

Worse than this was the position that Patricia had put him in by insisting they meet. His heart had stopped the moment Chelise walked into the tent. He'd put her from his mind a long time ago. But there she was, his flesh and blood, standing so beautifully in his doorway. The sight of her was brutal punishment. He'd exercised extraordinary self-control in making sure she didn't receive hope from him.

Then she told him she loved him, and he took a horse into the forest alone to hide his emotions.

He opened the door to the Thrall's sanctuary. "Where is Ba'al?" he shouted without bothering to look. If he had looked he would have seen the dark priest directly ahead, standing behind the stone altar dressed in his purple ceremonial robe. A red cape Qurong had never seen before covered Ba'al's shoulders.

A butchered goat lay on the altar, sacrificed already. The torches licked at the air, glancing off the serpent's wings on either side of the bleeding goat.

"I'm here," Qurong announced, striding forward. "And I'm in no mood to stay long. You called me from my army at the most inopportune time."

"The day before they are to be slaughtered?" Ba'al rasped. His eyes were red and there was blood on his lower lip. "You meant to wish them all well on their way to hell?"

Qurong drew up and closed his eyes, resolving to suffer through the man's games if he must. "Fine, my dear dark priest. What is it this time?"

Ba'al stared at him for a long moment. His usual coy grin was gone. Another quality about him gave Qurong pause. He looked more emaciated in the face, perhaps. Dirtier, as if he'd gone on this journey of his and returned without bathing. And he hadn't bothered to apply enough morst to hide his flaking skin.

"The world is crumbling about you, Qurong, and you don't have the decency to hear of it. I suggest you listen to the spirits of fear."

"I'll pass."

"Then I'll say what he told me to say and leave your fate up to him." Ba'al picked up a crudely fashioned glass bottle from the podium behind him and set it on the altar. It appeared to be filled with a black fluid.

"You're going to have to make a choice, my lord," Ba'al bit off.

"Tonight you will give all your allegiance to Teeleh, or you will suffer the same fate as the rest."

There was something different about his voice. Simple authority. No pretense. Qurong let him continue.

"At this very moment, the Eramites are gathering with the albinos to march on your army. Did you know that?"

Nonsense. But he would listen.

"Samuel, son of Hunter, has brokered a deal with Eram to fight together against the Horde."

"This isn't news to me."

"Janae, that albino witch from beyond, will convince many albinos to join. They mean to strike within days with an army of one hundred fifty thousand half-breeds and thousands of albinos."

Qurong felt his veins run cold. "That's not possible. I was with one of their leaders just today, and they said nothing of this."

"Your daughter, Chelise, knows nothing. If she did, she never would have come to meet with you."

Ba'al knew of Chelise's visit. More to the point, he seemed to know more than Qurong. There was no end to his spies!

"What I know comes directly from my lover, the queen Marsuuv, the twelfth of twelve who serve Teeleh. The day of the dragon has arrived, my lord. All those who do not bear the mark of the beast will die in the Valley of Miggdon—albino, half-breed Eramite, and full-breed Horde. I bring to you today the means to your salvation."

He'd heard similar words from Ba'al, but at this midnight hour, these words resonated with an undeniable quality that had Qurong's heart beating like a fist.

"We've all taken the mark of your beast," he said. "What more could he possibly demand?"

"Your heart, my lord."

"My heart? He has my entire body!" Qurong thundered. "What is this of Miggdon? We are gathered in Torun, not Miggdon."

"So you are. And I commend you on your plan; it was good thinking. But it won't be enough."

"You know all this how?"

Ba'al picked up the bottle and held it up to the flame. What Qurong had assumed to be black turned red as the light passed through the glass. Blood.

"You look up and you see only sky. I look up and I see the watchers of our souls perched in the trees, soaring over our heads. The Shataiki see everything."

"Only Shataiki? So Elyon is a fable."

"Only Shataiki," he said, bringing the vial to his lips. "For a time, only Shataiki." He kissed the blood and whispered lovingly, "I am your servant, my lover, Marsuuv."

"One hundred fifty thousand, you say." Qurong paced to his left, lost in the size of the half-breed army. "Less than one-third the size of our own."

"They haven't been sitting in the desert getting fat. And they will have albinos."

"A few thousand at most."

"Enough to tip the balance. Don't underestimate the albinos, my lord. They may have laid their swords down, but they were trained by Thomas of Hunter." Ba'al spit to one side and black saliva splattered on the altar.

"I'm listening."

The dark priest set the bottle of blood back down and slowly slid it across the altar until it rested in front of Qurong.

"Move your army to the east face of Miggdon Valley, where the terrain will play to your advantage. Hide three hundred thousand behind the valley and leave the rest on the hills to be seen."

"Bait."

"Eram will lead his army to the other side of Miggdon Valley." Ba'al drew out his plan on the dead goat's hide with a long, crooked finger in need of a nail trim. "He will take the bait and attack the army in the valley with enough men to destroy them."

"And we will descend with the two hundred thousand in plain sight."

"Which he will expect, naturally. He will then commit the rest of his forces against your army, not knowing that you have another three hundred thousand in reserve on the high ground."

"We take them out with a crushing blow, once and for all," Qurong said.

Ba'al smiled and stepped back. "If, and only if, you appease Teeleh."

Qurong didn't see the connection, and his face clearly betrayed his confusion.

"It is the day of the dragon, my lord. This isn't about you. You must believe me when I tell you there's black magic afoot. The Eramites aren't fools. They'll come with their own plans for victory."

"What plans?"

"Dark magic. If I knew more I would tell you, but I can't say what will happen if you don't take the side of my dark lover. In the end it is he who will rule. Not me, not you, not Eram, and certainly not Thomas of Hunter."

Qurong looked at the blood. The blood of Teeleh or Marsuuv, both equally terrifying. He lifted the glass container and held it up to the light.

"Drinking the blood will seal your vow," Ba'al said.

What madness could come from drinking blood?

"A vow?" Qurong asked.

"From your heart."

He could either refuse the rite, which would earn the rage of both Ba'al and whoever controlled him, or he could win their favor. The choice seemed simple enough.

Qurong twisted the stopper, lifted the blood to his nostrils and immediately regretted his decision to do so. The foul smell might have been an old open wound. He would have to drink quickly.

"Will you give your heart to my master?" Ba'al asked.

"Yes."

"Then repeat my words." Ba'al lifted both hands and called the pledge to the ceiling in a loud, ringing voice. "I, Qurong, supreme commander of the Horde, pledge my heart and my loyalty to the dragon called Teeleh, to do his bidding in accordance with only his will."

"I, Qurong, supreme commander of the Horde, pledge my heart and my loyalty to the dragon called Teeleh, to do his bidding in accordance with only his will."

"And I seal my vow with this blood, knowing that it comes from my master, Teeleh, maker of the evil that lives on our flesh."

The jargon of black magic was comical, but he knew every word would be important to Ba'al, so he repeated the vow exactly as instructed.

"Now drink!" Ba'al cried. "Drink of this blood in remembrance of the day you first embraced the evil. Drink to Teeleh, your lord and your master."

"I drink," Qurong said, and drained the blood into his mouth. He swallowed quickly, as if it was a hard drink, and slammed the glass down on the altar. He was tempted to spit, but he dared not. So he swallowed the last of it and steadied himself on the stone.

"Satisfied?"

Ba'al grinned at him. "More than you know, my lord."

"Good."

"Do you feel any different?"

"Only nauseated."

"No, you wouldn't. Your mind is already eaten by the worms."

More magic nonsense. And that was that.

"Then, if your lord requires—"

"*Your* lord," Ba'al corrected. "He's *your* lord now."

"Of course. If *my* lord requires nothing more, I have to leave immediately."

"To the Valley of Miggdon," Ba'al said.

"To the Valley of Miggdon."

WHILE QURONG was vowing his allegiance to Teeleh two thousand years in the future, Thomas Hunter, who'd come from that future, paced in Monique de Raison's personal library, slowly coming apart at the seams, aware only that this world was no longer his home.

"But it could be your home," Kara said. "Please, Thomas, sit down. I don't know how long I can take this pacing."

He spun around and threw his arms wide. "I'm lost, Kara! I'm stranded here in this"—he glanced about—"godforsaken place."

"This godforsaken place might very well be the only place you'll ever live. You've affected this reality as much as you've affected the other; it's time you acknowledge that. For all we know, this little jaunt of yours will have a profound impact on our future."

"Yes, of course, the apocalypse is just around the corner, and it's here because of me. Right."

She stood and crossed to him, intending to calm him. "You've said it yourself: everything that's happened there is a mirror image of what's happened here. It's a dim reflection that's anything but precise, but history is unraveling in almost perfect symmetry. What awaits you in the other reality?"

"Nothing much. Only the end of the world."

"And here?"

She had a good point. "Okay." He lifted both hands in surrender. "You're right, the same awaits me here."

"*Us* here," she corrected.

"Okay, us here."

"Eight billion people are on the cusp of either a tragic ending or a grand climax. And for all you know, you're here to usher it in. That doesn't sound like a rather important consideration to you?"

She was right, so right. But Thomas couldn't wrap his heart around the importance of any role he might play in this reality.

He turned from her, gripping his hair. His chest felt as though it might burst.

And then suddenly it was. Bursting. He shouted his frustration through clenched teeth and keeled over. "I can't be here! She needs me. Jake needs me. Samuel needs me!"

"I need you," Kara said softly.

Thomas faced her. "I will take you, Kara. I swear I will take you. Billy will come back with the books, because if anyone has a role to play in the end of this world, it's that redhead from hell! I won't leave this place. I don't care how long it takes, I'll eat here, I'll sleep here. The moment he appears, I'll . . ."

He'd what? Knock him out, take the books, and vanish? Yes, if that was what returning required.

"You never know how much you love someone until they're gone," Kara said. "When you left us, I thought I would die. I understand how you feel."

"They are my life, Kara. And Chelise . . ." He felt his eyes tear up. "I'm telling you, she is my breath. A constant reminder that Elyon longs for me the way I long for her. Without her I would dry up like an uprooted Catalina cactus." He spoke the words in a rush, feeding on his need to say what was eating him alive.

"She's water to me, my gift from the Giver of all that is good. She's my sky, my ground, my reason for waking and my reason for sleeping. She is my life!"

Kara's neck darkened a shade. "Wow."

"It's all about him; of course it is. But I see him in *her*! She's become the lake that I drown in!"

Overstated in a state of despair, perhaps, but hardly.

"I would rather die than stay here, separated from the woman I love, from the son who turned his back on me! I need to find them!"

Kara set her jaw. "Then beg Elyon to save you from a living death. Because from where I'm standing, you're stuck here. In this death."

She was right. Dear Elyon, she was so right!

Thomas turned around and fell to his knees. He squeezed his hands into two fists, faced the ceiling, and through streams of tears begged Elyon to send him the books.

Send him the books or let him die.

36

CHELISE HAD raced over the desert, expecting at any moment to see signs of stragglers converging on the Gathering in Paradose Valley, late-coming albinos who'd heard the summons that Thomas of Hunter was calling the Circle together for the first time in many years. And Eramite scouts, preceding Samuel.

But it wasn't until she was nearly in the valley that she saw any sign of albinos or Scabs, and the sight made her pull her mount up hard. The mare snorted.

A line of Horde, maybe twenty in all, turned to look at her. They rode in full battle dress over a dune not a hundred yards from where she'd stopped. Horde scouts, so deep?

But these weren't from her father's army, which she'd left last night. To begin with, their armor was a light tan and blended into the sands, not black like those she'd seen yesterday. And these warriors wore no hel-mets. Their hair blew freely, no dreadlocks.

Her first thought was that they were Eramite, though she'd never seen an Eramite warrior before. And she knew they couldn't be scouts. These twenty carried spears and maces, spiked steel balls, dangling from each saddle, not the lighter weapons of a fast-moving scout.

This was a contingent from a full army, riding without care within a half-hour march of Paradose Valley! That the warriors saw her and made no attempt to cut her off disturbed her even more.

She stared in stunned silence, lost for a moment. Thoughts of the Gathering crashed through her mind. All twelve thousand had surely arrived by now.

Did these soldiers know how close they were to the Circle's most prized tribe? But of course they must!

Samuel.

Samuel had done precisely what her father predicted. He'd brought a contingent of Eramites to the Circle. She'd fled her mother's tent with the scout Stephen as an escort and made the best possible time across the desert, hoping that Qurong's information was wrong, or at least twisted. Stephen had left at her insistence nearly six hours ago. She knew the way from here, and it was safe.

But here and now, she knew that there was only one explanation for the twenty nonhostile half-breeds on the dune to her right. She kicked her horse and galloped on, down the slope and up the far rise, heart pounding. Up the rise, begging Elyon for time. The elders knew about Samuel, but what would they say to . . .

Chelise slid to a halt atop the next dune and gawked at the sight that greeted her. The valley was alive, flooded by an army that stretched to the horizon.

Samuel had not only brought a contingent of Eramites, he'd brought the whole half-breed army! A massive throng, no less than a hundred thousand strong, capable of crushing the Circle under hoof without breaking stride.

And where was Elyon?

The world awaits you, Chelise. Michal's words whispered through her mind.

Chelise whipped her horse and cried out, urging it to run, to race as fast as was possible despite legs tired to the breaking point.

She had to tell them that Qurong had already gathered his army.

That they could not listen to Samuel.

That they could not make a move without Thomas!

A hundred thoughts pounded through her head, and she slapped the mare's hide harder, racing around the army. It didn't matter; not one seemed even slightly disturbed by the presence of an albino on a horse. Only curious. They'd already seen plenty today.

They were half-breeds, but their gray eyes and flaking skin were no different from full-breed Horde's. These half-breeds were as Horde as her own father.

They watched her from a distance, and the sheer scope of their enormity sent a shiver down her spine.

It took her less than twenty minutes to cut a line across the dunes, around the gathered army, into the canyon, and to the corrals behind the tents.

The camp looked deserted. But the albinos had to be around the corner, gathering in the amphitheater where Thomas himself had toasted the Great Romance not two weeks ago.

Then she heard his voice. Samuel's voice, echoing unseen from beyond the cliff. She ran up the path to the overlook and pulled up sharply.

The Circle had indeed arrived, all of them. They stood or squatted on boulders and sat on the cliffs, and their attention was firmly fixed on the flat stone surface where Marie had fought Samuel in the earliest bid to end this craziness.

And here he was again, this son of Thomas, Samuel of Hunter, standing next to an albino woman dressed in Horde battle armor and a red cape. Behind them, an Eramite leader, perhaps Eram himself, sat on his horse with a half dozen other half-breed fighters.

The elders stood to their right, arms crossed, watching with a mix of skepticism and interest. Why weren't they stopping this?

"Wasn't this day prophesied of old?" Samuel called. "It is said he will ride on a white horse and deliver those who swim with him to a new world, where there are no tears."

His voice rang out. "Where his fruit is heady enough to make the most pained heart laugh with delight. Where our children no longer fear that a Horde sword will gut their mother or drop their father's bloody head to the ground. For ten years we have fled this oppressor. Will Elyon never rescue us?"

"But he has," Mikil said.

"Let him speak!" someone shouted back. "This is Thomas's son, and what he says has merit."

Samuel continued without giving Mikil opportunity. "Mikil's right. Elyon has saved our hearts, and now he extends his hand to pull us from this wretched life on the run. Our enemy will not mock us, they will not ridicule us, they will only envy the Great Romance. I am Elyon's prophet and I say it is so."

"It is as he says!"

"He speaks the truth!"

"No, no, this can't be . . ."

The response was a cacophony of mixed sentiment.

"Do you doubt?" Samuel shouted, red-faced. They quieted slowly. "Do you think I was born to Thomas of Hunter for no reason? If he was here, would he deny the prophecies of old? We cannot escape our destiny."

"It is as he says."

"He speaks the truth."

"The day of Elyon's wrath against the Horde has come, my friends. We will destroy the Horde!"

"Through an *alliance* with the Horde?" Johan demanded. "This is ill-advised."

"Ill-advised," Samuel mocked. "Our elders are too intellectual to follow the passions of Elyon, who uses whomever he sees fit. Today that is Eram and the famed Forest Guard." He called the half-breeds as they were known before acquiring the scabbing disease. "I'm proposing we ally ourselves with Eram to this end. He needs us as much as we need him. Let me take five thousand of the strongest fighters here, and we will lead the army you've all seen just outside our canyon in one crushing blow against the Horde!"

It sounded perfectly reasonable, Chelise thought, except for what they didn't know. And according to the Roush, the world awaited her, Chelise, who'd been sent back by Thomas in his stead, to save them all.

The Circle awaited her.

She lifted both hands and stepped forward, overlooking them all. "I am Chelise, wife of Thomas, and I find fault with this son of mine!" she cried for the whole Gathering to hear. They tilted their heads up. A murmur ran through the Gathering as she hopped down and stood on a large boulder to Samuel's right.

"Hello, Mother," Samuel said.

She ignored him. "I have come from the east, where the Horde army is assembling in the Torun Valley. They know we are here at this moment, with the Eramites, and they beg us to come so that they can crush us and leave our bodies for the buzzards!"

"I love you, Mother, but you're wrong."

She whirled to face him. "You're saying the Horde will not slaughter many, if not all, if you march now?"

"Well, yes, there would be some bloodshed. But you're still wrong. Mother. You don't know everything. You don't know that Elyon has given me a supernatural means of victory."

She was at a loss for words.

Samuel stepped forward and addressed the assembly. "It's true, I'm a prophet for this day, but I don't come with words alone. How could I stand up to the quick tongues of the council or my own mother? But I come with another." He looked at the woman beside him. "I present to you the strong arm of Elyon himself, in the flesh, for our benefit." He reached for her hand, kissed it, and held it high. "Friends of the Circle, I present to you Janae, a messiah in her own right."

Applause started with a smattering and grew.

"Show them, Janae."

The dark-haired witch had the look of a seductress. There was a strange rash on her neck, similar to the one Chelise now saw on Samuel's neck.

Janae stepped forward and paced before them like a general surveying the troops. She motioned casually over her shoulder with a single finger. "Bring him."

Two of the half-breeds hauled a chained Scab into the clearing. Chelise recognized him immediately: This was Stephen, the very scout who'd treated her so kindly as an escort.

His gray eyes found hers. "Please . . ."

"Let him go!"

The witch twisted around. "We will! As soon as he shows everyone what I already know."

Janae pulled out a small vial and held it up for the whole assembly to see. "In my hand I hold Elyon's gift to us all." She plucked the stopper from the top of the glass tube and waved it in front of her nose like a precious perfume. "The scent of the most high. To you and I, who have bathed in the lakes, half-breeds and albino alike, it is a gift."

Chelise could smell the potent scent from where she stood, a mix of lemon and gardenia flower if she was right.

Samuel's seductress lifted it up and walked to the closest observers. She held it out. "It gives us only strength. But to this infidel behind me, the scent of Elyon is poison. Yes? If he comes within ten paces of me, as he is now, the scent will enter his nostrils, penetrate his blood, and excite the very scabbing disease that makes him Horde. To be more precise, the scent repels the worms that eat him alive, throwing them into a fit. They will wreak havoc . . ."

The scout began to whimper. He scratched at his skin in a growing panic.

". . . with his nerves," Janae finished. She nodded at the guards. "Release him."

They unlocked the scout's chains and pushed him forward. Stephen had gone from a terrified Horde who feared his captors to a debilitated man panicked by whatever was happening to him. He staggered forward, bent at his knees like an old man. "What's happening? Take it off me!"

"It's not *on* him," Janae said for all to hear. "It's *in* him, and it is Teeleh's breath, stimulating the worms eating his body." She paced before the crowd, scanning them with an even stare. "Yet I feel nothing. The half-breeds feel nothing. The council feels nothing. Those close enough to inhale this breath from hell feel nothing. Why? Because we have all bathed in the lakes at one time and are immune to my Raison Strain." Then she added, "Elyon's gift to us."

A mumble of amazement swept through the crowd with a few sharp expressions of protest, but even more cries of agreement. "She tells the truth, she tells the truth!"

Janae walked to Samuel, who gazed at her as if she might be his own personal goddess. She stood on her toes and kissed him on the cheek. Taking his hand, she turned back to the Gathering.

"Elyon's gift. He gave it to me and told me I would find Samuel with the Eramites. Together we would come to the Circle, in peace. We would extend the grace of Elyon, and then we would march on the Horde army, feed them Teeleh's breath, and slaughter them all in their weakened state."

Chelise stood on the boulder, bound by twisted cords of objection.

Where was Elyon in all of this? Janae spoke with authority. Could her son's new lover have come from Elyon? Her message was desperately needed by many in the Circle. They would drink it deep and satisfy their thirst for Elyon's power once again.

But this woman could not have come from Elyon! She was a seductress, a harlot with words that tickled the ears. And she was missing the most important element in Elyon's charge to them all.

Chelise yelled it now, shouting over both Johan and Mikil, who'd stepped forward as one and were objecting.

"Love the Horde!" she cried, pointing at the Horde scout who was now shaking in fear and pain. "This is our only charge regarding these poor souls. Judgment will be Elyon's to wield, not ours."

"What she says is true," Johan shouted.

"We can never take up a sword and cut down another human in Elyon's name," Chelise said. "Never!"

"So says the daughter of Qurong, the cousin of Teeleh."

She didn't know who from the throng of twelve thousand had made the point, but no one protested the comment. She stood high on the boulder, staring at the full assembly of albinos, and for the first time in many years she felt like a stranger in their midst.

She, who'd drowned in Elyon's love and been washed of the disease, felt more Horde than albino in this moment. What was the difference between them and Qurong? Between Samuel and Stephen?

The scabbing disease was the difference.

And the insight to acknowledge that the condition was evil, affecting the mind and heart as much as the skin. And the bravery to follow Elyon into the red pool, drown to this life of disease, and rise from the waters as a new creature.

Because wasn't her mother, Patricia, capable of love? Wasn't her father worthy of life? She would die before she considered taking up arms against any Horde!

All eyes were on her. Both Samuel and Janae seemed content to let her engage her own people. She silently begged Elyon to bring Thomas to them. *Now.* In these deserts, the people would follow him like no other. They needed him desperately.

She needed him. She required her lover by her side, for the warmth of his body and his soft words of encouragement and his tender kiss of love.

"Yes." Her voice was shaking. "I am the daughter of Qurong, and yes, my father is still deceived. He can't see the truth when it stares him in the face. But isn't this the way of the world? They can only see the ordinary, and Elyon is anything but ordinary. His love is extraordinary, extending beyond you and me to our own fathers and mothers and sisters and brothers who are still Horde."

"His love is extraordinary, Mother," Janae said. "But then so is his wrath." The woman stepped away from Samuel and drilled her with a stare. "Do you challenge my authority as the one who has come with this gift from Elyon?"

What if she was right? What if this really was Elyon's gift to them all? It was strange that this woman had come to them from nowhere, much like Thomas had first come. Strange that she had taken up with Samuel, son of Hunter. So similar yet so . . . different.

Before Chelise could answer the woman's question, Janae faced the Gathering. "And what say you?" She lifted the vial she claimed to be Teeleh's breath. "How many will hear the voice of one calling from the desert? 'Prepare the way of the lord, for every valley shall be filled in, every mountain made low. And the whole world will see the salvation of Elyon.'"

"Is it so impossible?" Vadal, son of the elder Ronin asked quietly.

"Sit down, Vadal," Marie snapped.

He looked into Chelise's eyes and she saw his confusion. When put this way, how could they deny?

Janae repeated her question. "Who will stand with me? And who will challenge me?"

Nearly half stood to their feet. A jumble of support and objection filled the canyon.

Chelise felt her world crumbling. It was too much. *Thomas, Thomas, Thomas. Where are you, my love?* She felt as though she might burst into tears.

She slowly lifted one hand into the air and spoke clearly. "I do."

Mikil, who'd been yelling the crowd down along with Jamous and Johan, looked up at her. But no one else showed they'd heard. The council argued among themselves. Even they were divided.

"I do!" she cried louder, shaking her fist at the sky. Then she screamed it, letting her emotions rally. "I do!"

Now they were listening. All of them. She breathed hard and pointed to Janae. "I do challenge your authority as the one who has come with this gift from Elyon."

She leaped from the rock, strode over to Samuel. Yanked his sword from his back where he'd slung it. Walked to the center of the stone slab.

"I do challenge you by the same rules invoked by Samuel, and I deny any to fight for me."

"What's this?" Janae asked whimsically.

Samuel explained that a challenge once settled disputes. The winner's way would be followed.

Chelise wasn't sure what she expected in the moment—some resistance from the council at least, a moment to judge the skill of her opponent as they squared off. Anything but what happened.

Janae handed her vial to Samuel, stepped over to Eram, who was still watching with amused interest, took his sword from the scabbard, and sprang forward.

But this was not just any ordinary leap. She took two steps, launched herself into the air like a cat, and flew a full ten yards before landing in a crouch directly in front of Chelise, sword on guard.

"Your first mistake, Mother," Janae said. "And your last."

Chelise lowered her sword by her side as if surrendering, but turned it in at the last moment and ran it up under Janae as she threw herself back into an aerial somersault with a loud cry.

It was one of Thomas's basic maneuvers, once taught to all Forest Guard, extremely effective because an opponent had to contend with both the blade and the attacker's feet at once. But Janae had something not even Thomas had.

The speed of a bat.

How did she manage to escape Chelise's sword and appear behind her? Chelise couldn't know; she'd been upside down when Janae moved.

But Chelise was no slouch, and she didn't waste any energy trying to understand what had just happened. She was swinging her sword with as much strength as she possessed before she landed.

Their blades met with a clang that echoed through the canyon. Chelise's hands stung with the clash of metal against metal. But they'd both escaped injury.

Each having earned the other's respect, Chelise expected they would hesitate in the crowd's silence for a moment before . . .

But Janae was moving already, this time with such speed that Chelise couldn't react except to gasp and attempt a block with a wild swing of her sword. Her opponent's blade sliced cleanly through the strap that held her chest armor in place.

Janae reached in and yanked the armor down. The leather thongs slipped free, and the chest guard fell to the ground.

"You've lost your top, Mother."

She felt naked with only a tunic between herself and this witch's blade. More to the point, she knew she was as good as dead. What kind of black magic empowered this woman was an easy guess, but unless Elyon himself granted her the strength and agility of the Roush, she would die.

She now knew that fighting this woman was utterly foolish, but Chelise was committed. And this fight was for her father, whom they sought to kill. If she must die, she would do so knowing she'd died for him.

"Come on, you little whore," she breathed. "Kill me. Or die trying."

Janae flung her sword to one side, easily evaded a thrust from Chelise's sword that would have connected with most mortals, and punched her soundly in the jaw.

Chelise's world spun. Faded. The ground beneath her feet tilted. She landed on the ground with a hard thud.

"I will not kill a child of Elyon," Janae was crying in the distance. "Our war is not between us. It is with the enemy of Elyon! Now this matter is settled. Samuel has joined Eram and the Forest Guard who wait over these hills."

Chelise's world began to right itself. She tried to push herself up but was still too weak.

"Today we will march on the Valley of Miggdon, where Qurong will move his army. In two days' time we will crush them with one blow of Elyon's wrath, and we will leave the blood of the dragon in the valley to feed the lust of all Shataiki. Then, and only then, will Elyon deliver us into his glory!"

A roar spontaneously erupted.

"Who is with me?"

Not all of them, *certainly* not all. But many were crying out in support. Chelise had to stop them! This could not be happening, not now with Thomas gone.

She tried to call out, tried to stand. But then Janae lifted her head by the hair and slammed it into the ground, and Chelise thought her skull may have broken.

Twelve thousand souls who'd drowned in the lakes and found new life were crying out, but to Chelise, the roar sounded muffled, like a voice from a large shell. Someone was shaking her, calling her name.

Then the sounds faded completely, and she lay in darkness for a while.

———∞———

COMPLETE AND utter solitude and contentment. Chelise was stripped of all worries for the first time since Samuel had ridden into the Gathering and slung the Horde head onto the ground. Just one moment of absolute peace, sweet and restful.

Where was Thomas?

". . . dead."

"No, no, don't speak that . . . more fruit . . ."

The silence gave way to this soft talk around her. Chelise's mind dragged itself from the solitude with gaining awareness. She wasn't alone. Two people were talking over her. One thought she might be dead. The other wanted to give her more fruit.

"We need to get the juice down her throat," one was saying. "Sit her up again."

"Why would she respond now? She's been like this all night." This was Marie's voice. Marie, sweet Mar . . .

All night? She'd been here all night? No. No, it had only been a moment.

"Dear Elyon, have mercy on them." Johan's voice.

Chelise tried to open her eyes. Failed. Then tried again. Firelight glowed around the edges of her sight.

"She's waking!"

A piece of fruit was pressed against her lips. Chelise bit deeply and felt the juice of a peach run down her throat. Then more, until she was eating large chunks of the flesh, ravenous for the healing nectar. Her mind cleared and the light grew bright.

They were in Marie's tent with Johan. It was dark outside, and one of them had said she'd been out all night. Janae had beaten her in the challenge while the sun was still high in the sky, many hours ago.

She could hear desert crickets singing outside. The camp was all peace and quiet. Which could only mean . . .

Chelise blinked. Tried to speak, then cleared her throat. "How many?"

Marie glanced over at Johan, who responded. "Nearly five thousand."

"Five thousand? Here?"

"No, five thousand left with Samuel and the half-breeds," Johan said.

"Vadal is with them," Marie said.

"Vadal?"

She bolted up in bed, but a headache of thundering proportions made her world spin again, and she dropped back down.

"No, Mother," Marie whispered. "It's too late, they're gone and you're hurt. Give the fruit some time."

Johan spoke in a soothing voice that failed to calm her. "We did all we could, Chelise. After you lost the challenge our footing was weak, but the council mounted a long defense that won many over to our side."

"And the rest? The five thousand?"

He shrugged. "They've been deceived by a compelling case."

"So they go against the Horde?"

"Yes," Johan said. "They go to Miggdon where they will die."

"Die?" But Johan would know more than most—before drowning he'd been a Horde commander of undisputed skill. "What makes you think Qurong will defeat them?"

"Because Qurong and the master he serves are far too crafty."

Chelise sat up, this time successfully. She looked around the room, saw no sign of Jake.

"He's with Mikil," Marie said. "Seven thousand are here, by the red pool. They're lost in tales of glory. And I'm here, lost in sickness over that fool who would be my husband."

"I'm sorry." Chelise pushed herself to her feet despite Marie's objections. "I know. Believe me, I know. And now I have to go."

"Don't be ridiculous, Mother. You'll go nowhere."

"They're going to kill my father," she cried. "Get me more fruit."

"And they're going to kill Vadal. I'll go with you."

"I'm not going to the Eramites."

Johan nodded at Marie. "Then I'll gather—"

"No," Chelise snapped. "This time I go alone."

They faced each other, knowing even a show of objection was pointless.

The same thought that had echoed through her mind for a day now came again: *The world awaits you, Chelise.* She'd failed to stop Samuel here—Michal's admonition clearly referred to something else.

Johan withdrew a vial from his pocket and handed it to her. "Then take this."

"What is it?" She took the small glass bottle, identical to the one the witch had called Teeleh's breath.

"We don't know. It fell from her cloak. The label says it's Thomas's blood. Maybe it has some power. Why else would she carry it?" Johan turned and lifted the tent flap. "If you see the harlot, shove it down her throat for me."

Marie was still pouting. "Mother, please—"

"No. I go to my father, and I go alone."

37

WITH EACH passing day Billy remembered more why he loved Marsuuv the way he did. In so many ways he was only doing what he was created to do: love himself.

Naturally. To love the beast was to love himself, because Marsuuv was as much a mirror of Billy's heart as a beast, born and bred to feed on the blood of mortal souls.

He wasn't sure how long he'd been in the lair following Janae's departure, a few days at least. The intimacy Marsuuv had shown Janae in both words and deed at first twisted a knife through his belly. Who was she to steal Marsuuv's affection after Billy's own long journey to find him?

When Marsuuv descended on her and thrust his fangs into her neck, he'd nearly cried out in protest. Seeing Marsuuv exchange his blood with her like that . . .

Billy had trembled with rage.

But then she'd been sent off and Billy had time to think about what happened.

Janae was a very small part, perhaps only one-hundredth, Shataiki, a descendant of someone bitten by Alucard generations earlier. A creature of the night.

Although the mythology surrounding vampires was sadly misinformed, there was some truth to the rumors. Vampires were real, of course, but they'd originated from this reality—not from Dracula in Transylvania but from a Shataiki queen named Alucard. *Dracula* spelled backward.

Crossbreeds between Shataiki and human were the *Nephilim* referred to in the Holy Bible itself. Billy had found the subject oddly compelling as a young boy.

While Janae was fulfilling her own destiny, Billy was preparing for his, as Marsuuv had promised.

"He comes," Marsuuv said, shifting his torso away from Billy.

They'd been reclining on the beast's bed with only their breathing and the occasional popping sound of Marsuuv's phlegm to accompany them. More accurately, Billy had been reclining, leaning against the queen's belly as he lightly stroked Billy's hair and cheek.

It struck him now and then, but less and less with each passing day, that he should be appalled by his environment. Instead, he was convinced he lay in heaven, and he found himself yearning to be even closer to his lover. They'd bitten each other several times, but Billy wanted to be bitten again. This was how Billos had become Ba'al, he thought.

He found himself dreaming of a blood transfusion. If he could only rid himself of all human blood and be pure Shataiki . . .

"He comes!" Marsuuv said again, brushing Billy aside.

He sat up groggily and came to himself. The scent of Marsuuv's breath wafted over him, and he fought off the desire to lie against the beast's belly again.

But the clack of talons on stone arrested his attention, and he forgot the thought. And then he remembered who it was Marsuuv referred to. Teeleh was coming.

The great beast himself?

Teeleh stepped into Marsuuv's lair, dragging his wings. He was taller than the queen, clearly the master here, though Marsuuv didn't bow or show respect other than to bare his fangs. He put a wing behind Billy and nudged him closer, as if to say, this one is mine, and Billy found the gesture as kind and loving as any Marsuuv had yet shown him. He swallowed a bundle of emotion that rose up in his throat.

"Billy . . ." Teeleh said.

Billy looked at him again, took in the mangy fur that crawled with tiny worms and flies. His large red eyes weren't glamorous like Marsuuv's, but terrifying. A quiver ran over Teeleh's shoulders, scattering a few flies.

"He is mine," Marsuuv said, and Billy felt better.

Teeleh ignored the queen. He stepped closer to Billy and examined him. "Stand up. Let me see you."

Marsuuv removed his arm. Billy scooted off the bed and stood next to the altar, five feet from the beast.

Teeleh's bulging red eyes studied him from head to foot. Billy was still dressed in the black robe he'd taken off the temple guard, but after days with Marsuuv it was badly stained.

"Take it off," Teeleh said in a soft, gravelly voice.

Billy glanced at Marsuuv, received a nod, and shrugged out of the robe. He stood naked except for his underwear. Sores from Marsuuv's fangs marked the inside of his arm and would be clearly visible on either side of his neck.

"Such a beautiful specimen," Teeleh said in a low, crackling voice. He reached a long claw for him and touched Billy's white chest. Then ran his talon down, leaving a thin scratch.

Billy looked at Marsuuv again, shaking with fear now.

"Be strong."

"If I didn't need you so badly, I would pull out your jugular now and have my fill," Teeleh said. "You humans make me sick. Why you were given such power . . ." He didn't finish, but his disdain was clear.

The beast lowered his claw and rested it on the altar, satisfied to stare at him for a moment.

"If you fail me, I will drain you." He flicked a fly off his cheek with a long pink tongue. "Do you understand this?"

"Yes. Yes, I understand."

"You will use the books and return with a single ambition. To deliver a time of tribulation in which *my* kind will reign. The Great Deception will leave humans desperate for a leader."

"What he says is true," the queen Marsuuv said with uncharacteristic reverence.

"In that day, many will flee and many will cower before me, and you will stand at my right hand."

The words washed over Billy as if carried by an electric current. He was shaking again, but not out of fear. Teeleh's words intoxicated him as much as Marsuuv's bite.

"You must not let the other one, Thomas, stop you. He will try. He will enter the Black Forest and all of humanity will stand in awe. But you, Billy, you can stop him. He must drink the water."

Teeleh spat to one side.

"Say it. He must drink the water."

"He must drink the water," Billy repeated.

"If he does not drink the water, I will crucify you. He must drink the water before he can save the world. You must go back to force his hand."

"I'm going back?" The idea terrified him. He wanted to stay here, with Marsuuv.

"Betrayal is written in the hearts of all, but you, Billy, will make betrayal your lover." Teeleh tilted his head back, swallowed the fly, then faced him again. "We will need to extract your . . . inner beauty and re-create you as two. One of you will go to Bangkok, the other will go back to the beginning to kill Thomas before he can cross over."

Billy looked over at Marsuuv and saw that the Shataiki had begun to tremble. The queen opened his jaw and cocked his head like a fledgling bird, then allowed Teeleh to spit into his mouth. Marsuuv settled with some satisfaction.

"I . . ." Billy didn't know what to say.

"Do our ways of evil disturb you, Billy?" Teeleh asked.

They did, but not as much as he would have thought.

"No," he said.

"They should." Teeleh faced Marsuuv, who seemed agitated, excited. "But you humans can't help yourselves. Blindness becomes you."

The queen sprang through the air and landed on the altar before Billy. He lifted a jar in which two large, slimy balls similar to fish eggs lay in a solution. Billy had studied the jar in his stupor these past few days and wondered what poor beast had given up their eyes as a trophy.

Now Marsuuv unceremoniously dumped the jar's contents on the table. When he spoke, his voice was strained with delight.

"Accept this as my gift to you and our offspring," Marsuuv said, lifting the black orbs. "Look into my eyes."

Billy already was looking. The queen leaned forward as if he intended to either bite him on the face or kiss him, and Billy really didn't care which. He only wanted to be held in a place of safety.

Slowly, the beast lifted his claw and traced his cheeks. "After I've taken your eyes and sent you back, you'll remember little of this. Only what you need to know. Only the impulses and the demands upon your life. And you'll be able to follow Thomas when he dreams." Marsuuv's breathing thickened. "May I blind you?"

Billy began to cry. He didn't want to cry; he knew shedding tears at a time like this must look weak, even foolish, but he couldn't help it.

"Yes," he said.

Marsuuv thrust two fingers into Billy's eyes, like prongs designed to blind in precisely this manner. White-hot pain flashed behind his forehead, and he heard himself scream.

Marsuuv yanked his fingers from Billy's head, then slapped something into his eye sockets. Clouded sight returned, then slowly cleared. The cavern was visible through two new eyes of his lover's making. The pain eased.

"Now you are two," Marsuuv said, drilling Billy with a hard look. "You will be called Bill."

Teeleh stood behind the queen, head tilted back, roaring with such ferocity that Billy thought the ceiling might collapse and crush them all. The great deceiver lowered his head and thrust a long talon toward Billy's left.

"And he will be Billy."

There, not five feet away, stood another Billy, nearly identical, right down to his red hair. His eyes were lined in red, and blood leaked from the corners.

I am Bill. Only Bill, not Billy, he thought.

Teeleh swiveled his head back to Bill. "Thomas must drink the water! Do not fail me this time."

The other Billy had his original eyes, Bill realized. Marsuuv had extracted his eyes—his inner beauty—and placed them in this copy of himself to duplicate his essence.

And the eyes in his face now?

He put his fingertips to his face. They came away bloody. He had new black eyes, from the jar.

"Stop Thomas," Teeleh growled in such a low voice that Bill's bones vibrated.

"I will," Bill whimpered.

"I will crucify you if you fail," Teeleh repeated.

The other Billy was crying. "What about me?" The man even sounded like Bill.

Teeleh stepped over to the other Billy, then around, examining him. He traced the man's flesh with his talon, stopped behind him, and marked him with three hooked claw marks at the base of his neck. Then he dug one claw deep into Billy's spine and twisted it slowly. Billy trembled, weeping.

"You, my friend, will be my antichrist."

Bill felt the man's pain as if it were his own. Because it was. He wanted to cry out and demand that Teeleh show more kindness, but he knew there wasn't a thread of tenderness in the beast.

"Do not fail me," Teeleh hissed in the other Billy's ear.

The redhead turned his head toward Bill. "Billy?"

"Bill. My name is Bill. I'm here."

"I can't see too well." This even though he had bright-green eyes.

"It's okay, neither can I. Our eyes are new. But I'm right here."

Marsuuv pointed at the four lost books stacked on the altar. "Go, and do what you must do." He slashed their fingers with a claw.

Marsuuv spoke to Bill. "Find Thomas in the place called Denver when he first crossed. Stop him. Kill him. Make him drink."

"In Denver? Please—"

"Do what you must do," Teeleh snarled. "Quickly!"

Both men stumbled forward, dripping blood. Together they put their hands on the exposed page.

For the second time in less than five minutes, the lair vanished, and white lights flooded Bill's mind. Billy, the one with green eyes, was returning to Bangkok to be Teeleh's antichrist. As for him, with the black eyes, he was supposed to go after Thomas. In Denver, right? If he remembered history correctly, Thomas had originally come from Denver.

Even as he left one world and entered the other, Billy forgot what he had seen. But he did know a few things.

He knew that he was the lover of Marsuuv, who'd shown him great kindness and gifted him with black eyes.

He knew that he must either stop Thomas or hang from a cross, where he would be drained of blood until dead.

And he knew that he was now Bill. Just Bill.

38

"I WON'T have it!" Monique insisted. "You can't hide in this room the rest of your life, waiting for some books to magically appear on the desk!"

"It has nothing to do with magic," Thomas pointed out. As promised, he'd remained immovable, eating and sleeping in the library. There was a bathroom off the main room, and he'd left only four times to shower.

He had accepted their offer to hook up a monitor and let them show him how to scan the Net using a small finger piece. He wore a pair of black cargo pants beneath his freshly laundered tunic rather than the jeans and T-shirts he'd become accustomed to wearing over the past few days.

Kara looked at the Net feed. "She's right, Thomas, we can't just keep you in here forever."

"It's only been a few days, not forever. Have you no mercy? I've suffered a death, for all I know. Chelise could be dead, slain by the Horde at this moment. My own son, Samuel, could be living with Eram. I have to find my son, for the love of Elyon. Time is of the essence. Michal was very clear!"

They stared at him as they always did when he began one of his tirades, which favored more poetic desert speak. He stuck one finger into the air.

"If there's but one chance in a million to bring my son back to my side, I will suffer all consequences. He is my son!"

"And now *this* is your world," Monique cried, pointing at the Net feed. "For all you know you're a prophet meant for *this* world."

"I'm no prophet," he said. "I've never claimed to be a prophet. I have no interest in being a prophet."

"Michal told you to make a way. Perhaps you've already done that."

Thomas hadn't considered the possibility. Michal had also said he might save his son if he returned quickly.

"Nonsense! Samuel is waiting for . . ."

It was as far as Thomas got. The room flashed with a bright light, like a strobe. He spun toward the desk.

Kara gasped.

There stood Billy, dressed in only a loose undergarment. Blood ran from several wounds on his arms and neck. A long scratch marked his white chest. And his green eyes . . . They were rimmed in blood.

Beside him sat the four lost Books of History.

Billy stared at Thomas for a few seconds, unmoving. Tearstains streaked his cheeks. The man looked as though he had come to them from either Ba'al's dungeons or the Black Forest itself. Even Teeleh's lair.

This was the same redhead who'd tricked them once, but whatever had happened to him seemed to have left his eyes empty. He'd lost his soul. He should be locked up, Thomas thought, and the key to his cell should be taken back to the desert. But that would stop nothing.

"I . . ." His voice was scratchy. "There's another one like me. He's going back to the beginning to kill you. He has black eyes."

Monique stepped forward. "Billy, where is Janae?"

"But I'm not him," he said. "I think I might be the antichrist."

Then Billy turned from them, walked to the exit, opened the door, and vanished into the hall, leaving black prints from his bare feet on the marble floor.

The books . . .

Thomas reacted without thought. He rushed forward, grabbed the knife on the desk and cut his finger.

"Wait!" Kara ran. "Wait!"

He wasn't fully versed in the rules of these books. The possibility that they'd been fixed so that he couldn't return swallowed him. Why else would Billy have left them unattended?

"Hurry!"

He reached for Kara's outstretched hand. Monique stood back, staring. He shoved the knife at Kara. "Cut yourself."

Springing across the room, Thomas took Monique's face in his hands and kissed her once on the lips. "Thank you. I am indebted. But I have to go."

"I know," she said. Tears misted her eyes. "Go to her. Find your son. Find Janae. Please. Save my daughter."

He released her, leaving a smear of blood on her cheek. Then he leaped back to the books, where Kara waited with a bleeding finger.

"Ready?"

Kara faced Monique. "You've been like a sister to me."

"And you to me. I think we'll be seeing more of each other."

Then Kara and Thomas pressed their hands on the opened page, and the world around them vanished.

THE FIRST clue that something different was happening to Thomas came almost immediately. The last time he'd vanished into the book with Qurong, he'd spun through a vortex that deposited both him and the Horde leader in Monique's library.

But this time, what started out as a tunnel of light suddenly expanded and then faded into emptiness. The violent transition from one world to the other or forward in time, depending on how it was seen, had been replaced by a perfect calm.

He hung in the air, completely weightless, like floating in the sky without a hint of wind. Sunlight warmed his back, though there was no sun that he could see. Far below him the curved desert reality slowly rotated, peaceful, undisturbed, as if asleep. There were troubles down there in that desert, but he felt no concern now. Only perfect tranquility.

It occurred to him that he was holding his breath, perhaps from the wonder of it all. He drew breath, but instead of air, liquid flooded his nostrils and he felt a stab of panic. Water? His alarm gave way to the thought that he was in a lake.

Elyon's lake?

He cautiously sucked at the water, allowing the warm fluid to flood his throat, his airways, his lungs. Forcing himself to ignore the instinct to panic, he drew the water all the way in, then pushed it out, an exercise that required a little more effort than breathing air.

Familiar pleasure swept through his chest, soft at first, then with more intensity until he couldn't hold back a tremble that overtook his whole body. He was floating in Elyon's lake a hundred miles above the earth as if it were heaven itself.

Elyon's presence lapped at his mind, and he found himself laughing with the pleasure of it all. He arched backward, arms spread wide, overwhelmed by an intoxication that he'd felt only twice before in his life, both times in the depths of this very water.

His laughter grew until his muffled cackles of delight spread throughout the water. It was as if he was being tickled by the hand of God. Of Elyon. Here in his great lake of breathtaking pleasures.

The colors came from his left, streams of red and blue and gold, rushing through the water like translucent paint. He slowly swallowed his laughter and watched as the colors twirled and circled him, stretching back the way they had come for a ways.

A very long ways. Thomas knew this because he could see the whole distance. In fact, there was no end to what his eyes could now see. The streams of color went on and on. They didn't stretch miles or light-years; they simply did not end.

Amazed, he reached out and touched a streak of red. It bent with the pressure of his finger. A shaft of electrical current rode up his arm and shook his body as if he were a rag doll that had stuck its finger in the wrong hole in the wall.

And with that current came raw pleasure so great that it could not, with any amount of human effort, be contained. So great that for a moment he thought it might overpower his life and leave him dead in the water. He had to pull his finger away from the color or surely die!

But he didn't. He let it consume him. Every nerve, every cell, every bone, screamed with a gratification that reduced all other pleasures to a mere grin in a room of rolling laughter.

And he knew then that he'd found the hope. This was Elyon's presence. This was a piece of heaven, only a piece.

He finally withdrew his hand. The colors veered away and ran in large circles a hundred yards distant, as if they had a mind of their own.

Thomas arched his back and dived backward, surprised to find he could pick up speed at will. He rushed toward the earth, feeling the waters rush over him. They caressed his skin and flowed through his lungs, flooding every fiber of his body with nearly uncontainable bliss.

The ground didn't seem to come closer, so he accelerated. But the farther Thomas dived, the deeper the lake seemed to run.

"Thomas . . ."

A child's voice whispered through the water, and he pulled up. "Hello?"

The voice giggled.

Thomas grinned. "Hello?"

"Thomas, up here."

He snapped his head back and saw that the lake above was brighter.

"Come up here, Thomas."

He clawed for the surface, desperate to be with the one whose voice spoke. He knew the sound. He had heard this voice.

"Thomas."

"Elyon?" He began to cry spontaneously. "Elyon!" He was screaming and weeping and laughing at once, as if his mind had forgotten how to separate the emotions that caused each.

He effortlessly swooped upward, but his desperation to be with the boy had him bawling like a baby. "Elyon! Elyon, wait!" he cried.

"I'm right here, Thomas." Then the boy giggled again, and Thomas rode the laughter to the light above him.

He burst through the lake's surface, rose all the way to his knees and faced a bright-blue sky, then splashed back down like a leaping dolphin. He searched the horizons for the boy.

Clouds drifted silently. Sand dunes surrounded him. It occurred to him that he was standing on the lake bottom, two feet under the water's red surface.

A red pool, no more than twenty feet wide on the top of a sand dune.

As he stared, the ground under his feet began to move. It rose upward. Not just the sand under the pool, but the dunes around him thrust upward toward the sky.

He crouched to steady himself, but quickly determined there was no threat. The desert rose hundreds, thousands of feet, and then slowed to a stop.

But it wasn't the whole desert, he could see that now. It was a circular section of the desert, perhaps a half mile across, that had risen toward the sky in a massive pillar.

And now all was silent. No movement other than a slight breeze.

Thomas turned around slowly, studying his new horizon. It wasn't until he'd finished a full circuit that he saw the boy, standing on a dune with his back to Thomas, staring over the edge.

He was a young boy, perhaps twelve, with black hair and dark skin, dressed only in a white loincloth, standing less than five feet tall. He was thin, and frail fingers hung by his sides.

Thomas's heart forgot how to pump in that moment. An old teaching ran through his mind, one that equated Elyon with a lion and a lamb and a boy in one telling. They all knew he wasn't a lake, or a lion, or a lamb. Neither was he a black boy, or a white girl, or a man, or a woman, or an eagle with eyes under his wings, for that matter.

He was Elyon, the Creator of all that was. He was the author and giver of life. And above all, he was their lover. The very essence of the Great Romance.

With a snap of his fingers, this boy on the dune ahead of Thomas could turn the world into a marble and crush all living things to sand. At a single word, a new world would roll off his tongue and spin into space.

A wink from this boy and the hardest heart would break into pieces, shattered by love.

Thomas thought it all in a moment, and then his heart began to crash in his chest. He had to move. He had to rush up behind the boy and throw himself to the sand in worship.

But before he could move, a fuzzy white creature waddled toward the boy from the left. Michal, the Roush.

Michal glanced back at Thomas once, then walked up to the boy. Without looking at him, the boy took the shorter Roush's hand, and together they looked down. At what, Thomas couldn't see.

Thomas found the courage to move, but carefully, thinking that sloshing through the water might be inappropriate. He walked out of the pool and had started down the depression that separated him from the dune on which the boy and Michal stood, when the first white lion walked into his peripheral view and settled on its haunches to his right.

Thomas twisted back and saw that a dozen huge, white lions had positioned themselves like sentinels around the entire edge, facing the boy. There was no threat, only a sense of honor. Elyon hardly needed such creatures.

Thomas walked up the dune and approached the boy's open side, opposite Michal. Neither turned to him.

He wanted to speak, ask permission, fall to one knee, something, but he was having difficulty thinking clearly in the boy's presence. And then Thomas saw the tears that darkened the boy's cheeks, and he felt the blood drain from his face.

Thomas sank to one knee, smothered by a terrible sadness. He didn't know why the boy was crying, but the sight of it flogged his mind and demanded he weep.

"What do you see, Thomas?"

Thomas? The boy had spoken his name? The boy knew him personally? Yes, of course, but to hear it . . .

What do you see, Thomas? he'd asked.

What do I see? I see you. I see only you, and it's all I need to see.

His weeping grew in earnest, changing from sorrow to gratitude for being in the presence of one so great. He knew he should answer.

Not to answer was a sacrilege worthy of eternal punishment. He wanted to answer, but he was too overcome by the boy's presence to avert his eyes, much less speak.

The boy reached out for Thomas's hand. Took his fingers.

The last reserves of Thomas's poise snapped. He slumped to one side and began to shake with sobs. The boy held his hand, and Thomas gripped the frail fingers as if they were his only thread to life. He wept with deep, air-gulping sobs.

Waves of gratitude swept over him, and he knew that he'd been wrong a moment ago. The waters were not the hope for which Elyon himself had died.

This . . .

He could hardly bear to think it . . . but this . . . this was the great hope for which they were all created. For *this* moment.

There was nothing else that could possibly matter other than to hold the hand of the one who'd formed you with his breath.

Thomas could not stop, he simply could not, and the boy made no attempt to suggest he do so. Thomas curled into a ball, clung to the boy's hand, and wet the sand under his face with tears.

It all made sense now. The pain, the death, the days and nights of fear as the Horde stalked them.

The ridicule, the disease, the fall.

The tears of the mother whose child had fallen and broken her jaw. The agony of the father who had lost his son to an arrow. For the pleasure set before them they, like Elyon himself, had endured it all.

Time seemed to stall.

When it occurred to Thomas that the boy had released his hand, he pushed himself up to his knees, meaning to beg forgiveness for his display, yet one more indiscretion. Because he was human, he might say, and humans stumbled over their indiscretions like oversized boots.

But the boy was gone. In his place stood a middle-aged man with a graying beard and a strong jaw. He wore a white tunic. Before Thomas could make the adjustment from Elyon the boy to Elyon the father, the man turned and stared at him with misty green eyes. "They're denying my love, Thomas," the elder said.

"No . . ." He looked at the desert below and for the first time saw what they were looking at. Far below them lay a great valley lined on all sides with armies that stretched far into the desert.

The valley of the miggdon figs.

"What can I do?" the man whispered.

But Thomas was still far too absorbed by the love that swam about them to consider any dilemma seriously. *Let them destroy themselves,* he thought. *Let those who deny your love slaughter themselves. Just let me stay with you.*

"They've turned away," the man said.

A white lion stepped past Thomas and gazed at the scene below. Thomas jumped to his feet. All of the lions had crossed the sand and now stood in two lines on either side of their master, fixated upon the gathered Horde armies.

The man turned away from the scene and paced. He ran his fingers through his gray hair, deep in thought. "I made them. I wove them together in the secret place, I knit them in the mother's womb."

Thomas recognized the words from a song the Circle sang. A psalm.

"All their days were ordained, written in my book. They are my poem, created for such wonders." His eyes lifted to Thomas. "But I gave them their own book and let them write in it. Now look what they have done."

Thomas thought he might tear his hair out.

"What have I done, what have I done?" The man spun back to the cliff and thrust his arm to the horizon. "Look!"

Thomas looked. Something else had been added to the distant mix of Horde ready to wage war. They were Qurong's army, gathered to battle Eram's army, and for a fleeting moment Thomas wondered if Samuel was caught up in the mix. But what he saw now swept the worry aside.

A massive black swirl of Shataiki circled over the valley—millions of the black beasts, ravenous for the human blood that nourished them.

"Look," Michal said, pointing to the west.

A flood of white approached like a wave of clouds. A sea of Roush.

Thomas could only think one thing now: This is the end. This is the end.

The man lifted both arms and wept at the sky. His shoulders shook with his sobs and tears ran down his face, wetting his beard. The lions turned to him and fell to their faces, hindquarters raised as they bowed. As one they moaned, a dreadful sound that filled Thomas with fear.

Elyon's wail began to run out of breath. Slowly he lowered his head, arms still raised, chest heaving to find air. But his stare began to change from one couched in anguish to a glare filled with rage.

His face flushed red and his cheeks began to quiver. Alarmed, Thomas tried to step back, but his feet would not move.

And then Elyon screamed, full throated, at the sky. His hands knotted into fists and he trembled from head to foot with such wrath that Thomas could not stop his own body from quaking.

The lions roared as one, and the whole earth was swallowed in a thunder of protest that shook it to the very foundations.

Still the cry raged with inexhaustible fury. Thomas fell to his knees and threw his arms over his head.

"Bring us home!" he cried. "Rescue your bride!"

But he was yelling at the sand and no one seemed to be listening. He could hardly hear himself.

"Bring"—the roar ceased midsentence—"us home. Rescue us. For the sake of the Great Romance, rescue your bride from this terrible day."

Silence hung around him, broken only by his own breathing. He snapped his eyes wide. Michal was flying off, fifty feet from the edge of the cliff. The lions were gone. The man . . .

Thomas stood slowly. Elyon was gone?

"Thomas?"

He caught his breath and spun to the voice. The boy stood by the red pool, staring at him with daring eyes. Had so much time passed?

"It's time," the boy said.

"It's over?"

The boy hesitated, then spoke without answering the question directly. "When it is, you'll know. And what you felt—that was only child's play, my friend."

He winked.

Elyon winked.

And Thomas could not keep his knees still.

"Follow me, Thomas!" the boy cried. He took three light steps down the bank, dived into the red pool, and vanished beneath the shimmering surface.

Thomas began to run while the boy was still in the air. It wasn't until he was aloft, falling toward the water, that he wondered how deep it was.

He plunged beneath the surface and knew that these were Elyon's waters, and his lake had no bottom.

39

THE VALLEY of Miggdon ran fifty miles through the high plains, where the fig trees that bore its name grew in abundance. But here at the head, it resembled more of a box canyon. Four sloping descents fell to an immense basin that was known to flood every few years when a rare rain visited this part of the world.

Samuel sat on a horse next to Eram and Janae, studying the lay of what would become their battlefield. Qurong had made no attempt to hide his army on the eastern crest. Their Throaters were mounted on steeds the full length of the valley, a thousand wide by his calculations. And at least two hundred deep.

Two hundred thousand cavalry on the far slope, only a thousand yards away.

The differences between the three armies were pronounced. Qurong's Horde used all manner of horses, no longer attempting to blend with the desert sands. Both Eramite and albino favored lighter-colored horses. The distinction extended to their battle dress. Where once the Forest Guard favored dark leather to blend into the forests, they now warded off arrows and blades in tan leathers, much like the Eramites, whose main infantry also wore helmets.

It was dark against light, the dark being Horde, the light being both Eramite and albino.

But beyond this distinction, the Eramites and Horde looked almost identical. They both used heavier armor that covered their joints, because the scabbing disease made quick movement in any joint painful. The Eramites who chewed the numbing beetle nut suffered less pain, but how much of an advantage this would prove to be on the battlefield was untested.

Tall scythes and spears carried by a full half of the Horde warriors rose like the charred skeletons of trees after a forest fire. They sat on their dark horses stoically, as if the mere sight of them could speak doom to any who dared not flee.

Qurong had divided his Horde army into four classes of fighters:

The Throaters. Qurong's elite fighters, who favored bows and long swords, almost always fought from their mounts. These were the Scabs that had hunted albinos for more than ten years with devastating results.

The grunts. Both cavalry and infantry, grunts were trained in long-reach hand-to-hand combat, using spears and maces or long swords—any heavy weapon that did not require speed in order to kill with a single blow. A spiked ball at the end of a five-foot chain didn't require quick reflexes to swing with any strength. But step into the arc of one of these maces, and either the sharpened chains or the spikes themselves would remove an arm or a head.

Infantry archers. Though their bamboo arrows could be deadly up to a hundred yards, they often found the wrong mark and were almost use-less once two armies collided. On this battlefield, Qurong would only use them when the Eramites were caught in the open, unless he was willing to sacrifice his own fighters in a fusillade of indiscriminate arrows.

The throwers. The final group was by far the smallest, perhaps two or three dozen catapults that hurled straw balls soaked in the resin of Qaurkat trees and ignited. The three-foot balls splattered upon impact, soaking a fifteen-foot radius with the sticky, flaming fuel. Samuel counted twelve of them on the eastern ridge. They tended to break, and would be quickly replaced by others in reserve.

This was the Horde army, similar to the Eramite army except for the variation in armor and the absence of artillery, which proved difficult to transport.

The skill of five thousand albinos, on the other hand, made a mock-ery of both Horde and Eramite. They left all joints free for ease of movement. Whether mounted or on foot, they depended on speed and strength and favored medium-length swords that could change direction almost immediately in the hands of a skilled fighter. They carried knives for throwing—a single warrior might carry as many as ten knives into a fight—and a deadly accurate bow with shorter arrows for short-range confrontations.

Never in history had all three enemies faced each other on one battlefield, and Samuel now considered his orchestration of the events with a mixture of pride and fear.

For months, Samuel had roamed the desert and skirted the forests with his loyal guard while envisioning the day they would return to war. But he'd never conceived of this massive gathering of armies for what could only be a brutal engagement. And yet here they were, because of his hotheaded defiance.

An image of his father entered his mind, but he pushed it out.

"He's there," Eram said, nodding at the southern ridge to their right. "With at least fifty thousand of his best warriors."

"I don't see the colors," Samuel said, looking for the tall purple flags that identified the supreme commander's guard.

"No, not now. But trust me, he's there. And he'll launch his first attack from there, not from the main body."

"How so?"

"He means to draw us in. His one advantage is size, but to use it he has to find a way to descend on my army."

"What size would you say?" Samuel scratched the rash that had begun to overtake his skin. The fact that his rash had worsened, whereas Janae's rash hadn't, wasn't lost on him. She still looked albino. His skin, on the other hand, looked very much like it had contracted the scabbing disease. Worse, he could no longer deny the pain spreading through his limbs.

It had been many years since he'd heard of any albino contracting the disease after drowning. He hadn't even known it was possible. For all he knew, it wasn't, and this was something else the witch had passed on to him, some foul disease she'd contracted from the Shataiki when she'd whored herself out to him. Either way, he couldn't breathe a word of it. Being albino was his one great advantage.

Eram spat red beetle-nut juice to one side. "Our scouts put them at three hundred thousand today."

Maybe he should try some of the beetle nut. Nearly all the Eramites ground the mild analgesic between their molars, turning their mouths red. They looked like they'd fed on blood, Samuel thought.

"So where are the rest?"

Eram scanned the desert. "How would I know? Back in Qurongi, nursing their wounds. Or suffering under one of Ba'al's curses. Even at half strength, they're twice as many as we."

Samuel looked down the line at their own army, stretching as far as he could see. The albino traitors were mounted on horses to his left, some looking fierce, others unsure. Regardless, they were all heavily armed, and once the first blow was struck, they would fight with the pent-up rage of a wounded pit bull.

"Half their strength," Samuel said, "but twice as strong."

"So you've claimed."

"And you've agreed. I would expect the other half of his army to be close by."

The crafty Eramite leader nodded his head slowly. "Perhaps. No report from our scouts. But I will say this for that old monkey: he's no fool. If I were in his boots, I would have chosen this very valley. These slopes will allow him to use his army to its full advantage. Honestly, if not for Teeleh's poison, I would reconsider."

Samuel glanced at Janae, who was looking at the valley unconcerned. Her beauty in the morning light quickened his heart. "But we do have the poison," he said. *And this woman is my poison*, he thought to himself.

Eram kept his eyes on the larger Horde army directly across the valley. "They'll send in a small force to lure us in, and we'll take the bait. We'll send twice as many, without poison."

"Qurong will crush them with a second wave."

"We'll commit our full force at that time, with poison. This breath of Teeleh had better work, because we face impossible odds without it. Ba'al's no fool. That old conniving wraith surely has a trick up his sleeve."

"For a daring leader who defied Qurong once—"

"I left Qurong to live, not to die! Don't question my judgment or I'll cut you down where you stand. The last thing I need is an insolent fool who's turning Scab."

The reference to the disease cut deeply, and Samuel was sorely tempted to lash out. But he couldn't engage Eram on the matter, not now, not when they were fully committed to a bloody end.

"You may not need Samuel," Janae said softly, "but you do need me. Now if you're done being men, we should get on with the rites. I want the albinos to come to me first. Then the rest, until every last warrior has made the vow and taken his poison."

Samuel looked at her. "Albinos? They don't need your poison."

Her eyes flashed, stopping him cold. "They *all* drink the bloody water. They *all* take the mark. They *all* vow their allegiance to me!"

He swallowed. It was so wrong. Yet so right.

"It's a disease, not blood," he corrected.

She studied him, then softened slightly. "The disease comes from his blood. We follow my instructions to the letter. Gather them now."

"Albinos first," Eram said, swinging his horse around. Naturally, he was no respecter of race at a time like this. "You're their leader; bring them to the pond." To his general: "Ready the others. If Qurong dispatches a division into the valley, engage them with twice his number. But none who've ingested this poison."

"Understood."

Samuel had given charge to Petrus, whom he trusted with his life, and Vadal, who served as a constant reminder to the five thousand that even the son of Ronin the elder had joined them. Each commanded half of the albinos, but at a moment's notice, Samuel could step in and take full control.

He signaled to both, and they ordered their fighters to the rear.

The horses seemed to sense the unique danger, where whole armies and peoples were in jeopardy of slaughter. No one spoke, but there were whispers among the albinos now. A thousand yards separated their army from one much larger, and by all appearances as bloodthirsty as any Shataiki legion. The fact that Qurong had chosen the battlefield and was here waiting didn't help either.

But they had this one gift from Elyon. Teeleh's breath, given to them by Elyon to slaughter the Horde. A bad thing for a good cause. War. The thought sickened Samuel.

But this was his lot. This was his destiny. He was Samuel of Hunter, and the whole world would know his name.

Forgive me, Father, for I have sinned.

It was with a sense of fatalism that the albinos encircled the large pond half a mile behind the valley and stood at ease, watching Janae's every move. They were two-thirds men and a third women, and all were better fighters than any Horde could hope to be in their wildest dreams.

They were also smarter, Samuel thought. They could not possibly miss the signs of the scabbing disease that covered his skin.

Vadal was the first to express what was on their minds. "What's the meaning of this disease, Samuel?" The man was chewing a beetle nut.

Janae lifted up the vial for all to see and answered for Samuel. "To test you, my love." She sniffed the bottle. "Do I have the scabbing disease? Do you?"

Vadal spit on the ground and glanced about without answering her.

"No? Yet you were in the proximity of this poison at the camp. You have no faith in Elyon's prophet?"

Vadal looked at Samuel. "And you?" he asked with a red mouth.

"You heard her," Samuel said. "Isn't it true that to defeat the evil, one must first die? To overcome the scabbing disease, we pay a price. If you doubt, leave now."

The albinos looked at him like ghosts lost on the plain. But none walked away.

"When you have all partaken, to the last warrior, Samuel will have paid his price and the disease will leave him. Take out your knives."

They hesitated only a moment, then did so.

"You too, lover," she said to Samuel.

He hesitated, then followed her order.

Forgive me, Father . . . Forgive me.

"As a sign of your loyalty to Elyon and his prophet, you will draw three marks on your forehead or your arm." She slipped out her knife and carved three lines on her own forearm. "Like so."

A rumble of objection spread, but rather than react, she looked at Samuel and winked.

"Three marks for the Maker, the Warrior, and the Giver, who has brought you this gift to make a mockery of the dragon. We use his own seed to destroy his devout, do we not?"

In different circumstances, some, even many, may have demanded a lengthier explanation. But they'd swallowed her reasoning in Paradose Valley, and the possibility of their enemy's destruction was finally within reach.

One, then a dozen, then all of them drew their blades over their skin as instructed. Blood flowed from their forearms, mostly. Some were bold enough to mark their foreheads.

With each cut into his own forearm, Samuel accepted the pain as a form of absolution.

Janae ceremoniously dribbled the vial of Teeleh's breath into the water as she walked along the pond's bank. "Each of you will drink. Be quick; the Horde awaits their final battle. With this poison in your own flesh, any who have never been washed by Elyon's waters will suffer their deserved fate when they draw near. You saw his judgment in your own camp, now you will see it again on a scale that will make all the world tremble with fear at the very name of Elyon."

As each red drop splashed into the water, it spread out with unnatural speed, turning the muddy pond a dark purple. Teeleh's breath looked to be alive and swimming on its own.

"Drink!" Janae cried, dropping the vial into the water. It landed with a loud *plop*. She lifted both hands and turned to face them all.

"Drink, my children. Drink his water and live!"

As if on cue, a terrible moan rolled through the sky far above them. A roar, a scream, rage and sorrow bundled as one. Samuel felt a stab of terror slice through his bones. The roar faded and was replaced by Janae's cry.

"The end is at hand, my children! Drink. Drink. Drink!" She smiled at the sky.

They hurried to the pond from all sides, fell to their knees, and drank. For fear, for revenge, for pain, for love.

But they loved the wrong beast, Samuel thought, facing Janae. Her eyes were on him, and his heart felt as though it might burst with desire for her. She tasted the blood from her forearm, making no attempt to hide her pleasure.

He could not resist her. Not now, not ever. Samuel dropped to the ground, walked to Janae, and kissed her deeply.

It was time for war. It was time for the slaughter.

40

MIKIL STOOD by the red pool in Paradose Valley next to Jamous, Johan, Ronin, and the rest of the council. She stared at the eastern horizon, where the sun had risen two hours earlier. The rest of the Circle lingered or slept in the natural amphitheater to their right, waiting for the council's decision.

All had drunk the red waters and eaten their fill of fruit and pork around a huge fire late into the night. Desperate to justify their reason for staying true, they'd danced hard and sung long and told a thousand tales of glory, many of which started with an element of truth, then spun into wild metaphors that delighted the whole crowd.

But when they awoke, the reality of their loss had robbed most of their passion, and they stared with tired eyes. What now?

"Maybe we should have gone," Tubin, one of the older council members, said.

"You doubt already?" Johan demanded.

"Thomas is gone. Chelise is gone. Samuel is gone. Half of the Circle is gone! But we stand here, waiting. I'm not suggesting we join the battle, but many of us have loved ones there, facing death." He glared, frowning with disgust.

Mikil didn't blame him. They all had dearly loved friends, and in some cases family, who'd been swept away by Samuel's call.

"Elyon knows, I thought about going myself," she said. "His case was compelling. And if we, who've seen everything from the beginning, could be so easily tempted, then think about what must be going through the minds of the rest." She looked at a mother who watched them while squatting on the ground with her daughter nearby. "They've stayed true, but we need to give them more."

"Then let me take a dozen of the fastest scouts and report back," Ronin said. He was eager to go after Vadal, his son. But they'd all lost dear ones to Samuel.

"No. We've already lost Chelise on a fool's errand. The people don't need to see more of their leaders running off. We should stay, all of us."

"And do what?" Ronin demanded.

Mikil walked to the edge of the pool and stared at her reflection in the red waters. So still, so unmoving. But there was something else here. She faced the rest of the council, then stared past them to a small, dark-skinned child on a rock, who also watched them. She didn't recognize the child. The Circle had grown so fast these past few years that she didn't recognize half of them.

A thin mother with long, straight black hair leaned against a boulder and nursed an infant. Boys too impatient to sit still kicked the skin of a bundled tawii fruit back and forth, keeping it in the air. A girl nearly of marrying age, perhaps sixteen, was braiding the hair of a younger girl, who sat with her back to them. A warrior—interesting that they still called the old Guard that—sat with crossed arms, lost in thought under the shade of a pond palm, named for its proximity to the red pools.

But no one was talking. Not even a breeze rustled the leaves. An odd silence hung in the air.

Mikil turned back to the pool and stared at the silky red surface. "When you look at this water, what do you see?" she asked.

The other nine eased over. "Water, like glass," said Susan.

"Water," Mikil repeated. "With these eyes, it's all we see at the moment. But if we open the eyes of our hearts, what do we see?"

"The drowning that made the waters red," Johan said.

Mikil nodded. "And our own deaths, which brought us life. Every day we look at this pool and see water. Beautiful water, but just water. Yet what kind of life has it given us?"

"The hope of a return to Elyon's playground," Johan said, using the metaphor the poets often used.

"Our entire hope is dimly seen through this glass," Mikil said, nodding at the water. "It's there, just below the surface, and we see glimpses of it every day. Isn't this what Thomas once taught us?" She bent down, picked up a small lemon, and tossed it in her hand. "Elyon's gifts to us are simply a foretaste to keep us eager for the banquet. Isn't that what our poets have told us?"

"It is as she says," someone said softly.

"She speaks the truth."

"So where is that hope?" Mikil said, dropping the lemon.

They stared at the pond in silence. Mikil couldn't put her finger on it, but there was an inexplicable stillness hanging over the waters. Easy to miss if she wasn't focused on it, but there just the same. It was easy to forget just how enchanted the red pools were.

"To many, the hope of winning peace through the sword is more real than what the poets have to offer," Rohan said, speaking for the first time.

No one disagreed. They all seemed strangely fixated on the water, perhaps sensing the same unnatural stillness that Mikil did. Or perhaps they wondered if Samuel's hope was more realistic than what lay beyond this still pool after all. Samuel had come with tangibles.

Words.

A sword.

The head of a Horde.

An *army*, for the love of Elyon. An army large enough to win the peace they required to live as normal human beings.

The pool at their feet, on the other hand, sat still as it did every morning. Just a red pool without . . .

Mikil's thoughts were cut short by a faint stirring in the pond, not ten feet from where she stood. Strange. There were no fish in this pool as in some of the larger ones. But the water was indeed moving, boiling gently, right there. She shivered.

"What's happening?" Johan asked, taking a step backward. "What . . ."

Water burst from the surface like a fountain. Only in this fountain there was a form. A blond-headed boy with chin tilted back, smiling wide as the water streamed off his face.

Mikil gasped and jumped back.

The pool thrust the boy above the surface, and he was laughing before his feet hit the shore. He was green-eyed, blond, thin, and clearly beside himself with whatever impossible force had brought him on such a ride.

He landed next to them with a slap of feet and looked up, grinning.

"Hello, Mikil," he said, but she didn't see his lips move. Water ran off his curved fingertips and wet the sand. She stood frozen, speechless.

The boy glanced at the others, and she knew that they were hearing him too, speaking each of their names. Mikil was so stunned by the boy's sudden appearance that she found her limbs immovable.

This was no ordinary boy. This was no boy at all. This was the one Thomas had spoken about many times.

This was Elyon, and the when the full realization hit her, Mikil could no longer breathe.

The boy leaped ten feet to a rock that overhung the pool, then bounced up to a precipice that overlooked the whole camp.

The water erupted again, and Mikil spun back. Their pool hurled another form from the depths, and this time Mikil half expected to see the Warrior. But it wasn't Elyon.

It was Thomas, and he was laughing with near hysterics as the water drained from his face and mouth. He landed on the shore, wetter than a freshly drowned albino, and jerked his head around, searching.

"Where is he?" His voice sounded muffled by water. He spit it out, more than could have come from his mouth alone, like those who emerged after drowning. "Where is he?"

"Follow him!" the boy cried, and Thomas snapped his head up.

The voice echoed down the canyon, and the whole camp spun to face the boy up on the cliff. He pointed down to the pool.

"Hear Thomas, your leader! Open your eyes and follow him to my playground!" he cried, swinging his fist through the air with infectious exhilaration.

The boy spun and ran into the desert, leaving breathless silence in his wake.

Were they to follow? Mikil turned to Thomas, who stood looking up at the empty cliff. But before he could tell them what the boy meant, the air around them began to move.

A breeze whipped up and swept after the boy, as if his invisible army was hard on his heels. A long streak of red swept over the canyon like a low-flying comet. A blue shaft materialized beside the red.

As if the sky itself were rolling back like a scroll to reveal its true colors, streams of every hue flowed directly over their heads, silent, but so low that a person on the cliff might reach up and touch one.

The colored streaks rose and parted to make way for a wide swath of white clouds rolling through the sky high above.

But these were not clouds, Mikil saw. They were Roush. Millions of the furry white creatures, flying in formation a mile over their heads.

The boy had opened their eyes to see what he saw.

Thomas was clambering up the same rocks marked by the boy's wet feet and hands. He crouched on the cliff, stared east for a moment, then faced the stunned crowd.

He shoved a finger at the eastern horizon. "This, my friends, is our hope!" he thundered.

The soft sounds of weeping filtered through the amphitheater. Mikil understood the sentiment, because her own chest was flooded with an emotion she'd never quite felt: a raw sensation of gratitude so intense that any cry of thanks would understate it tenfold.

Tears blurred her vision, and her breathing came hard. She felt weak and wanted to fall to her knees like some of the others; she wanted to thrust her fists into the air and cry, "I knew it, I knew it!"

Instead she let a sob shake her body.

"This is our day!" Thomas cried. "I have tasted and I have seen, and now Elyon is calling his bride to the great wedding feast."

A woman she'd never seen before, dressed in strange blue pants and a white blouse, stepped up behind him. Unlike him, she was dry. But then she hadn't come through the water.

"Thomas?" the woman said.

He spun and regarded her in a moment's shock. Then he grabbed her hand and held it up for them to see. "My sister from the histories. She's with me."

Two weeks ago it would have been a preposterous suggestion, but today it seemed perfectly natural. Yes, of course, this was Kara Hunter from the histories. Mikil should have known immediately.

Thomas sprang down to a lower boulder, practically dragging his sister with him. "Mount your fastest horses, every man, woman, and child. Leave it all behind. Everything! No water, no food, nothing but yourself and your children."

Thomas leaped to the ground, eyes bright with a fanaticism Mikil had come to know well. "Now!" he roared, sweeping his arm. "Follow me now!"

They ran as one. The raw intensity of the moment precluded more than a few cries as they swept up those too young or too old to match Thomas's sprint.

Colorful ribbons flanked the army of Roush high above. And now light shimmered on either side, reaching all the way to the ground, forming a tunnel that streamed directly east.

"Faster!" Thomas cried. "Run, run, run!"

Every albino was accustomed to quick flight, ready at a moment's notice to flee any Horde threat. And this . . . this call to follow Thomas to Elyon's playground made any threat of death seem like a child's mud pie.

They sprang onto the backs of unsaddled horses and whipped the animals to a full gallop, close on Thomas's heels. And he wasn't waiting, despite having to care for a sister unfamiliar with her horse. Likewise, she seemed too caught up in this mind-blowing encounter to worry about her lack of equestrian skills.

Mikil cried out to Thomas as he flew by, his eyes pinned on the horizon. He pulled up and looked about frantically. "Where's Chelise?"

"She's already gone to Qurong."

Without a word, he slammed his horse's sides and bolted forward. Then Mikil was hard after him, trying to catch up as they raced out of the valley.

"Faster!" Mikil hear Marie cry to those behind her. "Faster!"

They spilled from the canyon into the desert in a cloud of dust, and Mikil pulled up hard. Thomas sat on his black stallion beside Kara, staring at a rider mounted on a white stallion on the next dune.

The tunnel of light flowed around him, whipping his hair and a robe of red around his white battle leathers.

Elyon the Warrior.

The stallion under him reared and whinnied, pawing at the air. The warrior had a sword in his hand, and he now lifted it high over his head, pointing it at the massive formation of Roush.

Then Elyon screamed at the sky, and Mikil thought her ears might burst under the power of this one cry of victory. He swept his sword toward the eastern horizon and called out in a voice that no one within a mile could mistake.

"Follow me, my bride! Follow me!"

And then Elyon raced east, and the seven thousand rode after him with the colored wind in their hair.

East, my bride, east. Toward the Valley of Miggdon. Toward the Horde. Toward the battle.

41

"NOW, MY lord," Ba'al whispered, hunched beside Qurong at the top of the southern slope. "You must engage them now as he has instructed."

"I don't like it." Qurong stood on a flat rock ledge and gazed at the two armies—his to the right, three hundred thousand strong for all Eram could know, and the Eramite army to his left across the valley, half the strength of his own. But they had albinos with them, more than four thousand from what scouts had been able to determine.

"That old fox was right. This is his son's doing. They have something up their sleeves."

"*I* have something up *our* sleeves, you impotent old fool!" Ba'al shouted.

Qurong jerked his head to the dark priest, taken aback by his loss of control. A terrible sound rolled through the sky, high above. The sound of a strong wind moaning through a hollow, but there was no wind.

The sound passed.

"You see? It's a sign." Ba'al removed frightened eyes from the sky and bowed his head. "Forgive me, my lord. I beg your forgiveness. But victory is in our hands! You heard."

"I heard a wind. And I heard your insult."

"It's here!" Ba'al made a fist out of his scrawny white fingers and shook it. "It's right here, and my lover is ravenous for it. We must attack now!"

"Perhaps I should cut out your tongue first. And then we will see."

"You speak this way to his lover?" Ba'al demanded.

"I speak this way to my priest."

"I will remind you that you pledged—"

"To Teeleh, not to you."

Cassak stood by, wearing a frown. "The sun is high, my lord. We have eight more hours of light. I suggest we either execute our plan before nightfall or prepare for a long night of sparring with the albinos. And that won't be pretty."

"Be prepared for deception," Ba'al said. "Kill any albino who comes close, no matter what their intention."

"And if they mean to surrender?"

"Kill them!"

Cassak looked at Qurong. "My lord?"

"Yes. Kill any who approach. We trust no one."

"I'll pass the word. Should we deploy, my lord?"

Qurong fought through the fog of confusion that had not left his mind since his daughter dared to cross the desert to meet him. A week ago he would have refused to think of her as *Daughter*. But now . . .

It was maddening. The walls he'd successfully erected against love over so many years were crumbling around him. First Thomas had tricked him into a dream state, where nothing was as it seemed. Then Chelise brought news of his grandson, Jake.

Qurong had no other offspring but a grandchild fathered by his greatest enemy, Thomas. The supreme commander's inability to toss them all from his mind infuriated him.

Chelise, his feisty daughter whom he had once loved more than any treasure in his possession, was back—just there, on the horizon of his mind, calling to be loved by him once again. He stood overlooking a valley in which there would soon be more dead flesh than living, and he was thinking of only one person. No matter how absurd or naive her philosophy, she was still Chelise of Qurong.

"My lord?"

"I'm thinking!"

"We're running out of time," Cassak warned.

"They're up to something. I can feel it in my bones. They have something up their sleeves."

"As do we, my lord," Ba'al said. "As we most certainly do."

"What? What do we have besides another two hundred thousand men to send into the slaughter? I don't know your *real* plan, only that you keep insisting on some unseen magic."

"Have faith!" the dark priest screamed. He blinked, then settled. "Forgive me." He slipped his hands into the arms of his robe and turned a stoic stare at the Eramite army.

"They have broken their covenant," he said. "This harlot who's come to them has removed their covering, I am assured of that."

"That's it? I throw my army into danger on the back of a harlot and more religious jargon?"

Ba'al jerked his head around. "Listen, you fool." Spittle flew from stretched lips. "The powers of the air are far more potent than your little army. For many years the albinos have been untouchable. The half-breeds have all once bathed, like myself . . . we've all been protected till this day. All but pure-bred Horde have been under the covering of Elyon. But now that covenant has been broken!"

Qurong wasn't sure he'd heard correctly. A horse snorted behind him; a mace's chain rattled over metal. Ba'al's nostrils flared, unrepentant this time. But it was his claim that screamed at Qurong.

"You're saying what? That *you* were once Forest Guard? That you're half-breed?"

The dark priest faced the valley. "I am lover of Marsuuv, made whole by his blood. And now that you know, I will have to open your eyes so that you won't kill me."

He bent, grabbed a handful of dust at his feet, spit into it, and flung it at Qurong. The glob of mud slapped him square in the face and he stepped back, appalled.

"What's this?" he thundered.

"Open his eyes, Marsuuv, my lover."

Qurong wiped the mud off, face flushed with heat. And when he opened his eyes, he found that he couldn't see properly. The valley had darkened.

"Look above, Qurong. See what awaits all who have broken the covenant."

Qurong lifted his eyes and caught his breath. The Shataiki he'd seen at the high place were back. Thicker now. Blotting out the sun. Soaring through the sky not a thousand yards over their heads, with talons extended and red eyes glaring. Only at him, it seemed.

"Elyon help us."

"No, my lord. Elyon help *them*. But he won't. They've turned their backs on him. Now they will be flesh for the beasts."

"And what about me? Or you, for that matter? You don't think they would as soon tear us to shreds?"

"No. We've brokered a deal with the devils and pledged our allegiance, so that we will be spared along with our people. Do you forget already?"

It was beginning to make sense to Qurong. This was the reason behind his blood-drinking ritual. He didn't understand the full import of what he was seeing and hearing, but this must surely be the day of the dragon.

"So these Shataiki can only go after the half-breeds?"

"Yes. Unless . . ."

"Unless what?"

"Supernatural matters always have their caveats."

This would be the end, Qurong thought.

"Send the first wave," Ba'al said. "Send it while we still have their favor."

Qurong turned to Cassak, who was looking up, clearly lost as to what they were seeing. "Send in our first twenty thousand," he ordered. "Infantry. Ready the archers. Spare no one."

—∞∞—

SAMUEL KNEW beyond any doubt that he'd become Horde. His joints felt as though pins had been pushed into his bones, scraping with each movement. His skin burned, and when he tried to wash the pain away with water, it only worsened.

It was no wonder Horde generally shied from water and bathed only through pain. He tried some of the beetle nut, but the taste was too bitter.

Yet, even knowing he was Horde, he didn't resent his condition. It made him more like Eram. It fit into the greater world. And really, he wasn't sure why he'd been so offended by the scabbing disease to begin with.

It's taking your mind as well, Samuel.

Yes. Yes, there was that.

"They come!"

"Steady!" Eram called.

Samuel was jerked back to the moment. He leaped into his saddle and galloped to the front lines where Eram, Janae, and his generals were mounted, fixated on the valley. He pulled up between the Eramite leader and his witch, veins thumping with adrenaline.

"What is it?"

"Nice of you to join us, Son of Hunter," Eram said. "Qurong's finally grown a set and is sending his first men to die."

A sea of infantry was spilling over the crest, sweeping into the valley.

"How many have not taken the water?" Eram demanded of no one in particular.

"Fifty thousand, as instructed," his general said.

"The rest carry the poison in their blood?"

Janae responded. "Yes. All of them."

Eram spat, and his red spittle slapped into Samuel's boot before falling to the ground. Samuel caught the leader's eyes.

"Sorry about that." Eram studied the Horde army nearing the bottom of the far slope. "I'd say about twenty thousand men on foot. I'm surprised Qurong would be so obvious. Exactly as I predicted, he's trying to draw us."

"We can't show our strength yet," Samuel said. "Send fifty thousand."

"Yes, my new Horde general. That's exactly what I will do." He smirked at Samuel. "And you will lead them."

Samuel blinked at the man. "I'm sorry, I—"

"I need a general in the valley, my friend. Someone I can trust. I've decided you're the best choice." He snapped his fingers at his other general. "Send them now, General, the fifty thousand who have not taken the poison. Tell the captains they will take orders from Samuel once they're in battle. And tell them to send every last one of those Scabs back to hell."

"Yes, sir."

Samuel looked at Janae, but she didn't appear at all concerned by the decision. Her eyes were on the empty horizon to her left, where empty desert waited. And beyond the desert, the Black forest.

He still wasn't having great success wrapping his thoughts around Eram's decision to send him down. Naturally, he wasn't afraid. Far from it, thoughts of slaying Horde and taking glory were already pulling at him. But what motive did Eram really have?

"Samuel, you're questioning my judgment?" Eram asked.

"No, sir."

"I need your men to see you go down that hill, and I need them to see you kill Horde. I've just been informed that some of them are complaining about a rash. I would send them all down now, before they have a chance to realize they have the disease, but their presence on the battlefield now might spook Qurong, you understand? But one albino, the Son of Hunter—now that would tempt Qurong to send his whole army in at once."

"My men are turning Horde?"

"Are they?" He said it as if he'd expected nothing less. "They've taken the mark and given their hearts to its maker. What did you expect?" A gentle smile. "But the transition will take some time. We have to fight before we lose our physical advantage."

The thought that Eram was a brilliant tactician and the thought that Janae had betrayed the albinos entered Samuel's mind as one. But at the moment, only the former seemed terribly important. Had he expected anything less from his witch?

A flood of Eramite warriors broke over the crest to his left. Infantry. The ground rumbled with the footfalls of fifty thousand as the heavily armored warriors plunged down the slope. No cry yet. The two armies rushed toward each other.

Samuel's pulse surged and he nudged his horse forward, then brought it back around. "Just restrain those archers. I don't need an arrow in my back."

Eram nodded. "Watch for Qurong's next wave. He'll commit the bulk of his force; you'll know it's coming when he launches the fireballs. I'll send reinforcements as soon as he takes our bait, beginning with the albinos. Until then, hold them. Once they descend, the disease will spread. We'll see just how effective this poison really is."

The stampede of warriors still rushed over the crest. Janae still looked to the north, always to the north.

Now she looked at him and smiled gently. "Come here, lover."

"Say your good-byes quickly," Eram said, pulling his horse around. "Your battle awaits you."

Samuel pulled his mount next to Janae's, facing the opposite direction. He impulsively leaned forward and kissed her on the mouth. The smell of her breath drew him as the blood had. He knew that Teeleh had changed her into something less than any woman he'd ever known, and he wondered if he would be so fortunate as to have a similar experience.

"Good-bye, my love," she said. "It's been good to join with you for a while."

"I have no intention of dying," he said, looking into her lost eyes. "I'll be back."

"And I'll be gone. I've done what I was meant to do."

"Gone? No, no, you can't leave now!"

"But I must. I've finished my task here. They are deceived, all of them. Now my true lover calls me." She put her hand on his forearm. "Maybe when this is all over, you can join me, if he will allow it. I think you would like it."

"The Black Forest?"

"No," she said. "Earth. Two thousand years ago."

The histories. He didn't know what to say. A roar erupted from the valley behind him, and he twisted to see the two armies clash. Their leading edges feathered into each other like two black clouds meeting head-on. But here, the union was brutal and bloody, and already, screams of the dying mixed with cries of bravado and rage. He had to go!

"Then wait for me," he said, spinning back. But she was already headed away, sitting like an elegant queen on her pale mare. "Janae!"

She looked back, wearing her perpetual smirk. "Die well, Samuel."

"Janae . . ."

"General!" They were calling him. He could see Vadal watching him. As were all of the albino warriors. And another ten thousand Eramites. All eyes were on him. His army fought now, slaying the Horde as he'd always dreamed. Glory awaited.

Samuel spun his horse around, dug his heels into its flanks with enough power to crack a rib, and plunged into the Valley of Miggdon.

42

BILL REDIGER, who'd been called Billy before he received black eyes and a new name, stepped from the passenger ramp at the Denver International Airport, snugged his dark glasses to his forehead, and turned right, toward the trains that would take him to the street. To any ordinary passerby, he would look like a successful businessman with a taste for fine, dark suits and expensive watches, in this case Armani and Rolex. His red hair was neatly combed back, and a good tan softened the freckles on his cheeks.

None could possibly know who really walked past them on this otherwise plain summer day in middle America. They couldn't know that he had black eyeballs and could read minds.

It was a very good day to be alive, because in so many ways Bill was already dead. But now, having fully accepted his death, he could get on with the business at hand. He wasn't entirely sure what had happened to him, though he suspected that there was another man like him somewhere, living many years in the future.

Yes, that was right. To his recollection, he'd been in Bangkok in search of the Books of History, where he'd met Janae. They'd fallen into a trance of some kind. Gone somewhere he couldn't quite recall. It had left the taste of bile in his mouth.

Then he'd awakened in Washington, D.C., thirty-some-odd years in the past, which was technically before he'd been born. He'd been sent back for only one purpose: To stop Thomas Hunter. And the devil had given him the eyes to follow Thomas wherever he went, even into his dreams.

And once he stopped Thomas, then what? He would probably die some terrible death, because there couldn't be two of him running around.

Maybe he would become a monk, dye his hair black, find his way into a monastery somewhere, and wreak a little havoc. Help things along.

Or maybe not.

Getting the money he needed for his task had been easy. He'd simply walked into a Wells Fargo bank and taken what he needed from the manager's mind to make an unexpected visit to the vault before the bank opened the next morning.

He thought it a good idea to create an identity, so he got the necessary documents with some of his hard-earned dollars, bought a ticket under the name Bill Smith, and boarded a plane to Denver.

And here he was, in Denver. This is where he would change history.

This is where he would find and kill Thomas before he could do whatever he was meant to do that made all hell scream with rage.

Bill sighed and adjusted his glasses as he entered the train. Yes, it was good to be alive. Because really . . . most definitely, he was already dead.

43

THIS WAS the second time Chelise had made the eighteen-hour journey across the desert to save her father, but this time she was alone and she was scared, and this time she made it in a fourteen-hour sprint.

The sky was dark, and she was sure it wasn't by coincidence. Evil hung in the air, threatening to burst through the veil at any moment. Eram's army had left a wide swath of litter through the desert, traveling quickly without making camp. They'd eaten on the run and left the scraps from their meals scattered in their wake.

She approached Miggdon Valley from the northwest, following the Eramites' trail, but rather than cut south to the western slope as they had, she'd veered farther east. If Samuel and his witch were on the western slope, her father would be on the eastern slope.

The last thing she wanted now was to encounter Samuel and his band of fools. She had but one goal.

Qurong. Her father, leader of the world, awaited her. This is what Michal must have meant when he said *the world awaits you.*

These were the thoughts that ran through Chelise's mind as she closed in. But the moment she came upon the expansive scene in the Miggdon Valley, a chill swept over her.

She was too late!

The din of clashing metal joined with the roar of battle cries, rising from the valley floor like a hive of angry hornets.

"Easy." She patted her stamping mount's neck. "Easy."

But nothing about this valley was easy. She quickly took stock of the chaos.

The main battle had been joined on the valley floor by upwards of a hundred thousand warriors already. Of those, more than half were down, either wounded or dead.

One of a dozen Horde catapults launched a ball of fire into the air. It arced over the valley, trailing a long ribbon of oily smoke, and streaked toward the armies below like a comet. The projectile slammed into a sea of flesh and mushroomed. Resin splattered in all directions, spreading fire. Burning men from both armies fled in all directions.

Then another, then another, then a fourth ball, all launched in rapid succession, each floating lazily through the sky before smashing into the warriors below. Twelve balls were sent as Chelise watched, and each took the lives of at least fifty tightly grouped fighters—half-breed, full-breed, or albino, it didn't matter. They all burned like flies.

The main body of Qurong's army broke from their position on the eastern ridge and began to flow into the valley. The sight was enough to stop her heart for a moment. Two or three hundred thousand, maybe more, all in black, rushed down the long slope to crush the enemy. Dust rose about their horses as they pounded down.

Their cries then reached her, delayed by the great distance. A dull roar of rage from so many open throats.

Then the Eramites, a smaller army but still massive, broke from the ridge to her right and rushed to collide. Led by albinos! The whole army, leaving none to guard the hill.

She'd half expected the albinos to come to their senses and turn back. But the witch's tongue had clearly proven too crafty.

This was the final battle. When the dust settled, three or four hundred thousand would surely be dead on the ground.

She watched in horror as the two armies crashed into each other. It took a few moments, and then she heard the terrible sound of that initial clash, like two battering rams colliding head-on. She could see the thrusting lances, the sweeping maces bouncing surreally off bodies. From this distance, there was no blood, no flying body parts, only two massive walls of humanity tearing into each other.

And even as she watched, a third wave came from the Horde's slope. Another army to join the first, bringing their total to well over half a million. They outnumbered the Eramites three to one!

But the Eramites had the witch's brew. Teeleh's breath. And if they'd found a way to deliver it, the tide would turn quickly.

Chelise was so overwhelmed by the display of brute force that she couldn't think what to do. Then she saw the tall banners showing her father's colors on the southern slope, and she realized that he was there, commanding from above.

But this was Qurong, and he would join his men in battle if there was any hint that they needed his help. She had to get to him. She had to stop him and force him to use reason in this hour of endings.

She should approach from the east, where the Horde army had lain waiting. Her father's guard wouldn't expect anyone from that side, and she stood a better chance of reaching him. In a time of war, they would have orders to kill any albino on sight. If she died, then her father was hopelessly lost.

"Hiyaa!"

Chelise spurred her horse and forced it east against its will. It would take her half an hour to reach the far side, and then only if she went unnoticed. If she found a stray Horde mount and wrapped herself in Horde dress, perhaps.

Reaching her father was all that mattered now.

QURONG PACED the overlook, seething. "Ba'al!" He stopped next to a servant under the shade of the only tree on the southern ridge, an old miggdon fig that was leafy but barren. From this vantage, there was no sign of the dark priest.

He spun to the servant. "Get that dark witch! Drag him to me if you have to. Now!"

"Yes, my lord."

His servant fled, and Qurong doubted he'd be back. Cassak was down the hill already, as were his Throaters, leaving only a thousand guards to maintain a perimeter around him.

Qurong turned back to the runner sent by Cassak. "Tell me again what has happened to the warriors. This makes no sense, none at all."

"A spell, a sickness, I don't know. But our men in the valley are suffering, my lord."

"Suffering?" Qurong scoffed. "War is filled with suffering." Yet there was no denying the ease with which the half-breeds were cutting through his ranks. From what he saw, the albinos were virtually unstoppable, slashing through his men with such wickedness that his best Throaters might as well be bound by rope.

"Aches and pain." The runner turned frantic eyes down the hill. "They're baying like wounded animals."

"Cassak too?"

"All of them, my lord."

"And you? What of you?"

"No. But I haven't been in the fighting. The message was passed to me by another."

"And did he have this ailment?"

"I can't say. No, sire, I can't say."

This was impossible!

"Ba'al!" he thundered again. He loathed the man.

Then Qurong saw the high priest in the valley. He'd set up an altar in a protected enclave far to the east with a dozen of his wicked underlings. He looked to be sacrificing—of all things! A goat. Or a human, it was too far to see clearly.

Qurong watched in disbelief as the distant figure in purple raised both arms to an empty sky. Dark clouds had gathered, promising rain, but he could no longer see Shataiki. No magic in the air to slay the treasonous half-breeds.

When this was over, Qurong would sever Ba'al's head from his shoulders himself. The man might have some personal tunnel to Teeleh's lair, but he was a disgusting wraith, and a half-breed too. Let Teeleh feed on his flesh. The Horde needed a trustworthy man to guide them in spiritual matters.

He screamed his frustration into the valley, knowing that nothing could be heard down there but the clashing of metal and groans of men. "Ba'al!"

You're wasting your breath, Qurong. Your army is falling.

He stared at the battle, red-faced. An albino close enough for Qurong to make out his dark, smooth skin was on foot, wielding a sword in both hands. He swung his sword as if it were a feather, slashing up and across a Throater's chest, then sidestepping a thrown ax. Like a master among children. His own men looked far too sluggish.

It's over. In one fell swoop they destroy you.

His mind fled the valley for a moment and embraced an image of Patricia, the wise woman who'd loved him always. He would die for her. And Chelise . . .

Dear Chelise, forgive me. Forgive me, my daughter.

Qurong thrust out his hand, palm open. "Captain!"

The captain of his guard rushed forward and bowed.

"Give me my sword."

"Sir?"

"My sword, Malachi! Give me my sword. I'm going down. Order the rest of your men to the battle. Today we will live or today we die."

THE VALLEY of Miggdon might have been a burial pit and Samuel wouldn't have known the difference. That he'd managed to survive three hours of close battle wasn't a thing of glory as he'd imagined.

The blood of tens of thousands wet the ground; he could feel it squishing through his soaked boots. The valley was a butchering ground, pure and simple, and Qurong's army had indeed been the butchered. Horses could no longer navigate the carcasses underfoot and had taken to the perimeter, where those who'd lost their courage tried to flee only to be cut down. By the look of it, Qurong had lost over half of his army, and the rest were feeling the full effects of Janae's poison. Their own disease was eating them alive, and a wail rose on all sides as they dug at their flesh, desperate for relief.

But more than a third of the half-breeds lay dead as well. It was now only a matter of time before they cut down the last of Qurong's massive force, but they had already lost enough to leave many wives and children weeping for months.

Samuel ducked under a swooshing mace and swung his sword full in the face of the Scab connected to the other end of the chain. His blade cut cleanly through his neck, and the man's body took three more steps before tripping and falling over two other bodies.

Forgive me, Father, for I have sinned.

"Your back, Hunter!" a voice shouted.

Samuel spun in time to deflect a spear thrown by a young Scab now skewered at the end of Eram's sword. The half-breed leader caught Samuel's eye, then spun to ward off two Scabs who wielded long swords.

Samuel's own joints screamed with pain, and the albinos fighting around him were covered in the scabbing disease. With each swing Samuel felt his father's eyes on him.

There would be no men left. This wasn't an attack against the Horde. It was the *end* of the Horde. The carnage sickened him.

Samuel stopped and stood gasping in the middle of the battlefield, like a man caught in the eye of a storm, calm for the moment. He turned slowly and surveyed the butchery. The scene whipped by him with dizzying speed. A man with no arm, screaming, another staggering as he ran, blinded. An albino weeping. Weeping though he looked untouched by a blade.

The battle would be won soon. In thirty minutes, the great Qurong's army would be dead and rotting on the ground. Flies had already come by the hundreds of thousands. The stench of Horde flesh had become familiar to Samuel, but bleeding Horde flesh was much worse, and the smell now clogged his nostrils like so much rotting skin.

On all sides the massacre raged. Samuel moved to avoid a spear hurled at him. The Scab stared at him, then fell to his knees and began to weep. He was but a teenager, crying out his mother's name in a mournful wail. Martha.

"Shut up!" Samuel screamed. "Stop it!"

The boy either didn't hear him or refused. Furious, Samuel raced forward, leaping over the bodies in his way. He screamed his anger and swung his sword at a full run.

He stood over his kill, overcome by a wave of nausea. *Father. Please, Father.* He fell to his knees beside the slain body and touched the boy's warm flesh.

Mother . . . A deep sorrow welled up from his past. *Dear Mother, forgive me.*

And then the dam that had separated the boy in him from the man broke, and Samuel began to weep. He sat back on his haunches, clenched his eyes against the dark sky, spread his arms wide, and began to wail his anguish.

What had he done? What kind of deception had he ingested? How could he undo this catastrophe?

But it was too late. It was already done. He'd betrayed his father.

Samuel wept.

It would be better now if someone killed him where he sat, crying like a baby. How could he live knowing that this slaughter had been his doing? He'd been born in his father's image, destined to save the world. Instead he'd played the very Judas his father often spoke of. A traitor.

Slowly the sorrow became anger. Then rage. And then the sky above him became black and the battlefield around him grew silent, and the distant thought that he might be dead crossed his mind. He opened his eyes.

A host of Shataiki, a million strong if there was one, circled no more than a thousand yards above the valley, swirling black tar stuffed with mangy fur and red cherries. He could feel the breeze from their wings as they swept overhead in silence.

The battle around him had come to a halt; the horror painted on the skies above was laid bare for all to see. And Samuel knew the full truth then.

They'd broken their covenant with Elyon, leaving the way clear for the Shataiki to destroy them at will. What kind of evil Ba'al and Qurong were dealing, he didn't know, but he doubted they would be consumed. No, that honor belonged to the half-breeds, to the albinos.

Janae had convinced them all to turn their backs on the protection that came from bathing in Elyon's lakes. And in truth, Samuel had known all along, hadn't he? Deep beneath the disease clouding his mind, he'd known that the witch was Teeleh's handmaiden, because she'd come from the desert bearing his mark.

She was Teeleh's handmaiden, and Samuel, son of Hunter, was her fool.

He stood to his feet, staring at the sky, blinded by a debilitating rage. It was over. He'd come to kill Qurong, the father whom his mother loved more than she loved even her own kind. Instead he'd killed all *but* Qurong.

He'd slaughtered the world.

Samuel trembled, wishing death on himself. The dead were a feast, easy prey, blood and flesh for the Shataiki who'd waited for this meal since their captivity in the Black Forest. And Samuel, son of Hunter, was the one serving their meal.

Screams and chaos rose from the valley far behind him, and he turned slowly. To a man, the armies of both Qurong and Eram were gripped by the sight of a single stream of black bats flowing to the ground at the battlefield's far side, two hundred yards away.

Like a serpent reaching to earth, the Shataiki descended and began to feed. Talons first, ripping into head or backs. Then fangs, penetrating the skulls of any warrior standing. They went down in a tangle of blood and fur.

Warriors abandoned their weapons and tried to run, but the Shataiki caught them and hauled them to the ground. Darkness swallowed the battlefield as the evil creatures poured down through the funnel and spread slowly north.

The valley erupted in panic as the living, a hundred thousand strong still, fled. They could run . . . they *would* run, but they could not hide. Samuel turned his back and faced north, barely able to stay upright for the fear that shook his bones.

The ridge was empty. The Horde command had fled. And the lone tree that stood beside the tall banners was bare now. No leaves. An angular, burnt husk stood alone against the sky, reaching up like a black claw.

What was green was now black.

"Father . . ." Tears streamed down Samuel's cheeks as he turned back to the valley. "Father, forgive me! Forgive me, Thomas."

A small flash of purple streaked across the far southern slope, a warrior mounted on a black horse. It's Qurong, he thought, catching himself. And as Samuel watched, Qurong swung his sword at any enemy that stood in his way. He'd lost his mind and was attacking now, knowing all was lost. Loyal to the bone.

Even now, the reviled enemy of all that was good showed he was more of a man than Samuel would ever be. He blurted a cry of self-disgust.

Here was royalty, in the Horde. And Elyon's heir was a pitiful traitor soaked in blood.

Samuel screamed his frustration. He snatched up his sword, bounded over fallen bodies, and flung himself onto the back of a panicked Horde stallion.

He would die, they would all die, but first Qurong would die.

And then . . . then the end could come.

44

THE HORSE Chelise had taken belonged to a dead Horde warrior who was still slumped over his mount on the eastern ridge when she'd stumbled upon them. She'd quickly set her own horse free, shrugged into the fighter's dark cape, and pushed the fresher mount around the ridge at a full gallop.

Her father had committed his entire army, and from what she'd seen as she raced, they were suffering wholesale slaughter. Except for the few thousand albinos who were inflicting serious damage, the half-breeds' slight advantage as better fighters should have been offset by the Horde's numbers.

But even her father's Throaters were falling where they stood. Something was wrong. There was evil at work here, and the concern she had for her father's life grew with each passing breath.

The mighty Qurong was defeated! Five hundred thousand would be dead, leaving behind a city of weeping widows and children. And what would Samuel do, shove them all underwater until they drowned?

No, that wouldn't work. The drowning had to be voluntary to work.

She kept looking down the valley for any sign of her father's colors. Seeing his men fall like this, he would join. He would rather embrace death than go home stripped of his pride.

Dear Elyon, she had to reach him.

She rounded the southern ridge, whipping the snorting mount. She could see the banners far ahead, but the army was gone. No sign . . .

The sky darkened, and she reined in the horse. What was this?

Shataiki swept through the sky above in a massive, slow-moving vortex. The battle had stalled. Silence smothered the valley.

It was the end, then. Elyon would come. For a brief moment, she felt elation, because this had been foretold. The day of the dragon had come. How the rest would come to pass she didn't know or care to know any longer. Only that Qurong was saved.

And her mother? Yes, her mother as well, of course. But how?

The Shataiki suddenly dived at the far end of the valley, like the tail of a tornado. The damage they inflicted when they touched the earth was no less destructive. They began to devour the living, and Chelise began to panic.

"Father!" Her scream was hardly a whisper in the echoing din below. "Father! Fath—"

She saw him! Trailing a purple cape. Racing across the valley floor on a black horse. He hacked at a fleeing albino fighter, but his goal wasn't the main battle. He was going for a small grouping of boulders on the western side, where Chelise could just make out several priests in their dark robes.

She spurred her mount and dived into the darkened valley. "Hiyaa! Hiyaa!"

The Shataiki flooding into the valley were spreading out, like so many black hornets swarming through a crack in a cliff. Those who fled were being singled out and picked off as they clambered up the slopes. She still had time, maybe ten minutes, before the black beasts worked their way to this end.

There was a red pool one half mile east, but how would she get to it?

"Hiyaa!" She whipped the horse and raced to intercept Qurong.

Not until she was within a hundred yards did she guess his intention. Ba'al, the dark priest, was kneeling on a makeshift altar, stripped of his robe. His arms were stretched to the swirling Shataiki, and his jaw was wide in a scream of delight. Four other priests had discarded their clothing as well and were bleeding from deep cuts in their arms and ribs.

This was his finest hour. He was somehow behind the carnage as much as Samuel and Janae.

And now her father meant to take out his rage on the frail white skeleton of a man.

"Father!"

Qurong thundered on, sword raised over his head, roaring.

"Father!"

Movement far behind and to her right caught her attention, and she snatched a glance at a half-breed racing toward them like a dragon heading out of hell.

She spun back. "Father!"

Ba'al surely knew that his slayer had come, but he trusted only in his master, Teeleh, to save him. But Teeleh was clearly in no saving mood today.

Qurong rolled off his horse at a full gallop, came to his feet ten yards from the altar, and rushed Ba'al with both hands on his sword.

Ba'al was weeping at the heavens now, frantic with his own kind of pleasure.

"Father!"

Qurong planted one foot at the base of the altar and swung his blade like a club. The razor-sharp steel severed the nearest of Ba'al's raised arms, then slashed through his neck before glancing into the air.

The dark priest's head toppled off his body and landed on the stone, jaw still spread, silent now. Ba'al's priests fled, crying out to Teeleh like frantic women.

"Qurong!" Chelise pulled up and dropped to the ground. "Supreme Commander of the Horde, I beg you to hear me."

Her father turned slowly, bloody sword limp in his hand. He stared at her as if he didn't recognize her, lost.

"The end of the world has come, Father. Your army is gone. Your people are without husbands."

"Chelise?" Slowly his face wrinkled with anguish, and he sank to one knee.

"Yes, it's me, Father," she said, stepping closer. "And this is not the way of a mighty leader. You are called to Elyon's side as you once were."

He tried to stand but could not.

"You have to drown, Father."

"Never." His voice was weak, but his jowls shook with his stubbornness. "I will never drown like a coward."

"Stop this madness!" she cried. "It's life, you old fool! You're here on the edge of hell, and you still resist the call of your Maker?"

"I serve no one. Hell cannot touch me now." He tried to stand again, this time wincing. Was he in pain? Was he wounded?

She remembered the sight of Stephen, the Scab Janae had exposed to her vial of Teeleh's poison. Her father had come in contact with it when he'd entered the battle, and was dying already.

"The pain you feel is his betrayal. Teeleh's disease will kill you even if you're protected from the Shataiki. You've been betrayed!"

"I . . . will . . . not . . . drown!" He managed to stand, but shakily, like an old man.

She grabbed the bottle of blood that Johan had given her. Thomas's blood, which Janae must have carried knowing it would affect the disease. Why else bottle it up? She broke off the top, exposing a sharp jagged edge, and held it up to him.

"Blood, Father. Thomas's. Cleansed by the first lake."

"Don't be a fool." He spat to one side. "Ba'al makes me drink Teeleh's blood; now you want me to consume your husband's blood? We are in a battle here!"

"And you are dying! Your people are slaughtered by half-breeds and eaten by those who have a thirst for Teeleh's blood." She paused, not sure what to do. "I think that if Thomas's blood mixes with your own, it will stop the disease."

"I would spit on the blood of Thomas!" Qurong roared.

Chelise was so outraged by his abject refusal to engage common sense that she moved without thought. She rushed him and slashed his forearm with the vial.

He stared at his arm, aghast as Thomas's blood mixed with his own. Chelise stepped backward and dropped the vial. Behind her, the din of the slaughter pressed closer. But she was dressed as a Horde warrior and was with Qurong. They were safe for the moment.

"I don't know what else to do except pray that his blood will protect you. But you must drown, Father. Please, you must!"

He was looking down at his arm, breathing deeply. "I don't know what to do. I don't know what's happening." Tears welled in his eyes and spilled down his cheeks.

He sank to both knees and buried his head in both hands. "Forgive me," he wept. "Forgive me."

"I forgive you, Father." Now she was crying. She stood not ten feet from Qurong while the black beasts ravaged the Horde, and she begged like a mother pleading for the life of her only child.

"Drown, I beg you, drown. The Shataiki won't consume you now, you're protected by the blood. We can make it out, to a red pool nearby. Please, please, I beg you, Father."

She heard the faint pounding of hooves behind her, and an image flashed through her mind. The half-breed she'd seen.

Chelise twisted back and saw the horse upon her. Saw the sword on its way down. Heard the roar of protest from her father.

Saw in a fleeting glimpse that this was Samuel, turned Horde.

Felt the sting of the blade as it cut into her neck.

And then Chelise of Hunter's horizon went blue.

A brilliant sky rising from a perfectly silent desert. Nothing else, just a rolling white desert and a perfectly blue sky.

One moment—searing pain as the sword's metal edge sliced through her neck. The next—absolute peace in this bright world spread before her.

No pain.

No sorrow.

No blood.

Several long seconds slogged through the perfect silence.

A child laughed behind her. She turned around and saw that she wasn't alone. A thin boy of maybe thirteen stood on the bank of a green pool.

Yes, she thought, *there is the pool.*

"Hello, Chelise, daughter of Elyon," the boy said.

She knew at the first sound of his voice that he was far more than just any ordinary boy. Her voice trembled when she answered.

"Hello."

He grinned mischievously, looked at the water, then at her, then back at the water. Finally, his bright green eyes settled on her again.

"Are you ready?"

Are you ready? She couldn't find her voice any longer. And she suddenly couldn't see, because her eyes were blurred by tears of desperation.

Unable to contain his own excitement, the boy turned and dived.

Chelise tore her feet from the sand, gasping. She'd already taken three steps when his body splashed through the surface and vanished beneath the emerald waters.

Then Chelise dived headlong into Elyon's lake, and the pleasure of her first contact with him took her breath away.

———

QURONG HAD been so absorbed, so vanquished by his own misery, so consumed by self-pity, that he didn't see the danger. He'd seen the fleeing warrior earlier, but not until too late did he realize that he was coming in for the kill.

He leaped to his feet and threw out his hands, thinking one of his men was mistaking Chelise for an Eramite threatening him. "My daughter!" he screamed. "She's my . . ."

Then he saw that this was an Eramite warrior whose bloodstained armor made him nearly indistinguishable from his own warriors. Still, in the last moment, he thought the half-breed would heed his cry.

But it was too late. The momentum of the fighter's sword could not be stopped.

His blade sliced cleanly through Chelise's neck. Her head flew from her body, bounced off the attacker's horse, and fell to the ground, eyes still open.

Qurong didn't have time to consider the horror of this sudden change before the warrior swung again with a cry of rage, now at him. He ducked under the blow, aware that the pain he'd felt only a minute earlier was nearly gone. The attacker's sword clanged off the rock behind him, then the man was rearing his horse for another pass.

But there was Chelise, lying dead and bleeding from her neck, and Qurong could not manage the sight of it. He had killed his own daughter, as clearly as if he'd swung the sword himself.

She smiled in death. A pure, clean face, free of any blemish. This daughter, whose forehead he'd often kissed and who'd often strutted around announcing to all that her papa was the strongest, greatest man in the world—this daughter named Chelise was dead. On his account.

Qurong wanted to die. Let the half-breed end it now!

⸎

SAMUEL'S BLADE was in full swing when the guard turned and Samuel saw that the *he* was a *she*.

Saw that this woman was not one of Qurong's guards as he'd assumed from the cloak she wore and the horse she rode.

Saw that this woman was Chelise. His mother.

Terrified by the sight, he jerked his sword back and away, but the momentum was too great, and his blade slashed through her neck as if it were made of white clay.

His boot bumped her falling head as he rushed past. His mind lost track of his mortal enemy, the father of his mother. He was mistaken; this woman could not be his mother! He could undo this. Mother would never be cloaked as a Scab, riding a Horde mount!

But scream as it may, his mind drained of blood and reason as he struggled to force his horse around. He rushed back, pulled the horse up, and dropped to the ground. Qurong was there, on his knees, face white with shock.

And there on the ground, ten feet from him, lay . . . yes. Yes, it was her.

Samuel's world spun. The horizon started to fade, all but the green eyes staring at him from the face of this impetuous woman who'd scolded him so often, yet loved him as her son.

Chelise. Chelise! *Mother! Dear Mother.*

"Mother?"

He was facing the valley darkened by Shataiki, but in that moment nothing existed except for his own foolishness and the longing to join his mother on the ground, dead.

———— ∞∞∞ ————

THE HALF-BREED did not end Qurong's life. He made no attempt at a second attack. Instead, he dropped from his saddle and staggered forward. "Mother?"

Mother? *Mother?* Qurong felt his rage rise and his self-control slip.

Thunder crashed overhead, and Qurong turned to look at jagged lines of lightning that stuttered through the sky. The core of the black swarm circling the valley scattered as light cut through them. Thousands of Shataiki began to fall from the sky, screeching. It was as if a wide shaft of white-hot sunshine had bored through their middle and burned them to a crisp.

The light slammed into the battlefield, and the earth beneath Qurong's feet shook.

The world was ending.

Qurong slowly turned back to the half-breed. The world was ending, and there was only one task that would bring the smallest measure of peace to a man who'd lost everything.

Qurong reached for his sword, snugged the hilt tight in his fist, and rose from his knees, shaking from head to foot. He rushed the half-breed who was frozen by confusion. His wrath came out in a long bloody cry from the bottom of his chest, and he swung the blade with all of his strength, severing the man's body nearly in half at his chest.

The half-breed looked at him with wide eyes, then toppled dead at his feet, taking Qurong's sword down with him.

Qurong stood heaving over the two dead bodies, numb. Then he fell to his face by Chelise's head, and he wept into the ground.

45

THEY HAD raced through the desert for eight hours, and with each pounding hoof, Thomas's heart beat with an expectation that had been building for the last twenty-seven years.

This was it! This was everything.

Everything except Samuel and Chelise.

Their horses fell into a natural formation in a full, tireless gallop over the sand. A million Roush flew above, filling the sky as far as he could see. The streaming colored light formed a tunnel around them, ushering them forward. Thomas wanted to touch it again, to swim in those colors and dive into Elyon's waters of intoxicating power.

But these thoughts were whispers of promise; the Warrior on the white horse who rushed ahead of them stole his mind. He could not keep his eyes off Elyon, just there, a hundred yards ahead, sprinting full tilt over the desert with his red cape flowing behind him. As his horse passed, the sand came alive with light, so that by the time Thomas and Kara reached it, they looked to be rushing through a thin cloud of raw, white power. Maybe this is what gave the horses their unflagging strength.

They were being escorted in a vast display of wonder and power, and no one seemed able to speak a single word. They didn't stop to eat; this anticipation was their food.

This hope was their nourishment.

How had they missed it? Like children wandering in the desert, they'd lost sight of the promise, so easily consumed with finding reward in a daily feeding of crumbs from the sky. Elyon's Israel had lost its way.

But all along, this power crackled just beyond the skin of their world. If only they could have seen . . .

If only the other world could see. But they had, he thought. Someone named Johnny had shown them some things. The saint had opened their eyes. And soon Billy, the sinner, would blind them in an ultimate showdown.

How he knew this, he wasn't sure, because this was his home and he now knew little about the other world. Did Kara know about Samuel and Paradise?

The abstract thought distracted him for a moment. Samuel. What about Samuel? So complete was his preoccupation with the Warrior, he'd forgotten about Samuel and Chelise! He had to save them!

He had to find them and bring them with him!

But then he knew something else, like he'd known about someone called Johnny. There was a reason for their rush through the desert.

They were going after Samuel and Chelise.

Thomas leaned lower and pressed harder, but then the brilliant colors swallowed him again, and again he became fixated on his desire to reach Elyon's lake.

"Run, Thomas, run!"

He looked to his left and saw that Gabil, a fluffy white Roush he'd first met long ago, flew not ten feet from him. The creature's round green eyes sparkled with his mischievous nature. The flier flipped over midflight and executed what looked to be a karate kick at some unseen enemy. "Hiyaa!"

Thomas felt more than heard laughter bubbling from his own chest.

"Impressed, huh?" Then the Roush showed off more, and Thomas saw five younger Roush in his wake, mimicking his every move. "Hiyaa!" The warrior had found himself some apprentices.

He turned to Kara, thinking to show her, but saw that another Roush sat in front of her, holding the reins with her. Had he been there long? She couldn't keep her eyes off the creature's furry head.

Thousands of Roush had joined the seven thousand albinos, riding or flying with them all. And high above them all flew one. Perhaps Michal, following the Warrior who cut through the sand.

Thomas first became aware of the huge vortex of Shataiki when they were still far from the Valley of Miggdon. The beasts reached down to the earth through a funnel, a staggering sight even from this distance. The battle was there, raging, and he should have felt some alarm, but he couldn't seem to work up any.

Gabil and his young recruits, who'd grown to nearly a hundred, continued their antics nearby. No one seemed remotely concerned about this swirling black mass.

The Roush overhead suddenly rose higher, above the swirling vortex of Shataiki, and Thomas wondered if they were going to attack from above.

The Warrior had led them east, dead east, but he now veered south, where the Valley of Miggdon lay open. The light turned with him on either side; the Roush banked south; the seven thousand altered course hard on the Warrior's heels.

The Roush rose even higher, and the colored light swept lower. They were sweeping into the thick of the blackened valley, straight for the center of the Shataiki. At any minute, Chelise would join them. She would rush down from one of the slopes with Samuel by her side.

Thomas could see the whole valley now. Countless Shataiki littered the ground directly ahead. But they were not alone. There were bodies under the beasts.

The Shataiki were feeding on the fallen, a whole sea of death.

The scene took his breath away, and if his mount hadn't had a head for the Warrior alone, he would have pulled up. Gabil and his entourage were gone. The albinos' horses rushed forward, undisturbed by the carnage layering the valley floor.

Bodies lay upon bodies, and only a few thousand were left to flee the Shataiki, who methodically pulled them down and plunged their fangs into their heads.

The valley was screaming, a high-pitched inhuman wail from Shataiki throats. And in that moment, Thomas knew that he had made this very scene possible by creating a breach in time for Billy and Janae.

Michal's words flashed through his mind. *Go to the place you came from. Make a way for the Circle to fulfill its hope.*

But there was more. *And return quickly before it's too late. Do that and you might save your son.*

Where was he? Where was Samuel?

And where was Chelise?

The Warrior leading them didn't look back or slow. He thundered down the center of the valley.

"Thomas!"

He glanced at Kara, then followed her eyes up. The Roush were above the huge gathering of Shataiki swirling through the sky, and a thin stream of them were diving directly into the center of the black swarm.

The Roush cut into the beasts, and the whole swarm of Shataiki shifted, reacting to the intrusion.

The Warrior on the white horse stood in his stirrups and leaned into the wind, still at a full gallop. He thrust a finger from each hand into the air and screamed his charge, then abruptly clapped his hands together. The sound of his clap came as thunder, and it shook the valley.

Lightning stuttered through the sky.

And the bottom of the Shataiki swarm blew out as the first Roush broke through, red with blood. White light streamed through the hole they'd cut. A dozen, and then a hundred followed, each badly bloodied.

Black bats rained from the hole as the Roush punched through their center by the thousands now, creating a great hole at the heart of the vortex. Shrieking with terror, the exposed black bats on the ground abandoned their prey and flapped madly for the relative safety of those above. The whole swarm was off-kilter now, but they clung together like syrup, unwilling to flee alone.

The Warrior Elyon leaned over his white horse, sprinting faster, faster, head down. He was leading them directly into this bloodbath.

The Roush had created their own swarm, a tunnel through the center of the Shataiki, and the streak of light at the core suddenly swelled to a wide shaft and reached down, into the battlefield. It slammed into the ground below, vaporizing any flesh in its path.

The ground shook, then cracked. A chasm opened wide directly ahead of them. Roush streamed down into the great hole with the shaft of light and vanished. They flowed with the light, streaking through the angry swirl of Shataiki and those shrieking for safety, right into the wide gap, maybe a hundred paces across.

The earth was swallowing them all.

The colorful tunnel around the seven thousand narrowed as they entered the battleground, led by the Warrior. Whatever waited in their path was consumed by the light. The Warrior cleared a wide swath through the heaps of dead.

And then Thomas saw their destination, and his breathing stopped. Water was rising in the chasm. Red water, forming a new lake at the heart of the battlefield. The Roush still streamed into a swirling green hole at the lake's center, vanishing into the depths.

This was it. This was it!

But where was Chelise?

Thomas jerked his head around. Kara was there, ten feet to his right, beaming like a child. Mikil, Johan, and Marie were close behind, staring past him at the new lake. The seven thousand leaned forward on their mounts, eyes fixed on the water like dehydrated souls staring at their last hope.

But there was no sign of Chelise. Nor Samuel.

It occurred to him then that they might be lost. Lost! The mere suggestion of it shoved his heart into his throat. Above, the Roush flowed into the eye of this new whirlpool; behind, the seven thousand gave hard chase as the Warrior's horse galloped at full speed; ahead, the lake beckoned.

But Chelise was lost.

"Elyon!" he shouted. The Warrior didn't turn or slow. "Elyon!" Panic reached long fingers into his mind, and he screamed it this time. "Elyon!"

The last of the Roush vanished below the water's surface, and the hole at the lake's middle collapsed on itself. The water at the center swirled in hues of green, surrounded by a mirror of red.

The streaming light on either side of them reached the lake's edge. It curved downward and plunged into the water as if sucked by a powerful vacuum. A dull roar filled the valley, the sound of pure power. Above, the black Shataiki were scattering.

And then Elyon launched his horse over the slight rise that ran around the lake, catapulted himself from the white steed's back, and sailed through the air in a perfectly executed dive. His body followed his outstretched hands, and the moment his head entered the water, a brilliant white light spread out just under the surface like a shock wave.

Elyon vanished into the depths.

Thomas was going to follow as he had followed before—Elyon knew how desperately he needed to enter the water. But where was Samuel?

"Elyon!" He was crying out at empty water. "Elyon."

A lone Roush flew over his head, low enough to batter his face with wind, headed to the slope. He immediately recognized Michal, the leader of the Roush, fur red with blood. Thomas looked at the far slope in the direction Michal was flying and saw that a crude altar had been erected. A man was on his knees, fists raised at the sky, wailing.

Qurong!

"In," he cried to Kara. "Dive in after him! I'll come . . ."

He veered to the right, following the Roush. Kara hardly needed encouragement. She took her horse over the edge and fell headlong into the red lake with a mighty splash. Elyon's waters swallowed her.

Thomas followed the Roush to the west of the pool, tempted to turn back and dive in. But Qurong was there, just ahead, and Chelise had come for Qurong.

The seven thousand were now plowing into the lake, waves and waves, some of them clinging to their mounts, others diving midair, still others—mostly the young, squealing with laughter—tumbling through the air before splashing beneath the surface.

They all knew this was it. Elyon called to them from these intoxicating waters.

Thomas pushed his mount faster, oblivious to the dead underfoot. He rushed forward, aware that he was going in the wrong direction. The waters still called to him from behind.

But Chelise was ahead.

A wounded albino who looked like he'd caught the scabbing disease rushed past him, headed for the lake with tears streaming down his face. He stumbled to the edge and threw himself into the water. A half-breed rushed the waters on the opposite shore. Both vanished below the shimmering surface. Neither reemerged. Others left alive by the Shataiki followed.

Still others fled the lake, clawing back up the valley's slopes.

Thomas saw Qurong clearly now. The Horde leader had fallen on his face and was gripping an article of clothing. Behind him on a flat boulder lay the naked body of the dark priest, Ba'al, now headless. To his right, a fallen half-breed, facedown.

But no sign of Chelise. Or Samuel. None!

He pulled his horse to a stop, dropped to the ground, and rushed Qurong. "Where is she?"

The leader didn't look lucid. He'd been weeping for some time. Thomas grasped his dreadlocks and yanked his head back. "Where is my wife? Tell me!"

"Gone!" the man cried, shoving the clothing at him. "Vanished!"

Thomas was about to slap sense into the man in his eagerness to know, when he recognized the bloody tunic beneath the Horde cloak by Qurong's knees. And the riding pants, still stuffed into the tops of boots.

Boots . . . These were boots that he himself had made. Chelise's boots. She'd been here!

He spun back to the lake, and the meaning of what had happened filled his mind. Chelise had been here, slain in battle. But Elyon had taken her.

"My son!" he demanded, spinning back to Qurong again. "Where is my son, Samuel? He was with the Eramites."

Qurong's eyes snapped up, and realization spread over his face. He turned to his right and looked at the slain half-breed.

"There. There is your son, the one who killed my daughter."

Thomas stood slowly, fighting to stay steady as he turned to the body lying facedown. He walked forward, gripped the sword still sticking out of the warrior's chest, and turned the man over.

Disease covered his skin and his armor was patently Horde, but there was no doubting this man's face. Samuel. Samuel, who'd turned Scab, lay dead. And his body, unlike Chelise's body, was still here, trapped in this world.

Heat spread down Thomas's face and neck and then flashed down his body, squeezing off his breath. The strength to stand left him and he dropped to his knees.

How could this be? Chelise hadn't been able to save him?

The sky had emptied of Shataiki. Down at the lake, the last of the seven thousand plunged into the depths. The battlefield grew quiet.

But here, in Thomas's head, there was a moaning that washed over him like the voices of a thousand dead.

His heart was breaking and his mind was falling apart, and he no longer cared to live. He covered his face with both hands, lifted his chin, and wailed at the sky.

"Samuel . . . Samuel. Samuel, my son, my son!"

He tore at his tunic, ripped it wide open, and cried without reserve. "Elyon, save my son . . ."

The air was silent.

The vaguest notion of paradise without Samuel was more than he could bear. This was Teeleh's doing!

"Elyon has no ears," Qurong said to his right.

"No!" Thomas snarled, twisting around. "You're wrong." He shoved his finger at the red pool. "Drown! Drown, you fool. My wife and my son have given their lives; now, drown! Dive into the pool, draw his water into your lungs and drown!"

Thomas staggered to his feet, face hot, drawing energy from his sorrow. Then he faced the sky and screamed. "Elyon! Elyon, hear me. Save my son!"

The sky remained silent.

A new way came to him. He spread his arms and searched the sky. "Let me go back. Let me find my son. I beg you, Elyon. Anything . . . anything! Just let me save my son."

Nothing.

He clenched his eyes and threw both arms wide. "Elyon!" he cried. "Elyon!"

The words Michal had spoken a week earlier sliced through his mind: *Follow your heart, Thomas, because the time has come . . . he will give you what you ask in that hour when all is lost.*

With all of his strength, from the pit of his stomach, he screamed at the sky. "Elyon! Fulfill your promise!"

―—―∞∞∞―—―

QURONG WAS lost in his own black misery, but this simple fact pointed out by Thomas rose like a beacon of light on the dark horizon: Chelise, his own daughter, had given her life for him.

And she had demanded that he drown.

Thomas was demanding the same. *Drown, drown, you old fool.* Drowning was foolishness. But then, he was dead already, surrounded by the dead.

Drown, Father. Drown, drown!

Thomas spread his arms wide and screamed at the sky in rage. "Elyon!" And again, with such force Qurong thought the man might damage his lungs. "Fulfill your promise!"

Then it happened for the second time in the space of ten minutes. One moment Thomas was standing there; the next, nothing but air filled out his clothes. He simply vanished as Chelise had vanished. And now his tunic floated to the ground, empty.

Qurong stared at the heap of clothing, staggered by the unexplainable. Could it be that this wasn't Teeleh's doing? That both Chelise and Thomas knew what he did not? That the drowning was Elyon's gift to the Horde?

He turned and faced the red pool, heart and mind heavy with loss. Not a soul stood living. They had all either died, fled, or thrown themselves into the lake. The Shataiki sped south, high in the sky. Toward his city to feed.

By nightfall, every living soul would be consumed by Shataiki. This was Ba'al's gift to them. And yet he, Qurong, remained alive. Why?

He looked at the wound in his arm, where Thomas's blood had mixed with his own, offering him some protection against the disease and the beasts. And now that man had vanished before his eyes.

Drown, Qurong. For the sake of Elyon, drown!

He turned downhill, swallowed the lump in his throat, and walked forward. *This is what you were born to do. To drown. To dive into the lake and to laugh with Elyon.*

Desperation crept over him and he lumbered forward, running now. Over fallen bodies.

Drown, you old fool. Just drown.

He broke into a sprint, and now he couldn't get to the water's edge fast enough. Suddenly nothing else mattered. All was lost.

But there, just ahead, lay a red lake with a green core, and he couldn't run fast enough. Qurong started to weep as he ran, blinded by his own tears.

"I will drown. I will drown," he mumbled. "I will drown for you, my Maker. I will drown for you, Elyon."

And then Qurong, supreme commander of the Horde, dived into the lake. He inhaled the bitter waters of Elyon's death. He drowned in a pit of sorrow.

And he found life in a world swimming with color and laughter and more pleasure than his new body could possibly manage.

—∞∞∞—

THE WORLD around Thomas blinked off, then on, then he was standing on the white sand, facing a bright blue horizon in perfect silence.

Here? Alone? Like a fist milking his veins, his heart throbbed. Time seemed to have stalled.

But he knew he couldn't be alone. The boy . . .

The boy had to be here.

He turned ever so slowly. The boy stood twenty feet away, arms crossed, lips flat and gaze steady. Behind him, a green lake reflected the clear sky, like a shiny mirror.

"You want to save your son?" the boy asked.

"Yes."

"You want to save Samuel?"

His lover's face filled his mind. "Chelise . . ."

"Is with me," the boy said.

Which could only mean Samuel was not.

"I . . . I can't live without him."

The boy looked at him for several long seconds, then shifted his eyes to the horizon. "I know how you feel."

"I know this is within your power," Thomas said. "If you would save all of Sodom for ten souls, you would give me the chance to save my one son."

"It's much more dangerous than you realize," the boy said, looking back.

"I'll take that risk. I—"

"Not you, Thomas. The risk is to the rest. This isn't just about you and your son. If I send you back you might save your son, but at what cost? The cost of saving even one is beyond you."

He hadn't thought of it in those terms. But he couldn't back out, not now.

The boy uncrossed his arms. "Walk with me."

Thomas hurried forward on weak legs. He joined the boy, who reached up and took his hand as they walked along the shore of the lake.

"Every choice you make will have far-reaching consequences," the boy said. "You will eventually change everything."

"Will it be better or worse?"

"It depends."

"On what?"

"On you."

They walked ten paces in silence. The boy's fingers felt so small in his hand. Thomas looked at the water and for a few moments considered withdrawing his request to join the others. Chelise and Mikil . . . Kara. He could only imagine their pleasure now, dancing and tearing about like children.

"Okay, Thomas. But I have two conditions."

Elyon was agreeing? "Anything."

"I will send you back to the place and time of my choosing."

"Yes. Yes, of course."

"You will have no memory of anything that's happened. You'll have your chance, unlike anyone else in history, but you won't have the benefit of knowing it's a second chance. You won't have any of the knowledge you've gained here." The boy stopped and looked up at him with round green eyes. "Do you understand?"

Thomas tried. But did it matter? He wouldn't remember anyway. If Elyon required this, then he would agree, and quickly. "I think so, yes."

"You'll wake in a place called Denver without any memory of this reality. Your dreams will be touched."

"Dreams?"

"They'll be real. Unfortunately, you won't know it."

"How . . . how does that work?"

"Better than you might think." The boy smiled for the first time, though only slightly. Then his face fell flat again.

"The fate of the world will depend on every choice you make." He swept his eyes over the horizon. "We'll remake history together, Thomas. Is that what you want?"

"Yes."

He shifted his gaze back to Thomas. "Good. It's what I do with every human anyway. Let's just hope you make the right choices."

"What about Chelise?"

"I thought you wanted to start over?"

Confusion swarmed his mind. "But . . . what about Chelise?"

"I thought you wanted to save your son," the boy said.

"I do."

"By going back."

"Yes," Thomas said. "Unless there's another way."

"Not that I know of. And I know an awful lot."

He considered it all and came to his decision quickly. Impulsively.

"Yes. Send me back. For the sake of my son."

The boy stepped to one side and winked. "Then dive, my friend."

Thomas faced the glassy pool. "Dive? In here?"

"Dive deep," the boy said.

Thomas took one last breath, nodded at the boy, and dived deep. Very, very deep.

46

THE WATER cascaded over Thomas's head and ran down his face like a warm glove. It was just that, water, but it washed away all his concern and anxiety and set his mind free for a few minutes. He'd been here awhile, lost in a distant world that hung on the edge of his mind without any detail or meaning. Just escape. Pure escape, the closest he ever got to heaven these days.

A fist pounded the door. "Thomas! I'm outta here. You're going to be late."

A mental image of a much older Kara flashed through his mind. She was graying, perhaps in her fifties, and she was asking him to take her with him. Just that, "Take me with you, Thomas."

And then the image was gone. He blinked under streams of water, suddenly disoriented. How long had he been here? For the briefest moment he was at a loss as to how he'd even gotten here.

Then it all came crashing in on him. He was in the shower. It was late morning. His shift at Java Hut started at noon. Right? Yes, of course.

He shook the water from his head. "Okay." Then added, "See you tonight."

But Kara was probably already out the door, headed to her shift at the hospital. The thing about his sister: she might only be in her early twenties like him, but what she lacked in age, she more than made up for in maturity. Not that he was irresponsible, but he hadn't made the transition from life on the streets in Manila to life in the States quite as smoothly as Kara.

He stepped out of the shower and wiped the steamed mirror with his forearm. He ran both hands through his wet hair and examined his face as best he could with streaks of water clinging to the glass.

Not bad. Not bad. Chicks dug a little stubble, right? He'd lost some of his edge over the last couple years in New York, but Denver would be different. The troubles with loan sharks and shady import partners were behind him now. Soon as he got back on his feet, he would reenter society and find a way to excel at something.

In the meantime, there was the coffee shop he worked at, and there was the apartment, gratis, thanks to Kara.

He dressed quickly, grabbed a day-old sugar donut on his way out, and headed up Ninth, then through the alley to Colfax, where the boutique coffee shop better known as Java Hut waited. The Rockies stood against a blue sky, just visible between high-rise apartments as he made his way up the street. Mother was still in New York, where she'd settled in after the divorce. It had been a tough road, but she was set now.

Indeed, the world was set. He just had to put some time in, regroup, and let life come to him as it always had, with fistfuls of dollars and a woman who could appreciate the finer things in life. Like him.

Okay, only in his dreams at the moment, but things were looking up. Maybe he'd finally get back to one of those novels he'd written when his dream of conquering the publishing world was alive and well.

Thomas entered the coffee shop two minutes past noon and let the door slam shut behind him.

"Hey, Thomas." The new dark-haired hire, Edith, smiled and gave him a wink.

Okay . . . interesting. Pretty enough. But being a magnet for trouble, Thomas didn't make a habit of flirting with women he knew nothing about.

"Hey."

She tossed him a green apron. "Frank would like you to show me the ropes."

"Okay." He stepped around her and behind the counter.

"We close together tonight," she said.

Right. Frank had started up these ten-hour shifts a week earlier. "Okay."

"Yeah."

He refused to look at her, knowing what was on her mind already. It was the farthest thing from his mind.

⸻

TWO DAYS had passed, and Bill now knew what he needed to know, thanks to Tony, the two-bit crook with a New York accent who'd agreed to play by his rules for ten thousand dollars a day. Tony had studied Thomas's movements and knew he would cut through the alley when he got off work sometime past ten.

"Focus, Tony." Bill stood atop the building and motioned at the alleyway. "Just make sure he heads into that dead end."

"Please don't *Tony* me, Bill. Then what?"

He wondered if he'd regret hiring the fool, but this wasn't the kind of thing you advertised for unless you had time. "Then you go in after him. Stay on the radio, I'll direct you. I want him thinking we have the streets blocked. The only other way out is up one of the ladders."

"And then he's yours."

Bill adjusted his dark glasses, careful to keep his black eyes hidden, and studied the flat roofs across the alley. He nodded. "Then he's mine."

"What about cops?"

"What about them? We're using silencers."

The New Yorker nodded. "I may get some help. Just to be sure. We get the chance, you want me to take him out? 'Cause that'll cost you more."

"No, Tony. I want him up on the roof." The rifle case lay at his feet, where he would take up position and lie in wait. One bullet to the head, nothing more, nothing less. He couldn't risk jeopardizing the mission by winging Thomas and sending him packing.

He has to drink the water, a voice from his past whispered. He had no idea what it meant.

"Fine, Bill," the man said with a smirk. "When do I get paid?"

Bill forced a grin. "As soon as he's dead, Tony. As soon as he's dead."

———∞∞∞———

THE DAY passed quickly, and Thomas managed to close with Edith without either betraying his general disinterest in her or offering any encouragement. But showing her the ropes, as she called it, had taken longer than usual, and he didn't get out till ten thirty that night.

He headed down the street, headed for the apartment. Another day, another dollar. Not fistfuls, but at least it was steady. More than he could say for his, uh . . . more ambitious gigs. All was good. All was . . .

But then suddenly all wasn't so good. He was walking down the same dimly lit alley he always took on his way home when a *smack!* punctuated the hum of distant traffic. Red brick dribbled from a one-inch hole two feet away from his face. He stopped midstride.

Smack!

This time he saw the bullet plow into the wall. This time he felt a sting on his cheek as tiny bits of shattered brick burst from the impact. This time every muscle in his body seized.

Someone had just shot at him?

Was *shooting* at him?

Thomas recoiled to a crouch, but he couldn't seem to tear his eyes off those two holes in the brick, dead ahead. They had to be a mistake. Figments of his overactive imagination. His aspirations to write novels had finally ruptured the line between fantasy and reality with these two empty eye sockets staring at him from the red brick.

"Thomas Hunter!"

That wasn't his imagination, was it? No, that was his name, and it was echoing down the alley. A third bullet crashed into the brick wall.

He bolted to his left, still crouching. One long step, drop the right shoulder, roll. Again the air split above his head. This bullet clanged into a steel ladder and rang down the alley.

Thomas came to his feet and chased the sound in a full sprint, pushed by instinct as much as by terror. He'd been here before, in the back alleys of Manila. He'd been a teenager then, and the Filipino gangs were armed with knives and machetes rather than guns, but at the moment, tearing down the alley behind Ninth and Colfax, Thomas's mind wasn't drawing any distinction.

"You're a dead man!" the voice yelled.

Now he knew who they were. They were from New York. Right? He had no enemies in Denver that he was aware of. New York, on the other hand . . . Yeah, well, he'd done a few stupid things in New York.

This alley led to another thirty yards ahead, on his left. A mere shadow in the dim light, but he knew the cutaway.

Two more bullets whipped by, one so close he could feel its wind on his left ear. Feet pounded the concrete behind him.

Thomas dived into the shadow.

"Cut him off in the back. Radio me."

Thomas rolled to the balls of his feet, then sprinted, mind spinning. *Radio?*

The problem with adrenaline, Makatsu's thin voice whispered, *is that it makes your head weak.* His karate instructor would point to his head and wink. *You have plenty of muscle to fight, but no muscle to think.*

If they had radios and could cut off the street ahead, he would have a very serious problem.

One access to the roof halfway down the alley. One large garbage bin too far away. Scattered boxes to his left. No real cover. He had to make his move before they entered the alley.

Fingers of panic stabbed into his mind. *Adrenaline dulls reason; panic kills it.* Makatsu again. Thomas had once been beaten to a pulp by a gang of Filipinos who'd taken a pledge to kill any Americano brat who entered their turf. They made the streets around the army base their turf. His instructor had scolded him, insisting that he was good enough to have escaped their attack that afternoon. His panic had cost him dearly. His brain had been turned to rice pudding, and he deserved the bruises that swelled his eyes shut.

This time it was bullets, not feet and clubs, and bullets would leave more than bruises. Time was out.

Short on ideas and long on desperation, Thomas dove for the gutter. Rough concrete tore at his skin. He rolled quickly to his left, bumped into the brick wall, and lay facedown in the deep shadow.

Feet pounded around the corner and ran straight toward him. One man. How they had found him in Denver, he had no clue. But if they'd gone to this much trouble, they wouldn't just walk away.

The man ran on light feet, hardly winded. Thomas's nose was buried in the musty corner. Noisy blasts of air from his nostrils buffeted his face. He clamped down on his breathing; immediately his lungs began to burn.

The slapping feet approached, ran past.

Stopped.

A slight tremor lit through his bones. He fought another round of panic. It had been five years since his last fight. He didn't stand a chance against a man with a gun. He desperately willed his pursuer's feet to move on. *Walk. Just walk!*

But the feet didn't walk. They scraped quietly. He had to move now, while he still had the advantage of surprise. He threw himself to his left, rolled once to gain momentum. Then twice, rising first to his knees, then to his feet. His attacker was facing him, gun extended, frozen.

Thomas's momentum carried him laterally, directly toward the opposite wall. The gun's muzzle-flash momentarily lit the dark alley and spit a bullet past him. But now instinct had replaced panic.

What shoes am I wearing?

The question flashed through Thomas's mind as he hurtled for the brick wall, left foot leading. A critical question.

His answer came when his foot planted on the wall. Rubber soles. One more step up the wall, with traction to spare. He threw his head back, arched hard, pushed himself off the brick, then twisted to his right halfway through his rotation. The move was simply an inverted bicycle kick, but he hadn't executed it in half a dozen years, and this time his eyes weren't on a soccer ball tossed up by one of his Filipino friends in Manila.

This time it was a gun.

The man managed one shot before Thomas's left foot smashed into his hand, sending the pistol clattering down the alley. The bullet tugged at his collar.

Thomas didn't land lightly on his feet as hoped. He sprawled to his hands, rolled once, and sprang into the seventh fighting position opposite a well-muscled man with short black hair. Not exactly a perfectly executed maneuver. Not terrible for someone who hadn't fought in six years.

The man's eyes were round with shock. His experience in the martial arts obviously didn't extend beyond *The Matrix*. Thomas was briefly tempted to shout for joy, but if anything, he had to shut this man up before *he* could call out.

The man's astonishment changed to a snarl, and Thomas saw the knife in his right hand. Okay, so maybe the man knew more about street fighting than was at first apparent.

He ducked the knife's first swipe. Came up with his palm to the man's chin. Bone cracked.

It wasn't enough. This man was twice his weight, with twice his muscle, and ten times his bad blood.

Thomas launched himself vertically and spun into a full roundhouse kick, screaming despite his better judgment. His foot had to be doing a good eighty miles an hour when it struck the man's jaw.

They both hit the concrete at precisely the same time, Thomas on his feet, ready to deliver another blow; his assailant on his back, breathing hard, ready for the grave. Figuratively speaking.

The man's silver pistol lay near the wall. Thomas took a step for it, then rejected the notion. What was he going to do? Shoot back? Kill? Incriminate himself? Not smart. He turned and ran back in the direction they'd come.

The main alley was empty. He ducked into it, edged along the wall, grabbed the rails to a steel fire escape, and quickly ascended. The building's roof was flat and shouldered another taller building to the south. He swung up to the second building, ran in a crouch, and halted by a large vent, nearly a full block from the alley where he'd laid out the New Yorker.

He dropped to his knees, pressed back into the shadows, and listened past the thumping of his heart.

The hum of a million tires rolling over asphalt. The distant roar of a jet overhead. The faint sound of idle talk. The sizzling of food frying in a pan, or of water being poured from a window. The former, considering they were in Denver, not the Philippines. No sounds from New York.

He leaned back and closed his eyes, catching his breath.

Fights in Manila as a teenager were one thing, but here in the States at the ripe age of twenty-five? The whole sequence struck him as surreal. It was hard to believe this had just happened to him.

Or, more accurately, *was* happening to him. He still had to figure a way out of this mess. Did they know where he lived? No one had followed him to the roof.

Thomas crept to the ledge. Another alley ran directly below, adjoining busy streets on either side. Denver's brilliant skyline glimmered on the horizon directly ahead. An odd odor met his nose, sweet like cotton candy but mixed with rubber or something burning.

Déjà vu. He'd been here before, hadn't he? No, of course not. Lights shimmered in the hot summer air, reds and yellows and blues, like jewels sprinkled from heaven. He could swear he'd been . . .

Thomas's head suddenly snapped to the left. He threw out his arms, but his world spun impossibly and he knew that he was in trouble.

Something had hit him. Something like a sledgehammer. Something like a bullet.

He felt himself topple, but he wasn't sure if he was really falling or if he was losing consciousness. Something was horribly wrong with his head. He landed hard on his back, in a pillow of black that swallowed his mind whole.

And then . . .

And then Thomas Hunter dreamed, and the world would never be the same.

THE JOURNEY CONTINUES WITH BLACK . . .